Praise for *The Oversight*

"Exciting, exhilarating, scary and moving in equal measure, *The Oversight* is a teeming world of dark deeds and dark magics, brilliantly realised. This feels like the start of something amazing"
M. R. Carey, author of *The Girl with all the Gifts*

"Told in a kind of compelling and hypnotic poesie that I just lapped up . . . I'll certainly be reading the next one"
Cory Doctorow, *BoingBoing.net*

"*The Oversight* is – and let's be clear here – something very special . . . It's oh-so-moreish a morsel. I'd read a prequel this evening, a sequel as soon as"
Niall Alexander, *Tor.com*

"A highly entertaining fantasy that promises a trilogy worth sinking your teeth into"
SciFiNow

"Fletcher's Victorian London is juicily vivid, and laced with macabre Dickensian wit. There's a real sense of grim danger, both natural and unnatural, hungrily awaiting the slightest misstep" Frances Hardinge

"A richly atmospheric and intensely readable slice of Victoriana, with a splendidly eerie sense of the way the unearthly lies cheek-by-jowl with the mundane"
Adam Roberts

"A remarkable combination of British folklore, brisk pacing and wide-ranging imagination"
Kirkus Reviews

"Utterly enthralling: Charles Dickens meets Susanna Clarke"
Lou Morgan

"Richly atmospheric (the evil lurks in the background of every paragraph), the book should be a big hit with supernatural-fantasy readers . . . the second book can't come soon enough" *Booklist* (starred review)

By Charlie Fletcher

The Oversight
The Paradox

THE OVER SIGHT

CHARLIE FLETCHER

orbit

www.orbitbooks.net

ORBIT

First published in Great Britain in 2014 by Orbit
This paperback edition published in 2014 by Orbit

Copyright © 2014 by Charlie Fletcher

Excerpt from *The First Fifteen Lives of Harry August* by Claire North
Copyright © 2014 by Claire North

A CIP catalogue record for this book is available from the British Library.

ISBN 978-0-356-50292-2

Typeset in Bembo Book MT Std by Palimpsest Book Production Ltd,
Falkirk, Stirlingshire
Printed and bound in Great Britain by CPI Group (UK) Ltd, Croydon, CR0 4YY

Papers used by Orbit are from well-managed forests and other responsible sources.

MIX
Paper from
responsible sources
FSC® C104740

Orbit
An imprint of
Little, Brown Book Group
100 Victoria Embankment
London EC4Y 0DY

An Hachette UK Company

www.hachette.co.uk
www.orbitbooks.net

For Margaret Fletcher, with all my love

DRAMATIS PERSONAE

THE OVERSIGHT

Sara Falk – *keeper of the Safe House in Wellclose Square*
Mr Sharp – *protector and sentinel*
Cook – *once a pirate*
The Smith – *smith, ringmaker and counsellor*
Hodge – *Terrier Man and ratcatcher at the Tower of London*
Emmet – *a golem*
Jed – *an Old English Terrier*
The Raven – *an even older bird*

IN LONDON

Lucy Harker – *a lost girl*
Bill Ketch – *a ruffian*
Issachar Templebane, Esq. – *lawyer, broker and twin*
Zebulon Templebane, Esq. – *lawyer, broker and twin*
Bassetshaw, Sherehog, Vintry, Undershaft, Coram and
Garlickhythe Templebane – *adopted sons (unimpaired)*
Amos Templebane – *adopted son (mute but intelligent)*
Reverend Christensen – *pastor of the Danish Church in Wellclose Square*

Lemuel Bidgood − *parish magistrate*
William George Bunyon − *innkeeper and jailer of the Sly House*
Bess Bunyon − *his daughter*
The Wipers − *cutthroat gang from the rookery at Seven Dials*
Magor − *their leader*
Lily − *a rentable girl from Neptune Street*

RUTLANDSHIRE AND LONDON

Francis Blackdyke, Viscount Mountfellon − *man of science turned supranaturalist*
The Citizen − *a sea-green incorruptible, thought dead*
Whitlowe − *a running boy*

IN THE COUNTRYSIDE

Rose Pyefinch − *travelling show-woman*
Barnaby Pyefinch − *travelling showman*
Charlie Pyefinch − *their son*
Na-Barno Eagle − *stage magician, self-styled Great Wizard of the South*
Georgiana Eagle − *his daughter, an entrancing beauty*
Hector Anderson − *stage magician, self-styled Great Wizard of the North*
Charles John Huffam − *a showman and owner of an Educated Pig*
Harry Stonex − *bargee*
Ruby Stonex − *bargess*
The tinker − *a larcenous pedlar*

AT THE ANDOVER WORKHOUSE

M'Gregor − *superintendent*
Mrs M'Gregor − *his wife*
The Ghost of the Itch Ward − *female inmate, real name unknown*

BETWEEN THE WORLDS

John Dee – *known as The Walker between the Worlds*

BEYOND LAW AND LORE

Moleskin Coat, Woodcock Crown, Bicorn Hat, The Hunchback
– *Sluagh, also known as Shadowgangers or the Night Host*
The Alp – *a breath-stealer from the Austro-German borderland*
A Green Man – *run mad*

A Benefit of Mongrels

The natural and the supranatural inhabit the same world, intersecting but largely unseen to one another, like lodgers who share a house but keep different hours, only occasionally passing on the narrow stairs. They do not speak the same language, their customs are different and their views of the world and the laws and behaviours that govern it are wildly and mutually opposed.

It is only when they bump shoulders that they take note of each other, but when they do so, arcane and infelicitous things will happen. Because of this, it is necessary that the tight spaces where such friction may occur are governed by rules, and that those rules are policed.

For centuries there have been few more crowded nests of humanity than the great beast of a city which sprawls on either side of the Thames, and it was to regulate interaction between the natural and the supranatural that the ancient Free Company known as The Oversight of London was formed.

It is a paradox perhaps of passing interest only to those who collect quaint ironies that this shadowy borderland is best patrolled by those who carry the blood of both types in their veins . . . or to frame it differently: the unseen picket line which prevents one world from predating on the other is policed by mongrels.

from *The Great and Hidden History of the World* by the Rabbi Dr Hayyim Samuel Falk (also known as the Ba'al Shem of London)

PROLOGUE

She sat in the sun making daisy chains, happy in her own world, enjoying the warmth on her face and the simple spring beauty of the white May blossom tumbling overhead against a clear blue sky.

Her fingers moved steadily and expertly, a thumbnail splitting a short green stalk, then feeding the next one through the hole and splitting that one, then threading another. It was repetitive work but, as is the way with some manual labour, it freed her mind to think of other things, such as the little lost ones for whom she made the chains and how pleased they should be to be garlanded with them when they were all reunited. They would feel the tickle of the daisies round their necks and know she had never forgotten them, and they would also know she had always kept on believing that, no matter how violently the happy promise of past once upon a times had been betrayed and no matter how sharp the sorrow of the present, the future might still lead to a shared happy-ever-after.

In the other world, the unhappy one that was not her own, she sat in shadows, almost invisible, frequently forgotten (especially at meal times) on a wooden stool propped in that dusty corner of the Itch Ward reserved for the weak-brained and the addle-pated, the ones M'Gregor the superintendent called the moaners and dribblers. She neither moaned nor dribbled but just sat there, head angled slightly as if trying to catch some imaginary or distantly remembered sunlight, face slack and unexpectant and grey, her hair pulled loosely back from her forehead, her only movement a tiny repetitive business made by her fingertips working against each other, as if – said M'Gregor's wife – she was hemming her own grave-cloth.

She was well enough behaved, and only when given to shrieking fits (which afflicted her occasionally) was there any pressing need to discipline her, customarily with beatings and overnight solitary exile in the Eel House, on the other side of the water meadows.

She ate her slop when prompted, and washed and took care of her own privy needs according to some inner timetable, but she did nothing else, neither cleaning nor stone-picking nor bone-grinding, which made her a Useless Mouth in the account book and thus one that the M'Gregors visibly resented feeding.

"She does nothing," they said bitterly. "Nothing, by God. She does not even speak."

And it is true that as the world turned and the months and years ground away, she did not do anything at all. But one of the things that she didn't do, even in the depths of the coldest winters or the loneliest dead watches of the night, was this:

She did not die.

And that was the reason she did nothing else: the living ghost of the Itch Ward needed every ounce of strength in her body and mind to just remember to keep on living.

And who to kill.

FIRST PART

THE SCREAMING GIRL

CHAPTER 1

THE HOUSE ON WELLCLOSE SQUARE

If only she wouldn't struggle so, the damned girl.

If only she wouldn't scream then he wouldn't have had to bind her mouth.

If only she would be quiet and calm and biddable, he would never have had to put her in a sack.

And if only he had not had to put her in a sack, she could have walked and he would not have had to put her over his shoulder and carry her to the Jew.

Bill Ketch was not a brute. Life may have knocked out a few teeth and broken his nose more than once, but it had not yet turned him into an animal: he was man enough to feel bad about what he was doing, and he did not like the way that the girl moaned so loud and wriggled on his shoulder, drawing attention to herself.

Hitting her didn't stop anything. She may have screamed a lot, but she had flint in her eye, something hard and unbreakable, and it was that tough core that had unnerved him and decided him on selling her to the Jew.

That's what the voice in his head told him, the quiet, sly voice that nevertheless was conveniently able to drown out whatever his conscience might try to say.

The street was empty and the fog from the Thames damped the gas lamps into blurs of dull light as he walked past the Seaman's Hostel and turned into Wellclose Square. The flare of a match caught his eye as a big man with a red beard lit a pipe amongst a group standing around a cart stacked with candle-boxes outside the Danish Church. Thankfully they didn't seem to notice him as he slunk speedily along the opposite side of the road, heading for the dark house at the bottom of the square beyond the looming bulk of the sugar refinery, outside which another horse and carriage stood unattended.

He was pleased the square was so quiet at this time of night. The last thing he wanted to do was to have to explain why he was carrying such strange cargo, or where he was heading.

The shaggy travelling man in The Three Cripples had given him directions, and so he ducked in the front gates, avoiding the main door as he edged round the corner and down a flight of slippery stone steps leading to a side-entrance. The dark slit between two houses was lit by a lonely gas globe which fought hard to be seen in murk that was much thicker at this lower end of the square, closer to the Thames.

There were two doors. The outer one, made of iron bars like a prison gate, was open, and held back against the brick wall. The dark oak inner door was closed and studded with a grid of raised nailheads that made it look as if it had been hammered shut for good measure. There was a handle marked "Pull" next to it. He did so, but heard no answering jangle of a bell from inside. He tugged again. Once more silence greeted him. He was about to yank it a third time when there was the sound of metal sliding against metal and a narrow judas hole opened in the door. Two unblinking eyes looked at him from behind a metal grille, but other than them he could see nothing apart from a dim glow from within.

The owner of the eyes said nothing. The only sound was a moaning from the sack on Ketch's shoulder.

The eyes moved from Ketch's face to the sack, and back. There was a sound of someone sniffing, as if the doorman was smelling him.

Ketch cleared his throat.

"This the Jew's house?"

The eyes continued to say nothing, summing him up in a most uncomfortable way.

"Well," swallowed Ketch. "I've got a girl for him. A screaming girl, like what as I been told he favours."

The accompanying smile was intended to ingratiate, but in reality only exposed the stumpy ruins of his teeth.

The eyes added this to the very precise total they were evidently calculating, and then abruptly stepped back and slammed the slit shut. The girl flinched at the noise and Ketch cuffed her, not too hard and not with any real intent to hurt, just on a reflex.

He stared at the blank door. Even though it was now eyeless, it still felt like it was looking back at him. Judging. He was confused. Had he been rejected? Was he being sent away? Had he walked all the way here carrying the girl – who was not getting any lighter – all for nothing? He felt a familiar anger build in his gut, as if all the cheap gin and sour beer it held were beginning to boil, sending heat flushing across his face. His fist bunched and he stepped forward to pound on the studded wood.

He swung angrily, but at the very moment he did so it opened and he staggered inward, following the arc of his blow across the threshold, nearly dumping the girl on the floor in front of him.

"Why—?!" he blurted.

And then stopped short.

He had stumbled into a space the size and shape of a sentry

box, with no obvious way forward. He was about to step uneasily back out into the fog, when the wall to his right swung open.

He took a pace into a larger room lined in wooden tongue-and-groove panelling with a table and chairs and a dim oil lamp. The ceiling was also wood, as was the floor. Despite this it didn't smell of wood, or the oil in the lamp. It smelled of wet clay. All in all, and maybe because of the loamy smell, it had a distinctly coffin-like atmosphere. He shivered.

"Go on in," said a calm voice behind him.

"Nah," he swallowed. "Nah, you know what? I think I've made a mistake—"

The hot churn in his guts had gone ice-cold, and he felt the goosebumps rise on his skin: he was suddenly convinced that this was a room he must not enter, because if he did, he might never leave.

He turned fast, banging the girl on the doorpost, her yip of pain lost in the crash as the door slammed shut, barring his escape route with the sound of heavy bolts slamming home.

He pushed against the wood, and then kicked at it. It didn't move. He stood there breathing heavily, then slid the girl from his shoulder and laid her on the floor, holding her in place with a firm hand.

"Stay still or you shall have a kick, my girl," he hissed.

He turned and froze.

There was a man sitting against the back wall of the room, a big man, almost a giant, in the type of caped greatcoat that a coachman might wear. It had an unnaturally high collar, and above it he wore a travel-stained tricorn hat of a style that had not been seen much on London's streets for a generation, not since the early 1800s. The hat jutted over the collar and cast a shadow so deep that Ketch could see nothing of the face beneath. He stared at the man. The man didn't move an inch.

"Hoi," said Ketch, by way of introduction.

The giant remained motionless. Indeed as Ketch stepped towards him he realised that the head was angled slightly away, as if the man wasn't looking at him at all.

"Hoi!" repeated Ketch.

The figure stayed still. Ketch licked his lips and ventured forward another step. Peering under the hat he saw the man was brown-skinned.

"Oi, blackie, I'm a-talking to you," said Ketch, hiding the fact that the giant's stillness and apparent obliviousness to his presence was unnerving him by putting on his best bar-room swagger.

The man might as well be a statue for the amount he moved. In fact—

Ketch reached forward and tipped back the hat, slowly at first.

It wasn't a man at all. It was a mannequin made from clay. He ran his thumb down the side of the face and looked at the brown smear it left on it. Damp clay, unfired and not yet quite set. It was a well made, almost handsome face with high cheekbones and an impressively hooked nose, but the eyes beneath the prominent forehead were empty holes.

"Well, I'll be damned . . ." he whispered, stepping back.

"Yes," said a woman's voice behind him, cold and quiet as a cutthroat razor slicing through silk. "Oh yes. I rather expect you will."

CHAPTER 2

A WOMAN IN BLACK AND
THE MAN IN MIDNIGHT

She stood at the other end of the room, a shadow made flesh in a long tight-bodiced dress buttoned to the neck and wrists. Her arms were folded and black leather gloves covered her hands. The dress had a dull sheen like oiled silk, and she was so straight-backed and slender – and yet also so finely muscled – that she looked in some ways like a rather dangerous umbrella leaning against the wood panelling.

The only relief from the blackness was her face, two gold rings she wore on top of the gloves and her white hair, startlingly out of kilter with her otherwise youthful appearance, which she wore pulled back in a tight pigtail that curled over her shoulder like an albino snake.

She hadn't been there when Ketch entered the room, and she couldn't have entered by the door which had been on the edge of his vision throughout, but that wasn't what most disturbed him: what really unsettled him was her eyes, or rather the fact he couldn't see them, hidden as they were behind the two small circular lenses of smoked glass that made up her spectacles.

"Who—?" began Ketch.

She held up a finger. Somehow that was enough to stop him talking.

"What do you want?"

Ketch gulped, tasting his own fear like rising bile at the back of his throat.

"I want to speak to the Jew."

"Why?"

He saw she carried a ring of keys at her belt like a jailer. Despite the fact she looked too young for the job he decided that she must be the Jew's housekeeper. He used this thought as a stick to steady himself on: he'd just been unnerved by her sudden appearance, that was all. There must be a hidden door behind her. Easy enough to hide its edges in the tongue and groove. He wasn't going to be bullied by a housekeeper. Not when he had business with her master.

"I got something for him."

"What?"

"A screaming girl."

She looked at the long sack lying on the floor.

"You have a *girl* in this sack?"

Somehow the way she asked this carried a lot of threat.

"I want to speak to the Jew," repeated Ketch.

The woman turned her head to one side and rapped on the wooden wall behind her. She spoke into a small circular brass grille.

"Mr Sharp? A moment of your time, please."

The dark lenses turned to look at him again. The silence was unbearable. He had to fill it.

"Man in The Three Cripples said as how the Jew would pay for screaming girls."

The gold ring caught the lamplight as the black gloves flexed open and then clenched tight again, as if she were containing something.

"So you've come to sell a girl?"

"At the right price."

Her smile was tight and showed no teeth. Her voice remained icily polite.

"There are those who would say *any* price is the wrong one. The good Mr Wilberforce's bill abolished slavery nearly forty years ago, did it not?"

Ketch had set out on a simple errand: he had something to sell and had heard of a likely buyer. True, he'd felt a little like a Resurrection Man skulking through the fog with a girl on his shoulder, but she was no corpse and he was no body-snatcher. And now this woman was asking questions that were confusing that simple thing. When life was straightforward, Bill Ketch sailed through it on smooth waters. When it became complicated he became confused, and when he became confused, anger blew in like a storm, and when he became angry, fists and boots flew until the world was stomped flat and simple again.

"I don't know nothing about a Wilberforce. I want to speak to the Jew," he grunted.

"And why do you think the Jew wants a girl? By which I mean: what do you think the Jew wants to do with her?" she asked, the words as taut and measured as her smile.

"What he does is none of my business."

He shrugged and hid his own bunched fists deep in the pockets of his coat.

Her words cracked sharply across the table like a whiplash.

"But what you think you are doing by selling this girl is mine. Answer the question!"

This abrupt change of tone stung him and made him bang the table and lurch towards her, face like a thundercloud.

"No man tells Bill Ketch what to do, and sure as hell's hinges no damn woman does neither! I want to see the bloody Jew and by God—"

The wall next to her seemed to blur open and shut and a

man burst through, slicing across the room so fast that he outpaced Ketch's eyes, leaving a smear of midnight blue and flashing steel as he came straight over the table in a swirl of coat-tails that ended in a sudden and dangerous pricking sensation against his Adam's apple.

The eyes that had added him up through the judas hole now stared into him across a gap bridged by eighteen inches of razor-sharp steel. The long blade was held at exactly the right pressure to stop him doing anything life-threatening, like moving. Indeed, just swallowing would seem to be an act of suicide.

"By any god, you shall not take one step further forward, Mr . . ."

The eyes swept over his face, searching, reading it.

"Mr Ketch, is it? Mr William Ketch . . . ?"

He leaned in and Ketch, frozen, watched his nostrils flare as he appeared to smell him. The midnight blue that the man was dressed in seemed to absorb even more light than the woman's black dress. He wore a knee-length riding coat cut tight to his body, beneath which was a double-breasted leather waistcoat of exactly the same hue, as were the shirt and tightly knotted silk stock he wore around his neck. The only break in the colour of his clothing was the brown of his soft leather riding boots.

His hair was also of the darkest brown, as were his thick and well-shaped eyebrows, and his eyes, when Ketch met them, were startlingly . . . unexpected.

Looking into them Ketch felt, for a moment, giddy and excited. The eyes were not just one brown, not even some of the browns: they were *all* the browns. It was as if he was looking into a swirl of autumn leaves tumbling happily in the golden sunlight of a blazing Indian summer.

One look into the tawny glamour in those eyes and Ketch forgot the blade at his throat.

One look into those eyes and the anger was gone and all was simple again.

One look into those eyes and Bill Ketch was confusingly and irrevocably in something as close to love as to make no difference.

The man must have seen this because the blade did something fast and complicated and disappeared beneath the skirts of his coat as he reached forward, gripped Ketch by both shoulders and pulled him close, sniffing him again and then raising an eyebrow in surprise, before pushing him back and smiling at him like an old friend.

"He is everything he appears to be, and no more," he said over his shoulder.

The woman stepped forward.

"You are sure?"

"I thought I smelled something on the air as he knocked, but it didn't come in with him. I may have been mistaken. The river is full of stink at high tide."

"So you are sure?" she repeated.

"As sure as I am that you will never tire of asking me that particular question," said the man.

"'Measure twice, cut once' is a habit that has served me well enough since I was old enough to think," she said flatly, "and it has kept this house safe for much longer than that."

"Are you the Jew?" said Ketch. His voice squeaked a little as he spoke, so happy was he feeling, bathed in the warmth of the handsome young man's open smile.

"I do not have that honour," he replied.

The woman appeared at the man's shoulder.

"Well?" she said.

The chill returned to Ketch's heart as she spoke.

"He is as harmless as he appears to be, I assure you," repeated the man.

She took off her glasses and folded them in one hand. Her

eyes were grey-green and cold as a midwinter wave. Her words, when they came, were no warmer.

"I am Sara Falk. I am the Jew."

As Ketch tried to realign the realities of his world, she put a hand on the man's shoulder and pointed him at the long bundle on the floor.

"Now, Mr Sharp, there is a young woman in that sack. If you would be so kind."

The man flickered to the bundle on the floor, again seeming to move between time instead of through it. The blade reappeared in his hand, flashed up and down the sacking, and then he was helping the girl to her feet and simultaneously sniffing at her head.

"Mr Sharp?" said Sara Falk.

"As I said, I smelled something out there," he said. "I thought it was him. It isn't, nor is it her."

"Well, good," she said, the twitch of a smile ghosting round the corner of her mouth. "Maybe it was your imagination."

"It pleases you to make sport of me, my dear Miss Falk, but I venture to point out that since we are charged with anticipating the inconceivable, my 'imagination' is just as effective a defensive tool as your double-checking," he replied, looking at the girl closely. "And since our numbers are so perilously dwindled these days, you will excuse me if I do duty as both belt and braces in these matters."

The young woman was slender and trembling, in a grubby pinafore dress with no shoes and long reddish hair that hung down wavy and unwashed, obscuring a clear look at her face. At first glance, however, it was clear she was not a child, and he judged her age between sixteen and twenty years old. She flinched when he reached to push the hair back to get a better look at her and make a more accurate assessment, and he stopped and spoke quietly.

"No, no, my dear, just look at me. Look at me and you'll see you have nothing to fear."

After a moment her head came up and eyes big as saucers peered a question into his. As soon as they did the trembling calmed and she allowed him to push the hair back and reveal what had been done to her mouth to stop the screaming.

He exhaled through his teeth in an angry hiss and then gently turned her towards Sara Falk. She stared at the rectangle of black hessian that was pasted across the girl's face from below her nose down to her chin.

"What is this?" said Mr Sharp, voice tight, still keeping the girl steady with his eyes.

"It's just a pitch-plaster, some sacking and tar and pitch, like a sticky poultice, such as they use up the Bedlam Hospital to quiet the lunatics . . ." explained Ketch, his voice quavering lest Mr Sharp's gaze when it turned to add him up again was full of something other than the golden warmth he was already missing. "Why, the girlie don't mind a—"

"Look at her hands," said Sara Falk.

The girl's hands were tightly wrapped in strips of grubby material, like small cloth-bound boxing gloves.

"Nah, that she does herself, she done that and not me," said Ketch hurriedly. "I takes 'em off cos she's no bloody use with hands wrapped into stumps like that, but she wraps whatever she can find round 'em the moment you turn your back. Why even if there's nothing in the rooms she'll rip up her own clothes to do it. It's all she does: touches things and then screams at what ain't there and tangles rags round her hands like a winding cloth so she doesn't have to touch anything at all . . ."

Sara Falk exchanged a look with Mr Sharp.

"Touches things? Then screams?" he said. "Old stones, walls . . . those kind of things?"

Ketch nodded enthusiastically. "Walls and houses and things in the street. Sets 'er off something 'orrible it does—"

"Enough," said Mr Sharp, his eyes on Sara Falk, who was stroking the scared girl's hair. Their eyes met once more.

"So she's a Glint then," he said quietly.

She nodded, for a moment unable to speak.

"She's not right in the head is what she is," said Ketch. "And—"

"Is she your daughter?" said Sara Falk, clearing something from her throat.

"No. Not blood kin. She's . . . my ward, as it were. But I can't afford to feed her no more, so it's you or the poor-house, and the poorhouse don't pay, see . . . ?"

The spark of commerce had reignited in his eyes.

"Don't worry about that blessed plaster, lady. Why, a hot flannel held on for a couple of minutes loosens it off, and you can peel it away without too much palaver."

The man and the woman stared at him.

"The redness fades after a couple of days," he insisted. "We tried a gag, see, but she loosens them or gnaws through. She's spirited—"

"What is her name?" said Sara Falk.

"Lucy. Lucy Harker. She's just—"

"Mr Sharp," she said, cutting him off by turning away to kneel by the girl.

"What do you want to do with him?" said the man in midnight.

"What I *want* to do to a man who'd sell a young woman without a care as to what the buyer might want to do with or to her is undoubtedly illegal," said Sara Falk almost under her breath.

"It would be justice though," he replied equally softly.

"Yes," she said. "But we, as I have said many times, are an office of the Law and the Lore, not of Justice, Mr Sharp.

And Law and Lore say to make the punishment fit the crime. Do what must be done."

Lucy Harker looked at her, still mute behind the gag.

Mr Sharp left them and turned his smile on Ketch, who relaxed and grinned expectantly back at him.

"Well," said Mr Sharp. "It seems we must pay you, Mr Ketch."

The thought of money coming was enticing and jangly enough to drown out the question that had been trying to get Ketch's attention for some time now, namely how this good-looking young man knew his name. He watched greedily as he reached into his coat and pulled out a small leather bag.

"Now," said Mr Sharp. "Gold, I think. Hold out your hands."

Ketch did so as if sleepwalking, and though at first his eyes tricked him into the thought that Mr Sharp was counting tarnished copper pennies into his hand, after a moment he realised they were indeed the shiniest gold pieces he had ever seen, and he relaxed enough to stop looking at them and instead to study more of Mr Sharp. His dark hair was cropped short on the back and sides, but was long on top, curling into a cowlick that tumbled over his forehead in an agreeably untidy way. A single deep blue stone dangled from one ear in a gold setting, winking in the lamplight as he finished his tally.

". . . twenty-eight, twenty-nine, thirty. That's enough, I think, and if not it is at least . . . traditional."

And with that the purse disappeared and the friendly arm went round Ketch's shoulder, and before he could quite catch up with himself the two of them were out in the fog, walking out of Wellclose Square into the tangle of dark streets beyond.

Ketch's heart was soaring and he felt happier than he had ever been in his life, though whether it was because of the unexpectedly large number of gold – gold! – coins in his pockets, or because of his newfound friend, he could not tell.

CHAPTER 3

A CHARITABLE DEED

If the fog had eyes (which in this part of London it often did) it would not only have noticed Mr Sharp leading Bill Ketch away into the narrow streets at the lower end of the square, it would have remarked that the knot of men who had been unloading boxes of candles into the Danish Church had finished their work, and that the carrier's cart had taken them off into the night, leaving only the burly red-bearded man with the pipe and a wiry underfed-looking young fellow in a tight fustian coat.

The bearded man locked the heavy doors and then followed the other across the street, heading for the dark carriage still standing outside the sugar refinery. If the fog's eyes had also been keen, they would have noticed that the red beard over-hung a white banded collar with two tell-tale tabs that marked him out as the pastor of the church whose barn-like doors he had just secured. There was a crunch underfoot as they reached the carriage and he looked down at the scattering of oyster shells with surprise. The wiry youth, unsurprised, reached up and rapped his bony knuckles on the polished black of the carriage door.

"Father," he said. "'Tis the Reverend Christensen. 'E wishes to thank you in person."

There was a pause as if the carriage itself was alive and considering what had been said to it. Then it seemed to shrug as something large moved within, the weight shifting it on its springs, and then the door cracked open.

The reverend's beard parted to reveal an open smile as the pastor leant into the carriage apologetically.

"So sorry to discommode you, Mr Templebane, but I could not let the opportunity of thanking you in person pass me by."

"No matter, no matter at all," said a deep voice from inside. "Think no more of it, my dear reverend sir. My pleasure indeed. Only sorry we had to deliver at so unholy an hour."

"All hours are holy, Mr Templebane," smiled the pastor, his English scarcely accented at all. "And any hour that contains such a welcome donation is all the more blessed."

"Please!" said the voice, whose owner remained hidden except for the appearance in the carriage window of a fleshy hand carefully holding an open oyster with the smallest finger extended politely away from all the others. The shell was full of plump grey oyster meat that bobbed and spilled a little of the shellfish's liquor as the hand airily waved the thanks away.

"You will embarrass me, sir, so you will. To be honest, the bit of business that resulted in me taking over the unwanted deadstock from the unfortunate, not to say imprudent, candle-maker left me with enough dips to gift all the churches in the parish."

The fleshy hand retreated into the shadows and a distinct slurping noise was heard.

"But a lesser spirit might still have sold them," said the pastor, working hard to make his thanks stick to their rightful target.

The fleshy hand reappeared as the carriage's occupant leant further forward to drop the now-empty oyster shell daintily on to the pavement, revealing for just an instant the face of Issachar Templebane.

It was a paradox of a face, a face both gaunt and yet pillowy, the skin hanging slack over the bones of the skull with the unhealthy toad's-belly pallor of a fat man who has lost weight too late in life for his skin to have retained the elasticity to shrink to fit the new, smaller version of himself.

He wiped a trickle of oyster juice from the edge of his mouth with the back of his thumb before reaching forward to grip the pastor's hand in a brisk, hearty farewell.

"I could, I could, but my brother and I are lawyers not tradesmen, and I assure you our fees in the matter were more than adequate. Besides, money isn't everything. Now, good-night to you, sir, and safe home. Come, Coram, we must be going."

And with that he released the hand and retreated back into the carriage as the wiry young man sprang up to the driver's seat, gathered the reins and snapped the horses into motion with a farewell nod to the pastor, who was left standing among the debris of Templebane's oyster supper feeling strangely dismissed, rather than actually wished well.

As the carriage turned the corner a panel slid back in the front of the vehicle, next to Coram, and Templebane's face appeared.

"Did you draw the reverend gentleman's attention to the man Ketch and his suspicious bundle?" he asked, all the cheeriness in his voice now replaced by a business-like flat-ness.

"Yes, Father. I done it just as 'ow you said, casual-like."

If the fog had ears as well as eyes, it might by this time have noted a further paradox regarding Issachar Templebane, which was that the boy who called him Father did not have anything like the same deep, fluid – and above all cultured – voice as he. Coram's voice had been shaped by the rough dockside alleys of the East End: it dropped "h's" and played fast and loose with what had, with Victoria's recent accession to the throne, only just become the Queen's English. Issachar spoke with the smooth polished edges of the courtroom; Coram's voice was sharp as a docker's hook. If there seemed to be no familiar resemblance between them, this was because although Issachar Templebane had many children, he had no blood kin beyond his twin brother Zebulon, who was the other half of the house of Templebane & Templebane.

Issachar and Zebulon were prodigious adopters of unclaimed boys, all of whom grew up to work for them in the chambers and counting room that adjoined their house on Bishopsgate. It was their habit to name the boys for the London parishes from whose workhouses (or in Coram's case, the foundling hospital) they had been procured. This led to unwieldy but undoubtedly unusual names: there was an Undershaft, a Vintry, a Sherehog, a Bassetshaw and a Garlickhythe Templebane. The only exception was the youngest, who had been taken from the parish of St Katherine Cree, and he, it being too outlandish to call the boy Katherine, was called Amos, a name chosen at random by letting the Bible fall open and choosing the title of the book it opened at. If Amos had anything to say about the matter he might well have remarked that he had as well been called Job since, as the youngest member of the artificially assembled family, with brothers who shared no love between them, he got more than his share of grief and toil. He didn't remark on this because he spoke not at all, his particular affliction being that he was mute. Coram, by contrast, was garrulous and questioning, a characteristic that his adopted fathers encouraged and punished in equal measure depending on their whim and humour.

Coram cleared his throat by spitting onto the crupper of the horse in front of him and went on.

"And 'e remarked, the pastor did, that the 'ouse Ketch gone in was the Jew's 'ouse, and that she was a good woman, though not of his faith."

Templebane nodded approvingly, his hands busy with a short-bladed shucking knife as he opened another oyster.

"Quite, quite. He has no malice in him, none at all. As solid and upright and clean as a new mast of Baltic pine is the Danish reverend. Which will make his testimony all the more credible, should we require it."

Here he paused and slurped another oyster, tossing the shell out into the road. He chewed the unlucky bivalve once, to burst it, then swallowed with a shiver of satisfaction.

"Mark it, Coram: there is no better instrument of destruction than an honest man who has no axe to grind."

And with that the panel slapped shut and Coram Templebane was alone with the horses and the fog that thinned as he drove up towards the higher ground of Goodman's Fields.

CHAPTER 4

HAND IN GLOVE

Sara Falk crouched in front of the trembling young woman and smiled encouragingly at her.

"Lucy," she said.

Lucy Harker just stared at the door through which Mr Sharp had led Ketch, as if expecting them to walk back in at any moment.

"Lucy. May I?"

She reached for Lucy's neck, pushed away the hair, and then lifted the collar of the pinafore as if looking for something like a necklace. Finding nothing she sucked her teeth with a snap of disappointment and shook her head.

The eyes stayed locked on the outer door. Sara Falk moved into her field of vision.

"Lucy. You must believe the next three things I tell you with all your heart, for they are the truest things in the world: firstly, that man will never walk back through that door unbidden and he shall never, ever hurt you or anyone ever again. Mr Sharp is making sure of that right now."

Lucy's eyes flickered and she looked at the slender woman, her eyes making a question that her mouth could not, her body still tense and quivering like a wild deer on the point of flight.

"Secondly, I know you have visions," continued Sara Falk, reaching out to touch the pitch-plaster gently, as if stroking a hurt away. "It's the visions that make you scream. Visions you have when you touch things. Visions that make you wonder if you are perhaps mad?"

The eyes stared at her. Sara smiled and raised her own hands, showing the gloves and the two rings that she wore on top of them, one an odd-shaped piece of sea-glass rimmed with a band of gold, the other set with a bloodstone into which a crest of some sort had been carved.

"You are not mad, and you are not alone. As you see, others have reason to cover their hands too. And if you come with me into my house, where there is a warm fire and pie and hot milk with honey, we shall sit with my glove box and find an old pair of mine and see if they fit you."

She removed the rings, reached for the buttons at the wrist of one glove, quickly opened them and peeled the thin black leather off, revealing the bare hand beneath. She freed the other hand even faster, and then reached gently for Lucy's bound hands.

"May I?"

Lucy's eyes stayed locked on hers as she gently began to unwrap one of the hands.

"I have something that will calm you, Lucy, a simple piece of sea-glass for you to touch, and I promise it will not harm you but give you a strength until we can find you one of your own—"

Lucy pulled her hand sharply away but Sara held on to it firmly and smiled as she held out the sea-glass ring: the glass, worn smooth by constant tumbling back and forth on a beach, matched Sara Falk's eyes perfectly.

"You need to touch this—"

Lucy goggled at it, then ripped her hand out of Sara Falk's, shaking her head with sudden agitation, emphatically miming "No!"

"Lucy—" began Sara, and then stopped.

Lucy was tearing at her own bandages, moaning excitedly from behind the tar and hessian gag. It was Sara's turn to watch with eyes that widened in surprise as the rags wound off and revealed their secret.

Lucy freed one hand and held out a fist, palm up, jabbing it insistently at the older woman.

Then she opened it.

Clenched in her hand was another piece of sea-glass, its light hazel colour like that of Lucy's own eyes.

Sara Falk's face split into a grin that matched and made even younger the youthful face she carried beneath the prematurely white hair. It was a proud and a mischievous grin.

"Oh," she gasped. "Oh, you clever girl. Clever, *clever* girl! You kept your own heart-stone. *That's* how you survived that awful man unbroken! Oh, you shall be *fine*, Lucy Harker, for you have sense and spirit. The visions that assault you when you touch things are a gift, and though it is not an easy one to bear, believe me that it *is* a gift and no lasting blight on your life."

A tear leaked out of one of Lucy's eyes and Sara caught it and wiped it away before it hit the black plaster.

"And this heart-stone, I mean your piece of sea-glass, does it glow when there is danger near?"

Lucy again looked startled and on edge, as if she was on the point of breaking for the door. Sara put a hand on her shoulder, gently.

"Did you know that only a true Glint can see the fire that blazes out of it when peril approaches?" said Sara. "Ordinary folk see nothing but the same dull piece of sea-glass. Why, even the estimable Mr Sharp who has abilities of his own cannot see the fire that guards the unique power that you and I have. It is not glowing now, is it?"

Lucy looked at the dull glass in her hand; it was like a cloudy gobbet of marmalade.

"Then if you trust it, trust me," said Sara. "And we shall find a way to soften that pitch and peel this wretched gag off without hurting you. Come to the kitchen and we shall see what we can do."

She smiled encouragingly at the gagged face. Her grandfather had indeed once sought out oddities like Lucy Harker and other people with even stranger abilities. The Rabbi Falk had been one of the great minds of his time, and though not born with any powers of his own, he not only believed in what he termed the "supranatural" but also toiled endlessly to increase his knowledge of it and so harness it. He had been a Freemason, a Kabbalist, an alchemist and a natural scientist, obsessively studying the threads of secret power that wove themselves beneath the everyday surface of things and underpinned what he called "The Great and Hidden History of the World".

It was perhaps proof that Fate had a sense of humour in that his granddaughter had been born with some of those very elusive powers which he had spent a lifetime searching for and trying to control.

Sara reached for Lucy's hand and gave it a reassuring squeeze.

"You are a Glint, Lucy, and you have fallen among friends," she said. "You are out of danger here, for this is the Safe House, the most secure house in all London, safer than the Tower itself for it was made so to guard a grave secret, a key of great power, and because of that you can rest, secure that none may enter unless I let them, and so none shall harm you. Now come with me, for you are cold and the kitchen is warm and altogether more welcoming."

With that Sara led Lucy from the room so that all that remained was the echo of their footsteps walking away down a stone-flagged passageway, and the sound of her voice saying, "The third thing you must believe, Lucy Harker, is that the world in general, and London in particular, is a far, far stranger place that most people ever know."

And as if to prove that fact to the empty room, the hollow clay mannequin stood up, walked across the room and quietly closed the door behind them, before returning to his seat and sitting as motionlessly as before.

CHAPTER 5

THE BLOODSTONE BADGE

Ketch felt woozily happy, despite the chilling fog blanketing the gas-lit streets.

The companionable arm over his shoulder steered him past the King's Arms at the edge of the square, and he looked sideways at the fugged windows and the inviting glow of firelight and candles within. It was a large building, and an observant passer-by might have noticed the horseshoes nailed up above all of the windows as well as the more customary main doorway. Ketch was not of a mood or disposition to observe small details: he was glowing and sentimental and he felt the tavern exerting a magnetic tug on the heavy jingle of coins in his pocket, and then he had a marvellous idea.

"Tell you what," he said, looking up into the face of his wonderful new friend, "tell you what! I should like to stand you a drink to round off a mutually profitable night's work. We could slide in here and have the landlord make us a nice hot ale, or maybe a steaming jug of bishop, yes, bishop's the thing for a chilly night like this, wouldn't you say?"

He was so taken with the idea of sharing a warm glass or two of spiced port with his companion that he could already hear the sizzle of the red-hot poker the landlord was going to plunge into the jug to heat it. In fact he was imagining the lovely smell of orange and cloves and strong wine so intently that he didn't notice Mr Sharp had walked them into a dark side alley until it was too late.

"No," he said. "No, the door's over there——"

His voice was strangled by a fleeting moment of worry, triggered both by the knowledge that this particular alley was a dead end and the sudden memory of the alarming knife this man carried somewhere beneath his coat. But the moment dissolved and he instantly relaxed as the eyes turned on him again: even in the Stygian black of the blind alley he could see their tawny glow and felt flushed and content, as if bathed in the warmth of a thousand summers.

"Nah, but this is fine too," he smiled, with a look on his face that was quite as blurred with happiness as if he had already drunk that imaginary jug of fortified wine.

Mr Sharp gently slid his hand off Ketch's shoulder to grip his chin in such a way that the man could not look away.

"Indeed it is. But it is also goodbye. And it is also this . . ."

He raised his other fist to show him the gold ring he wore. The ring was set with a bloodstone like the one Sara Falk wore, into which was carved a rampant lion facing an equally wild-looking unicorn. He held it out, and when he spoke again there was a distinctly official tone to his voice.

"By the Powers, Mr William Ketch, and as a Free Companion of the London Oversight, I charge you that you will go now, and you will forget what you did with the girl Lucy Harker, and you will forget us, and you will forget the house we have just left: if asked, you will remember she ran off while you were drunk. And because of that," he continued, with a sparkle of cheery malice in his face. "Because of that you will never touch liquor again, and you will be kind to the needy——"

Mr Sharp's nostrils flared slightly and his head came up as he scanned the darkness around them for whatever smell had interrupted his thought. Ketch just nodded, his mouth smiling so sloppily that a thin line of drool dribbled out of the side and spattered on the ground by his boots.

Mr Sharp shook his head and his eyes returned to Ketch. Ketch opened his mouth to say something, but Mr Sharp gently pushed the chin up and closed it again.

"—and because of what you did to the girl's mouth, you shall be unable to speak from now until the first day the dog roses bloom next spring, and when they do you will go and offer your services at the very Bedlam Hospital you spoke of, and help with the washing and cleaning of the poor turned minds who are locked within. That shall be your own punishment and means of rectification."

He reached forward and pressed the ring to Ketch's head. When he took it away, the image of the lion and unicorn was indented on the skin, and for a moment it seemed to glow a mottled red and green like the bloodstone itself, and then it was just a temporary dimple, and then it was gone.

Ketch opened his mouth to speak, and then found he couldn't. He sneezed three times, looked a little confused, then shrugged and scratched his forehead as he turned and stumbled off down the alley, back into the street.

As he walked he rubbed at the itch above his eyes, and then forgot it as he felt the jingle of coins in his pocket and pulled a handful out, pausing to examine them beneath the first gas lamp he came to. He saw a scrabble of tarnished copper ha'pennies and farthings and felt an unaccountable pang of surprise: surely these coins were meant to be something else? But then he couldn't quite remember what or why he might think they would be anything other than they were.

He pocketed the change and was swallowed up by the fog.

CHAPTER 6

THE MISSING UNICORN

Lucy Harker could not keep her eyes still. She sat at the huge wooden table at the warm heart of Sara Falk's kitchen, her neck craning and swivelling as she tried to take in the extraordinary room that ran across almost the whole basement of the house. The only clear space was the table itself, a big five-sided thing with age-darkened oak legs supporting a deal top almost white with the repeated scrubbing it had received over the years.

At the centre of the table burned a single candle surrounded by five leafy twigs, all of different woods, laid in a rough star: an oak twig bearing an acorn crossed another bearing the distinctive keys of an ash, which crossed a sprig of white hawthorn resting on a spray of pink apple blossom that supported a hazel stick heavy with green nuts. Beyond this calm half-acre of scrubbed wood there was an ordered mayhem of shelves and racks and cupboards, with alcoves and pillars leading into glimpsed side-larders and pantries all crammed with boxes, bookcases and bottle racks.

Wherever the eye looked, it found a bewildering variety of things in which the unfamiliar comfortably outnumbered the familiar: apothecary jars with ancient gilt lettering on them fought for shelf space with irregular ziggurats of spice tins while below them on a groaning dresser bucket-shaped stone crocks sprouted explosions of spoons, spatulas and porridge spirtles like exotic wooden flower arrangements. Lowly potato sacks slumped next to metal-trimmed tea chests which in turn supported a regiment of black japanned canisters emblazoned with yellowing paper squares stamped with impressive red Siamese chop marks that made them look more like battle pennants than labels.

One windowsill was piled so high with jars containing such a multicoloured variety of liquids and preserves that the gas lamp shining in from the street above turned it into a three-dimensional stained-glass window.

Even the ceiling was full; every spare inch was jammed with bunches of drying herbs hanging next to smoked hams and strings of onions, and something that looked suspiciously like a blunderbuss. There were recognisable kitchen tools scattered about – homely, useful things like graters and colanders and rolling pins and very up-to-date mechanical devices like hand-cranked apple-peelers and sausage-stuffers. There were also indeterminate contraptions made of metal, wood or glass which seemed as if they'd be equally at home in an alchemist's laboratory, a mechanic's shed or even perhaps a very experimental dungeon.

Knives, hatchets and blades of every shape, size and age (including a notched cutlass and a very hacked-about boarding axe) fanned across one wall next to a similarly bewildering profusion of pots, pans and chafing dishes, all scoured and polished to a high copper sheen, which reflected the fire glowing red in the centre of the huge cast-iron range at the heart of the room.

The range was a great contraption of stove-blackened metal and brass-bound hinges, in the centre of which a fire crackled happily behind the bars of an open grate. "THE DREADNOUGHT

PATENT RANGE" was embossed in blocky lettering across the back of the fireplate, and a kettle the size of a baby hippo-potamus hissed and bubbled on the hotplate beneath.

Next to it on a leather-topped club fender sat Cook, dobbing a mixture of sugar, currants and allspice into the centre of six pastry circles laid out on a small table beside her.

Cook had been introduced to Lucy as just Cook, as if no further name was necessary or indeed available.

She definitely looked at least *part* of the part: she was built on a heroically stocky scale, and the expanse of white pina-fore straining across her ample bosom combined with her generous wide-set curves to give her both the cut and jib of a small galleon, one that had been built at a time when the broadest of beams were in fashion. The part of her that didn't look the part was her face: the wisps of greying and once-blonde hair that escaped from the white cotton mob-cap were ladylike enough, but the black eye patch and the scar that emerged from it to dent her nose and the opposite cheek gave her a wild, buccaneering air. It was an impression entirely supported by the fearless sparkle in her one blue eye, and perhaps explained to the curious and associative mind how a blunderbuss and a boarding axe had become part of her eccentric *batterie de cuisine*.

Despite her size, Cook seemed to have something of Mr Sharp's ability to move fast because Lucy thought she had only glanced up for a moment to examine a duck carcase which appeared to have been run over by a lawn roller before being hung from the roof to dry, but when she dropped her eyes she saw Cook had placed six pastry lumps on a baking tray in front of her. They were the shape (and almost the size) of cannonballs and had been rolled in sugar.

Lucy looked at them, then at Sara Falk, who was sitting on the other side of the table with a bowl of hot water, some flannels, a towel and a box full of old gloves.

"Now, my lovely, these are Eccles cakes," said Cook. Her voice was rough but kind. "We shall bake them for twenty minutes or so, and while we wait for them to come out of the Dreadnought, I will try my best to free your mouth without any distress. I expect the smell of them baking will encourage you to bear any small pain we may accidentally inflict, knowing once we're done you can enjoy eating them, all of them if you wish, perhaps with a nice slice of Lancashire cheese. I assure you they will be worth it: I have used the estimable Mr Henderson's receipt."

She offered Sara a small knife.

"No," said Sara. "Lucy may do it, for the luck of the thing."

Cook expertly spun the blade between her fingers so the handle faced towards Lucy.

"Three slashes across the top of each one, no more, no less," said Sara Falk, giving Lucy an encouraging and mysterious wink. "Threes are powerful things, Lucy, almost as powerful as fives: some say the triple cut is for Mecca, Medina and Jerusalem, some say it's for the Trinity. Others say it's for the Maid, the Mother and the Crone. Wise King Solomon said—"

Cook made a short explosive snort like a boiler blowing a safety valve.

"If Wise King Solomon knew anything about baking, he'd have known it's to let the steam out and stop them exploding sticky mincemeat all over the inside of my nice clean oven."

She jabbed the knife handle at Lucy.

"Come on, girl, let's get this done. My tummy's rumbling."

"Your tummy's always rumbling," said Sara Falk with a smile. "It's like living with a permanent thunderstorm."

"Why—" said Cook, and then cut off abruptly as Lucy snatched the knife from her fingers.

"No!" said Sara, reaching across the table, too late to stop the girl.

Lucy stretched her jaw as far away from her nose as she could manage, like a silent scream, then sliced the tip of the knife into the hessian plaster, the sharp edge of the blade facing away from her, and ripped outwards, wincing as she did so.

"*Aie!*" She said, her voice escaping through the ragged hole she had cut. She stabbed the knife into the wood tabletop where it quivered with the force of her blow as she reached inside her mouth. Her finger came out with a smear of blood on the tip. "*Merde. Je me suis coupée. Ce salaud—*"

Cook blew her cheeks out in shock.

"Hell's teeth!" she exploded. "She's a bloody Frenchy!"

Lucy worked her mouth, trying to spit something out through the hole in the gag.

"Lucy," said Sara, reaching across the table with the flannel while Cook surreptitiously reclaimed her knife and examined the tip for signs of damage. "Do you speak English? *Parlez vous—?*"

The girl managed to spit the thing out of her mouth. It bounced on the scrubbed deal table and came to a halt between them. It was a gold ring and even though it landed face down, they could see from the back that the stone it was set with was broken and half was missing.

Lucy tugged at the hole in her pitch-plaster gag, wincing again and grimacing as she made it bigger. She took several deep breaths and looked at them as if what she had done and the thing she had produced as if by magic from her mouth was perfectly normal.

"*C'est l'anneau de ma mère,*" she said with a shrug. "*Ils ont lui cherché partout, ces salauds avec leurs visages bleus—*"

She reached for the ring and wiped her spit from it on the flannel.

"*—je pensais que j'allais avaler le truc foutu!*"

"What did she say?" said Cook. "She speaks so fast—"

"She said it was her mother's ring. And they searched everywhere for it, those blue-faced, um, bastards. And she thought she was going to swallow the, er, damned thing." Sara raised an eyebrow at Cook. "I must say she swears quite a lot."

"Spirited and clever though, hiding it in her mouth," said Cook with a gleam of approval in her eye.

"And reckless," said Sara Falk. "She could have choked."

"Well, she is a Glint," said Cook. "Just like you. And you were reckless at her age . . ."

"But if she can only speak French . . ." said Sara Falk, ignoring the raised eyebrow that accompanied Cook's observation, "why is she called Lucy Harker?"

Lucy stretched across the table, indicating she wanted Sara Falk's right hand. She let the girl take her glove and turn it to look at the ring she wore outside the glove.

"Lucy," said Sara Falk, "what—?"

Lucy turned her mother's ring over and held it next to the other one. The former's gold setting was an older and thinner style, but the stone, of which half remained in the setting, was also a bloodstone.

And more than that, it was a lion.

Exactly the same lion as the one on Sara Falk's ring. The only thing it lacked was the half of the stone that had cracked and fallen out.

All that was missing was the unicorn.

"Sara," said Cook very slowly, stretching her hand forward and showing another matching bloodstone ring on her flour-covered finger. "Her mother was one of us."

They stared at the girl. She looked at them, then at the rings, then back at Sara.

"*Mais* . . ." Lucy said, hope and distrust fighting for control over the smooth planes of her face. "*Qui êtes-vous?*"

CHAPTER 7

BRIGHT KNIVES IN A DARK ALLEY

Mr Sharp did not see Ketch count his gold under the gaslight and find that it was copper. He didn't see him shrug and forget why this should disappoint him, nor did he see the man walk on and disappear into the gloom. He did not see any of that.

He was still in the alley by the pub, but was standing with his back to the fog-muffled lights of the square. His nostrils were flared, like a hunting dog testing the wind, and he was staring into the pitch-black dead end waiting for something to move. His right hand was cocked beneath his coat, fingers ready over the handle of his blade.

Seconds passed, then minutes, but he did not move a muscle.

After five minutes had passed, he decided he had imagined whatever he thought he had sensed and was about to turn when the side door of the King's Arms slammed open. It was a high door and above it a horseshoe had been nailed, just as on the windows and door at the front of the tavern. A shard of candle-light jagged across the dark alley, far enough for Mr Sharp to see something on the cobbles, and then a red-faced man in a barman's apron peered out and his shadow blotted out whatever it was again as he shouted.

"Bessie? Bessie? Where are you, girl?"

He cocked an ear for a moment but there was no reply. He disappeared back inside, slamming the alley back into darkness.

Mr Sharp moved quickly across the cobbles and picked up the thing he had seen in the brief slash of light.

It was a woman's shoe.

He looked at it for a moment and then carefully placed it on the barrelhead of one of the empty casks stacked up against the side of the building. He stepped back to the middle of the alley and drew his blade.

"Let her go," he said quietly.

Time seemed to go very still in the dark slot between the pub and the blank-faced house next door.

Nothing happened.

Nobody answered.

And Mr Sharp did not move.

And still nobody answered.

And still Mr Sharp did not move.

And nobody went on answering and nothing moved until the shadows shifted and an ugly laugh tumbled out of the darkness, followed by a harsh voice that was angular and somehow northern.

"I wondered if you could see me."

Mr Sharp nodded.

"So did I."

A whimper followed the ugly voice into the light, a whimper that came from a young woman's mouth and was immediately stifled with a hand. The unseen speaker laughed again.

Mr Sharp reached inside his coat and pulled out a candle. He held it upright and snapped his wrist. The candle ignited by itself, and when he tossed it into the darkness it remained alight, even as it bounced and rolled on the ground and came to rest at a pair of slender top-boots.

The boots were made of some close-cropped fur, like seal-skin, and they emerged from a long moleskin coat. Thanks to the candle, Mr Sharp could see that it wasn't the kind of tough velvety moleskin material woven in one of the cotton mills sprouting up all over the newly industrialised Midlands. It was the other kind, the old kind, and old in two ways: not only was it worn and greasy with age, it was made from the skins of hundreds of dead moles, stitched together. The flattened heads had been left on and hung downwards, which gave the tight-fitting coat a scaly look like a kind of soft chain-mail. In place of buttons it was fastened across the chest with the bones and skulls of small animals, bleached and yellow with long use.

The coat wasn't the strangest thing, nor the fact that its owner was holding a young serving girl gently by the hand, her clothes unbuttoned and dishevelled, her flushed face slack and happily drooling with an expression very much like the one on Bill Ketch's face when he had been with Mr Sharp: what was strangest was the man in the moleskin coat's own face.

He had a forked beard which jutted untidily forward of his chin like a goat, and his hair was swept back off a high forehead and tied in two braids strung with more bird skulls and tiny animal bones. From the hairline to the tip of his nose his skin was covered in writhing blue tattoos so dense that his eyes peered brightly out of them as if he were wearing a mask.

He cocked his head at Mr Sharp.

"What are you?" he asked, his voice hissing softly in a way that reminded Mr Sharp of the sound that winter waves made after they had broken and were draining back off a cold shingle beach.

There was something majestic about the man, but there was also something grotesque and corrupt; he was somehow smaller than he appeared to be at first sight. His smile was regal and arrogant until he spoke, when his teeth showed through the tangle of his beard, brown and mossy like neglected tombstones jumbled at the back of an overgrown churchyard.

"I am the person asking you to let the girl go inside to her father, who is looking for her," said Mr Sharp. His voice remained even and reasonable.

"Go away, *boy*," spat the man, waving a hand dismissively.

"I cannot. Not now I have seen you."

The bones rattled as the man shook his head in irritation.

"You carry a familiar blade, and yet you are not what the marks on it say you should be. You can make light, but you need a candle to hold it. And you held the Ketch man's mind and bent it to yours, but only to punish him for some trifle."

"It wasn't a trifle," said Mr Sharp. "Now please let the girl go, mind and body."

"Well, it wasn't much of a punishment either, truth to tell," continued the man with a short bark of laughter, quickly strangled. "Now if I was *punishing* a man I'd slit him up the back and skin him slowly, then make him put his pelt back on inside out and dance a jig in it until his feet wore out or he ceased to amuse me: that's a *punishment*."

"No. That's an abomination."

"Abomination?" he snorted with derision. "You exaggerate. I'm just talking about a *man*. At best it's a diversion . . ."

"Abomination or diversion, I can't allow that, or anything like it."

"Who are you to allow or disallow anything to a Pure One?" rasped the tattooed man. "I do not even know what you are, aping us and yet talking like one of them, like some cross-bred mongrel everybody kicks—"

"I am Sharp," he replied calmly. "And I know you are going to put the girl down and step away from her."

"Or?"

"Or you will have a chance to kick this mongrel and find out exactly how hard it bites."

"You think you can better me, a half-breed runtlet like you?" he spat. "Slink away now or I'll hurt you so bad you'll skin yourself to make me stop . . ."

Mr Sharp didn't blink.

"I cannot leave. I am sworn to this. And if you try to harm the girl it will be my pleasure to enable you to read the marks on this blade much, much closer than you will find comfortable."

The tattooed man's hand snuck inside his coat and emerged with a blade of his own, flashing gold in the candlelight, a thick strangely recurved thing like a broken-backed sickle made of bronze. He hooked it round the girl's neck. She just smiled dreamily and giggled as if the razor-sharp edge were tickling her like a feather.

"Ah now, boy, I had only thought to sport with this girl and be gone, but if we're to play at blades, I think I shall wet mine first, and this pretty will be on your dainty conscience. So perhaps you should just put up your knife and walk on. I have no mind to do anything with the girl which she has likely enough not done already, and if she has not, well, she will do it often enough in the future. There will be no permanent harm to her, unless you persist."

Mr Sharp looked at the girl.

"Bess?" he said. "Bess, are you all right?"

Her eyes wandered and then found his and for a moment seemed to focus, but then went dreamy again.

"Her mind's not her own for now is all," said the strange man. "Now, you don't want to cross blades with me, mongrel boy. My sword was singing long, long before the bitch that bore you was whelped, and will sing on long after your grave's grown over and the headstone gone to dust in the wind."

"Ah. You're trying to provoke me," said Mr Sharp. "You're trying to get inside my head."

The tattooed man snarled angrily.

"I'll be inside your guts in a min—"

And then, before he could finish, the dreamy girl moved so fast that he had no time to defend himself as she twisted and ducked and rolled, spinning her neck clear of the hooked blade.

Her left hand clamped round his wrist, yanking his arm straight while her right smacked up into the elbow, sending it the wrong way with an ugly crack.

The blade dropped from his convulsing fingertips, his mouth opening to emit a shriek of pain as her remaining shoe kicked his knee sideways.

He dropped lopsided to the cobbles while her right hand calmly snatched the tumbling dagger from the air and held it to his neck.

Stilling him wide-eyed on the ground.

Killing the yell in his throat.

"If he so much as blinks, cut his damn head off," snapped Mr Sharp, already in motion. He ran and jumped, boosting off the barrelhead and seeming to run sideways along the wall of the pub as he snatched the horseshoe off the lintel above the door and then leapt across the width of the alley to land at Bess's side, slamming the open ends of the horseshoe on either side of the tattooed man's neck, pinning him to the ground.

"No!" squealed the man. "No, please – it burns!"

"Cold iron," said Mr Sharp. "I lied. I know *exactly* what cruel stock you come from. Now be still a moment."

He held his hand out to the girl. Her eyes brightened for a flicker and then dulled to a sleepy happiness again. She handed him the bronze blade.

"Thank you, Bess," he said as she gazed into the autumnal

tumble of his eyes. "Now forget all this. You went for a walk because your head was hurting but it's better now and you heard me calling for assistance, and now you're going to go in and tell your father that Mr Sharp sends his compliments and has a customer for the cells in the Sly House for the night."

She shook her head as if coming out of a sleep and then sneezed three times. She wiped her eyes and smiled at him clear-eyed.

"Why, Mr Sharp," she said as if seeing him for the first time. "You've apprehended yourself another miscreant. Shall I get my father to open the cells?"

"That would be a considerable kindness, my dear," he said with great seriousness, and watched her run inside.

"You got inside her head while I was trying to get into yours," hissed the tattooed man. "You made her do all that fighting. You could never have beaten me in a fair contest."

He was looking smaller and older by the minute, as if the iron in the horseshoe was leaching the power from him. The dark blue tattoos on his face were beginning to fade, bleaching out to a pale blue as his power waned, revealing the tired and washed-out eyes of a very old man.

"Ah well," said Mr Sharp, keeping him in place with the horseshoe round his neck like a giant staple. "Mongrels don't fight fair, especially not with the foul."

"You call me foul because you have tricked me into a disadvantage," he wheezed. "But you do not know what enemy you have just made, you mannerless puppy. Our blood is Pure, our blood is One and I am *Many*!"

His eyes flashed for a moment, then faded again. Mr Sharp smiled down at him.

"I know who you are. I recognised the smell and the tattoos. You are one of the Night Host, a Shadowganger. You are one of the Sluagh," he said, pronouncing the word "sloo-er", his lip curling with an evident distaste as he did so. "But your place is in the north. Your place is the wild lands. That is the Law and the Lore."

The Sluagh shook his head and winced as his neck touched the iron on either side. His voice was weakening and fading as fast as his tattoos were washing out but there was still a flicker of defiance within him.

"That is your Lore, not ours. We live wherever we will and always outside the Lore. What is this Lore anyway?"

"The heart of the Lore is simple," said Mr Sharp in a measured voice, the kind a teacher might use to a slow but excitable child. "It says you cannot come among defenceless men, women and children and prey on them. If you do, we will stop you."

The Sluagh tried to snarl but only had the energy to curl his lip.

"What almighty 'we' is this?"

"You know who those of us who carry this badge are. We are the Free Company. We are Law and Lore . . ."

Mr Sharp made a fist and held the ring in front of the Sluagh's eyes.

". . . we are The Oversight."

CHAPTER 8

THE SHADOW GUARD

"*Qui êtes-vous?*" said Lucy again.

"Are you going to tell her?" said Cook. Lucy was trying to keep still as she fussed about her with cloths and a bowl of warm olive oil, softening the plaster and carefully pulling it off her face in small increments. Sara stood behind, gently keeping her from squirming with a firm grip on each of her shoulders.

"Why not?" said Sara. "I've already tried to explain that she's a Glint. And if the ring is hers, she has a right to know."

"She's listening," said Cook without looking at Lucy. "I think she understands us."

"Do you speak English?" said Sara, gripping the shoulder-blades a little harder and turning to peer closely at her. Lucy kept her face blank.

"Lucy. *Parles-tu anglais?*"

"*Non. Je veux seulement savoir qui vous êtes!*"

"She just wants to know who we are—" said Sara.

"I can speak French quite as well as you can, thank you," said Cook sharply. "Especially when she speaks slowly. I just don't think now is the time to tell her."

"She's a Glint," repeated Sara. "And now she knows what she is, sooner or later she will have to know who we are."

"Later will be better," said Cook. "Once we know more about her."

"Once The Oversight welcomed and protected those who were as unaware of their powers as she is until they could master them and put them to good use."

Cook shook her head.

"Once The Oversight was many Hands strong. Once we had so many members in so many Hands that I could not have fed them in six shifts seated round the great table upstairs!" she said, jabbing her finger at the ceiling. "Now we can fit round this small table with room to spare. These are not the old days, Sara. Now there is just you and I and Sharp and Hodge and The Smith, and no others. We are the Last Hand and we cannot behave as we did before the Disaster. Do you understand what I'm saying?"

Sara saw not just the flint but also the flicker of worry in the older woman's eyes.

"Sara," repeated Cook, "do you understand what I'm saying?"

"Yes," said Sara. "You are saying there is room for one more at the table."

Cook exhaled like a porpoise clearing its blowhole.

"You are ungovernable and incorrigible . . ."

"Thank you," said Sara with a smile.

Sara began to speak in French. Lucy swivelled and craned her neck round to watch her, lips closed to avoid getting a mouthful of oil as Cook dabbed away at it.

"We were founded long ago," Sara said, "when the world was less crowded and people liked to fill up the space with four or five long words where one simple one would do: we are the Free Company for the Regulation and Oversight of Recondite Exigency and Supranatural Lore."

"What?" said Lucy, feeling like she'd just been hit by a landslide of words that buried any meaning deep beyond her reach. Sara Falk smiled.

"Amongst ourselves we're known as The Oversight. For short."

"Or The Lore," said Cook. "For shorter."

"What does it mean?" said Lucy, hackles of suspicion rising. "The words are too confusing . . ."

"It's simple: 'recondite exigency' just means strange, hidden things that happen without a normal explanation. 'Supranatural lore' is knowledge and customs that apply to those things. 'Regulation and oversight' means we watch the shadows and police what goes on there. And a 'Free Company' means we band together and do this of our own free will, and are subject to no king or government."

"Or queen," said Cook.

"Or queen," agreed Sara Falk.

"God save her," said Cook stoutly.

"Indeed," said Sara Falk.

No question, thought Lucy. Both of them were mad.

"This does not make sense to me," she said. "And I still don't understand who you are . . ."

Sara took a deep breath.

"Long ago, before the idea of history had even been born, there were many different kinds of people: some were very fast, some were very strong, some came out at night and slept in the day, some could silently 'think' to each other the way we talk out loud. They weren't unnatural because they were part of nature. But if you take nature as what is normal, and normal as what *most* people can do, well, they were perhaps 'supra'-natural—"

Lucy nodded, although she wasn't listening as closely as she appeared to be. She was thinking that there were two doors between her and the outside door through which she had been brought into this odd house. She was retracing the steps which had brought her here, thinking that she could probably outrun Sara if she got a head start.

"'Supra' means above and beyond. Or extra. It's Latin," said Cook helpfully. "Powerful stuff, Latin."

Her nose twitched, smelling some subtle change in the baking smell emanating from the Dreadnought Range. There was an alarming creak of stressed wood as she swivelled in her chair, grabbing a potholder as she turned.

Lucy watched as the Eccles cakes were pulled from the oven and slid onto the table in front of her. They now looked like small golden cannonballs. The sugary baking smell and the odour of nutmeg and clove swirled slowly around her like a warm blanket.

Her stomach gurgled despite herself as Sara continued:

"They had extra abilities which most 'normal' men have forgotten about, abilities which people might make up stories about and call 'diabolical' or 'elvish' or 'dwarfish' or things like that, you see?"

Lucy shrugged a "yes", thinking she could probably turn chairs over as she ran to the first door, and that these obstacles would buy her the time she needed to escape.

She had frighteningly large blanks in her memory, especially about the recent past, and was feeling woolly-headed as if she had been drugged, but the body remembers things the mind doesn't and she knew she had the ability to move unusually quietly and speedily. She knew she had staved off hunger in the past by catching rabbits in the fields, being quiet enough to get very close to them and fast enough to catch them when they ran. That fragment of memory made her stomach rumble again. She had not eaten in a very long time.

Then she noticed they were both watching her as if expecting another question.

"Oh. So, er . . . where did they go?" she said quickly. "These people with 'supra' abilities?"

"They didn't go anywhere," said Cook in English.

Lucy caught her piercing look and again had the thought that this deceptively fat lady might move unexpectedly fast. There was steel in her eye, and that fat was more muscle than it seemed. Lucy remembered to appear baffled, as if she hadn't understood. Cook repeated her answer in French, and Lucy let her face uncloud and nodded. She would definitely need to throw chairs down behind her, and not just to trip Sara Falk. She would also grab a cleaver from the knife rack as she passed in case she needed to make them both keep their distance. Lucy knew about running and she knew about fighting. Sometimes it felt as if she'd been doing both all her life.

This talk of supranatural powers had confirmed her resolve to get away from these two women who were, despite being outwardly friendly, clearly mad, even madder than she knew herself to be.

And the homely, seductive smell of the baking was far too nice to be real.

Sara Falk rolled down her glove and pulled back the cuff of her dress, exposing an elegant wrist which she flexed and held, palm up, towards Lucy.

The room was very still. Perhaps because Lucy had now worked out how she was going to run for it, both halves of her mind came together and focused on what was being told her. It seemed to her that the only thing moving was the pulse bumping the blue artery beneath the tautness of Sara Falk's skin.

"They went there," Cook said. "Into the blood."

"They went into your blood?" Lucy began.

"They went into everyone's blood," said Sara. "They mixed. And married. And bred. And the supranatural blended with the natural, and just became part of us all. Most supranatural abilities just got diluted down the generations and are barely noticeable if indeed noticed at all. But some strains stay strong in the blood and are passed mother to daughter or father to son, like you and I and glinting, and others, well, just as two normal white sheep sometimes throw a black lamb, sometimes old blood comes back strong and you get a throwback."

Cook slid an Eccles cake towards Lucy. The smell wrapped round her and threatened to loosen her resolve to escape, so she told herself to ignore it, that it was a lie, that these people were liars, that everyone lies.

"Don't touch it until it's cooled a bit," Cook said. "Mincemeat will still be hot enough to scald you."

"But not *all* the supranatural peoples mixed," said Sara Falk. "Some kept themselves apart. They call themselves things like the Pure, the Clean or the Saved. Depends where in the world they are hidden."

"But how can they be in the world and we don't see them?" said Lucy. "How can they not be known about? This is stupid."

"As there are always more shadows than light, and more layers in the shadows than you can imagine, they choose to live in the layered darknesses of our world," said Sara Falk. "And if they come out of the shadows and harm normal men, we put them back."

Cook pushed a knife and fork across the table and lurched to her feet.

"Cut it open; it'll cool faster. But don't eat a mouthful until I get you some cheese. Can't eat an Eccles cake without a slice of nice crumbly cheese."

Lucy no longer had to think about any of this: chance had again put a knife in her hand and Cook was disappearing into a larder at the far end of the kitchen. It was as if fate had suddenly arranged all of this to allow her escape. All she had to do was distract Sara, and her hand was moving before she'd fully thought about how to do it. She was a natural survivor and sometimes her body seemed to think for itself while her conscious mind caught up later on, when she'd got to a place of greater safety.

She grabbed the piping hot ball of sugar-hardened pastry and threw it into Sara's face.

She heard the gasp of surprise, but by the time she heard it she had toppled a chair and was sprinting for the door. She scrabbled at the handle and felt a flash of relief as it opened. Her fear that it had been locked behind her evaporated and she saw the key was in the outside—

—because of that she allowed herself a fast look over her shoulder to see if she had time to slam it shut and lock them in so she could make her escape more safely.

Cook was fast.

She was out of the larder and already halfway across the kitchen. But she stopped next to Sara, who was wiping the smashed Eccles cake off her face, trying not to wince at the heat of the mincemeat in her eye.

Neither of them was chasing her.

"Sara—" said Cook.

"I'm fine," said Sara tightly.

"You're burnt," said Cook. "Stupid. I told you it was too soon."

The calmness with which they looked at her but did not follow was somehow more chilling than if they'd rushed pell-mell after her.

She would have to lock them in before they got over the shock. Without taking her eyes off them she sprang backwards through the door.

And bounced straight back into the room.

She stumbled, lost her footing and sprawled on the floor.

It was her turn to gasp in surprise.

The door was blocked by the massive clay-faced coachman, immoveable as a brick wall.

She was trying to think how the statue had been moved

into place when it – impossibly – raised a finger and shook it slowly side to side, as if to say "no". And then scowled and bunched it into a fist as it took a half step forward—

"No, Emmet!"

Sara's voice cracked across the table, angry.

"Emmet! No. She didn't understand. She didn't mean to harm me."

The clay giant seemed to emit some kind of subsonic growl which Lucy felt rumbling through the scrubbed floorboards as much as heard, and then stepped back and closed the door.

"What's wrong, girl?" said Cook with a grim smile. "Never seen a golem before?"

CHAPTER 9

THE TRIPLE-WOOD CELL

It wasn't just the horseshoes nailed up over every opening which made the King's Arms especially outlandish in a city full of unusual taverns and alehouses: what made it unique was the fact that it was not merely a busy pub but also a working jail.

There had long been a small courthouse in the building next door and it had become customary to lodge prisoners in the adjoining cellars, known as the Sly House, which meant that the landlord drew both beer and a jailer's salary. Most of the people sent through the door between the court and the King's Arms were petty debtors who remained incarcerated until their debts were paid off, and their accommodation was unremarkable for anything other than Spartan discomfort and the damp that rose from the ground at night, as if the twenty acres of water penned in the New London Dock just two streets to the south was trying to soak its way back up into the city proper.

These were the public cells.

Behind them was the ale cellar where the beer barrels were stored, and beyond that was a secret door that led to a low brick-lined tunnel known as the Close Passage.

The Close Passage led to the Privy Cells.

The Privy Cells did not belong to the courthouse; indeed the officers of the court knew nothing of them, nor did they know that the Close Passage actually continued past the cells and through a pair of locked doors to a junction, where it split. The left fork led south, taking a short journey down to the Thames at Hermitage Dock, while the right fork burrowed west across the corner of the square, under a secret entrance to Sara Falk's house and onwards through increasingly thick sets of subterranean doors, all the way to an anonymous and little-opened culvert gate within the Inner Ward of the Tower of London itself.

William George Bunyon, father of the recently dishevelled but thankfully largely unmolested Bessie Bunyon, was the present landlord-jailer of the King's Arms, and he had never gone – or thought to go – beyond the double doors at the limit of his property. He was a cheerful and outgoing man, naturally hospitable yet firm, in short both an exemplary landlord and a benevolent jailer. Above ground, behind the bar or beside the crackling fire in the snug, he displayed a talent for talking and joking, a gift that not only put everyone at their ease but had the not unprofitable side-effect of usefully encouraging customers to stay longer and buy more beer. Underground, in the Privy Cells, he talked much less and only rarely asked anything other than the one question.

He asked it now, as Mr Sharp pushed the Sluagh into the cell ahead of him.

"Bad 'un is he, Mr Sharp?"

"Yes, Mr Bunyon. A right bad 'un," confirmed Mr Sharp as he in turn always did.

Bunyon nodded as if he understood everything now, which he neither did nor minded about.

He wore, in addition to the high apron of his profession, a pair of dark-lensed spectacles like the ones Sara Falk wore. He had been trained by Mr Sharp never to enter the passage without them because some of the guests in the cells had the disturbing ability to turn men's minds if they could only look them straight in the eye. This was an undoubtedly queer thing but William Bunyon never thought it so, precisely because Mr Sharp himself had looked him in the eye a long time ago and diverted his normally wide-ranging inquisitiveness so that it flowed quite around the narrow matter of the Close Passage, the Privy Cells and their occasional strange residents without touching on it at all. If asked who Mr Sharp and his colleagues actually were (which he never was) the jovial landlord would have put a knowing finger to the side of his generous red nose, dropped an eyelid and muttered something about "officers of the law", which was not a million miles from the truth, especially if you spelled things a bit differently.

The cell was lined in wood, floor and ceiling, like a rougher version of the anteroom in the basement of Sara Falk's house. Mr Sharp was controlling the Sluagh by the horseshoe held round his neck. The Sluagh now seemed impossibly old and frail, his once-dark tattoos reduced to a thin scrabble of blue lines that could have been mistaken for broken veins beneath his paper-thin skin.

Mr Sharp hooked a wooden stool out from under the cot with his boot-tip and dragged it into the middle of the room.

"Sit," he said, forcing the Sluagh down on it, facing away from the doorway. "The tray, Mr Bunyon, if you please."

William Bunyon slid a wooden tray onto the floor just inside the door and withdrew his hand quickly.

"There is ale and water and bread," said Mr Sharp.

"And cheese," said Mr Bunyon, who had stepped safely back out of sight.

"And cheese," said Mr Sharp.

"And a nice apple," Mr Bunyon's voice insisted.

"And an apple," sighed Mr Sharp. "Indeed, Mr Bunyon

spoils you. Now, I shall take the iron from your neck and you will not move until you hear the door lock. Understood?"

"Yaass," hissed the Sluagh, and the voice that slithered weakly out of his mouth sounded every bit as ancient and corrupt as he now looked.

Mr Sharp yanked the horseshoe free and flickered out of the door in no time at all. The lock snicked shut before the Sluagh could even raise his head.

"Well," he said, gazing round. "Well. You think this box can hold me?"

"Yes," said Mr Sharp from the other side of the door. "Look at the woods that surround you."

The Sluagh stumbled to his feet and staggered to the wall. His good hand stroked across the panels and recoiled slowly.

"Oak . . . ash . . . and thorn," he breathed. "You are cruel."

"We are not cruel. We are modern and humane. Hence the bread and ale and water and Mr Bunyon's very fine and somewhat superfluous apple," smiled Mr Sharp. "But we *are* also cautious."

The Sluagh spat weakly at the wall and watched the phlegmy gobbet dribble down the planking.

"Woods of protection, woods of binding," he wheezed. "And something else too, something I cannot see that is making me as slow and rudderless as the men you protect, something like the cold iron you burned me with—"

"The back of each plank is carved with words against such as you, for extra protection," said Mr Sharp. "Your abilities will not, I'm afraid, work at all in there. I only mention it to save you later disappointments."

The Sluagh turned and looked into Mr Sharp's eyes through the narrow viewing slit in the door.

"You are very dainty for a mongrel. What are you going to do with me?"

"I am going to check across the metropolis to see if you have been up to any other mischief or viciousness. If you have, you will answer to The Smith's Court and be punished. If not—"

The Sluagh threw back his head with a rattle of small bones, and chopped out a short bitter laugh.

"The Smith? What of him? The Sluagh do not answer to anyone or anything, neither mongrels like you nor a turncoat cripple-foot like him. We are Pure. Besides," he wheezed, "The Smith's Court may still exist in name, but The Smith himself is no longer seen, we hear. He is gone and lost in the wind like the rest of your company."

Mr Sharp's nostrils flared a little, but apart from that there was no sign that the barb flung by the Sluagh had found its mark.

"If The Smith is not seen by you and yours, it is because he chooses not to be seen," he said.

The Sluagh laughed.

"And the mighty Oversight? You talk as if you are still something. But you are almost extinguished. Your great days are gone."

"If the Sluagh think our misfortunes have weakened us to the point where you can come into the cities and prey on normal people, then they and you are much mistaken," said Mr Sharp.

The Sluagh smiled nastily.

"Why else would we come into a city? A city is an abomination to us, a place of iron and steel, just as a brick-built farmyard with its fenced-in chicken run is a blight to the open countryside a fox loves. But like the fox and the chicken run, we have learned that a city has the single virtue of concentrating and controlling the quarry in one place . . ."

"And because you cannot control yourselves, just as the fox once inside a chicken coop cannot stop his blood frenzy, Law and Lore forbid you from entering and limit you to the Wild Lands," said Sharp.

"But our wild land is not protected from your cities!" snarled the Sluagh. "And year by year the stink of iron and machinery begins to spread into our domain, with forges and manufactories, and rails of steel hammered into the ground like great metal snakes that run for hundreds of miles, caging the wild beneath it, breaking the flows of the older lines. And your precious Law and Lore do not protect us from that!" He spat again. "You are pets; we are Pure—"

"You are many things, I'm sure," cut in Mr Sharp. "But what you are *now* is in here for the night. I suggest you get some sleep."

"We do not sleep."

"My mistake. Of course you don't." Mr Sharp bobbed his head in apology. "Sit quietly then and wait until morning. I will come back then."

The Sluagh looked round his cell and waved a dismissive hand at the viewing slit.

"Don't trouble yourself. There is no window here. By morning I shall have stifled."

"You exaggerate," said Mr Sharp. He was in a hurry to get back above ground because he wished to see what was happening with the strange girl whom Ketch had deposited with Sara Falk, and he had one more thing to do before he could return home, which was to patrol the area in case the Sluagh had had any accomplices lurking in the fog. Mr Sharp did not like leaving any unpleasant possibility unexamined.

He turned on his heel and nodded at the landlord.

"Lock him up, Bunyon. I will be back in the morning if not before." He headed away down the corridor. Bunyon bent and slammed home the first of the three heavy bolts that added security to the lock on the door. When he had shot them all he peered in one last time, his hand rising to close the slit on the judas hole. As he did so he caught the Sluagh's eyes which were staring right back at him, and paused.

"I am a creature of the air." The Sluagh's voice wheezed in complaint. "Not some shadow-fed dirt-burrower. And you say you are not cruel."

Bunyon watched him through the viewing slit for a long beat. The Sluagh stared palely back, his shoulders heaving as he tried to get air into his lungs. With each breath Bunyon could hear them crackling and popping like a small twig fire. It was a sad and pathetic noise, and Bunyon was a kind-hearted jailer.

"Very well," he said. "I will leave this slit open. That will allow more air in. Goodnight to you, sir. You may as well rest. Nothing has ever escaped these cells. Your mischief is over for the night."

The Sluagh watched the lantern light bobbing away through the slit, listening as the footsteps diminished until they were cut off by the sound of the door to the ale cellar opening and then slamming him into darkness.

He listened some more, heard nothing and knew he was alone.

Then – and only then – did he reply with a nasty smile containing such a distillation of malice in it that for a moment he regained the malign vigour of a much younger version of himself.

"Oh no, my fine fellow: the mischief has just begun."

CHAPTER 10

BREAKING THE LIP

The black carriage had pulled into a stable in a mews behind a tall house just off Bishopsgate. Coram slithered from the driver's seat, turned up an oil lamp on the wall and opened the door of the carriage.

"We're 'ome, Father," he said unnecessarily. Issachar made no move to emerge. He sat on the leather bench with a small basket on each side of him. Coram could see the oysters in them and his mouth watered. His father, who made his living by missing nothing, saw this and smiled. He wore a stained leather apron which served as a bib and napkin, protecting the sombre lawyer's clothes beneath it. He pointed from one basket to the other with the stubby knife in his right hand.

"Whitstables and Colchesters, my boy. Whitstables for meat, Colchester for cream."

His eyes, which had seemed so cheerful when talking to the pastor, had now deadened to something altogether flatter and more calculating. For a moment he seemed to be staring deep into the distance and seeing something only visible to himself.

"My grandfather's grandfather burned witches at Whitstable."

As he spoke, he tossed an oyster and the knife to Coram

with the unconsidered condescension of a man tossing a bone to his dog. Coram moved fast and caught them both with either hand.

"Burned 'em did 'e?" he said.

Templebane nodded. And this was one of the hidden truths of the Templebanes – more than a century and a half before Issachar and Zebulon and their polished carriage, they had been Puritan witchfinders and witch-prickers, riding the countryside searching for the unnatural and the abnormal and bringing those they found to trial and death by hanging or burning.

The Templebanes had been cunning men with a nose and an eye for the strange and the vulnerable, especially those who existed in the shadowy margins of even the most simple and sunlit agricultural communities. Their progress through the eastern counties of England had added a dark streak of blood and ash to the misery of a country torn by civil war. But they had been Puritans in dress only and had understood that, since fortune swings over men's lives like a pendulum, the witch craze that attended the Roundheads' victory and the following Commonwealth would pass, and that those who had prosecuted it would likely end up themselves pursued. The most successful witchfinders had a habit of ending their lives accused of the very dark powers they claimed to be able to search out in their victims, by a process of reasoning that said their success was itself unnatural and that the information they were privy to could only come into their possession through uncanny means.

The Templebanes certainly did have a network of informers and other stranger and more questionable allies, and perhaps because of this, they remained alert to the dangers of outstaying their welcome as Cromwell's Puritan protectorate dwindled and the return of a less judgemental monarchy became increasingly inevitable.

Ever adaptable, they had quit the rural stage before the curtain fell and moved to London, where the large amount of money they had earned for finding witches (paid by the government or the parish) and the even larger sum they had earned for *not* finding witches (paid by the accused witches and their families) was put to good use buying property and setting up a broker's house in the City of London.

Within two generations, the Templebanes were wholly respectable: they were not only owners of a brokerage but also lawyers or, as Issachar and Zebulon's father had once said with a disconcertingly uncharacteristic chuckle, "Poachers *and* gamekeepers, my boys, poachers and gamekeepers both, and all the world to play for."

Respectability might have sat on them like a well-lined cloak, but beneath it they remained cunning men, and cunning men know that information itself is power. So they had never wholly given up on the shadowy contacts made by their forebears as they had travelled the hedgerows and remote villages of England, nor had they forgotten what they had learned about the gap between the natural and the supranatural worlds, not least the incontrovertible fact that both existed, and that there was often a profit to be turned brokering the exchanges between the two when opportunity presented itself.

Issachar watched Coram trying to open the oyster, saw him slip and bloody his knuckles on the sharp shell, and noted with approval that he did not cry out.

"You must break the lip," said a voice from the doorway, "then the knife goes in easier."

The voice was Issachar's, but he was still in the coach and his lips had not moved. Coram looked across the stable and saw what appeared to be the spitting image of Issachar, minus the apron, step heavily into the light. Coram nodded.

"Father," he said.

And this was another hidden truth about the Templebanes:

the bloodline tended to throw identical twins, and this was not Issachar, but Zebulon Templebane. In this way the orphan boys adopted into the house of Templebane may have lacked a mother, but gained two fathers in lieu. The current twins came by their archaic names due to a combination of professional foresight – the Templebanes holding that biblical names added a veneer of gravitas to their chosen line of work, though they were not, in truth, remotely religious – and uncharacteristic whimsy, their own father being a Jacob Templebane, and Issachar and Zebulon being listed in the book of Genesis as sons of the first Jacob.

In earlier times, previous twins had ridden the countryside separately, gaining the reputation among a rural and credulous populace, who were unaware of the fact there was a pair of them, for uncannily being able to be in two places at once. Since the current twins had long ago agreed it would be more efficient to keep different hours, in order that Templebane & Templebane would gain the enviable distinction of being "the house that never sleeps", their adoptees called them Day Father and Night Father.

Zebulon, the Night Father, reached for the knife and oyster, which the boy relinquished with visible regret. He had hoped for food, and knew now that he was going to get a lesson instead. Issachar spoke as Zebulon demonstrated how to open the oyster.

"There is a man, an ordinary man, a man with no abnormal powers but certainly abnormal wealth who wishes to possess something in that house on Wellclose Square."

"And he has commissioned us to help?" said Coram, eager to show he was catching on. "Catching on" was one of the qualities his adoptive fathers valued above anything else, bar a closed mouth to strangers and complete loyalty to the house of Templebane & Templebane.

There was a beat of silence as Zebulon cracked the lip of

the oyster and slid his knife inside, working it round, audibly severing the strong muscle keeping it shut.

"So it would . . . appear," he said.

"Ah. He *thinks* he has commissioned us," said Coram.

Zebulon jabbed at the oyster with the knife, seeing it flinch with an approving smile.

"Alive, alive-o," he said. "Never eat a dead one, boy, or you'll shit yourself into the grave."

He didn't, at that moment, sound at all like a lawyer. He stared thoughtfully at Coram, who was unable to read that thought and avoided the resulting uncomfortable feeling by repeating himself.

"So he *thinks* he has commissioned us, Father?"

The Night Father snorted and swallowed the oyster. His dead eyes lit up with a flash of life as he chewed down, extinguishing the oyster between his teeth, squirting its juices down his throat.

"Any conjurer or card sharp knows the only freedom about will is the freedom to manipulate it," he said.

He held his hand up to forestall interruption.

"But in this business we are, as ever, mere honest brokers. Our patron wants something in that house, a powerful key that only someone with extraordinary powers can have a chance of obtaining. We do not have those powers, God be thanked—"

"God be thanked," said Coram, his eyes following the flash of steel as Zebulon tossed the oyster knife back across the stable to Issachar. There was something unnerving about the way the twins behaved when in the same room, a disconcerting thing which the boys only occasionally felt unwatched enough to discuss among themselves: the twins often talked and moved as if they shared the same brain, and did not need to speak to know what the other was going to do. In this moment, the uncanny synchronicity between the twins showed itself in the way Issachar reached out and caught the knife without seeming to need to look for it.

"Indeed," said Issachar picking another oyster – a Colchester this time – from the basket at his side. "That house is sealed tighter than this oyster. So we needed a tool to get in."

He broke the lip of the oyster with the brass butt plate on the knife, and then twisted the stubby blade, opening the flat top half of the shell with a small cracking noise. He smiled across it at Coram.

"Now, it happens that our patron has, among his many treasures, another item that others who do happen to possess such powers want, but may not have. So I have brokered things in order that they will help us in acquiring the key in the Jew's house, in return for which they will be given the object they wish."

"Is it a valuable object?" said Coram, eying the oyster meat hungrily.

"They call it a flag, but it is no more than a tattered rag," said Issachar.

"And the key?"

"A thing of great value," said Zebulon.

"Rags for riches then, Fathers?" said Coram, licking his lips.

"So it seems. To the great man . . ." said Issachar.

Coram had played enough of these games to know he was being given an opening to "catch on", and that catching on was not only praised, but often greeted with a reward. His eyes had not wavered from the oyster glistening so appetisingly in the lamplight.

"The rag is powerful too?" he said.

"So it seems to the others," smiled Zebulon.

"And for this we get a fee?"

"For this we get an opportunity."

Issachar held out the oyster. Coram reached for it, but as

his fingers brushed the shell the Day Father pulled it away and stared at him with a look Coram knew to fear. It was a look that seemed to pierce through one's eyes and see the truth of your soul. It was a look the Templebanes had used in their earlier trade at the very point when they wanted to break some poor country simpleton and have them confess to sins that they had not committed.

"So. Now. Your brothers are in position?"

"No one can leave the Jew's house without us seeing them," said Coram.

Issachar stared at him.

"If the girl succeeds at first stroke and emerges with the key, and the people within the Jew's house do *not* give chase, you know where to bring her?"

Coram nodded.

"And if they do give chase?" he said.

"Let them catch her. If you have *any* suspicion that they may be following, let them catch her up again. Do nothing. They must not on any account know we are the invisible hands who move against them."

"But what of this key?" asked Coram. Issachar looked at the oyster, then into the young man's eyes as Zebulon spoke.

"If you remember one thing of this conversation, Coram, remember this: every plan is a gamble against the unforeseen, and the unforeseen happens more than is strictly comfortable. So always have a contingency."

Coram was about to nod, then realised he did not know the word and, more than that, knew the Templebanes knew he likely did not, and he also knew that pretending to knowledge was one of the crimes for which he was apt to be punished. When either Templebane told the "sons" things the lessons were usually laced with traps for the unwary. Coram had not achieved the position of most trusted son without being wary.

"What's a contingency, Fathers?" he said.

The Templebanes smiled, though whether with pleasure at Coram's guilelessness or at their own cunning it was hard to say. Issachar reached into his pocket beneath the apron and produced a small rectangle of paper fastened with a wax seal. He held it out.

"An openness to the play of chance, a second plan, a fall-back: for if the first stroke fails, the next may do just as well. If the girl is taken back, or does not emerge by dawn, take this envelope to the magistrate."

"And then?" said Coram, taking the letter but keeping his eyes on the oyster.

"And then we shall, if all goes well, have the freedom of the house and *all* its contents. There are more ways to open an oyster than a knife. Some you pry open," said Zebulon. "Some you boil."

"You will boil it open?"

"With the full heat of the law. As I said: the best tool is an honest man, and who is more honest than a magistrate or a policeman – or a pastor?" smiled Issachar.

"And inside the oyster?" ventured Coram.

"Meat," said Issachar, finally holding out the oyster. Coram stepped forward and let him tip it into his mouth.

"Sweet meat," said the Day Father, his eyes glittering with something close to warmth as he watched the young man suck the fluids from the shell. "For what could be sweeter than the destruction of an old foe who was once powerful and is now reduced almost to nothing. Once they nosed into every shadow in London and obstructed us at every turn, but now you can count them on one hand, I'm told."

"And as soon as there are fewer than five, as soon as they cannot muster a Last Hand, they cannot serve their sworn purpose, and then their control and their power is gone," continued Zebulon.

Issachar nodded.

"And what could be lovelier, my boy, than delivering the very final blow of extinction."

Coram's eyes rose to meet his in sudden understanding.

The Day Father wiped the trickle of brine from the boy's chin and smiled at the Night Father behind him.

"And so, for me, to bed. You go and join your brothers and watch for the girl."

CHAPTER II

THE GREEN MAN

The clay giant was a trick.

Statues don't move.

Lucy had been picked up from the floor and led back to the table, and by the time she was seated again she had worked it out for herself: the head was just a mask worn by a real man inside the clothes. That's why it was such a big head. She didn't know why they relied on a guard dressed up in a clay mask, but it must have been something to do with frightening people. She'd certainly been frightened by it, and her mind and body had frozen until she had worked out the only rational explanation.

Now she was unfrozen and angry: angry that they had foiled her escape attempt, and angry that they thought her feeble-minded enough to believe that the guard was a golem, a clay statue made to move by some kind of magic.

Angry and something else: she was a little ashamed as she watched Sara Falk scrubbing the mess off her face, her slender body bent over the kitchen sink while Cook pumped water from the spigot in the wall above it. The Eccles cake had been hot enough to scald her, and the red splash-mark throbbed across the white skin like an accusation. She had got hot mincemeat in her eye and held a wet cloth to it as she wiped the rest of the mess away with her free hand under the spurting water. Lucy was ashamed because they had not hit her or punished her, but just put her back at her place at the table. She could see that the thin one was not only controlling her own anger but also trying not to show the pain she was in.

Lucy didn't like feeling ashamed. It was unfamiliar and uncomfortable, and the silence of the other two was a void into which the shame seemed to grow. Her face was hot and her eyes treacherously moist. Lucy did not cry in front of other people, but if she didn't do something, if this void of silence went on, she might betray herself. So she asked a question to fill it with something else.

"*Que veut dire* 'Glint'*?*" she said quietly.

They ignored her. Cook handed Sara a dry towel and she dried her face. Her eye was swollen and red.

Lucy repeated the question, louder this time.

Sara Falk exchanged a glance with Cook, and then turned slowly and answered her in French.

"When you touch something and the world around you jumps, and suddenly you see a vision that's so real it's not a vision but the thing itself? That's glinting."

Lucy gaped at her, as if to ask how could she know this private thing.

"Things that happen, important things, terrible things, they leave an imprint in the stones around them, as if they are leaving a record of the event. A Glint is someone with the gift to be able to read what is recorded."

"It does not feel like a gift. It feels like a curse. It feels like a dream but I am awake. And then I feel sick," said Lucy, her voice beginning to accelerate with remembered panic. "Sometimes I do vomit. People say I am having a fit because I scream. I mean, they *say* I scream, but I never remember screaming – I remember being frightened but I do not think these are things that happened. Some of the things are too bad to be real. These things are in my head. They are things I imagine because my head is bad. Because I have done bad things. I do bad, bad things . . ."

Her head bowed over and she stared down at her knotted fist, which was now thumping at her knee, as if trying to hammer her heel through the black and white tile on the kitchen floor.

"What bad things?" said Sara Falk.

"Things I cannot remember doing, like the screaming. I know this is true. This is why they beat me. This is why they say I am bad!"

"You are not bad," said Sara Falk as Cook gently but firmly trapped Lucy's fist in a hand the size of a small ham and stopped her hitting herself. "I am your friend, Lucy, so believe me—"

Lucy was letting the gusts of panic and shame blow her where they would, making no attempt to control herself now.

"I must be! They would not beat me just because I see the past. I cannot control the past or seeing it," she cried excitedly, trying to wrench her hand free. "They would not beat me for something I cannot control—"

"They beat you for something they cannot, um . . . understand," said Cook, her French failing her for a moment and making her stutter as she reached for the right final word.

"NO!" Lucy cried, smacking the table with her free hand so hard the bowl bounced and spilled oil. "They beat me because I am *bad*. They say so!" She was breathing hard now, her eyes hot, face flushed with a rising tide of distress.

"If I can prove to you that you are seeing the past, and not something made up in your own head, will you stop saying you are bad?" asked Sara, her voice betraying the irritation she was trying to control.

"You cannot," she spat, anger swirling again, feeding on the shame. "You cannot know what is in my head! You are stupid—"

"If I can . . ." said Sara Falk.

"You *cannot*!" Lucy cried, her free hand sweeping the earthenware bowl across the table, toppling the candle at its centre and bouncing off it towards the hard tile floor.

For a woman built on such generous lines, Cook moved with a speed that was in its own well-padded way as eye-bending as Mr Sharp's, catching the bowl so deftly a bare inch from the floor that she scarcely seemed to hurry. Olive oil splashed everywhere.

The candle rolled across the table and fell.

Sara caught it. Curiously the flame was not extinguished but began to burn brighter and much more fiercely, so fiercely that Lucy could feel the heat coming off it from the other side of the table.

"Sara," said Cook, a warning growl at the back of her voice. "The Wildfire—"

"I know," said Sara and quickly replaced the candle in the holder, which she then placed back in the centre of the star made from the five different twigs. As soon as she had done this the unnatural flame dwindled back to that of a normal candle.

"I . . ." began Sara Falk, visibly trying to control herself. "Oh, to the devil with it – come here."

She grasped Lucy's arm and pulled her away from the table, towards the door at the side of the room.

"Wait," protested Cook in English. "Sara! She has had too much to take in already; she needs time—"

"This won't take long," said Sara Falk grimly, opening the door and revealing the steep flight of carpeted steps beyond.

"Right," she said, taking Lucy's hand. "We're going to touch the wall. You're going to glint."

"No, please!" cried Lucy, wriggling like a netted salmon as she tried to escape her unshakeable grip. "Please no – you said you were my friend, you whore's bitch!"

She had known they would punish her. They had just been waiting their time. Sara raised an eyebrow at Cook, who was standing in the doorway watching.

"Don't worry," she said. "I know every inch of this house. I was born in it. And only one truly bad thing happened on these stairs."

"What?" yelled Lucy, kicking at her in fear. "What happened, pig's co—?"

"This."

And Sara Falk slammed Lucy's hand against the wall.

The girl felt the flat face of the stone, the fine grit cool against the soft skin of her fingertips. For an instant everything stopped.

Then she did the thing she did, the thing where there was a small jolt and the world lurched with such a shock that her eyes wouldn't close, couldn't even blink as a horribly familiar feeling of nausea punched a hook into her gut and the past tugged itself deep into her, slamming home like an axe, and in shattered fragments and glints of time she saw

The same wooden stairs

No carpet now

But a candle on a sconce on the wall where there had been a gas globe

A low white-painted gate across the top of the steps

Then a little black-haired girl in a nightdress running out of the dark and grabbing the gate

Shaking it

Too small to climb over

Screaming down the steps at her

"Mummy! Mummy! Cook! EMMET! Please! There's a man in my room! A green man behind the door!"

The child looks back into the dark hall behind it.

Listening. Shaking with fear

"No, Mummy please! Please! It's real! Mummy! I'm not

lying! PLEEEASE! I'M NOT LYING THIS TIME! IT'S COMING! EMMET!"

Nothing follows her out on to the landing.

Nothing.

Then shadows shift and rearrange themselves in the dimness behind her

As if something is moving past candles in the unseen room

The candle on the stair gutters.

The little girl stops rattling the gate and stares at that something that is still out of sight in the hall.

Something only she can see

Something bad

Her only movements are

Her eyes getting wider

Her teeth biting her lower lip in terror

The tremor in her knees riffling her thin nightdress like a breeze

Wetness spattering to the floor between her feet

Her mouth shrinks to a quivering dot

two words

"Please no"

squeezing out on a tiny breath

"Please . . ."

and then it's there

behind her

the bad thing

green man

green hair

green skin

red mouth

white teeth

green fingers

clawing for her

touching her shoulder

missing their grip
tangling in her hair
hair black as a raven's wing
leaching the colour from it
the black flowing from the roots to the tips,
twining into the greenness of his skin
bleaching the little girl's hair snow-white
as
she turns
and
jumps
and
twists
in mid-air
leaping at the gate
little hands
reaching scrabbling gripping
pulling herself
(impossibly)
up and over
and then she is diving headfirst down the steep steps
her scream cut off brutally as the ridge of bone behind
her eyebrow hits the unforgiving right angle of a step with
a *thunk* that Lucy felt through the soles of her boots
and as the diving girl tumbles and slumps down like a rag
doll
the thing
the green man
at the top of the steps boots the gate open
comes after her
green riding clothes swirling round him
long green pigtail swinging behind the sharp-fanged snarl
of his head
then a blur, close to

white, silver, pink
a roar of red rage
coming fast from the kitchen
a smear of black eye patch
Cook

snarling like a mastiff as she bounds at the stairs, miraculously scooping and saving the tumbling girl with one hand as she hurls silver through the air

her heavy ladle spinning like a tomahawk

hitting the green face with enough force to cancel his forward momentum and knock him backwards

and then a second figure overtakes her
brown coachman's coat
tricorn hat
hollow eyes
unmistakably hollow
not a man in a mask
an irrefutable real live moving statue
a clay landslide charging uphill

falling on the green man and making his neck do a very sudden and final snap

green boot-heels spasm and drum on the steps
Cook cradles the little girl, looking at her face
her hair now horror-white
eyebrow split and swelling

bright bloodstream beginning to delta down the death-pale curves of her face

her eyes fluttering open
grey-green eyes opening wide as
The world kicked again.

And Lucy was yanked back to a gas-lit stairwell now carpeted and monster-free.

All different and safe.

Except she is looking into the same grey-green eyes.

The little girl's eyes.

In Sara Falk's face.

"But—" Lucy began.

Sara Falk pushed aside the renegade lick of white hair and leant forward to show the silver scar that parted her eyebrow.

"*Merde*," said Lucy. "It was you?"

"You believe me now?" said Sara Falk. "The bad things you see? They *happened*. They are not from your imagination. And *certainly* not because you are bad. You are a Glint, and someone should have told you this before now."

The girl's eyes stayed on Sara's face, and Sara could see the weather change behind them as Lucy adjusted to the new truths of her world: the clay man was not a trick, the green man was something awful and she, Lucy, had a power to conjure the past out of stones. What she had thought was madness in her head, an assault of made-up things, was not madness at all, but a different kind of reality.

And so everything the two women had tried to tell her before she ran must be true.

Shock turned to wonder and wonder cooled to something more guarded in her eyes, and Sara knew that she had done the right thing but done it too abruptly, out of her own impatience, maybe out of anger at the pain the girl had caused her by flinging the hot mincemeat and pastry into her face. Whatever the reason, she had brought about the very result she had begun by hoping to avoid: telling Lucy the truth like that, showing her the world as it really was meant that she would now never really be liked by this girl, this lost child who her heart had so instinctively gone out to.

And so she steeled herself, as she had done before, to the lonely fact that it was not her lot to be liked, but only her duty to protect.

"Lucy," she said. "I realise that until you adjust to what you now understand, the world will seem frightening and hostile, but know this for a truth: I will not let harm come to you, and all in this house shall be a friend and the house itself will always be a haven to you. I swear this, and give you my hand on it."

She held out her right hand, and after a hesitation Lucy swallowed, nodded slightly, reached out her own hand and shook.

CHAPTER 12

THE HORSE WITH NO SHOES

Mr Sharp retrieved the Sluagh's bronze blade from where he had left it, hidden behind the ale barrels in the alley, and then walked back out onto the pavement.

Once more his nostrils flared and he smelled the fog. He cast this way and that trying to find a scent trail and then stalked off down the east side of the square and round the bend into Neptune Street.

Neptune Street may have been named after a deity, but there was nothing godly about it. The narrow shambles of mismatched houses was a ramshackle catalogue of the various building styles that had superseded each other as the city had stumbled its way forward over the past few centuries: ancient half-timbered edifices leant drunkenly against jerry-built brick houses standing cheek-by-jowl with narrow four-storey tenements faced with age-warped clapboarding. Most of the dwellings were rooming houses, some with two or more families to a room; others accommodated those who were happy to rent by the hour to the furtive customers of the brazen ladies who loitered on the street corners outside.

There was a swish of skirts as one of these lurched out of the fog and put a hand on Mr Sharp's arm.

"Looking for something, dearie?" she said in an alarmingly gravelly simper.

"A horse," he replied.

The hand released him quickly.

"Sorry, Mr Sharp. Didn't recognise you in this blessed murk," she said. "It's as thick as cheese out here."

"Yes," he agreed. "It's a not a good night to be out. There are bad things abroad."

"I know," she giggled, "but I'm damned if I can get any of them to come inside with me. Tuesdays is always devilish slow . . ."

"Any of them on a horse?"

"No," she said after a beat. "I mean yes. Little Timmy Goodbehere come by saying there's an old nag tied up next to his uncle's shop and it kicked him when he went close—"

"Goodbehere's," said Mr Sharp. "Thank you, Lily."

"Always a pleasure, Mr S," she called after him as he strode away into a murk that erased his outline within six steps.

"Or it could be if you weren't always in such a blessed hurry," she continued under her breath with a distinctly unprofessional hint of wistfulness.

He found the horse in the dank cut-through between Goodbehere's Hardware Shop and Ship Alley. It was a small mud-spattered thing, more pony than horse, hard-ridden and haggard, with an unmistakably mad look in its eye. It snorted and shied away from him as he approached, but he held out a hand and gentled it into stillness with a few soft words. He kept talking to it as he came close enough to see the shaggy mane was twisted into braids and elf-locks, and the harness was patched together from woven sea-grass and plaited leather. Hollow sections of bones and topless limpet shells were used anywhere where metal would have been used on a normal bridle, and the skulls of animals and birds hung from the end of the braided mane and clattered against each other as the horse shifted uneasily.

Mr Sharp leant and whispered something in the horse's ear, his hand stroking its neck as he spoke. The horse stilled again, and remained calm as he bent and lifted a foreleg, curling it upwards and confirming his suspicion that it was unshod.

"Right," he said, dropping the hoof as he straightened. "This may hurt, but it's the only way to free you, my dear."

The horse rolled an eye sideways at him, a demented sliver of white flashing on the rim of the socket, matching the sharp silver edge now glittering through the air as Mr Sharp drew the blade from his coat and grabbed a handful of mane. He wrenched the horse's neck towards him and slashed at it, three, four, five eye-defying times.

The horse whinnied and jerked in fear, but Mr Sharp held tight as he cut the skulls from their plaits and sliced through the bridle and harness with the precision of a surgeon, moving so fast that the last skull had not hit the ground before he stepped back with the shreds of harness in his hand.

The blade disappeared into his coat and he whipped out a large red kerchief and crouched over the scatter of small skulls, moving swiftly but carefully to drop them into it, like a man picking hot potatoes out of a pot with his fingers. The last skull was a puffin's, and even though he moved fast and gripped tightly, the skull still managed to gimbal sideways and catch his finger in its short hooked beak, drawing blood. He winced and tugged it free.

The beak chattered and snapped at him even as it fell, but stopped the moment it hit the red silk. He quickly gathered the corners of the kerchief and knotted them together, making a small bundle. He shook it and held it to his ear, as if listening for movement. Satisfied that there was none, he sucked the blood from his wounded finger, spat on the ground and led the horse out into the street with nothing more than a hand on its neck. It was calm and happy to go with him, and the mad look was gone from its eye.

"Emmet will put iron on your hooves," he said. "And you shall be protected."

CHAPTER 13

A HARBOUR AND A HAVEN

Sara led Lucy back into the kitchen. The girl was still trembling with the shock of glinting and what the past had shown her.

"But such things do not exist," said Lucy weakly, because she now knew she was wrong. "That green man—"

Cook plonked two things on the table in front of her.

"Well, you're right about him: he *certainly* doesn't exist any more," she said with satisfaction. "That's my best ladle. Three and a half pounds of solid silver."

And there it was, lying there on the scrubbed pine in front of her. A ladle like a sledgehammer. Next to a long pigtail. A green pigtail.

Sara felt her heartbeat catch for an instant at the sight of it. Then she reached for it and held it up to the light.

"I didn't know you kept this . . ."

"Well," said Cook gruffly. "He stole the lovely raven colour from your hair. It seemed only right to keep his."

Sara smiled, matching the banked-up warmth in the older woman's eyes. She turned to Lucy.

"Cook has a highly developed sense of fair play. It comes out in the strangest ways."

"What was it?" said Lucy. "That devil."

"A Green Man," said Sara, feeling the weight and the oily density of the plaited hairs in her hand. It still felt like a living thing to her, and she put it back on the table, controlling her sudden revulsion so that she appeared to be in no hurry to do so. "They're not normally dangerous. Just mischievous. This one had gone mad."

"But how—?" said Lucy, looking from one to the other.

"Her grandfather left a door open," said Cook.

"He unlocked a great many doors that should have remained shut," said Sara Falk grimly, crossing to the sink and pumping water over her hand, washing the greasy feel of the green hair from her skin as casually as she could. "But I think we have closed all of them again."

"But just in case," said Cook, and tapped the blunderbuss hanging from the pot rail. "Loaded with clipped Spanish pieces-of-eight from the old Potosi mine in the New World, before it became South America. Purest and most powerful silver I know, with nasty sharp edges. So no need to worry."

She patted Lucy's arm and gave it a reassuring squeeze, but her eyes were on Sara.

Lucy looked at the broken ring on her finger, then at Sara's unbroken one, then down at Cook's pudgy hand, which had the same ring on it.

"I'm not mad," she said. "Or bad."

"No," said Sara, drying her hands and feeling her burned face. "No, you are clearly quite bad when you want to be. Just not in the way you meant."

And she grinned.

Despite herself, Lucy smiled back.

Cook disappeared into one of the pantries and returned with a slab of crumbly white cheese on a blue-striped plate. Another plate was pushed in front of Lucy, and then a new Eccles cake was placed on it. The golden pastry case was streaked with dark dribbles of mincemeat which had bubbled out of the three slits on top. She took a knife from the rack behind her and carved a neat triangle of cheese from the slab and put it beside the cake.

Sara Falk, whose eyes were trained to miss as little as possible, could see that Lucy was very hungry. She saw her swallow reflexively at the juices beginning to run in her mouth. Sara, a connoisseur of self-denial and self-control, saw the younger woman steel herself, as if before she allowed herself to eat she had to ask another question. Sara shook her head and presented her with a fork.

"You eat. Talk later."

The smell of the baking won. Lucy used the side of the fork like a knife, breaking a section of the pastry shell and shovelling a portion of the dark brown filling into it before putting both in her mouth.

Sara saw the smile of animal satisfaction twitch on the side of Lucy's mouth before she suppressed it. And in truth the Eccles cake tasted wonderful. The nutmeg and the cloves and the raisins and the hard yet flaky sugary pastry all mixed together as she chewed and ended up tasting like she had a dark but happy Christmas Day in her mouth.

"Have the cheese too," said Cook.

So she did. And Sara could see Lucy realise it was perfect, so perfect that she didn't remember to hide her smile this time. The cheese was like the opposite of all the other tastes and textures, smooth not flaky, firm not crumbly, one curiously flat cheesy taste instead of a mix of spices and fats and flour and fruits, adding up to the missing half that made sense of it all.

She smiled at Cook and then at Sara, and they smiled too, and for a moment that was enough, that this instant was the first time they had all three shared a smile.

"Supranatural," said Lucy, mouth full. "This 'glinting'. It is supranatural, yes?"

"It is a supranatural power, yes," said Sara Falk.

"So how will you regulate me?" said Lucy.

Sara made herself pause and choose the right words. Having raised the first smile she had no wish to lose the barely kindled flicker of trust it betokened.

"Carefully. Kindly. As a friend."

"Why?" asked Lucy. "Why would you do that? You do not know me."

"Because we all have supranatural powers of our own, child," said Cook. "We have all been you, in our own way, when we were younger."

"Set a thief to catch a thief," said Sara. "But we're on the side of light. Not of shadows. And this house, this is the Safe House. No harm will come to you here. The Green Man was an accident. He did come to us out of the shadows with malice, but he came because my grandfather unlocked a door and, as I said, left it open. That does not happen any more. He came because there is something in the house that is a key to both the natural and supranatural worlds, and it is our duty to guard it, and to guard the inhabitants of the natural world from supranaturals who would wish to harm them. It is a key of great power, but it is safe here now. This house, the Safe House, is a bulwark and a bastion against the darkness."

"A harbour and a haven," said Cook.

"They have sometimes tried to find us, when they remember us, and they have tried to harm us," said Sara Falk with a smile. "But do not worry, Lucy Harker. You are protected and secure here. They likely do not know where we are, and if they do, then they do not know how to overcome our many defences."

"And with luck they do not know how reduced our numbers are," added Cook.

"Numbers are not everything," said Sara. "As long as five

stand together to make a Hand, The Oversight remains. It is the oldest law of the Free Company. It's known as the Rule of Five. And there are still five."

"And when there aren't," said Cook, reaching to the centre of the table and rearranging the oak twig so that the five-wood star around the candle was more symmetrically shaped, "things go bad so fast you don't have time to worry because you're so busy trying to outrun the flames. You don't believe me – go and have a look at the Monument and see what happened last time."

"The Wildfire hasn't been loosed to take the city for nearly two centuries, and The Oversight, like the city itself, was made better and stronger after the Great Fire," said Sara, the light from the candle dancing in her eyes. "Even now, even after the Disaster that befell us, we are better if fewer, and in this place of all places, we are safe. There is nothing in London that can harm you."

She caught Lucy's eyes and for a moment considered whether she had just lied to the girl, for she had just glimpsed a kind of cloaked reserve in them that made Sara wonder if there was in strict truth one thing in London that might harm Lucy, and that was Lucy herself.

CHAPTER 14

HOWEVER . . .

. . . thirteen hours of hard riding north of London, it was raining with a peculiar viciousness, as if the blustery night had a score to settle with the small and often overlooked county of Rutlandshire, and had determined that if it couldn't drown it by dawn it would at least wash it away into the featureless oblivion of the neighbouring Lincolnshire fens.

On an exposed stretch of the Great North Road, five miles out of Great Casterton, a solitary carrier's cart was making slow progress through the relentless squalls, horses head-down and hunched against the downpour, the driver so tightly wrapped in his oilskin coat that he appeared no more human than the lumpy bales and boxes lashed down beneath the tarpaulin behind him. The only illumination on this lonely road came from the dim lanterns swinging from the front and back of his cart.

A sudden flash of lightning turned night to day for a jagged moment, revealing a stark T-shape by the side of the road made from a tall pole topped with a horizontal crosspiece.

The oilskin bundle pulled back on the reins, slowing the horses, and then took his whip and reached backwards, prodding the tarpaulin at the rear of the cart.

"Bowland's Gibbet!" he shouted in. "Bowland's Gibbet!"

The tarpaulin shifted and coughed, and then something slithered out from beneath it, two boots splashing into a deep puddle as a hidden passenger dropped off the tail of the cart.

For a moment the carrier could see him quite clearly in the glow of the tail-lantern, a thin youth, a little taller than average, his body wrapped in a high-collared serge overcoat that was clearly a worn hand-me-down from a much larger man. He wore a battered hat pulled low over his forehead, and the lower part of his face was swathed in a chequered muffler wrapped several times round his neck. His eyes were the only visible features, flashing briefly in the dull lantern-light as he bobbed his head and raised a hand in silent thanks.

"Bowland's Gibbet!" repeated the carrier, "and the main gate to Gallstaine Hall beyond."

He pointed his whip at the roadside gallows, and then aimed it across the way to a high wall topped with iron spikes. Fifty yards further on the wall was broken by an ornate pair of gates set back from the highway, clearly the main entrance to some great estate beyond. He turned and cracked his whip and the horses leant resignedly into the wind-driven rain again and headed on into the foul night.

"And good luck to you, young man," he shouted over his shoulder, already re-swaddling himself in his oilskin.

The youth watched the tail-lantern swinging away, leaving him alone and lightless in the centre of the road, and then he drew his coat more tightly round himself and ran down the wall until he got to the gate.

There was no lodge house and the gate was, on closer inspection, unusual: beyond the thick wrought-iron bars, where you might have expected to see a driveway snaking off towards some large house hidden in the elegant parkland beyond, there was only a blackness even darker than the surrounding night.

It was not the gate to a driveway.

It was the entrance to a tunnel.

The young man found a brass bell handle set in the stone gatepost and yanked it hard several times. In the distance he heard a bell jangle, and a dog started barking. A door opened in the side of the tunnel and light slashed across its width, revealing that it was floored with coconut matting and vaulted with brick. It was also wide enough to easily accommodate a carriage being driven down it.

A large brindled mastiff hurtled out of the door and charged the gate, barking and snarling with such gleeful savagery that the boy stepped back a yard, even though the bars kept the animal from him.

"Down, Saracen! Down, you devil!" snarled a man's voice, every bit as ferocious as the dog. The gatekeeper limped up behind the brute and wrested it back from the bars. Behind him a small child with a dripping nose appeared, rubbing sleep from his eyes and carrying a bull's-eye lantern. The gatekeeper snatched the light from him and held it up to the bars.

"Who is it?"

The young traveller stepped forward, bobbed his head in a silent greeting, and then reached inside his coat, fumbling for something. He produced a letter and took off his hat to keep the rain from it as he held it out through the bars, keeping one eye on the barely restrained dog. The gatekeeper took the folded paper and looked at the name inscribed on it in thick slashes and curlicues of black ink. It read, "To the Viscount Mountfellon – By Hand – Most Urgent and Private."

He flipped the envelope and examined the crimson blob sealing it on the reverse. The wax bore the imprint of a grinning skull above a deeply incised motto reading *"As I am, you will be"*.

Most skulls grin because the lack of any skin robs them of any viable alternative: this skull not only grinned, but positively gloated.

"Right," he said. "Whitlowe! Running Boy! Letter for his Lordship; cut along sharpish!"

And he handed the letter and the lantern to the small child, who sniffed once more, wiped his nose and then turned and sprinted down the tunnel, the circle of light bobbing around him steadily diminishing as he sped away from them into the dark.

The gatekeeper turned back to the soaking youth on the other side of the gate. He leaned forward and peered at Amos through the bars.

"See your face?"

Amos unwrapped the muffler. His green eyes were a startling counterpoint to the burned caramel colour of his skin. The gatekeeper nodded as if he'd made a great discovery.

"You're a darkie."

This wasn't news to Amos. Nor was it something he ever forgot, indeed his "brothers" made a point of reminding him of the fact at every opportunity, the only variation in the monotony of their practice being the seemingly endless litany of new and unkind words they dredged up from the teeming docks and market gutters to describe the visible effect of the mixed strains in his ancestry. So he didn't react to the gate-keeper's comment. He just looked back at him with an entirely neutral expression.

"You to wait for a reply?"

He nodded. The gatekeeper gave him a sly smile.

"So who's the letter from then?"

The youth shrugged and said nothing.

"Come on, cully," said the man in a wheedling tone. "Just a natural interest as to what must be so important to be delivered so late and in such weather . . . ?"

The messenger again kept quiet. The gatekeeper scowled at him.

"Don't say much do you, cully?"

He shook his head.

"You stupid or something? Cat got your tongue? Or just haughty, like?"

The youth shook his head again, shivering at the rain runnelling down his neck as he unwound his muffler and pulled out an oval brass plate he wore around his neck on a worn leather strap. There was just enough light from the door in the side of the tunnel for the gatekeeper to read the letters stamped into it:

My Name is Amos Templebane and I am Mute but Intelligent.

The gatekeeper's lips moved as he read the words slowly, then gave a snort of unkind mirth as he stepped back and looked at the dripping boy.

"Not intelligent enough to stay home and dry on a wet night though, are you?"

Amos rolled his eyes and made a dumb show by which the gatekeeper was invited to open the gate and allow him inside the mouth of the tunnel, out of the weather. The gatekeeper in turn made a pantomime of shaking his head.

"No one inside the gates without his Lordship's permission. Don't worry though, darkie: you just stop there until we see if there's a reply. You can't get any wetter."

With that he turned on his heel, leaving the dog to sit and stare at Amos on the other side of the bars, and disappeared back into his cubby and closed the door, cutting off the slash of light so that all Amos could see was a distant glow from the running child, who was now out of sight beyond the initial incline of the tunnel. He put his brass badge back inside his coat with a well-practised and fatalistic sigh, shook out his muffler and made a kind of hood which he then tied over his hat, and retreated into a natural recess made by the gate-posts that gave at least the illusion, if not the strict reality, of protection from the unending downpour.

CHAPTER 15

THE BONE PET

The Sluagh did not move for a very long time, his ears straining to catch the tiniest creak or murmur of breath from the darkness in the corridor beyond the cell. He was good at staying still because for him time was a very different thing than it was for normal beings. He had also been so weakened by the iron Mr Sharp had put round his neck that he'd felt his vigour drain away like blood from a butchered pig at the slaughterhouse. He had never felt this bad, this bled-out, this *mortal*.

Not even when he had been alive.

When he was sure there was no trick, and that neither Mr Sharp nor the bulbous-nosed innkeeper was standing in the dark waiting to spy on him, he began to move. First he knelt, and his fingers started to pick at his clothes, the hand on his uninjured arm removing the bones used instead of buttons, then working at his beard and hair, untwining the plaits and freeing the other small bones and vertebrae which had been braided into them. He put them all on the floor in front of him as he worked, and once they were all laid out on the wood, he bent over carefully and began to read them with his fingertips, searching through touch alone until he found the ones he was looking for.

He sorted as he went, grouping the thicker neck bones next to the long column of thoracic and then sacral vertebrae, a chain that then diminished further in size as he recreated the tail all the way down to the tip of the last tiny caudal vertebra. Next he made separate piles of ribs and radii, the tiny phalanges and the almost impossibly miniscule metatarsal bones of the paw, matching long tibias to fibulas and tarsals. Once he had laid everything out, he counted the bones twice, his face wrinkling in frustration when the count came back wrong both times, until he remembered his ears and removed the two miniature shoulder-blades of a stoat that hung from his earring like sycamore keys carved from yellowing ivory and added them to the piles.

Next he painstakingly took the bones from the piles and placed them in a different sort of order on the floor. If there had been a light in the room he would have been seen to be spreading out the seemingly random collection of bones to reveal an exploded diagram of a strange rodent's skeleton. It was no rodent that had ever walked the earth, however, mainly because he was mixing a stoat's skeleton with that of a red squirrel, which gave it a lopsided appearance. And the thing that topped it off was not a stoat or a squirrel's skull but a woodcock's, with a long beak like a needle.

Once he was satisfied that all the parts were there, he neatly scooped every bone into his cupped right hand. Then he took the woodcock's beak and jagged it into the fleshy part of his left hand, just below the thumb. Once this was done he spat three times on the bones, and then squeezed his left hand over the spittle-flecked pile, splashing blood on them.

He rose carefully and went to the door, taking care not to spill the bone pile. He flattened his palm and slid it through the judas slit so that his hand stuck out of the room and into the brick-lined hall. He pushed his arm as far as it could go so that it was clear of the damping influence of the triple-wood cell and flexed his palm open, bending it back like a child preparing to feed a horse.

Then he whistled into the dark.

At first nothing happened. Then the bones on his open palm began to slither around, slowly at first, seemingly randomly, then faster and with more purpose. There were snicks and crunchy noises as the skeleton began to join itself together, starting with the ischium and the pubis. The ripple of something close to life spread and fizzed outwards along the hind legs, then back into the backbone, and in a very short time – had there been any light – he would have seen the fully self-assembled skeleton of a rodent with a stiletto beak standing on his hand, now unmistakably alive. The ribs opened and closed as if there were invisible lungs penned within their yellowing bone cage.

The eyeless skull swivelled and a blank socket stared back at him as the beak gaped, like a fledgling waiting for food to be dropped into it.

The Sluagh hissed through the slit.

"It is done. They have taken the girl in. The bone pet will lead you back to me. Free me soon."

The bone pet snapped its beak shut as if trapping the words.

The Sluagh squeezed his other hand through the slit and awkwardly jammed it forward far enough to be able to stroke the strange creature's skull with something like affection. It arched its back with pleasure as his hand ran down the tiny vertebrae, like a cat.

"They wait for you. Go."

The bone pet flexed and jumped, landing on the floor with a scrabble that diminished into a skitter of claws as it ran for the gap beneath the ale cellar door and the stairs beyond.

The Sluagh slumped against the cell wall and smiled.

CHAPTER 16

THE SUMMONS

Far north, beneath the rain-soaked Rutlandshire soil, the letter Amos had brought up from London was proceeding at speed down the tunnel towards Gallstaine Hall. Whitlowe the Running Boy's feet made muffled slaps on the coconut matting as he carried his sphere of light towards the house at the end of this strange subterranean driveway.

The tunnel began to slope gently uphill again after half a mile, and he ran back above ground and into a covered turning circle which swept around beneath a glass roof held in place by cast-iron pillars. He cut across the circle and up the steps to the main doors of a great sprawling manor house built from dark ironstone.

He paused to get his breath and then knocked on the door. Almost immediately it opened and a footman regarded him with a raised eyebrow.

"Letter . . . for . . . his . . . Lordship," panted the child.

The footman just nodded and stepped back.

Whitlowe trotted past him, through another set of double doors and into the entrance hall of the house.

It was a cavernous space, two storeys high, and the child shivered and sniffed as he passed through it. He was an impressionable creature and though he had only once been in a cathedral, on a market day holiday in Lincoln, he felt there was something cathedral-like in the vaulting space around him. It was, however, a cathedral peopled by ghosts, or at least it appeared to be, since every piece of furniture was covered with dust cloths. Even the large mirrors and the pictures on the walls were draped, and the chandeliers were bagged in protective muslin, so that they hung overhead like spectral hot-air balloons, half deflated and frozen in mid-fall. All the windows were shuttered, and the doors to the rooms which ranged along the hall's outer perimeter were closed.

The child jogged up the grand sweep of the stairs two at a time, the sound of his feet on the cold marble his only companion in the emptiness of the silent house.

He slowed when he came to the landing and walked very deliberately down the long corridor ahead of him as if this final leg of his journey required a sudden brake and injection of weighty formality. In truth, the important fact that his Lordship detested the sound of Running Boys had been beaten into him from the earliest time he could remember. So he edged stiffly down the long dark corridor, sniffling his way past draped chairs and paintings, carrying his lantern ahead of him and clutching the white letter to his chest as if scared it might hop out of his grip and lose itself in the shadows closing in behind him.

This was the very part of the journey that the boy always wanted to get over quickest, and the urge to run was strong. The reason lay in the glass-fronted specimen cabinets which lined the walls from the polished floor to the high ceiling above. They were not draped in dust cloths but he never got more than a few paces into the endless corridor without wishing that they were. The first few yards of wall were innocent enough, and on the few occasions when he'd been here in daylight (his Lordship being a man of studiedly nocturnal habits) he had paused to enjoy the ranks of brightly coloured butterflies which were pinned neatly in matching cabinets. A yard or so of sombre moths with wings like mottled patches of fusty velvet followed. Then the horror began to itch beneath Whitlowe's skin as the homely moths gave way to spiky battalions of segmented centipedes, and millipedes frozen in regimented order next to shiny-dark phalanxes of scorpions and armoured beetles, some of which were nearly as large as the primordial-looking horseshoe crabs hung like half-helmets on the wall beyond them. In his mind the boy called this section the "Black Bone Yard" to distinguish it from the truly unnerving final section of bleached skeletons which followed it.

The last length of the hall seemed narrower because the specimen cases got increasingly thicker so as to accommodate the larger fish and then the mammals whose flayed and cured skins were pinned to the backboard behind their white and yellow bones, as if the animals had flung them off as carelessly as a coat.

Whitlowe sniffed and tried hard not to focus on any of this as he passed. This was where his nightmares came from. The ordered squadrons of spiny-boned fish were separated by banks of eel skeletons ranging in size from small cutthroat eels, through garden congers to the giant morays that were just simple spinal columns with hideously fanged jaws attached to them.

The eels were bad enough, but the bare bones of the primates were what really haunted him. They went from tiny prosimians, starting out with neatly ordered eviscerations of lorises, lemurs, night monkeys and tarsiers, some no bigger than a baby rabbit, all the way through to the larger species, and then the simians proper. Monkeys were splayed in cabinets with their tails precisely curled between spatchcocked legs, and then in the narrowest section of the corridor the tailless primates began with the lesser apes, a graded platoon of skeletonised gibbons giving way in turn to the great apes. The chimpanzees and orang-utans and gorillas rose up to loom over the boy, the sightless sockets of their eyes staring down at him out of increasingly human skulls in which yellowing teeth were bared in forever-smiles of rage and pain.

There were other things beyond the last of the gorillas. Their bones were not pinned and stapled to the back of the cabinets. They were splayed out and held by rusting iron shackles to wrist and ankle. Some of the skins stretched behind them had unnatural markings which he had thought – on the only occasion he had mistakenly noticed them – looked distinctly like tattoos but were, he decided, probably just regular monkey markings made to appear like that by the curing process. Possibly all apes had marks like that under their fur because these later primate pelts were smooth and hairless, and so must have – surely – been shaved prior to being stretched out and preserved by the taxidermist.

A footman sat on a stool at the end of the corridor, and did not move until Whitlowe had walked the whole length of it and stopped in front of him, sweating more from the effort of controlling himself while walking down the ghoulish hall than the two-mile underground run which had preceded it.

"Letter," snivelled the child, holding it out.

"Wait," grunted the footman, and took the envelope into the doorway beside him.

Whitlowe saw the tall double doors open and close and then stood there trying to re-snort the persistent dewdrop hanging off the end of his thin nose.

Inside the double doors the footman crossed a small anteroom to another door. This door was ironbound with a lattice of metalwork, and in its centre were a wide ledge and two letterboxes, marked IN and OUT. A tray was positioned under the OUT slit, standing ready to catch whatever paper was pushed through it. The footman knocked three times on the door and then slipped the letter into the second slit.

The room on the other side of the door was cavernous and almost empty. Once it had been a great ballroom. Now the walls were stripped, the shutters closed and the whole interior was gridded – walls, floor and ceiling – with a lattice-work of iron bands, spaced a yard apart.

At one end of the room, the wall was entirely taken up to its twenty-foot height with a bookcase. The other three walls were unembellished and stark white behind the regular criss-cross of metal caging the room.

In the centre of the great chamber was a dark oak piece of furniture, a heavy-legged thing which might once have done service as a dining table before the Restoration, but was now a huge desk covered in neat stacks of paper. At the centre of it sat a powerfully built man with granite-grey hair brushed back from a cliff-like forehead, dark eyes gleaming on either side of a savagely hooked nose of heroic proportions.

Francis, Viscount Mountfellon, was writing by candlelight, and his steel-tipped pen did not cease its rhythmic scratching as he heard the rap on the door and the sound of the envelope falling into the tray. Instead he continued to the end of the sentence before looking up. He blew on the page to dry the ink and put it beneath a leather-bound paperweight on top of a tall pile of identical pages, and only then stood, stretching the kinks out of his back and striding across to the door. He read the front of the envelope and glanced at the green wax seal, returning the skull's smile with an equally bony grimace of his own. Then he took a knife from the tray and slit the letter open in one fast cut, as if he couldn't wait to gut it and read the contents.

In an angular copperplate hand which appeared to have been slashed rather than written and was so peppered with random capital letters that the writer might as well have loaded them into a blunderbuss and fired them blindly at the page, this is what he read:

> *Your Lordship,*
>   *The Trap is Sprung and the Game is Afoot . . .*
>   *By the Time you receive this Letter, the Certain Girl shall have been delivered to the House on Wellclose Square by Our Northern Confederates in such a Manner and State of Mind that will make her arrival Unimpeachable and herself Instantly Trusted by those of that Free Company whose Downfall and Ruination we both so Earnestly Desire.*
>   *If you will meet me Tomorrow at Midday at the Magistrate's Chambers as previously discussed, I will have Constables standing by and we shall by the Operation of our Ruse gain Entrance to the House and you may take Possession of The Discriminator, that Great Key to All Bloods for which you have Sought for So Long, with the Full Appearance of Probity and Legality, as if it were indeed Merely your Lordship's own Purloined Property that we were Repossessing.*
>   *Please bring that Certain Fragmentary Token by which we shall Prove your "Guardianship" of the Apparently Abducted Girl, and the Sketch of the Hitherto Unattainable Key so that we can Prove Title to the Magistrate as we have Previously Planned.*
>   *I send this to you with Best Wishes of my Brother and Myself in the Discreet and Confidential Safety of our Boy Amos's Hands, and request that you Be So Good as to Bring him back to London, if it Be Not Too Burdensome upon You,*
>   *Ever Loyally Your Servant,*
>   *Issachar Templebane, Esq.*

Mountfellon passed a hand down his face, from forehead to chin, as if scrubbing the possibility of a smile from it, but as he crossed back to his table his eyes were sparkling.

He opened a casket and took out a folded sheet of paper and a small ring box. He opened the sheet of paper to check it: it was a sketch of a key whose bow, or handle, was made to look like the flared hood of a king cobra. He refolded it and slipped it into an inner pocket of his coat. Then he opened the ring box. There was no ring inside, only another fragment of paper with a wax blob into which a lion and a unicorn seal had been pressed. He snapped the box shut and slid it into his waistcoat pocket.

He dipped the corner of Templebane's letter into the candle and lit it, holding it until the flames consuming it reached his fingertips. Then he dropped it onto a pewter plate on the tabletop, watching until all the fire was gone and only black ash and a gobbet of twice melted sealing wax remained.

He snuffed the candle and strode to the door, unlocked it and walked out, leaving the caged room to itself.

CHAPTER 17

NIGHT ON MARE STREET

There are two ways to get from A to B across a crowded
city: as the crow flies or as the rat runs.

The bone pet had a beak but no wings, so it was tied to
the earthbound route, and its stoaty-squirrelish body parts
meant that it scuttled and zigzagged north like a rat. Rats
don't run in straight lines or in plain sight, so its journey
took place in shadows, as much below the ground as on it.

It found its way out of the cellar through a broken airbrick,
and scrabbled along the side of the wall and through a back
area hung with damp washing which floated like ghosts in
the fog over its head as it ran towards Cable Street.

Though it was night, there was still horse-drawn traffic on
the road. The bone pet paused behind the crook of a down-
spout, and then crossed in a mad dash which took it between
the slow-moving wheels of a brewer's dray and across the
litter-strewn corner, where it plunged immediately into the dark
maw of the bridge carrying the iron tracks of the Blackwall
Railway overhead. It hopscotched from street to alley to
drying green as it made its way through the densely packed
grid of two-storey workmen's houses leading up to the
Commercial Road.

A drunk lying in the gutter opened a bleary eye and saw a small and bony nightmare skitter across the pool of vomit he had just added to the pavement and shrieked in fuddled terror, but the thing was gone, into a drain system that took it on a short dog-leg into the grounds of the London Hospital. As it splashed relentlessly north, it surprised the rats who were the normal occupants of the pipes and sluices and sent them scurrying ahead of it, chittering in fright.

A porter was standing in the open ground behind the hospital, feeding some bloodstained gauze and other waste into a roaring iron brazier which sent spirals of bright sparks into the starless sky above. He heard the rats before he saw them, turning with an armful of dirty dressings to see a sudden wave of black bodies erupt from the ground and sweep towards him. He yelled in fright and stumbled back into the brazier, bouncing off it and tripping himself so that he went down in a festoon of soiled bandages as the scared rats overran him and swept into the door he had left open to the hospital basement.

He never saw the bone pet break off to follow the perimeter wall to the Mile End Road, which it passed beneath in another drain that came up right under the nose of a brindled terrier which was worrying a cabbage stalk that had fallen from a passing cart earlier in the day. This flash of white was much more exciting than the cabbage stalk and the terrier reacted as terriers do – instantly giving chase, firing a fusillade of excited barks ahead of it. It kept pace all the way north to the Jews' Burial Ground, where the bone pet shot through the iron bars of the gate, a space too narrow for the dog. The dog yelped in frustration as the thing raced over the jumbled gravestones, sending flying the pebbles and prayer stones which grieving friends and family had neatly stacked on the top of them. It hurled itself over the ivy-choked northern wall of the graveyard, dropping into the ordered planting of the market gardens on either side of the Eastern Counties Railway, which it passed beneath as a goods train thundered above, couplings shrieking as it began to slow down for the terminus ahead.

The skeleton passed Bethnal Green on the Paradise Row side, and then plunged into a hole and skittered underground for half a mile before emerging behind another stampede of panicked rats which fled ahead of it until they splayed off each way down the towpath either side of the humped bridge over Regent's Canal.

The bone pet hurtled straight ahead along the bridge's parapet and off into the less built-up land north of the water. It slalomed between rows of neatly planted cabbages and hurdled sprouting carrot tops all the way to the scrabble of cottages bordering the junction between Mutton Lane, Essex Place and Mare Street. And there, at a smouldering tinker's fire beside a rough shelter on the tip of the triangle of grass in the centre of the junction, it stopped.

There were two horses standing by the tent, small beasts, ill-used and hung with skulls and bones plaited in their manes. The bone pet passed between their hooves and approached the meagre warmth of the fire.

The tinker was stone-drunk, sprawled out against his pack. Two tall figures sat easily by the flames, each with a face writhing with blue tattoos and matted hair and beards wound with bones and twigs. The taller of the two wore a ruinous billycock hat with the top punched out, around the brim of which was a garland of woodcock skulls arranged with their beaks pointing skywards so that the effect was that of a bony crown. He was whittling a rowan twig into a stiletto-like point. His companion was finishing the delicate work of attaching a sharp bronze beak to a hawk's skull using gut thread sewn through carefully bored holes in the bone. He tied off the gut and leant in, neatly biting off the thread hanging beyond the knot with his front teeth.

They both stopped as the bone pet edged into the firelight and stood in front of them.

The one with the woodcock crown nodded and touched it on the head.

Immediately the beak opened and the voice of the imprisoned Sluagh emerged from it:

"*It is done. They have taken the girl in. I am taken but the bone pet will lead you back to me. Free me soon.*"

The tall man nodded again and looked at the other with a grim smile of satisfaction.

"Free him."

The other leant across and neatly twisted the head off the bone pet. Just as neatly he snapped on the hawk skull. He then tossed the woodcock skull over the fire to the tall man, who in turn threw him the sharpened rowan twig. He held it out and the hawk's beak gripped it.

"Go," he said. And with no more ceremony than that, the bone pet scuttled south again.

The two Sluagh looked at each other across the fire and shared a smile.

"Yes," said the one in the crown. "Now it begins."

CHAPTER 18

FIRST LAW

Everything, including the stars themselves, hangs on this – the First Law of Motion: a body persists in its state of being, either at rest or of moving uniformly straight forward, unless it is compelled to change its state by a force acting on it.

As above, so below.

Imagine a child, an intelligent child, an inquisitive child – a child of the Enlightenment. Imagine that child is privileged and rich and denied nothing, least of all the best of teachers. Imagine that child is educated to believe that the world is a scientifically explainable place, a machine governed by provable rules of cause and effect. Imagine that child as he grows and is taught the immutable laws which govern the world in a universe illuminated by the great and supremely rational minds of Galileo, Boyle and, above all, Sir Isaac Newton, the very author of that First Law of Motion.

Imagine that child who thus knows that the sun, the planets and the very world upon which he stands swing through the cold void according to a grand celestial clockwork. Imagine the child now a youth, a hard-minded product of the Age of Reason, what half a century before would have been called a

Natural Philosopher, now become a self-proclaimed Man of Science.

Imagine his steely eye surprised by a fairy.

Or rather, specifically, imagine this young man sees another beautiful young person escape both a locked room and his unwanted attentions by calmly walking into a mirror and disappearing as completely as if she had simply passed through a door.

Imagine his mechanical mind thus presented with another set of rules which disproves the very system by which he held the world works. The young man, little used to being wrong and wholly unused to being thwarted, has two choices: to believe he has run mad, or to understand that the rational mechanism which he thought underpinned the world is no more than a first layer hiding a second, more arcane, clock-work by which the universe is *really* governed.

Imagine all this and you have the pattern and model of one Francis Blackdyke, Viscount Mountfellon.

In his case, befitting a solitary young man steeped in wealth and the unthinking truculence which often attends great privilege, he did not limit himself to one choice. He chose both, embracing madness of a sort, and devoting his life to mastering this other, secret clockwork. He did all this with the ruthless zealotry of a convert: he did not lose the habits of science or the conviction that given the right set of rules and tools he could explain and control the world and what happened in it – he now merely applied that mode of thought to the new system whose occult working he had just glimpsed through the cogs and springs of Newtonian mechanics. He was possessed of a mind trained to remember and categorise everything he experienced, what in a later era would be known as a photographic memory. He was an obsessive reader, note-maker and collector, and had drilled himself to become a detailed and accomplished draughtsman as well. His fanaticism matched even that of the great Newton, his first and now discarded hero, a man who had the mad rationalist will to stick a steel bodkin into his own eye socket to prove his theories about optics.

Imagine that the beautiful young person who had escaped into the mirror was the only person Mountfellon had ever loved, and that she was also, infuriatingly, a childhood playmate, the daughter of one of the people who had educated him in the "rational" truths of the natural world, truths which themselves proved that her walking into mirrors was a categorical impossibility.

Imagine Mountfellon deducing that it might well be possible that the rational world was connected by a secret honeycomb of passages running between all the mirrors across the globe.

Imagine him realising that what he would have previously called magic actually worked.

If you think that there are men of science who are happy enough to understand and discover the clockwork which swings the stars in their courses, and are satisfied enough with that knowledge for and of itself alone, you are imagining men who are not like Mountfellon.

He belonged to the other tribe, those who delight in the hidden nature of that clockwork and in its immense power: the power of the machine is the thing, and they wish to own the very key that winds it. Even in this tribe there are the sane ones who want the key for the greater good of all humanity. The mad ones want the key for themselves.

And Mountfellon was, perhaps in this way only, the maddest of the mad.

Taking his experience with the girl in the mirror, a case might be argued that the First Law applies not just to physical objects but to personalities, indeed not only to motion, but emotion: it could be reformulated to state that everybody persists in their state of being, unless they are compelled to change their state by a force acting on them.

Mountfellon had been acted upon: the child of reason thus became irrationally consumed by the need to control the supranatural world and all of its hidden clockwork.

Amos Templebane knew none of this as he stood trying to keep out of the worst of the rain. He had been shivering too hard to sleep, but the exhaustion of his journey north had dragged him more than halfway there when the hinges of the iron gates shrieked as the gatekeeper threw them open. Amos had to move fast to avoid getting flattened against the stone walls by the heavy metal bars, and had to leap backwards as six black horses thundered out of the mouth of the tunnel pulling a closed carriage. The coachman roared and threw himself simultaneously back on the reins and the wheel brake.

"Whooaa!" he thundered, and the coach came to a stop with the shuttered door level with Amos.

The shutter cracked an inch and Mountfellon's eye looked him up and down.

"You are the Templebanes' creature?" he said, voice dry as autumn leaves rustling across a crypt floor.

Amos met his eyes and did not flinch. He nodded.

"Speak when you're asked a question, damn your eyes!" snarled the coachman and flicked his whip so that it cracked an inch above Amos's head. He jumped.

Mountfellon scowled at him.

"Are you an idiot? My man in London told me the Templebanes had a half-breed simpleton or some such . . ."

Amos scrabbled inside the collar of his coat and pulled out his brass badge, holding it up to the window. Mountfellon's eyes skated briefly over it and then he nodded in satisfaction.

"Ah. I knew it was some species of crippledom. Well, boy,

defective though you are, your father would have me return you to him."

Amos smiled and nodded. Mountfellon's scowl only deepened.

"I am not a common carrier, nor do I deliver packages on instruction. Since I am at present obliged to your father for his continuing good offices, I shall, however, condescend to agree to his request. Have you pissed?"

Amos's smile faltered at the unexpected question.

"If you have not pissed, do it now, for by God I will be in London before noon strikes, hell or high water, and tonight we will not stop for the devil himself, except to change horses at Hertingfordbury."

The shutter slammed shut. The coachman looked at Amos. Amos turned to the wall and quickly unbuttoned and added to the downfall drenching the ivy hedge. Then he hurried across to the carriage and climbed in.

With a yell and another crack of the whip over the lead horse's head, the carriage lurched into motion and Amos fell back in his seat.

There was a further flash of lightning in which he saw the gatekeeper closing the entrance to the underground drive, and then all was lost in the spray kicked up by the rapidly accelerating wheels.

Mountfellon sat opposite him, motionless as a statue, his eyes reflecting the small flame in the lamp mounted at his shoulder. A book lay on his lap, which was wrapped in a blanket lined with dark fur.

Amos shivered, not so much at the cold but at the unblinking gaze he was now subject to. He looked away but calmed his mind enough to listen for Mountfellon's thoughts. Amos lacked the ability to speak but he had a secret, one even his adopted family knew nothing of, and this was his ability, sometimes, to hear people's thoughts. At least that's what he felt he was doing: sometimes he wondered if he was just imagining what they *might* be thinking, but imagining it very vividly, since he had never been able to talk to anyone about it. If it was imagination then he felt it was a very accurate imagination, since he usually heard them thinking of doing something and then saw them do it. So it was a skill he relied on, particularly while trying to avoid his brothers when they were in a malicious or spiteful mood.

Mountfellon's thoughts were precise and analytical: *he's a strange-looking boy. Dark skin, but not too dark. Could pass for a gypsy in some lights. With a different nose. Mulatto? Quadroon? Octaroon? At least half negroid, I think. Bright eyes. Green. Not a blackamoor's eyes. White blood showing through. Too bright. Too much life in them. Not beaten as frequently as he should have been. Children are like dogs. Respond to the whip. Not enough to eat as a young creature. Effects of malnutrition visible. A certain delicacy of bone. Not much meat on him. Nine stone wet, if that. Five feet ten inches at a guess. How old is he? Could be anywhere between fifteen and nineteen. Won't meet my eyes. Hiding something. Why would Templebanes send a mute? Why should I believe he is such? So I can't question him? Templebanes no fools. The boy is likely dissembling. Sent to deliver but also to watch. Test him.*

The carriage jolted and lurched and he heard the thrum of the wheels throwing water against the mudguards. When he looked up again he saw Mountfellon was holding his hand out.

"Give me your hand, boy."

Amos instinctively didn't want to.

"I am a man of science. I wish to examine your hand."

Amos reached across the narrow gap between them. Mountfellon's cold fingers gripped his hand and turned it palm up. He grunted and switched his grip so that he held Amos's thumb.

"Close your eyes."

Amos gave him a questioning look. Mountfellon's face just clenched a little more, like a fist tightening.

"Close your damn eyes or you can walk to London."

Amos closed his eyes. There was a moment's darkness, and then a sudden sharp agony in his thumb. His eyes flew open and he tried to yank his hand out of the older man's grip, but Mountfellon was unyielding.

Amos's thumb was cut across the pad, ribboning a dark trickle of blood. Something shone in the other man's free hand. He held it up.

"Just a penknife. Just a little prick."

He folded the blade and pocketed it and then released Amos's thumb. Amos immediately put it in his mouth and pressed his tongue to it to stop the bleeding. He stared across the carriage in undisguised fury.

"You did not cry out," said Mountfellon.

And Amos heard the rest of the sentence in Mountfellon's thoughts.

He really is a mute. QED.

Amos scrabbled in his pocket and came out with a damp handkerchief that he wrapped tightly round his thumb.

"I take no man's word for anything," said Mountfellon. "I am an empiricist. All that I know I get by experience or experiment. I make no apologies for that."

Amos glared at him.

"Lower your eyes or I shall have the coachman toss you into the ditch."

Amos looked away.

"Good. You are biddable. Your fathers have broken you to the harness, I see."

Amos kept his eyes on the side of the road.

"Your fathers are cunning men."

Amos nodded.

"But are they always trustworthy?"

Amos felt the eyes on him like heat off a lamp. He neither nodded nor shook his head. Instead he just smiled. Mountfellon returned a smile of wintry insincerity.

"Why are you disloyal to them?"

Amos shrugged as if it were a thing of no matter.

"Why?" insisted the older man.

Amos reached into his coat pocket and brought out the small wood-framed slate he always carried there for such moments. There was a stylus attached to it with a thin piece of twine. He wrote, "Honest," and showed it to Mountfellon, who read it and shook his head.

"No. I think you are clever. I think the brass plate round your neck is right. No cunning man is entirely trustworthy, for as the world changes he must adapt to it. I think you know that saying they are always trustworthy would have damned them and made you a liar in my eyes . . ."

He opened the door. The wet night hurtled past outside.

"You may travel in the boot with the luggage. I do not choose to be observed as I sleep. And hold on tight, for if you bounce overboard you must swim home by yourself. I will brook no delays this night."

Amos took a deep breath and clambered out into the downpour, managing to find straps and handholds by feel alone which allowed him to work his way back along the side of the carriage. The door slammed shut behind him and he spent a very wet couple of minutes trying to worm himself in under the tarpaulin covering the boot without tumbling into the road ribboning away beneath the thundering wheels. When he finally did, he spent the next ten minutes trying to find a way to sit or lie comfortably among Mountfellon's bags and boxes. Unfortunately they were as hard-edged and intractable as their owner, so he wedged himself between a trunk and a hatbox and jammed his arm under one of the luggage straps so that he would not fall into the wet highway in the unlikely event that he managed to forget his discomfort enough to fall asleep.

The sound of the wheels and the irregular bumping of the luggage as they flew along made that impossible, so he closed his eyes and tried to see what Mountfellon was thinking inside his metal-banded carriage.

CHAPTER 19

THE REEKING BLADE

Sara Falk sat talking quietly to Lucy Harker at the corner of the kitchen table, just as Mr Sharp had left them. Cook was watching from her seat by the stove, peeling chestnuts into a bowl held between her knees. It was a warm and welcoming scene after the cold fog of the street.

They all stopped and looked up at Mr Sharp as he entered and closed the door carefully behind him.

"And . . . ?" said Sara Falk.

He placed the bronze blade on the table, and gently put the knotted kerchief next to it. Cook picked up the weapon and examined it.

"This looks like—" she began.

"Indeed," said Mr Sharp.

Cook looked a question at Sara Falk, who sat very still, eyes locked on the red silk bundle.

"Well, let's see, shall we?" grunted Cook. She disappeared into one of the alcoves and came back with a carving board on which sat a half-eaten pink ham with a dark brown skin studded with cloves and glazed with marmalade. She took the blade and cut the remaining chunk of meat across the grain.

For an instant nothing happened, and then each side of the newly cut wound darkened to a sudden and startling green-black that blossomed with dull grey eruptions of rot in slow explosions through which white maggot heads began to writhe and poke like hundreds of tiny fingers reaching out of the corrupted flesh.

The smell was as swift and if possible even more shocking. Lucy Harker slipped off her chair and ran to the far end of the room gagging, her hands clamped over her nose, staring at the rotting ham as if it were a personal insult.

"*Jésus chiant!*" she cried, one finger clamped on her nose while the other pointed in outrage. "*Cela sent comme le cul d'un mendiant mort. Faites quelque chose!*"

"We're really going to have to do something about her language," said Sara Falk. "But she's right. Can you do something about that, Cook?"

Cook picked up the ham, which had shrivelled halfway back to the bone already, and dropped it decisively, board and all, into the fire. The fire crackled and roared and then kicked up unnatural red and green flames which shot three feet above the grate and curved savagely backwards into the catch-all hood and up the open flue, racing one another in their fiery eagerness to get to the open sky beyond the chimney-pot three storeys above.

"Well," said Sara Falk, taking her eyes off the bundle and finding Mr Sharp.

"I told you I smelled something," he said. "I thought it was Ketch or the girl—"

"But it was something else?"

He nodded.

"One of the Sluagh."

Cook exhaled sharply in an explosion of disbelief.

"The Sluagh? This far south?"

"Yes."

"In a *city*?" she spluttered.

"He was in it," said Mr Sharp. "Now he's under it. I have him in the Privy Cells. I found his horse."

As if on cue there was the sound of a hammer clinking against metal out in the alley.

"Emmet is shoeing it," he said.

"Shoeing it?" said Sara. "Surely it would have been kinder to just put it out of its misery?"

He shook his head.

"It had been Sluagh-rid for a long time, but it was still just enough itself behind the madness to be worth the saving. Besides . . ." – he looked at the floor for an instant – "you know I don't like to kill."

Cook snorted again.

"There's a long line of dead men would be spinning in their graves if they could hear that!"

"None the less," he said. "You know it is so."

He pointed at the red handkerchief.

"I cut the beaks and skulls off its mane. One of them was faster than I was . . ."

He held up his finger and showed the wound with a rueful smile.

"We must talk," he said, widening his eyes and tipping his head very slightly to indicate Lucy.

"You can talk freely. She speaks only French," said Sara.

"How do you know?" said Cook. "All we know is that she hasn't spoken English yet."

"It doesn't matter," said Mr Sharp. "What matters is that it is not safe to have her in the house."

"I have just given her my word that she will be safe here," said Sara.

He shook his head.

"There is something in the manner of her arrival I do not like—"

"Is there a connection between her and the Sluagh?"

"I do not yet know of one——"

"I gave her my word."

"As I gave my word to protect you and this house," he countered with the faint exhaustion of one for whom this was an overfamiliar exchange. "Have Emmet take her to The Folley. Have her guarded by The Smith if he has returned. If not Emmet can keep her there. She can do——"

"One night here will do no harm, Sharp," Sara cut in. "Look at her. It is not even a full night for it will be light soon enough and she is dropping in her tracks."

Lucy's eyes were drooping, it was true. Mr Sharp took a deep breath.

"My nose tells me something is wrong——"

"Something is always wrong," said Sara. "We would not be necessary if it wasn't."

"That argument does not improve with your incessant repeating of it," he bristled. "She cannot stay here. It is not safe."

"It is the Safe House. If not here, then where?"

"I mean it is not safe for the house to have her here," he said.

There was a pause as he looked at Cook, who in turn looked at Sara.

"It is not safe for us," he finished.

Sara shook her head slowly, tired at having to rejoin an old battle.

"Why was the house made safe in the first place?" she asked.

"To guard the library," said Cook.

"To guard the key," corrected Mr Sharp.

"And why must the key be guarded?" continued Sara wearily.

Mr Sharp looked at Cook again. She didn't meet his eyes. He smiled with icy politeness.

"Sara Falk. With respect, I am not a child to be pulled through his lessons by you."

"I am not schooling you. It is a serious question which applies to the girl."

His smile tightened up a notch. Then he exhaled.

"The key's power must be kept out of the hands of those who would misuse it."

"Why?" she persisted.

He shook his head and looked at Lucy. She was head down on the table, eyes closed, fast asleep.

"I will not play this game with you, not now and not in front of her—"

"It is no game and the child is asleep."

He leant in and looked closely at Lucy.

"I put something in her milk," said Cook.

He straightened and looked into Sara's face, whose chin was tipped up in a defiant manner.

"Very well," he said. "I will play but you will not like my answer: the real key is the Discriminator. It discriminates. It shows who is normal and who is not. It reveals those who have supranatural characteristics to those who don't. It even reveals those who have abilities which are latent or unsuspected—"

Sara opened her mouth but he raised a finger to stop her and rode implacably over her attempt to interrupt.

"We are here to protect the unaware from the unseen, but also to protect the unseen from the attentions of the unaware. We know what the unaware can do when in the grip of one of their occasional fits of religion or other zealotry. Burned girls, men tortured and foolish old women put to the rack or drowned in the village pond."

"My father—" she began.

"Your father said the last witch craze under Cromwell killed scores of innocents, most of whom had no real powers anyway. The persecutors lit their fires without a means of truly distinguishing who was actually who. Just imagine the immense harm they could do with a Discriminator like the key—"

"If I might—" began Cook. He shook his head.

"I have not finished. The last witch craze would seem like a mild diversion when they set to work in earnest with a tool like that. The next fit of enthusiasm could be on a horrible scale – it would be like comparing the meagre output of the humble weaver working his handloom in the back of his cottage to the torrent of fabric emerging from the new steam-driven mills. It would be death wholesale and persecution by the yard—"

"Mr Sharp," said Sara, eyes hot.

"No, Sara Falk," he said, stabbing at her with his finger. "It would not be a mere temporary tipping of the very balance we are sworn to maintain; it would be the scales themselves knocked over and smashed in the rush to blood and vengeance. Man is too fearful to embrace difference. One day this may change, once poverty and ignorance are banished, but as long as the passage of most men's lives remains a struggle against hunger and insecurity, difference itself is a threat because those who are alien to you, those whom you do not know, might come and steal your food and do worse to your family. The key is not merely the Discriminator: in the wrong hands it is a tool for finding difference and thus identifying an enemy. Cromwell's men kept dissent at bay in the shires by scourging the 'different' and blaming them for the ills his war brought to the peasantry. Prejudice is a strong fire, Sara Falk, and the Discriminator is too easy a means of finding it fuel."

He smacked his hand on the table and looked up into the attendant silence, almost immediately ashamed at his unchar-acteristic vehemence.

"And now who is giving lessons?" said Sara quietly.

He coloured slightly.

"I am reminding you why it is my duty to go against your wishes and insist the girl is taken from here tonight."

"She stays," she said.

"This is the Safe House. It is my charge to keep it – and you – so. I cannot understand why it pleases you so much to check me on that, unless it is a wilful obstinacy that—"

"Don't continue this old dance," said Cook. "Sometimes I think you bring out the worst in each other: Sara never reckless except in reaction to Sharp; Sharp never so cautious except in relation to her. It is quite exhausting as a spectacle, especially this late at night. I swear sometimes the pair of you make me feel like an old gooseberry forced to watch two mooncalves stumbling through a flirtation—"

Sara's pale face tightened and flushed pink at these words, and her voice rose.

"I frightened the girl!" she said. "I have an obligation. I overstepped myself. She panicked and threw hot food in my face, and because it hurt I got angry, which was an unpardonable lack of self-control, and I gripped her hand and made her touch the wall and so made her glint against her will!"

She looked down at the floor, as if too ashamed to meet anyone's eyes.

"I hurt her instead of being patient and explaining things in a slow and measured way. It was unforgiveable."

"Nonsense," said Cook, nudging Mr Sharp.

He didn't say anything. So she nudged him again, harder, the kind of nudge that leaves a bruise. He looked at her in surprise. She raised an eyebrow and drew her arm back a third time.

"It was . . . understandable," he said.

"Nevertheless," she went on, raising her head and pointing at Lucy. "She was hurt and drained because of me. She can stay one night."

He opened his mouth. She carried on with a placatory wave of her hand.

"If you have a Sluagh in the Privy Cells, then The Smith will want to see it. I suggest we send Hodge to fetch him. He will be here at first light, and then can take the girl back to The Folley afterwards. One short night will do no harm."

He held her gaze, seeming on the point of retorting, then winced as Cook trod on his foot. He dropped his eyes into a shrug of acceptance.

"Very well." He looked at his hands and wrinkled his nose in distaste. "I will go and wash my hands at the pump."

The door bumped loudly behind him as he walked out, making Lucy raise her head and look sleepily round the room before sinking back into sleep.

"What?" said Sara without looking at Cook. "He agreed with me in the end. It's fine."

"Nothing," said the older woman.

"That's a rather pregnant nothing," said Sara after a long beat. "Spit it out or go to bed."

"I was just observing that you are, as ever, the one blade he cannot defend himself against," she replied with an unconvincing innocence.

"And what does that mean, you old pirate?" said Sara, a dangerous edge to her voice.

"It means, young lady, that one day you and he are going to have to have a conversation."

Sara's eyes bored holes into Cook's ample back as she watched the older woman examining the Sluagh blade.

"I don't know what you mean," she said.

"Yes, you do. Even if you don't know you do, you do. But that's for another day," said Cook with a shudder. "I don't want this filthy cleaver in my kitchen for a minute longer. It has a charnel-house reek to it."

"Yes, I think it and these need to be placed out of harm's

way," said Sara Falk, relieved that the conversation had tacked back into safer waters. She reached over and picked up the bag.

"I think they shall have to be put in the Red Library."

CHAPTER 20

QUIETUS

The lock to the cell door wouldn't budge. No matter how insistently the Sluagh worried at it with the bronze pin he had secreted in his sealskin boots, the mechanism just wouldn't move at all. It was iron, and cold iron was stubborn, alien stuff for the Night Host at the best of times, and this was far from a good time for the Sluagh. He knew it was pointless, but his pride kept him at it until the pin bent and re-bent and then finally snapped.

Only then did he stop, tossing the pieces away and slumping to the cell floor, his back against the door. He could feel the discomfort of the power in the alternating oak, ash and blackthorn planks fizzing against him like a very mild static electricity, but he was much too tired to move. Instead he sat in the dark and remembered his life. Not the short life before First Death, but the much longer life he'd led after that. He remembered the wild rides and the companionship of the Night Host and the sense of excitement in the mastery of the dark they shared.

Before First Death, in his day-lit life, he had been as cautious about the dark and what it might hide as any other man or woman living in a solitary spot at the edge of the world would sensibly be: he smiled at the memory, dim and distant though it now was. The dark was his element now, as essential and unnoticed as water to a fish. It was hard to be afraid of what the darkness might hold when you know you are almost always the most dangerous thing abroad after the sun goes down.

He shook himself to erase the memory of his Day Life, funny though he found the idea of the dark ever having held terrors bigger than those he was now blood-kith and bone-kin to: other Sluagh never mentioned their Day Lives. For them it was as if escaping the tyranny of light had rubbed out all memories of their earlier selves, their friends, their families. He wondered, as he often did, if he had perhaps done something incorrectly on that cold midnight so very many Beltanes ago as he stumbled bloodily through the twin fires which marked his First Death. He knew the Sluagh chieftains, who saw everything even in the darkest corners of a man's soul, noticed this in him, and though nothing a Sluagh did was condemned by another Sluagh as a point of honour, he sensed they saw his taste for day-drenched girls as a weakness. He viewed it differently, this coupling with girls fat with sunlight a demonstration of his power, but he never spoke of it. He enjoyed playing with the girls' minds as much as he perversely thrilled to the unwholesome warmth of their flesh against the vital chill of his own. And in the end he also knew the thin thread of connection he had with the daywalkers was a tool the Sluagh were happy to use when it suited their purposes. Most of them were so removed from the light-locked that they scarcely noticed them as they rode past their lit windows or darkened doorways, paying them no more heed than a man does who rides past a wood and fails to see the birds in the trees or the rabbits and field mice hidden beneath the hedges and brambles. He always noticed, and his noticing of the daywalkers was a bridge between them.

That is why he had been sent into London to do what he had done. That is how he came to play the part he had in the game that was now running. He'd felt the power and the life in the girl in the sack, and an old fire had kindled in him even as Ketch had shouldered her and set off for the Jew's house with his story, and he had sought out the soft-minded girl in the tavern as a vessel within which to quench that heat.

He should have kept apart and waited and watched, but he had done what he had done and nothing was to be regretted. Nothing except that he had not had time to do more because the man in the midnight-blue coat had seen him where others couldn't.

His lip curled at the memory. The first thing he would do when he was released by his bone-kin was to find the man and skin him.

He knew he would be released. Before he had ridden into the city he had asked what would happen if he fell foul of the Lore, and his chieftain had sworn a blood oath that he would be released. He might be in a cell of oak, ash and thorn, but the Sluagh had their own woods, their own metals, and any moment now he expected to hear the sound of bronze blades on rowan handles hacking their way through to save him.

He didn't hear that. What he heard was a smaller though no less welcome sound. He heard the scrabble and skitter of bony feet on the corridor floor outside, and then the slow careful scratch of tiny claws pulling a skeleton up the outside of the door-frame.

He smiled and unfolded from the floor. It was not a smooth movement as he gasped to his feet and leant against the door.

"Hello, my dear," he croaked. "Brought them to rescue me, have you?"

And he laughed, the dry wheezes tumbling from his lips like dead insects.

"Come in then," he croaked, and slid his hand out of the judas hole, palm up, ready. "Come in, pretty one, for by the bone you have run far tonight and you deserve rest."

His good hand trembled in the dark as he waited for the familiar weight to drop into it. It was true, he thought, he had never felt so old. The cold iron and the mongrel puppy with the fast blade had done this to him: he knew his strength and the vigour of his youth would return to him as soon as his kin had freed him from the woods lining the room and whatever words had been hidden on the back of them. He would celebrate his returned strength by dancing in the mongrel's blood. It would happen so soon that he could almost feel it was happening already, and his voice was stronger as he spoke to the bone pet outside.

"Come, my dear, for we shall soon be free."

Unseen by the Sluagh, the bone pet turned its head, still gripping the sharp rowan twig in its bronze beak as it gauged the distance and then leapt from its perch on the door-frame and landed on the waiting hand.

"Good," laughed the Sluagh. "Good . . ."

He began to draw his forearm back inside the cell.

The bone pet turned its head sideways so that the sharp end of the rowan pointed downwards, and then ratcheted its neck backwards before striking towards the floor in one sharp decisive movement.

The small stick went through the Sluagh's arm just below the wrist, right through the gap between the radius and the ulna bones and out the other side, so that there was more than four inches of wood sticking out above and below the arm preventing the hand being withdrawn back into the cell through the narrow slit.

The Sluagh grunted in surprise as much as pain. He squinted out into the dark and saw the stick and the bone pet beyond.

"What . . . ?" he choked, his eyes trying to make sense of

the familiar skeleton and the unfamiliar skull with its bronze raptor's beak crouching on his trapped hand. "Why . . . ?"

The beak opened and the Sluagh chieftain's voice answered him.

"*As I swore, by the blood and by the bone, you are released.*"

"No!" shouted the Sluagh, and tried to crush the skeleton in his palm, but his fingers were too old, too tired, too human to beat the inhuman speed of the bone pet as it leapt out of his grip and landed athwart his wrist, the beak open, the sharpened edges slashing right and left and then right again. And where it cut, the blood came, but not the bright blood, the red blood of life, but the inky blood of Last Death, blood turned as black as the wound itself as the bronze blade brought the outer darkness into the body of the Sluagh, and in its own way, did release him.

CHAPTER 21

THE RED LIBRARY

The Red Library was on the first floor of the house, at the top of an elegant staircase which swept up round the panelled walls of the entrance hall onto an upper landing covered in murky green and brown murals depicting a marshy coastline dotted with strange buildings and ships in distress on a dark, rising sea. The double doors to the library were, in contrast, covered in rich scarlet silk. Each door had a large animal outlined upon it in shiny brass upholsterer's tacks: on the left a rearing unicorn, on the right a matching lion.

Lucy, having been roused from her doze in the kitchen, was feeling unnaturally sleepy despite wanting to remain alert. She looked at the seven-foot-high animals and then at her ring.

"Yes," said Sara Falk in French. "The same unicorn."

"I do not understand," said Lucy, looking around at all of their hands and the rings on them.

"Well," said Sara. "It's late . . ."

Lucy opened her mouth to protest, but Sara continued firmly.

". . . it's late and you must go with Cook and, if you wish, have a hot bath, but you must then sleep. Your eyes say you are exhausted, whatever your mouth might claim. Sleep, and then you will be in a better condition to understand things. But until then I will tell you this: the lion and the unicorn represent the one truth behind the great and hidden history of the world, and that is that there is more than just one way to see. View the world in one way, it's a day-to-day place where wonderful things like lions are possible, but if you can see it the other way you notice it contains other realities, layers if you will, in which there are 'impossible' things, things like—"

"Unicorns," said Mr Sharp, jogging up the stairs behind them.

"Exactly."

"But unicorns *don't* exist," said Lucy, yawning despite herself.

"You're right," said Sara, exchanging a look with Mr Sharp. "At least as far as I know. But they certainly do exist as symbols."

Mr Sharp pointed to her hand.

"You have one on your ring," he said.

"Yes. But it is broken—" she began, her chin rising in defiance. He pointed to the animals outlined on the door.

"But when it is whole, like this, and faced with a lion, like that, it says the different realities do exist and are, like this lion and this unicorn, in balance," said Sara, showing her ring. "And those who wear this seal are sworn to keep that balance."

Lucy nodded, not because she fully understood, but because she was running out of energy and was filing all this away to be unpacked later. She had one final question.

"Why are the doors so red?"

"For safety," said Cook firmly. "Now: bath and bed."

"I thought red was for danger," said Lucy.

"Danger. Safety. Two sides, same coin," said Sara with a smile. "Balance, you see."

Lucy yawned. She really was very tired. She wanted to ask more questions but Cook's large hand was steering her towards the next flight of stairs, so she just nodded sleepily instead.

"Sweet dreams, Miss Harker," said Mr Sharp. "You are safe and among friends."

Lucy turned, remembering the rest of the question.

"But why silk? On the door?"

"My grandfather found a passage in the Talmud which told of the power of a red thread to ward off the evil eye," said Sara Falk. "Thinking that if one single thread had such power, many must have much more, he decided to line this whole room – floor, walls and ceiling – in silk, which is of course woven from uncountable numbers of threads, so making it infinitely secure."

"To ward off the evil eye?" said Lucy.

"Yes," said Sara Falk as Cook steered her out of sight round the next curve in the stair. "Sleep well."

Mr Sharp unlocked the door and pushed the lion part open.

"Of course she wouldn't sleep any better if we were to tell her it's as much to stop the evil getting out as getting in, would she?" he said quietly.

"She'll sleep fine," she said, pushing past him. "Cook's hot milk has its virtues."

He followed her in and locked the door behind him as she turned up the gas globes on the wall.

"Well and good," he replied. "If she can stay asleep until The Smith gets here, so much the better."

"She means us no harm," Sara said as the light flooded the room, revealing walls covered in ceiling-high glass bookcases crammed with ancient leather-bound volumes of every shape, size and colour. The shelves were also lined in red silk, as was every visible surface not covered by a book, an artefact or a cascade of manuscripts. The ceiling was red, and the thick Chinese silk carpet beneath their feet was of the same hue. The shutters were closed on the tall windows and were also, of course, lined in silk like the doors.

There were tables down the centre of the room covered in books, papers and maps, and there were glass cabinets filled with an extraordinary mixture of objects: bones, weapons, jewellery, cups, idols, fragments of pottery and much more, all assembled with no visible rhyme or reason, but all, when you looked closer, carrying a handwritten label, tied on with red silk string.

In the middle of the floor, between two long tables, there was a blocky pedestal made of glassy obsidian so black that it was like a square hole sucking the light into itself from the four corners of the library. On top of it was a three-foot-square wickerwork cage made from flexible strips of raw steel. An ornate key with a handle made to look like the flared hood of a cobra hung from the roof of the cage at its dead centre. As Sara walked past it, something hidden hissed at her, and she paused for a moment with her gloved hand stretched wide against the woven metal wall.

The floor of the cage was covered in black volcanic sand, and in one corner an obsidian urn had been half buried on its side, next to a shallow pool of water the size of a saucer. It was from the dark mouth of the urn that the hissing emerged, but it died down quickly, as if Sara's hand was calming it.

"There is not much in the natural world that makes me shudder," said Mr Sharp, pausing behind her and nodding at the cage. "But I will confess the thing guarding that key never fails to do so."

"Put the bones over there by the Murano Cabinet," Sara said, pointing at an empty shelf in a far corner next to an ornately panelled cupboard. The panels were covered in delicate paintings of Venetian canals, and each panel was outlined in twirled rods of hand-blown glass which caught the lamplight as they moved towards it. "And give me that damned blade."

"I shall keep the bones for now, and try them with Jed's nose," he said, handing it over.

"I told her about The Oversight," said Sara, looking at the cruel bronze edge in her hand. "I didn't tell her how few we are, or how fragile the balance."

"Or what power we must protect?" he said quietly. "I wager you told her nothing of that."

"No," she said, looking at the Murano Cabinet. "She has no need to know about the real key."

"And who is she?" he said.

"The Smith will know," she said. "And then I want to know who has been in The Three Cripples saying the Jew wants screaming girls."

"There was a time——" he began, turning.

"That was before *our* time," she said, cutting him off.

He watched her put the Sluagh's blade on a red shelf in a glazed cabinet set on the wall between the bookcases.

"None the less," he said calmly. "Old stories get repeated, and so the past comes back with a different face: it's how the city builds its legends, out of misremembered realities and old wives' tales."

"My grandfather used to say that men always deceive themselves when they remember their own pasts," she replied, "so why should a city be different?"

"Why indeed?" he agreed, pausing by the cage and looking at the small key hanging at its centre. "And what after all is wrong with a little deception?"

"In the right place, at the right time? Nothing," she said. "But I would prefer a little clarification and truth about the night's proceedings, and so we need to alert the others."

He stepped to the door and unlocked it. He paused to look back at her.

"You're sure The Smith will know who she is?"

She had her back to him, hands on her hips, scanning the high shelves above her.

"Wayland makes all the rings. He'll know if anyone does. He'll at least know who he made it for. And that's a start."

He watched her flex her back and roll her head from side to side, unconsciously stretching away the pain and fatigue he knew she always carried with her, but never spoke of.

"It's on the next shelf," he said.

"What?" she asked.

"'S'," he said, smiling mirthlessly. "For 'Sluagh'. But now you need to go to bed. I will find Hodge, who is as ever on the trail of an interesting bitch, and send him for The Smith, and then, since you will have your way about the girl, I think I will go and ask the Sluagh some more questions, questions I should perhaps have already asked . . ."

"You have nothing to worry about," Sara said, her voice soft. "I know I may betimes seem wilful and hard to govern, but I am no more a fool than you, old friend."

He looked at her and shook his head, still not quite ready to smile.

"Since I am at present still cursing myself for a weak-minded idiot for letting you keep her here until dawn, that does not recommend you much, I am afraid."

Silence hung between them, and then he shook himself like a man waking up from a doze.

"No matter. Hodge will not come in to make his report until breakfast, and then The Smith will be here and we can move forward." He inclined his head to her in the ghost of a bow. "Sleep well and sleep safely, Sara Falk."

CHAPTER 22

THE TERRIER MAN

Mr Sharp had been right. There was an interesting bitch under the Thames, and that was where he found Hodge the Terrier Man. The bitch was a young Irish terrier with bright eyes, good strong teeth and a beautiful red-coloured coat of rough broken hair. That was the good news. The bad news was that the bitch's owner was an out and out rogue who worked as a pimp and who, perversely, was as unwilling to sell the services of his terrier as he was keen to profit from the bodily attentions of the not so convincingly youthful stable of ladies he cared for. Unfortunately for him, Hodge was not, nor had ever been interested in ladies, negotiable or not, and he was presently and with characteristic single-mindedness much more interested in contracting an exclusively canine conjunction.

He had been on a rooftop earlier in the day, investigating a mysterious outbreak of mortality in a crowded series of pigeon houses, when he'd seen the man and his dog on the outside staircase of the building opposite. His eye had been so captured by the man's dog that his mind had been quite taken off the ramshackle coops full of pigeons which appeared to have been methodically crushed to death. He had curtailed his investigation and made enquiries about the man and the clutch of women he was shepherding around instead, and had determined he was a trader in ladies' favours.

He was now under the Thames because it was there, after dark, in the new tunnel between Wapping and Rotherhithe that the pimp's charges patrolled the already dank and dingy arcade of retail booths with which the speculative developers had lined the tiled underpass. These emporia had been advertised to potential investors as a subterranean replacement for the legendary cavalcade of shops that had once lined the great mediaeval London Bridge, which had been demolished ninety years before: the promoters had puffed the prospect of jewellers and cabinet-makers and fine craftsmen of all disciplines moving into the passage in order to cater to "the Quality", who would flock in high-class droves to the novel sub-riverine thoroughfare. The truth was that by day the tunnel was full of gaudy booths full of every kind of gimcrack operator working to take money from the passers-by, from conjurers dressed up as "Egyptian necromancers" to several lesser species of cardsharps, hucksters and pitchmen, as well as sweetshops, toy-sellers and dancing monkeys. At a certain late hour, the stores shuttered up, the gas globes seemed to dim, and – to the inattentive eye – the shop-girls appeared to stop selling souvenirs and start selling themselves, though in truth the actual shop-girls left as the ladies of the night arrived.

Hodge wanted a wife for his dog Jed, and he was arguing his suit with a tenacity that matched the stubborn, never-say-die quality he so admired in the dog himself. He was a distinctive and muscular man, built low to the ground, with bright blue eyes and a shock of wiry copperish hair brushed back from a weatherbeaten face which – in conjunction with a rolling gait caused by his slightly bowed legs – gave him the air of permanently walking into an invisible wind.

Jed sat obediently at his feet as Hodge tried to make the

match, studiously ignoring the charms of the comely Irish bitch with a lordly unconcern, as if the whole thing meant nothing to him. He himself was an Old English Terrier, black and tan with an equally broken coat and a lively and alert eye.

He saw Mr Sharp before Hodge did, but when Hodge noticed his friend he made his apologies, engaged to come back later to continue the negotiation and joined him as they walked out of earshot towards the galleried entrance shaft. They both moved fast and with purpose, Jed never straying more than a foot from Hodge's heels.

The shaft was an impressive cylindrical space, well lit and floored in a chequerboard mosaic of blue and white, more than fifty feet in diameter. It rose from the tunnel mouth to a marbled rotunda high above. Marble stairs zigzagged up the curved walls, and there were two landings on which tired pedestrians might rest on their way up or down. Neither Hodge nor Mr Sharp paused as they jogged up the steps. Hodge's head inclined towards the other's as he listened to what he was telling him.

"A Glint?" he said at one point, and as they neared the brass turnstile at the top he stopped and looked at Mr Sharp in amazement. "Sluagh? In the city?" But apart from that he was all attention, as was the dog, who followed him but seemed to watch Mr Sharp's every move.

They emerged into the fog and only then paused.

"So," said Hodge. "Something's afoot."

Mr Sharp nodded. Hodge pulled a stubby cut-off clay pipe from his jacket and lit it with a phosphor match, staring at his friend over the flame as he did so. The hand that held the pipe showed a bloodstone ring with the lion and unicorn incised in it.

"And you are unhappy," he said.

"I smelled something in the air, but I let the man Ketch in," grimaced Mr Sharp. "That may have been a mistake."

"And he never makes mistakes," said Hodge to the dog sitting expectantly on the ground between them. The dog barked once.

"I make them," said Sharp. "I just don't like them. I don't like this. I need you to go and fetch The Smith. Ask him to join us for breakfast. Then see what you can find out about Ketch's movements tonight."

"This Ketch may not have been what he seemed?" said Hodge.

"He may have been acted upon. If I'd known there were Sluagh abroad, I would have considered that. I would have asked more questions about the man at The Three Cripples who told him the Jew wanted screaming girls."

"I'll get The Smith and then go to The Three Cripples," said Hodge. "They don't close. What did this Ketch look like?"

Mr Sharp looked at him. Hodge held his gaze for a beat, then nodded although no audible words passed between them.

"Not the face of an angel, is it?"

Mr Sharp shook his head. "Walked a hard road and shows every mile, I'd say."

"I'll find him," said Hodge. "And the Sluagh?"

"Here," said Mr Sharp. "Start outside Bunyon's tavern, the side entrance. He was there for a long while."

He unwrapped the bones he had taken and crouched on the ground. Jed stiffened and began to quiver with a low whine of excitement as he filled his nostrils with the smell of the Sluagh's trophies. The sharp-beaked puffin skull that had bitten Sharp began to vibrate and turned towards the dog, chittering menacingly, but Jed just curled his lip on one side, showing his fangs, and rumbled a low warning growl. The puffin skull stopped chittering immediately, turned away and was very still.

Hodge scratched the dog's head affectionately.

"Good man," he said. "See you back at the Tower."

Jed yipped once and then bolted into the night.

"You could put the Raven up," said Mr Sharp, retying the bundle.

"At night, in the fog?" said Hodge. "Jed's lower to the ground and his nose is almost as good as mine. You worry about Sara and the house. We'll backtrack your visitors and see who met whom and when."

Mr Sharp clapped him on the shoulder.

"I'll see you later," he said, and was about to turn when Hodge took his sleeve.

"Sluagh. Do they kill animals? Birds and the like, say pigeons, wholesale killing for pleasure or maybe just pure malice like a fox? Just crush 'em and leave 'em?"

Mr Sharp thought and shook his head.

"Not really. No. I mean they'll kill easy enough, but always to a purpose. What have you seen?"

Hodge grimaced.

"Raven saw a child this afternoon crying on a rooftop among some pigeon coops. Coops were full of dead squabs."

"Birds die of many things . . ." began Mr Sharp, clearly eager to be on his way.

"Raven draws my attention to something, I take it seriously," said Hodge.

"Wise," said Mr Sharp. "Where?"

"Farringdon way," said Hodge. "Not close to us but the birds had all been crushed. Little chests a tangle of broken bones. Pitiful to feel it."

"People do strange things," said Mr Sharp. "Normal people."

"Strange things do strange things too," said Hodge grimly.

"Should be checked out, no doubt," agreed Mr Sharp. "But it can wait until tomorrow. If it's some kind of breath-stealer or Mara we should find it and deal with it. But for now, I don't think it relates to the Sluagh, and it's the Sluagh and this girl that we must deal with. First things first."

Hodge nodded, but from the look in his eye he was wondering if he'd been distracted by the comely bitch a little too easily. He watched Mr Sharp disappear into the fog in the direction of Wellclose Square and took a deep draw on his pipe, before knocking it out on his boot-heel.

"Come on then," he said, and set off up a different street. "We'll run this errand to The Smith then maybe have another look at that rooftop."

There was a flutter from the top of the octagonal rotunda above the tunnel shaft and a mass of oily black feathers dropped out of the gloom and landed deftly on his shoulder. The feathers shook themselves as the wings folded and resolved into a large raven.

The Raven turned an unblinking eye towards him, and then very precisely bit him in the ear.

"Ow," said Hodge, swatting the bird's beak away from the side of his head without any evident rancour. "I was just telling the truth. You hate the fog and Jed can follow with his nose what your eyes can't see."

The Raven clacked its beak and looked away. Hodge rubbed his ear.

"You're getting very easily offended in your old age," he said. "Positively crabby."

Hodge had no real idea of how old the Raven was, and the Raven had forgotten long ago, so long ago that it was before the river they were at present walking away from had had a bridge or even anything more than a scrabble of huts alongside it, let alone a whole teeming city. He wasn't a very normal raven, but then Hodge wasn't a very normal Terrier Man. He had an innate ease with animals, being able to see into the minds and often through the eyes of the less sentient ones, and able to communicate with the more intelligent like

Jed or the Raven, though the Raven was, he knew, something even more than merely sentient.

Hodge did not live at the Safe House since he was, officially, the Terrier Man of the Tower of London. It was an ancient, little known but vital office of state, for the Tower was home to the ravens, and if the ravens left, legend had it that the city and the Tower would fall.

The Tower, being eight hundred years old, had acquired many unplanned-for residents, the most significant for Hodge and the realm at large being the rats. Ravens lay eggs, and rats eat them. The Terrier Man's job was a constant war against the hungry rodents, and Jed joyfully scoured the undercrypts and the hidden foundations of the Tower every day, never happier than when pouncing on an unwary rat, some of whom were so ancient as to be nearly his own size, and breaking their necks with one rough shake of his head, throwing the lifeless corpse over his shoulder and leaping forward to the next one. Being a terrier he was only following his nature, and being a terrier he would never stop fighting forward, even when severely outnumbered, as he often was. Hodge, who was not his master but his companion, had the same resolute determination and inability to back off, no doubt acquired by long association with the battle-scarred dog. Where Mr Sharp had speed and elegance on his side in a fight, Hodge had a battle-rage which would have been familiar to the Vikings whose blood ran in his veins and whose clear blue eyes he shared.

His Norse blood also explained the affinity he had with the Raven, whose black pinions had fluttered like dark pennants over long forgotten battlegrounds and the narrow ships of the warriors who fought on them.

CHAPTER 23

A THIEF IN THE NIGHT

Lucy Harker lay in bed and listened to the dark.

Earlier she had stood over a basin while Cook washed her hair with a solution of rosemary water and borax. She had then been given a scrubbing brush and a bar of Castile soap and allowed to enjoy the luxury of a long hot soak in a high-backed copper bath, on the strict understanding that if left to herself she would use both brush and soap with vigour. She had dried herself behind a screen in front of a fire, and had been given a cotton nightdress so sharply ironed that it snapped and crackled as Cook shook out the folds and held it out for her.

The linen sheets above and beneath her were so white and crisp and smooth, and tucked in so tightly that she felt like a flower pressed between the pages of a heavy book. She stretched her feet to the edge of the bed, enjoying the cool feel of virgin sheets beyond the area already warmed by her body.

She had, she decided, never felt so clean.

Not on the outside.

On the inside where her thoughts and her memories lived she didn't feel clean at all, and that was why she couldn't get to sleep.

The knowledge that she was going to do something bad spread through her like a stain. She didn't know exactly what the bad was, or why she was going to do it, but the inevitability of it loomed over her as if the future was impossibly casting a shadow backwards onto the present. She tried to banish this feeling of impending doom by thinking of her past, but that didn't help much because there weren't that many happy memories lurking back there and, more importantly, she had recently found the past had alarming holes in it, bits where her recollection just seemed to run out of road and hit a blank drop-off.

Those blanks frightened her almost as much as the certainty of the unknown badness she was about to do. She felt her heart beginning to trip-hammer with panic, and tried to slow it down by joining up what she could remember of her life into an orderly chain: she remembered being very little in the big city in France, in a tall pale house with blue shutters which folded around a courtyard garden with a big tree in the middle of it. She remembered her mother, and sitting in her lap in the shade beneath the generous green spread of leaves, and she remembered watching herself hanging upside down from a low branch and sticking her tongue out at herself, which was strange and maybe a dream memory, because the herself who stuck the tongue out had shorter hair than she did, and how could she be sticking her tongue out at herself anyway since being in two places at one time wasn't possible?

She did remember her mother's hands, always busy, sewing or making as she sang to her or told her stories. They were strong, nimble hands, and the smallest finger on the right hand was missing the top joint. Whenever she had asked about it her mother had said a little bird had taken it one day when she wasn't looking, and when Lucy asked if it had hurt she had shaken her head and smiled and said no, and anyway the bird must have needed it more than she did, so she mustn't mind at all.

Lucy remembered the finger and the smile, and the smell and the warmth of her mother's body, but she couldn't quite remember her face, not all of it at one time. When she tried to put the bits she could remember together to make a complete face, when she tried to join the crinkle at the edge of her eye with the freckles across her cheek and the smile and the hair, it never made a whole person, not sharp and distinct: the smile seemed to blaze out and blur things, so that it was like trying to look at a street-lamp through a haze of rain. And the last time she had seen her mother, it had indeed been raining, the cobbles wet and slippery beneath Lucy's bare feet, giving no purchase or chance of stopping herself as she was dragged away and lifted into the back of a closed carriage, and her very last glimpse before the door slammed shut was doubly blurred by rain and tears as she saw her mother on the steps of the house with the blue shutters, arm outstretched towards her as two men in darker blue dragged her back into the black mouth of the hallway.

That hallway not only swallowed her mother, it seemed to have devoured a large portion of her past because it left an almost perfectly blank hole in her memory after that, but it didn't trouble her because instead of falling into it, she fell asleep instead, and now that she was no longer listening to it, the darkness that filled the house listened back . . .

CHAPTER 24

THE SMITH'S FOLLEY

Hodge, as one of the perquisites of his official job, drove a dog cart. It was a small two-wheeled open carriage painted a dull green with two cross-seats back to back, the rear one cunningly contrived to open up if needed, so as to form a box for the transport of dogs.

Jed being a terrier, and thus proud and of an independent mind, never rode in the box. Instead he always sat beside Hodge on the front seat and watched the horse pull them through the streets with a proprietorial air, quite as if it was he who was driving and not the man who held the reins at his side.

This late at night, and so far east of the city, most people would have kept a careful eye on the figures loitering in the shadows, but Hodge gave them little thought, knowing he had unusually acute reflexes, a stout blackthorn cudgel close to his right hand, not to mention the comfort of the black and tan terrier to his left. The city thinned as they passed through Limehouse to Poplar on their way to the Isle of Dogs, and what lights remained visible through the increasingly grimy windows of the passing houses and drinking dens became dimmer and fewer.

Hodge had ratted across the landscape ahead as a boy when

it had still been known as Stepney Marshes, and as an even younger child he had watched the butchers slaughter the marsh-fed cattle on the great field known as The Killing Ground. The Killing Ground was now gone, dug up and filled with water to create the West India Docks. He knew it was fancy, but whenever he passed the black water at night he still smelled the flat tang of blood in the air.

The Isle of Dogs was an unlucky place for him. He had lost his first little terrier Jig there when he was ten, after the bank of the old inlet known as The Gut had collapsed and swallowed the dog and the rathole he had gone down in one heavy slump of mud and gravel. He had dug all night to try and rescue Jig, bloodying his fingers and tearing his nails. He had found the dog in the dawn light, seven feet down, smothered and lifeless, his jaws still locked on a huge rat. None of his friends could understand why he stayed and dug for so long, and one by one they had left him to it. He could not tell them that he knew the dog was alive and where it was trapped because he heard it, because what he was hearing was not audible to the normal ear. What he was hearing, at least for the first few hours, was the dog telling him he was still there and waiting trustingly for rescue. He had wept over the dog, said some fumbled words and then reburied him where he'd fallen. He had sworn to Jig that he'd never lose another dog, and he never had. He had sworn that he would die before he'd let that happen.

He had also never returned to the spot. It was no consolation to Hodge that the docks and the canal had in time swallowed The Gut too as they cut off the neck of the land, turning the marsh into an island in reality as well as name.

The Smith chose to live on the east side of the marsh, below the docks. His house was known as The Folley for reasons lost in time, but it was certainly thought a foolishness to set up a forge on what was still an out-of-the-way stretch of wild land overlooking the forbidding waters of Blackwall Reach and the dank Greenwich marshes beyond. Folly it would have been if The Smith had need of trade to justify his workshop, but the truth was that he had a workshop because he was The Smith, not that he was a smith to make a living. It was more than a living: it was his life. It was what he was to the core of his being: a maker. His workshop was also more than a smith's forge, though it was that too: to the undiscerning eye it looked like the aftermath of a bad explosion in a well-stocked ironmongers, a great muddle of tools of every shape and size slung promiscuously on hooks which covered every available space, garlanding the walls, spilling out of wooden racks and dangling from the roof-trees.

To the discerning eye, it was clear each tool had its place and was arranged according to an idiosyncratic plan. The workshop was set up with a section in which to work metal and a section for woodwork, and it was clear that the tools ranged in age from great antiquity to the most modern mechanical devices: there were dark hammers which had formed hot iron into swords long before the Romans came, and burnishers which had brightened the metal on Saxon shields; there were chisels and block-planes and spokeshaves and adzes and saws which had built wagons and half-timbered houses; there were pliers and moulds and sala-manders which had formed rings of gold and silver for courtiers in Tudor times; and there were screwdrivers and augers and wrenches which had mended Hodge's own dog cart on at least two occasions in living memory. There was also a flint knife.

The sharpest of the discerning eyes would have enjoyed the symmetry of the fact that the flint knife, perhaps the oldest tool in the workshop, rested on a shelf above the newest tool, a Holtzapffel Rose Engine lathe. The Smith sat in front of it, his foot working the treadle that powered the great cast-iron flywheel which in turn, via a cunning arrangement of pulleys and rope loops, drove a razor-sharp cutter whirring happily as it made shallow geometric cuts in a block of ivory. The ivory was held steady in the jaws of a chuck attached to one of a series of great brass rosettes which slowly moved in a pumping rhythm against a bumper as he turned a crank with his left hand.

He was so rapt in what he was doing that he appeared not to hear Hodge pull up outside, or feel the cold air fan the fire in the forge as he entered. Jed stopped to sniff at some long metal boxes stacked against the wall. They were as tall as a man, and had hinged lids. Hodge looked at them and tapped the metal. It made no sound other than a dull thud.

"What are you making?" he said.

The Smith gave no sign of surprise, just peering even closer at the pattern the whirring blade was cutting into the ivory.

"A five-pointed star. Of a new sort. It's quite fascinating how it happens, it quite stretches my understanding of geometry from two dimensions into three! I find it most relaxing trying to work out what will occur . . ."

"Not that," said Hodge, and rapped the boxes again. "These coffins."

The Smith turned from the lathe and looked up at him through a pair of half-moon glasses. He was a powerful man with thick, dark eyebrows and long greying hair brushed back from a high forehead. He wore a bushy moustache which had something of the Viking about it in its extravagant length and proud curve. His face had all the dark components of a storm cloud, betrayed by the flash of happy sunlight in his eyes as he turned them on his friend.

"Hodge," he boomed, his voice deep as rolling thunder.

"Wayland," said Hodge, his hand still testing the boxes.

"Not coffins, you fool. Chests!" growled The Smith, rising from his seat. The only sound was the crackle from the fire and the declining whirr of the blade as the great flywheel slowed to a halt once he had taken his foot off the treadle.

"Made from lead," said Hodge. "They do seem coffin-like."

The Smith stretched and walked over to the chests, pausing to scratch Jed's head as he passed. Jed had made straight for the heat of the fire and was warming his bones alongside it.

"They can be soldered shut and made watertight. Being so heavy they will sink directly. It is a solution to our problem if we are further reduced in number."

"I was not sure you would be here," said Hodge, accusation hovering in the background of his voice.

"I returned yesterday," said The Smith.

"You returned empty-handed."

The Smith grimaced and wiped his hands on his apron.

"No new recruits."

Hodge's brow creased in incredulity.

"You found *no one*?"

"I found people. I found plenty of people, several Glints as it happens, some others like Mr Sharp, a couple of families with your gifts with animals and so on. If you know where to look, the strong mixed blood is still out there. There's no mystery in that. But I found no one who would join us. And there's the rub: since the Disaster happened The Oversight is far from trusted."

"But it wasn't our fault!"

The Smith laid a great hand on Hodge's shoulder. His fingers were blunt and scarred.

"It was our fault. That it was not you nor I nor Sara nor Cook nor Mr Sharp who made the decision is irrelevant to the others. That those who made the decision did so out of the most admirable intent carries no weight either. They have heard what happened, felt the loss and have no desire to join us."

"Sharp could persuade them," said Hodge.

"He could turn their minds, but that is not how we recruit. You know that. You speak out of desperation. Have some warm ale. The nights are damp out here on the Isle."

He took a tall jug from the sideboard, limping as he walked back to the fire. It was an old limp, something which he clearly didn't think about, something which had become a part of him. He rested the jug on the edge of the forge as he gave the bellows a couple of hearty squeezes. The red coals paled as they heated up, and he grabbed a rag and pulled a poker from the fire, quenching its hot tip in the jug in a sizzle of steam. The room filled with the scent of warm ale and spices.

"I can't think how you favour it," said Hodge. "It truly is a place for ghosts and little else."

"I have always sat ill in the city, you know that," rumbled The Smith. "And these marshes are close to, but not of the city. And then again, it is the only island in London, with the Thames on three sides and the old Running Cut and the new docks on the other: there is much to be said for being surrounded by the protection of running water. I am safer here than they are in Wellclose Square, almost as safe as you in the Tower. Why have you come?"

He handed Hodge a pewter tankard, which he filled from the jug.

"A girl was brought to the Safe House this evening."

"A girl?" he said, raising an eyebrow.

"A Glint. Though she knows little of what she is and seems as if her mind has been turned. Sharp found one of the Night Walkers close by . . ."

The Smith choked on his ale and sat back against the anvil in the centre of the room.

"Sluagh? In the city? But they hate the city. Too much light and iron, too many people, too much flowing water in sewers and culverts, the place must be a maze to them . . ."

"Sharp has him in the Privy Cells. You can come and see him if you don't believe us," said Hodge, holding out his mug for more ale.

As The Smith poured he watched his face.

"They want you to come and see the girl's ring."

"Why?"

"They want to know who you made it for."

The flow of ale jerked and splashed onto the ground. The Smith looked up into Hodge's face.

"She has one of our rings?"

"So Sharp says. And she doesn't know a damn thing about us."

The Smith walked to the back of the workshop and opened the door to a cupboard. The shelves within were lined with books and scrolls. He took a thin green leather-bound book from the top shelf and riffled through the pages. They were full of drawings of rings, all similar in that they contained a bloodstone carved with a lion and a unicorn, but each subtly different in the way the stone was set, the style of the ring and the way the creatures were carved.

"I will bring my book."

"Come in the morning," said Hodge. "I have an errand in the city and the girl is sleeping now. You can give them the bad news about your recruiting drive first hand. Don't see why I should be the bearer of bad tidings."

CHAPTER 25

WHAT THE HOUSE HEARD

As Lucy slept, the house was still and silent. And for a long time there was no sound at all . . .

. . . and then there was a noise so quiet that it was not a creak or even the ghost of a creak, but maybe the memory of a ghost of a movement – and a very dim memory at that.

It was the air riffling past Lucy Harker walking through the night, silently. Her eyes were open but unseeing, as if still asleep. As she walked her gloved hand flexed repeatedly, as though loosening up for some delicate operation, like a pianist before a recital, and then closed purposefully on the door-handle to the Red Library and began to turn it.

CHAPTER 26

BUNYON'S BLESSING

Mr Sharp could see that Emmet was finishing nailing the last horseshoe into place on the Sluagh's horse as he entered the small stable adjoining the Safe House. The horse was still slick with sweat and quivering as if all its nerves were on the surface, but the giant clay man held it still with the foreleg clamped between his knees as he worked with his customary blend of speed and tirelessness.

A golem is a rare thing. Mr Sharp knew for a fact that this was the only one that had ever been made on this island, and he knew that Sara's grandfather had made him. Mr Sharp was never quite comfortable with Emmet, perhaps because the power that made him had bound him to protect and serve Sara just as Mr Sharp had been charged – in his case of his own free will – with the same task. There was a love of freedom buttoned tight behind Mr Sharp's leather waistcoat and somehow he could never quite get himself comfortable with the idea that Emmet was bound to his particular task as a slave. A long time ago, The Smith had tried to explain this to Mr Sharp, that Emmet was not alive in any meaningful way: "a mere automaton without visible internal workings" was how he described him, as if Emmet was some species of marionette or puppet, just a piece of showman's trickery such as to be found in the sideshows of any large county fair. Mr Sharp did not have that sense of Emmet. Rather he sensed that whatever the animating power was that moved the clay man, it was a power bound rather than a power given. And in that difference lay his unease.

Emmet could move and obey orders. He could understand, but he could not speak. Nor could he write, which Mr Sharp knew because he had once provided him with pen and paper and ordered him to do so, something he had not managed. Yet despite all this he believed there was more to Emmet than anyone had realised, or perhaps divulged. Mr Sharp had an affection for him which he could not imagine feeling for a mere thing, the kind of vital affection one can only have for a fellow being. As a man who needed less sleep than most normal people, Mr Sharp had spent long watches of the night sitting companionably with the golem and never felt alone while so doing. In fact he found the golem's presence relaxing and strangely comforting to his nerves whenever they were frayed or stretched by too much activity or worry. Because of this he never gave Emmet an order, certainly not in the abrupt and harsh tones in which Samuel Falk had addressed his creation. Instead he asked him to do things in the same tone as one might use to address an equal. It was this tone he adopted now as he walked into the stable.

"Emmet, would you be so good, once you have put the horse in a stall, to watch the house with extra care tonight. And if The Smith should come before I return, give him this note?"

He held out a piece of paper that had been first folded into a narrow strip and then been bent through a series of right angles to produce a sort of flat knot.

Emmet nodded, pocketing the note. And turned back to

the horse, taking a blanket off the stall side and beginning to rub it dry.

Mr Sharp tried to remember if he had told Emmet to dry the horse before putting it away. It was undoubtedly the correct and humane thing to do. Then, secure in the knowledge that whatever happened in his absence, the golem would guard the house, he turned his feet towards the Privy Cells, but not before picking a new iron horseshoe off the small farrier's table close by the door.

He entered the public house by the side door and slipped down to the cellar without troubling William Bunyon, who was entertaining a small smoke-wreathed knot of regulars with a humorous tale about his earlier career in the late king's navy. One of Mr Sharp's many abilities was that of not being noticeable when he wished it by blending in with the shadows as if he were one himself.

He passed through the main cellar and into the dark passage beyond without even the slightest clink from the keys he used to open the door. He twirled the horseshoe in his hand as he walked, and then rapped it on the wooden wall as he approached the cell.

"I have some questions for you. I hope you weren't sleeping," he said cheerily. "Oh, of course. I forgot. You don't sleep, do you?"

Something crunched under his foot and he stopped dead.

"Hello?" he said, his hand slowly drifting inside his coat as his nostrils wrinkled at something wafting towards him from the floor. His hand emerged clutching a candle.

"Light!" he said.

The candle snapped into flame, filling the narrow passage with a bright flickering light.

There was a thunk as the horseshoe dropped from his fingers and a snick as the hand that had held it darted inside the other side of his coat and came back with a blade in it.

"I've been a fool," he hissed.

The fragments of the bone pet were spread across the floor like a scrabble of white islands in the sea of black that was the Sluagh's blood.

He raised the candle and saw the arm of the Sluagh sticking out of the judas hole into the passage, pinned in place by the wooden spike between a now visible radius and ulna, blackened flesh rotted back to the very skeleton within. The Sluagh's hand was frozen in a gesture that might have been a blessing or a curse, pointing at the blank wall opposite.

"Damn you!" said Mr Sharp, stepping through the pool of blood and quickly unbolting the door. He jerked it open to see the body suspended on the other side like a sagging animal hide hung on a hook. The shells and bones in the rotting dreadlocks rattled against each other with the sudden motion. Mr Sharp yanked the head back and looked into the already rotted face of the Sluagh, into eyes that were already just empty holes in a skull.

He shook his head as he put the knife away and let his finger touch the judas hole thoughtfully.

"William Bunyon," he said sadly. "Your kindness is blessing for some, but for this poor creature it was a curse. Though why he would kill himself, or indeed why anyone else might want to stop him talking I do not know."

A thought hit him with the suddenness of an arrow from the dark.

"Sara . . ."

And he turned and ran for the door with such speed that the blood on the floor was still splashing from his passage through it by the time he hit the street above.

CHAPTER 27

THE MURANO CABINET

Lucy did not enter the dark library like a thief in the night: she didn't skulk or sneak or even tiptoe, but walked straight in as if she had every right to be there, though she did turn and click the door closed behind her, calmly picking up a chair and wedging it beneath the door-handle.

She had no need to light a candle to see her way through the cluttered space because of an orangey light which kindled and blazed out from her sea-glass the moment she crossed the threshold. This unnatural brightness threw stark shadows that lurched threateningly across the walls as she threaded her way past the tables and cabinets, making inexorably for the black cage at the centre of the room.

When she got to the obsidian plinth she stopped abruptly, her hands splaying out and moving across the slick enamelled surface of the woven metal cube as if they were doing the seeing for her eyes, which were fixed and open, but still somehow asleep and not focused on anything in particular: indeed if she hadn't moved with such clear purpose (and if there had been anything other than the dark to witness her progress) it might have been thought she was either stone-blind or trance-walking.

She found the door in the side of the lattice, and a second later the lock and catch. Her fingers moved in a light exploratory dance across the mechanism, and then nimbly manipulated it so that something pinged and the door jumped open a crack. Her fingertips quickly found the edge of the door and pulled it open.

An angry hiss emerged from the depths of the cage.

Lucy instantly went still.

But a very thin wire attached to the door on the inside had been pulled upwards by the action of the door opening.

The path of this wire descended through a small tube in the floor of the cage and continued on a zigzag path – via an intricate series of pulleys, quadrants and tubing – all the way downwards through ceilings and floors and walls to the main servants' bell-board in the basement. On this rectangle of polished mahogany were lines of curlicued springs attached to shiny brass bells. The lines of bells were split into floors, and each bell had its own label describing the room from which it was being rung. There was only one bell that was different. It was a dark iron bell, larger than the rest, and its label, reading "LIBRARY", was not written in black but red ink.

This bell clanged into life as the wire was pulled taut, the sound shattering the deep quiet of the sleeping house.

It was so loud that the bell could be heard two floors above, though Lucy's head was cocked and listening to something else entirely: the angry hissing coming from the half-buried urn in the floor of the cage.

Something was flowing out of the urn like a black river crossing the dark volcanic sand. The light blazing from her sea-glass cast a grid of shadows across the interior of the cage, which made it hard to see precisely what the thing was until it began to coil its body beneath the hanging key and rear up, its hood flaring out in warning.

It was a black cobra, jaws stretched wide, revealing the shockingly pink interior of its mouth and the needle-white bone-jag of two venomous fangs held ready to strike.

Angry red eyes looked at her.

The snake was unmistakably guarding the key.

Lucy did not step back.

She didn't close the cage door.

She didn't show any fear at all.

Instead she leant in and put her face to the opening, her eyes still dreamy and half seeing, and she spoke very softly.

"*Shhh,*" she whispered. "*Shhh. Soyez calme, mon petit. Tout va bien . . .*"

The snake continued to hiss at her, quivering with the tension of muscles held ready to strike its blunt nose forward and bite.

Lucy held the stillness for a long time, waiting for it to set.

Then she took a deep breath.

And reached carefully into the cage.

The snake didn't move.

Her hand slowly approached the key.

And still the snake didn't move.

The red eyes seemed hypnotised by the soft pink flesh on the hand reaching between it and the key.

The hissing stopped.

Lucy's fingertips reached the key, felt iron beneath them.

And the snake struck.

Death-filled fangs stabbed at the back of her hand.

Whiplash fast.

Her hand moved faster.

The cobra hit the key exactly where her hand had been, but that hand had lifted out of the way and now dropped to grip the snake on either side of its head before it could swirl around and bite at her again.

"*Non, non. Soyez calme, j'ai dit . . .*" she whispered.

And with a final muscular convulsion all the tautness left the snake and it went limp in her hand.

She carefully withdrew the cobra from the cage and held it clear of her body as she reached in with her other hand and lifted the key from the hook in the roof of the cage.

She grunted in surprise at the weight of the thing, which was more than its size hinted at, and as the weight came off, the hook sprung upwards and the cage simply fell to bits in a tinkling shower of metal, revealing that it was a cunning construction of short pieces of sprung steel that had been interwoven with each other and only held in place by the heft of the key, which had acted as a kind of anchoring keystone or counterweight.

More cunningly, or perhaps just more maliciously, those pieces of steel had razor-honed edges.

Three pieces of metal sliced cuts into her forearm as they fell, and the damage would have been worse had she not been wearing Sara's gloves.

The pain seemed to cut through the sleepiness in her eyes and she winced and looked round as if seeing things for the first time.

Her eyebrows cocked in surprise at the nightmare into which she had woken.

In one hand she held a snake.

In the other a key.

Blood dripped onto her bare foot from her arm.

And the floor around her was now strewn with scalpel-sharp strips of curved steel.

"*Merde*," she breathed. "*Quel bordel* . . ."

The cobra began to move in her hand, its tail curving upwards and finding her arm, trying to wrap around it as if it too was waking up again.

She stepped back and winced sharply as one of the metal shards cut into the ball of her foot.

"*Salopard!*" she hissed.

There was the sound of feet outside the door and a crunch from the chair wedged under the handle as someone tried to get in.

"Lucy!" shouted Sara Falk. "Is that you?"

Lucy grimaced silently. The cobra writhed against her firm grip, and its hood began to flare again as she looked desperately around the room for a place to hide.

"What are you doing, child?" shouted Cook. "It is dangerous in there!"

Lucy saw the shuttered windows next to the ornate glass cabinet at the far end of the room. She took a deep breath, swore under her breath one last time, then flung the writhing snake far into the shadows behind her and leapt forward onto the manuscript-strewn tabletop beside the black plinth.

Her feet skidded on the loose paper but she kept her footing and ran the length of the room, nimbly hurdling piles of books and jumping from table to table towards the windows.

Outside, on the landing Sara was pounding on the door as Cook leapt to the bannisters, red flannel nightgown billowing round her like a spinnaker, and roared down the stairs.

"Emmet! You lollygagging lump of useless sod, shift yourself!"

In the library Lucy skated to a stop by the shutters and reached up to unbar them, only to discover they were padlocked shut.

She hissed in frustration and looked round.

Something else hissed at the far end of the room.

And then hissed again. Closer.

Lucy bit her lip in frustration. And then her eyes fell on the Murano Cabinet.

Outside, Cook heard heavy boots clattering up the stairs so she turned back to the door and joined Sara's efforts to break it open by throwing her shoulder against it. She only managed to bounce off and drop the blunt end of the boarding axe held in her free hand onto her shoeless foot.

"Bugger," she winced.

Inside the library all was now dark.

There was the sound of someone large clumping up the stairs onto the landing, and then a sharp crack as the chair wedged under the door-handle smithereened shards of wood in all directions as the door flew open and Emmet tumbled into the room, followed by Sara Falk and Cook.

The room was pitch-black, bar the shard of light now lancing across the room from the door behind them.

"Lucy?" said Sara.

Emmet snapped his fingers and pointed.

The shard of light fell across the obsidian plinth, revealing the urn and the sand and the complete absence of cage.

"The bloody key's gone," said Cook. "Damnation—!"

"LUCY!" shouted Sara. "Where are you?"

There was no reply.

Lucy was crouched in the darkness inside the Murano Cabinet, her head smarting from an unexpected collision with something hard and angular. In one hand she held the stolen key. In the other she held her sea-glass tightly so its light would not betray her. As she adjusted her grip a sliver of light did flash out, and she covered it quickly. In the flash of vision it afforded she saw the inside of the cabinet was entirely mirrored, her reflection multiplied to infinity as the parallel sides reflected themselves back and forth in each other, and there was a bracket with a candlestick on it screwed to the back wall of the cabinet, the thing she had banged her head on as she entered the confined space. She did not have time to think how strange it was that a cabinet should be lined with mirrors, nor why it was equipped for internal illumination.

"Right," said Cook, hefting her axe and looking suspiciously around at the shadows beneath the tables. "I hate snakes. Emmet, if you see that blasted cobra you have my permission to stamp it into a pancake."

"It won't attack her," said Sara. "The snake's protective. She's one of us—"

"*If* she's one—" began Cook.

Emmet snapped his fingers again and pointed to the far end of the room.

There was a very thin line of light just to one side of the shutters. Emmet ran towards it, Sara half a pace behind him.

Inside the Murano Cabinet Lucy tightened her grip on the sea-glass. Then she realised that the light was not coming from her at all. Instead to her dismay she saw that far away down the chain of infinitely reflecting Lucys there was a bright light, harsh like a naphtha flare, and it was approaching as if someone or something was able to step from one reflection to another, and each time it or they did the light bounced and the figure got closer.

Her heart missed a beat – and then kicked back in at triple speed.

Her mouth was dry and the glass at her back was cold and hard as she scrunched against it, instinctively trying to get as far away as possible from whatever was approaching down the tunnel of reflections.

Her head turned and she saw to her growing distress that the figure with the lantern was only visible in the mirror ahead of her. Although the glass mirrored her on both walls, the light-bearer was not reflected in the mirror behind her, as if the laws of physics covering reflections didn't apply to him.

She instinctively knew that this was a very bad thing.

Lucy could think fast.

Whatever she was doing, whyever she had woken up to find herself in this forbidden room with a stolen key and a deadly cobra in her hands, she did not know, but she did realise that explaining this to the people outside the cabinet was going to be infinitely less unpleasant than meeting the thing calmly walking towards her through the layered reflections in the mirrors.

So she kicked at the doors, but they opened an instant before her foot made contact, so she fell backwards onto the floor of the cabinet and stared up at Emmet.

"Get her out of there NOW!" Sara shouted, running towards Emmet as Mr Sharp ran into the room behind her.

Emmet hesitated a moment, his attention taken by the growing light blazing out of the left-hand wall of the cabinet.

"Emmet!" cried Sara.

Emmet turned and reached for Lucy and three other things happened at once:

The cobra lunged past Cook and flew between Emmet's legs, heading for the mirror in front of Lucy like a black javelin, striking at the approaching lantern bearer.

Lucy, flinching away from Emmet, stumbled and fell back into the mirror behind her: it happened so fast she only had time to catch Sara's eye in panic as she – impossibly – disappeared through the glass without breaking it, just as the cobra struck at the other mirror.

Sara threw herself past Emmet, diving for Lucy, her outflung hand reaching deep into the mirror after her as if plunging into a vertical pond just as the snake hit the other mirror like a blunt-nosed hammer.

The glass of that mirror shattered.

Mr Sharp leapt through the air and caught Sara's collar, stopping her falling further into the mirror which Lucy had tumbled back into.

She grunted in shock.

The stunned cobra dropped insensible to the floor of the cabinet as the approaching light in the mirror it had shattered smithereened into a thousand points of light which snapped off as the tunnel of reflections cut off in an instant.

"Sara—?" said Cook, puffing up behind Emmet and stopping dead with a terrible gasp of shock.

Sara lay across the floor of the cabinet, her arm flung towards the mirror through which Lucy had been dragged.

She pushed off and scrabbled awkwardly to her feet, helped by Sharp, who gasped at the sight of her wrist.

There was no blood.

But there was also no hand.

The arm was sheared off cleanly at the wrist.

Sara stared at the stump as if the limb suddenly no longer belonged to herself.

There was still no blood, no gore, no inner flesh, no white flash of neatly severed bone.

"Sara," said Mr Sharp, his voice strangely choked.

There was just a mirrored oval.

Glass seemed to have fused itself to the cut end of her arm.

"Oh," she said, staring dully at it. "Oh . . ."

Sara Falk looked up at the older woman and the golem and the young man with the brown pain-filled eyes, and for a moment her face was visited by that of the uncomprehending little girl who had been scared from her bed by the Green Man so many years before.

For a beat of time the house was again silent.

Then her eyeballs rolled white as she fell forward into a dead faint, and Mr Sharp and Emmet caught her as bells shattered the quiet as the clocks struck midnight, marking the moment they all knew to their horror that Lucy, the key and Sara's hand – gloves, rings and all – were abruptly, brutally and irretrievably gone.

SECOND PART

THE LOST HAND

THE POWER OF FIVE

The material world beyond our minds is made from the Five Elements and perception of it comes in through Ears, Eyes, Tongue, Nose and Hands, known as the Five Ports of Knowledge, without which we would be locked within the purblind prison of our skulls, unable to use the Five Senses, viz. Hearing, Sight, Taste, Smell and Touch . . . the significance of Five is manifest in the Five Wounds of Christ, the Five Pillars of Islam, the Five Poisons of Cathay, the Quincunx, etc. . . . In 'apotropaic' magic (that which practises to 'ward off' evil) there is no more widespread periapt[1] or sigil[2] than the five-fingered hand, the *Mano Pantea* which the Ancient Egyptians knew as Hand of the All-Goddess. It is a symbol so powerful that it has been adopted by all subsequent societies, so that what was once the "Hand of Aphrodite" to the Ancient Greeks was the "Hand of Tanit" to the Phoenicians, and is to this day the "Hand of Miriam" for the Jews, the "Kef Miryam" or the "Hand of the Virgin Mary" to Levantine Christians and the Khamsa or "Hand of Fatima" to the Mussulman . . . As Sir Thomas Browne wrote in *The*

---

[1] An amulet or charm worn on the body

[2] A sign, a mark.

Garden of Cyrus (or *The Quincunciall, Lozenge, or Network Plantations of the Ancients, Artificially, Naturally, Mystically Considered*,1658): "To enlarge this contemplation unto all the mysteries accomodable unto this number, were inexcusable Pythagorisme, yet cannot omit the ancient conceit of FIVE surnamed the number of JUSTICE . . ." It is thus not surprising that The Oversight with its interest in preserving equity between the natural and the supranatural has traditionally organised itself by interlocking cabals of Five, known as Hands . . .

. . . The Rule of Five is the foundation stone on which The Oversight is built: every year, on the fifth day of the fifth month a Hand of five members must sit round a table and contain the Wildfire. If five are not found, then The Oversight is disbanded for its own protection and the remaining few disperse and travel the wider country until they each find five new recruits to take up the challenge again.

This is done because the weight of The Oversight's obligations are judged too heavy for less than a single Hand, and a weakened Oversight is deemed worse than none, as it gives the *illusion* of safety and vigilance where none is possible. This has happened at least twice in its long history, and consequences of a suspended Oversight have scarred the city and the outlying country so badly that it took more than a century in each case to return things to equilibrium.

One given reason for the rump of The Oversight dispersing to the four corners of the country is to make it harder for their enemies to find the weakened remnant unprotected in one place . . . in the past the secrets and powerful objects normally protected by them are said to have been dropped into the Thames where salt water meets fresh, so as to always be covered by running water, and thus stay safe until a resurgent Oversight returns to reclaim them. At the

Great Fire of London it is said the secrets were not put in the river in time, and that indecision led to the conflagration that followed . . .

Extract from *The Great and Hidden History of the World* by the Rabbi Dr Hayyim Samuel Falk

CHAPTER 28

THE PIG-HEADED WOMAN AND THE HAND OF GLORY

Lucy twisted and grabbed handfuls of air as she tried to stop herself falling into the mirror, but it did no good. She hit the glass hard, but instead of a hard crack she felt no more than a slight but distinct *pop* as she passed through it, tumbling right out of the Red Library as if the mirrored surface was a thin membrane like a soap bubble – and then the bright light was gone and she was falling into a dark space full of shouting and crashing and pitching lanterns which seemed to throw more shadows than light.

And as she sprawled onto what felt like grass she saw a completely different mirror ahead of her being toppled sideways by a big woman in a calico dress and matching bonnet.

In the instant before it crashed and smashed, she saw the reflection of Sara Falk reaching for her out of the Red Library within a second mirror behind her – the mirror in fact out of which she had clearly just tumbled. Sara was calling her name while being held back by Cook and Mr Sharp – then she saw the blur of the cobra striking the other side of the cabinet beneath Sara's arm, and the Red Library shivered and dissolved into fragments as the falling mirror hit a barrel and splintered, destroying the vision entirely. In its place she saw the woman who had knocked it over looking at her, and Lucy choked back a scream because the woman was not a real woman at all but a nightmare thing in a dress.

The eyes that met hers were not human. They were pig's eyes and the head within the bonnet was pink and jowly and snouty, the blunted animal nose snuffling, the ears flapping wildly on either side as the thing showed its teeth and roared at her in red-mouthed anger.

In a snatched moment of clarity she realised she was looking at a full-grown woman with the head of a pig and the snarl of something darker and more insistently feral.

She wanted to scream but knew escaping danger was always better than screaming at it, so she turned to flee, only to find herself facing a small crowd of people running at her out of the dancing shadows, at the front of which was an impossibly wasp-waisted woman, her mouth a perfect "O" of shock, framed between a lush moustache and a beard like a spade.

She paused and in that moment was lost, as her foot skittered on a piece of broken mirror and she fell again. The pig-headed woman snarled and lurched forward, straddling her.

For an instant she thought it was all over as the woman drew back a hand to strike her, and then someone jumped between them, a wiry young man stripped to the waist, carrying a flaming torch in one hand and a mop in the other.

"No, Nellie!" he shouted. "Back, I say!"

Lucy's rescuer faced down the pig-headed woman, who was now roaring and slashing freakishly large gloved hands at him as he backed her away from Lucy's prone figure. He took a quick look down at her, and she saw his face was shockingly different from his lean torso, being smeared in white paint with black crosses painted over his eyes above a large red nose like a tomato.

He nodded at her and then dodged round to shout at the pig-headed woman in a voice that was unexpectedly cheerful and full of good humour.

"No, Big Nellie. No! Leave her alone you great puddin'. She don't mean no harm!"

He turned and waved impatiently at the gathering crowd beyond Lucy.

"Oi, someone cut along sharpish and get Big Nellie a bun; buns always calms her down, don't it?" He turned back to the pig-headed woman and smiled. "We'll get you a nice iced bun with a cherry on top, Nellie girl, only give the little lady space to breathe, eh? You're frightening the life out of her!"

He flicked a wink at Lucy, who was as disconcerted enough by his distinctly friendly tone as everything else around her.

"Be right as spanners in a minute, my girl. Big Nellie'd rather a bun than a bust-up. It's just her nerves, see?"

And true to his words, the pig-headed woman grunted and backed away further, her mouth closing and her head dropping as if she were ashamed. Lucy took the young man's outstretched hand and allowed him to pull her to her feet. Only then did she remember to breathe.

"*Cauchemar*," she said. "*C'est un cauchemar . . . ?*"

"What she say?" shrilled the bearded woman.

"Nightmare," said a cultured voice from the back of the crowd. "She said it's a nightmare."

"Didn't sound like that," said the young man.

"She said it in French," said the voice.

"French?" said her rescuer. "Blimey."

He reached up and pulled off his red nose, just as politely as if removing his hat, and then swept into a theatrical bow.

"Well then — *bong-joower, mamzel*," he smiled. "And what are you a-doing at the circus in your nightdress at this late hour?"

Lucy caught the word "circus" and for a moment allowed herself to believe she was not trapped in a nightmare, that Big Nellie and the clown-faced boy and the bearded lady were explainable denizens of a travelling show. She was about to smile in relief when she saw, behind the boy, something like a crab spidering across the broken glass towards her.

It was a disembodied black hand, and it was trying to get to her.

For the first time in her life, and one that she would not forgive herself for, she stumbled back and fainted.

What she missed, as her eyes rolled back into her head, was seeing someone dart out of the shadows and scoop up the hand before anyone else had had a chance to notice it.

The person with the hand swiftly bundled it under their jacket and slipped through the crowd of circus folk, sliding through a gap in the tent wall and out into the fairground beyond, a sea of tents and wagons set up on a patch of common ground outside a village, bounded by a rough thorn hedge.

There were smoking oil lamps and pitch torches by the tents and even, at the very centre of everything, some of the new bright naphtha lamps.

Most of the wagons were painted in varying degrees of garishness, and so were the tents and even some of the people, for they were clearly showpeople and, where they were not, they were villagers and country-folk dressed up for all the fun of the fair.

But there was now no sign of fun to be had at this fair. The day was over and the showmen's booths were closing up.

The person walked fast, holding the hidden hand tightly to their chest, moving from shadow to shadow with the kind of controlled speed of someone who wants to escape, but not be seen to be escaping.

Moving away from the centre of the fair, the figure picked

up the pace as it reached the less well-lit cordon of show-people's wagons arranged around the perimeter as if confident that no one was now going to observe it.

No one was.

But there was a dog.

The dog chained to a stake outside a tent saw the person passing and ran forward without warning, like a shadow suddenly solidifying into a snarl of teeth, muscle and wild eyes, barking excitedly.

The person kicked the dog. Hard.

There was a yelp of pain.

The dog rolled on the grass.

The person looked back.

The barking did not attract attention. No one saw the dog or the kick.

The person slipped through a gap in the rough hedge and scrambled up into the hooped canvas tent covering the back of the last wagon on the very edge of the camp.

There was no light in this wagon but the person didn't need it. At the far end of the cramped space there was a small iron stove bolted to the floor. Behind the stove was a tin box, and in the box there was sea-coal.

The coal was scrabbled aside, revealing another box, a padlocked iron case hidden beneath the fuel.

The person unlocked the lid and lifted it, swiftly tipping the rag-bundled hand into the case with a light but meaty thump. The lid slammed down, the lock clicked, the key was removed, the coal scrabbled back and then there was only the creaking sound of the person sitting heavily back on the low-slung rocking chair in front of the fire and the words, spoken so low, and the glee in them so whispered that anyone overhearing them would have been hard-pushed to say if the speaker was a man, woman . . . or even perhaps a child:

"*Manus Gloriae, Manus Gloriae* indeed. We are saved."

But no one overheard. Nothing moved in the wagon.

Nothing except the hand, scrabbling blindly in the pitch-black darkness of the iron box hidden beneath the jumbled sea-coal.

CHAPTER 29

NIGHT RIDERS

It was while they were changing horses at the White Hart at Hertingfordbury that Amos realised that they were being followed. He'd stepped beyond the lights in the yard in order to relieve himself behind the stables when he heard them. There was no one visible, and the jingle of harness and clatter of hooves on the paving stones behind him almost drowned it out, but he heard the word "Mountfellon . . ."

His eyes swept the darkness beyond the ring of light. His eyes were very good in the dark once they adjusted. He could see the distant copse of elms in the centre of the field more than a hundred yards away. He could see the shape of the trees where the cattle had neatly cropped off the bottom branches to a uniform height so that the dark leafy mass seemed to hover in mid-air. There was, he concluded, definitely no one there. The hearing had been a trick of the night, and he should get back to the coach before it thundered southwards without him. He had been warned he had two minutes and no more.

And yet there was something that kept him where he was, staring across the thorny hedge and the dinted grass towards the elms. He just couldn't see what it was, and then the air between the trunks rippled and the leaves, or what he had taken to be leaves, moved across the grass. Three horsemen seemed to materialise out of nothing and trot towards him, and as they came he heard not the sound of their hooves, which in truth made no sound, but the conversation running between them.

A voice said, "We cannot take Mountfellon. The coach is bound in cursed iron . . ."

A second scratchy voice replied, "But we may take the boy who rides beyond the safety of iron in the boot beneath the leather curtain."

Amos's heart stuttered and a cold abyss seemed to open inside him as he realised they were talking about him. He also suspected they were Sluagh, for though he had never seen one in person he had heard much about them. He might not speak in the Templebanes' counting house, but he listened to everything, and nothing he had heard of them filled him with pleasure at their current closeness to him. He remained motionless in the shadows.

"Why will we take the boy?" said the third in a voice that was less a whisper than the frozen ghost of one.

"Because he brought a message from the Templebanes," spat the first. "He is the broker's boy."

"We can use him," agreed the second voice.

"We can hurt him . . ." whispered the third, a flicker of restrained glee kindling in its voice.

"We can do both," agreed the first decisively. "We will take him as they slow going up the long sharp hill two leagues hence, as they pass through the dark of the wood. They will see nothing and hear nothing and not know he has gone until they get to London."

They grunted in agreement and there was a rattle of bone as the leader pulled hard on the reins of his pony, yanking its head round, and then he kicked his heels into its ribs so hard that Amos heard the hollow thump of it as the three

Sluagh wheeled round and cantered off towards the ambush point.

At that moment he heard the coachman call his name with a sharp crack of the whip, and he knew he must make a decision, and fast.

He knew that the safest thing to do would be to run back into the courtyard and tell Mountfellon what he had seen, and do it now. It was clear that if he rode on the boot he would be taken and hurt by these riders. But what if Mountfellon wouldn't let him ride within the coach?

As he thought this he felt a twinge in his thumb, and he thought of the smile on the gaunt viscount's face after he had jabbed the blade into it and watched him flinch and bleed. He heard the coachman say something, and heard Mountfellon's reply.

"If he's not here, he can shift for himself. I've better things to do than hunt for a blackamoor in the dark."

And so Amos did a very unusual thing.

He took Mountfellon at his word. He stayed in the shadows and did not return to the coach in time and, true to that word, the coachman cracked the whip and without bothering to call him a second time, drove the coach back out of the courtyard and into the night, leaving Amos alone in the dark. He didn't move until he heard the ostler put the used horses into the stable, and then stomp off back into the welcoming warmth of the inn.

And then Amos moved very fast and decisively.

He knew that he needed cold iron in his hand to protect himself in case the Sluagh came looking for him, and then he needed to put running water between him and them. Even though he had never been this far away from London, he knew the things that would help ward against the attentions of the uncanny.

He slipped back into the stables and pulled a twelve-inch

bastard file from its place by the anvil. He felt the rough edges and the weight of the thing, and stuck it in the waistband of his trousers. Next he stuffed both pockets of his coat with oats, and finally he stole a horse-blanket which he wrapped around himself as he slipped out into the road and headed in the direction he had come from.

Not wanting to stand out as the only traveller on the empty road, he slipped through the hedge at the first opening and jogged doggedly along the field edge, keeping parallel to the road but protected from view by the hedge itself.

It was wet plough beneath his feet, and it soon felt like he was taking most of Hertfordshire with him as his boots clagged into heavy balls of clay, but he kept going.

He knew what Templebane said the Sluagh were capable of doing to those who fell foul of them. Indeed Issachar had used the very thought of the Sluagh as a threat to keep his boys on what he called "the straight and sensible road": it was this childhood fear of the Shadowgangers who would skin small boys for their sport which propelled him away from London with his heart thumping wildly in his chest.

He had almost been bounced out of the coach's boot half a mile back as the coachman had taken a humpback bridge at breakneck speed, and he had had a glimpse of a canal, its moonlit surface ribboning off into the darkness on either side. If he could cross the canal, it would be an added safety. He did not know how the Sluagh hunted, but he was certain that the night was entirely their element and not his at all, at least not in the rural version that he was hurrying through.

There were no lights to be seen now since the inn had dropped out of sight behind the curve of the field, and the moon, which had revealed the canal as he had hurtled over it on the coach, was itself also hidden behind a thickening bank of sky.

He was beginning to feel he could slow down when he

heard something move behind him. Without looking back he started to sprint for his life, heavy-footed through the clay, running blind from the things breathing hard behind him.

He missed the canal entirely, although it did not miss him. He stumbled off the plough through a thin band of long grass, and then just as the thing behind him snatched wildly at his neck, catching the strap of the brass plate, his feet clomped into thin air, and he was pitching forward, his momentum snapping the leather as he plunged face first into the water.

The cold wet hit him like a knife and he gasped and filled his mouth with the flat silty taste of the canal. He coughed and spluttered it out before he filled his lungs, but as he flailed for a handhold he instead wound the heavy horse-blanket round him like a shroud. His arm was pinned by the wet material and, worse than that, the weight of his clay-balled feet pulled him inexorably below the water.

If he had continued to flail, Amos may well have drowned.

But one thing he was was a survivor, and the way he survived was by thinking fast. He realised that he was fighting himself, and so he just went still and didn't move. He let his feet sink until there was a good six feet of water over his head. Even though his lungs were burning with oxygen star-vation he kept calm, squatting as he was carried slowly along by the flow of the canal. His feet dragged along the bottom as he went. As soon as he had enough bend in his legs he straightened them explosively, powering himself up towards the air. His head burst the surface of the canal and he sucked a lungful of the night air, shaking the water out of his eyes to try and get a bearing before sinking again.

And then he went under.

CHAPTER 30

SINGLE-HANDED

"It is my fault," said Mr Sharp, looking down at Sara Falk, who was stretched on her bed with her eyes still shut, lying just as motionless as she had been ever since he had carried her up the stairs and into her bedroom.

"That's not how she'll see it," said Cook.

"It was a trap," he said, bitterness spiking his words. "The girl was a trap."

"Well," Cook agreed, "she was a something, that's for sure."

"I should have insisted she didn't stay in the house," he said.

"You did," said Cook, looking down at Sara. "Unfortunately as you well know, she has never been particularly . . . insist-able."

Sara lay there between them, so drained that her face was as colourless as the starched linen of her bed. The sheets were pulled up to her shoulders and her arms hidden beneath the covers.

The room itself was perhaps the plainest in the house: the walls once painted a pale violet were aging back to a bleached-out white, and what furniture there was – a cupboard, a bedside table and a desk and chair in front of the window – were simple light-coloured things made of limed oak. No pictures intruded onto the blank walls, and there was no mirror. The room was plain because this was the room into which Sara retreated to sleep and be calm. The only splash of colour came from the intricate Kashgai rug; a meadow of once bright yellow, blue and green flowers on a pinkish ground, all now faded with time and wear. Mr Sharp mashed his foot into one of the green blooms and scowled.

"I should have known. I did know. The Sluagh wasn't a coincidence—"

"Are you going to whine or do something?" said Cook, her words brutal as a slap. His head came up and he looked at her, his face as close to surprise as he ever allowed it to get.

"I mean, you can whine if you like, but I do not expect that will help Sara much," she said. "Her ring was on that hand. And a Glint without a heart-stone, an adult Glint, will sicken and go mad."

Mr Sharp opened his mouth to say something, and then bit down and clenched it off. The muscles round his jaw worked for a long beat, and then he spoke with a controlled, glacial voice through which tension shivered like a crack in the ice about to unleash an avalanche.

"If I could give her my hand for hers, I would cut it off instantly," he said. "Without thought. Willingly. But I cannot . . ."

"And a good thing too," said Cook. "You are becoming positively histrionic."

"What happened?"

Sara's voice rose from the bed like a wisp of smoke, thin as cobwebs. Her eyes were open and for an unguarded moment they darted between Cook and Mr Sharp, bright with shock.

"How much do you remember?" said Cook.

Sara's eyes locked on to Mr Sharp's as if trying to pull an answer from him. He said nothing, but his eyes slid off hers and down to the end of her right arm, hidden beneath the sheets.

Her eyes seemed to go away for a long moment, and then she shuddered and they came back older and less bright.

"All of it," she said.

"So you know about your hand?" said Cook.

Sara nodded and slowly pulled her arms out from under the covers. The sight of the truncated wrist silenced them all. Mr Sharp's throat worked but no sound emerged and they waited as she looked at the clean-sheared stump, turning her forearm this way and that, and then finally reaching across to touch the mirrored oval where the arm stopped. She winced as her fingers skated across the glass.

"I will go and wake the pharmacist on Ratcliffe Highway," said Mr Sharp. "I will bring laudanum for the pain."

"There is no pain," she said flatly. "And I do not require poppies to dull my faculties at this time of all times."

"Child," said Cook, coming forward now the silence was broken. "Your . . ."

Whatever she had been about to say remained unsaid, because something large and unswallowable rose in her throat and made it impossible to speak. She rested her hand on Sara's cheek instead. Sara looked up at the big woman.

"I have not been a child for a long time," she said.

"No," snuffled Cook, pulling a red and white spotted handkerchief from the inner recesses of her pinafore and blowing her nose with a thunderous series of detonations like a rolling broadside.

Sara patted her hand and sat up.

"Besides, there is no pain," she repeated.

"Good," said Mr Sharp.

"But there is something else," she said, the catch in her

voice betraying the strangeness of what she was feeling. "I have a great sense of . . . loss. And I can feel the hand."

"As if it's still there?" said Mr Sharp, looking at Cook.

"In a manner, yes," she said. "Yes. I see it has quite gone, though I revolt against the thought of it, and yet . . . and yet . . . I feel . . ."

Her voice trailed off as she closed her eyes and concentrated on exactly what it was she seemed to be feeling.

"You feel it?" said Mr Sharp.

"Yes," she said, eyes still shut, moving her arm a little from side to side. "Yes, that, and yet more than that I feel . . . I mean, it is as if I can also feel *with* it. As if it is still connected to me . . ."

She opened her eyes.

"It is not a painful sensation, but it is also not quite a pleasant one. In the circumstances."

Cook blew another cannonade into her handkerchief.

"Had a shipmate once," she said. "French chain-shot took his leg off just below the Tortugas, carried it clean over the side in an instant. As gone as any limb could hope to be, buried fathoms deep and lost to man. And yet, ever after, when it was cold he said his toes was freezing off, except it was the toes on the foot that were already long gone under the waves that he felt. It's a trick the body plays on the thinking part of you. It's just your mind not quite caught up yet."

"It's not that," said Sara, her voice gaining strength. "It doesn't feel like it's here."

She raised the stump again and looked at it wonderingly.

"It feels like it's somewhere else."

"In the mirror?" guessed Mr Sharp.

Sara shrugged and shuddered again. "Wherever it is, it's distracting. Not painful. Just distracting. It feels like it's in a . . . box."

She moved the stump but looked at the void above it, as if she was moving an invisible hand.

"It's your mind, girl," said Cook. "Like I said: it's the shock."

Sara fixed her with eyes that had now regained their usual sharpness.

"You know it isn't."

Cook wiped something out of her eye.

"Don't," said Sara softly.

"I'm not," said Cook, blowing her nose with a final thunderous series of detonations.

"The girl . . ." began Mr Sharp.

"Lucy. Lucy Harker. I told her she was safe," said Sara.

"She's a thief. The key from the black cage is gone," he replied.

"The key in the cage was false bait, you know that. So no harm done," she replied. "It has served its purpose. The Discriminator is secure still, and since the stratagem was yours in the beginning, you are to be commended for your cunning and foresight in installing the decoy all those years ago."

The long speech clearly drained energy from her that she could ill afford. He opened his mouth to say something but she shook her head and carried on.

"We must still find her and get her back to safety."

"Sara Falk," he snorted. "You gave your word to a thief."

"It doesn't matter what *she* is," she snapped back. "My word is my word. Besides. She may not have known what she was doing . . ."

"She knew exactly what she was doing, and so did those who sent her to us."

"We must find her," she said.

"I have sent for The Smith. He and Hodge will be here at dawn. You may decide with them what is to be done. I have one thing to do, and one only . . ."

He was already stepping to the door.

"Mr Sharp—" she said.

"Miss Falk," he said, cutting her off. "I will find your hand or—"

"Find the girl," she insisted.

"No," he said. "I must find the hand. If the girl is still wherever the hand is, then I will drag her back too, but the hand is the thing."

"You are . . . ungovernably obstinate," she said, rising off the pillows. "Do as I say. It is my hand!"

"It is not just the hand," he snapped. "It is my duty to protect not just this house, but you above all."

She shook her head in irritation.

"This is not about some quaint chivalry, Mr Sharp, this is . . ."

"No," he said. "It is not: it is about life or death."

"I can live with one hand if need be," she snorted. "I can li—"

"But you cannot live without your heart-stone."

She stopped as if slapped.

"It is not just the hand that is gone, Sara Falk," he said. "Your rings were on it too."

She remained frozen, propped on her good arm halfway between pillow and upright.

"I will find the girl. I will return your heart-stone, or . . ." He stopped himself, unable to say what the alternative might be, nodded a curt farewell, and closed the door behind him.

". . . or die trying," finished Cook quietly.

"I had not thought of the heart-stone," said Sara, wonderingly. "It was stupid of me. But the loss of my hand makes me, made me . . ."

She looked at Cook, her eyes suddenly wild with a new fear.

"The mirrors: he cannot—!"

"He is distressed," said Cook, easing her back onto the pillows. "He blames himself. But don't worry. He cannot get lost in the mirrors like— Well, he cannot get into the mirror anyway, not in through the Discriminator since one of the inner mirrors is in shards, so the direct road to the girl and the hand are gone for ever."

CHAPTER 31

SNICKERSNEE

Amos did not drown. He plunged into the canal just as something snatched at his neck. He felt the leather strap that held the "Mute but Intelligent" brass around his neck yank his head back and then snap, and then he was underwater and breathing in river until everything went black . . .

. . . and then he was out of the river and flat on his back and somewhere on the other side of the water from where he had gone in, coughing and spluttering, aware that someone was sitting on his chest and pumping him as if he was some kind of engine. His rescuer was emptying his lungs of river by squashing his ribcage and then releasing it again; he felt like some kind of human accordion.

He waved his hands and sat up.

His rescuer stepped away and looked at him in the light of a meagre camp-fire, which was smoking fitfully and throwing more light than warmth. The man who had saved him was a tinker. That much was apparent from the large pack drawn up to the fire, hung with tinware of all shapes and sizes, with a small knife-grinding machine strapped to the back of the pack. The tinker prodded him.

"You all right, matey?"

Amos nodded.

"You might have drownded, weren't for me," said the tinker. "Would have, more like. Dead as a stone. Saved you."

Amos looked at him. He was not a pretty man. His head was bulbous at the top and fell away in an alarmingly triangular fashion to an undershot jaw which was almost indistinguishable from the neck it disappeared into. As he swallowed, Amos saw his Adam's apple was more prominent than his chin.

"Might thank a fellow as has plucked you from a watery end?" said the tinker. His tone was both querulous and demanding. "A fellow as has got himself wet through in the process."

Amos signed that he could not talk. The tinker looked at him.

"Cat got your tongue?" he said.

Amos nodded and pantomimed his inability to speak for the second time. Then he took the man's hand – cold and boneless, like a wet sock – and shook it enthusiastically to show his thanks.

"You're a simpleton, are you?" said the tinker. "Well, there you go. You sit there by the fire and get what wits you do got back, eh?"

Amos moved closer to the mean fire. A cast-iron pan sat in the embers at the side with a blackened pair of sausages in it. He was conscious of the tinker looking back across the river. He wondered if the Sluagh were there. He tried to see them or hear anything that might give a clue.

All he could hear were the tinker's thoughts, like a whisper.

"*Something strange out there in the night. What was he running from? Maybe he's a thief. Maybe it was bogles. Never seen a bogle. Don't want to see a bogle. Mind, if it is a bogle we're safe enough. Always safe we are, carrying so many iron knives in our pack. Never hear of any tinker getting bogle-led or taken. Enough iron in that*

*pack to scare off a whole squadron of bogles. Bogles don't like iron is
what the old dad said, and he never got bogled any . . ."*

Amos felt something slippery in the way the tinker thought,
word tumbling after word, like a barrel of fish being poured
onto the slab at Billingsgate market. He was used to judging
people as much on how they thought as on what they thought,
and people who thought like the tinker, people whose
thoughts were a cascading babble, were not usually trustworthy.

A point proved by the tinker's next flurry of thinking.

*"What about the idiot then? Strange looker. More'n a touch of
the tar-brush in him. Someone's darkie, a servant, likely, slave blood
from the West Indies or such. Stolen something and on the run maybe.
Money in his pocket. Felt it go clink. Good shoes. Belt is new. Get
something for his coat. He can't talk. Who's he going to tell? Knock
him on the head and by the time he wakes up in the morning we'll
be long gone. No. No. Maybe he's clever. Maybe he's a one as can
write. If he can write he can tell on us. Not good. So cut him. Cut
him fast after he's taken his coat off. Don't want blood on it. Snickersnee
across the throat and skip away sharpish cos it always sprays so. Don't
look till his heels stop drumming on the ground. We done it before.
Trick is don't think too much. Do it quick and don't look till he's
gone and the body's still. Then we'll have his money and his shoes
and that belt and we'll plop him back in the water with a big stone
round his neck and the eels can have him.*

Tidy night's work.

*And it's not like real murder cos if we hadn't picked him out of
the water he'd have drownded anyway and all that money and his
nice things would have been no use to anyone. Eels don't need nice
shoes. No more'n a darkie does. No feet on an eel. Now, quiet now
as we opens the knife and then snickersnee quick as thought once we've
told him to take the jacket off. Tell him we'll a-dry it for him, before
he catches his death . . ."*

"Tell you what, matey," said the tinker solicitously. "Why

don't you take that jacket off and hang it over the fire so it can dry quicker, before you take a mortal chill?"

Amos nodded and slipped his arms out of the wet coat one at a time.

"*Wait till he turns to hang the jacket over the fire. Then snicker-snatch at his throat from behind. He won't feel a thing. And he can't scream anyway, dumb idiot as he is.*"

Amos knew about fighting and moving fast from his uncomfortable fostering with the other Templebane "brothers".

He only turned long enough to grab the handle of the iron pan, and then swung back as hard as he could.

The tinker was closer behind him than he had thought, and his elbow hit the man's hand, knocking the knife wide, while the arc of the heavy cast-iron ended in a thunk against the tinker's head.

Something cracked nastily.

The tinker staggered back stiff-legged, something unnatural in the angle of his neck. He stumbled out of the ring of firelight, and then suddenly disappeared with a splash.

Amos went to the edge of the river and looked down.

No more splashing.

No body.

No tinker.

The river had taken him.

He watched the water flow past for a long while. He was shaking, and trying to think if he'd done a bad thing.

Then he shrugged, unable to decide, and went back to the fire.

He felt a little sick at what he'd done.

But not too sick to look for those two sausages.

CHAPTER 32

THE TRAP SPRUNG

The watchers outside the Safe House saw no one except Mr Sharp leave by dawn, and so followed Templebane's instructions about what they should do if Lucy failed to emerge with the key: Bassetshaw Templebane, who had never been seen by the Reverend Christensen and was therefore unknown to him, went to the pastor's house and interrupted his breakfast by showing him the folded paper he claimed to have picked up in the street, having seen "a young girl" signalling from one of the windows prior to tossing the note. The note was weighted with a half-crown (which he begged to be allowed to keep) and a small fragment of bloodstone in which could be seen a distinctive carving of a unicorn. The note claimed that one Lucy Harker had been carried into the house by a man on the night previous, and was being held captive against her will, having been kidnapped from the safety of her normal care under the protective wing of one Francis, Viscount Mountfellon, a man who would, if shown the fragment of bloodstone, attest to the truth of what she said (it being part of a ring with which he was well acquainted).

By no coincidence at all, at exactly this time Mountfellon's coach arrived at the home of Lemuel Bidgood, Magistrate, to be met by Issachar Templebane, refreshed by a short night's sleep, who had been waiting in his carriage at the corner of the street for the last hour.

The coaches pulled up side by side and neither alighted, the conversation taking place through the two open windows.

"Did the girl escape with the key?" Mountfellon said with no regard for the niceties of a greeting.

"No," said Templebane. "But we knew it was a long shot, my lord. Now we shall proceed with the contingency, which is, as I explained, a sure one."

Mountfellon clicked his teeth in irritation.

"You appear to have lost my son, sir," added Templebane mildly.

"Lost be damned. The boy was told to hold on, and warned we would stop for nothing," replied Mountfellon without a shred of apology. "I am not a parcel delivery service, Mr Templebane—"

"Never got back on after we changed horses," said the coachman with a half bow to his master, as if apologising for having overheard.

"There you have it," said the noble lord. "Probably went for a pot of ale which he is even now sleeping off in the inn's stables, I shouldn't wonder."

"He does not drink," said Templebane, "but just so, just so, my lord. It can't be helped and he will no doubt roll back home soon enough. He is an enterprising boy."

Templebane was not especially irked by the cavalier treatment of his messenger. He knew Mountfellon to be a driven man who was on the very point of achieving a long-held ambition, that of obtaining what he called the Blood Key, or the Great Discriminator. The Templebanes had not achieved the things they had by holding the wrong kind of grudges, or letting personal matters interfere with business. Amos would find his way home, and by the time he did, Mountfellon would be satisfied and the Sluagh paid back with their own flag, and beyond the formal fee he was to be paid by the viscount, Templebane would have struck his blow against The Oversight. If Amos were lucky, he would arrive home in time for a celebratory dinner.

Magistrate Bidgood was startled out of bed by the sound of his great brass door-knocker hammering away as if the devil himself were on the tail of the person trying to gain entry to the house. He was further astounded to arrive at the head of his stairs, rumpled and unshaven, to be greeted with the worrying news that a great lord was now waiting in his parlour with suspicions that his young ward had been abducted along with some valuable property, and was being held at some unspecified house in the parish.

Bidgood dressed quickly and not well, and tumbled down the stairs, still unshaven and almost as rumpled as when he had risen, to greet his visitors. He was not a tall man, and since Mountfellon not only was, but also refused the offer of a chair, Bidgood had to conduct the interview looking awkwardly up into a face which looked back down at him like the overhanging brow of an incoming thunderstorm. In this way a badly cricked neck was added to his discomfort and disorientation at such a rude awakening.

It was explained that Templebane was Mountfellon's London agent and had brought the viscount to Bidgood's door immediately on receiving his distressed patron in the pre-dawn hours, straight from Rutlandshire.

In support of the story Mountfellon provided a sketch of the unique cobra-shaped key that he claimed had been stolen from him, and further identified the girl by explaining that though she would be, in Bidgood's eyes, somewhat indistinguishable from any other well-formed young person with reddish hair, she wore a distinctive ring, whose seal he was able to show, being a blob of wax on a fragment of old letter, a lion and unicorn facing each other.

When Bidgood, with suitable deference and hesitation, asked how the noble gentleman knew that in all the great haystack of London his own particular needle was to be found in Wellclose Square, he was told coldly and with a degree of condescension that the lord's footman had been tied up and knocked about the head during the theft, but had managed to overhear the kidnappers laughing about how pleased they should be to get the booty back to the house on Wellclose Square.

"Wellclose Square is in your parish, is it not?" said Mountfellon. "Or am I mistaken?"

Magistrate Bidgood stuttered his confirmation and thought no more about it, since at that moment his overworked knocker mounted a fresh assault on his front door which, when opened, revealed an out-of-breath Danish reverend and the innocent face of one Bassetshaw Templebane, who gave not a sign of recognition when he was shown into a room containing both his father and brother. Bassetshaw was, among other things, a very good actor.

Pastor Christensen (alerted by Bassetshaw and his story of glimpsed faces and notes thrown from windows) had immediately abandoned his customary morning bloater, put on his good coat and hurried through the streets to Bidgood's house hoping to enlist his aid and that of a squad of sturdy constables.

His story was told, as was Bassetshaw's. The scribbled and much-folded note was reopened and read several times. Bassetshaw again asked if he might keep the half-crown and it was agreed that he might. He went on his way, having given a false address and an undertaking to return and give evidence should Bidgood later require it. As this was happening Coram, no mean actor himself, turned to the reverend gentleman as

if struck by a sudden bolt of wonderment out of the clear
blue sky and asked if he thought that the "strange cove" they'd
remarked on carrying a sack last night as he slunk past them
might indeed have been *the very thief and kidnapper in question*?
Pastor Christensen became inflamed with guilt and conviction
at the same moment, grabbing the magistrate's sleeve, and told
him he had, by chance, seen exactly such a figure and bewailed
the fact that, had he but known it, he had had a chance to
save the poor, poor abducted girl from whatever indignities
she might have been subjected to in the night just past.

Quite inflamed himself by now, and convinced that he not
only had the chance to foil a vicious (and no doubt soon to
be infamous and prestigious) crime but also to ingratiate himself
with one of the greatest aristocrats in the land, the energised
Bidgood sent for the constables, who came at once. They
brought ladders and crowbars, and set off at a jog for Wellclose
Square.

Templebane at this point faded into the background of the
moveable scene as Mountfellon and Bidgood followed the
long and brawny arms of the law through the narrow streets,
which were beginning to fill as the city awoke, hurrying
towards the docks in the viscount's own coach.

The door of Sara Falk's house was, in very little time,
subjected to the same percussive indignities as Pastor
Christensen's and Magistrate Bidgood's. The insistent rapping
on the wood brought, at first, no reply. A second fusillade
was cut off in mid-attack as the door swung suddenly inward
to reveal Cook.

The more perceptive constables stepped back half a pace,
having noticed the cleaver she was carrying in one hand. One
of the others stepped officiously forward.

"Open in the name of the law!" he said.

"I have," said Cook. "Otherwise we couldn't see each other,
could we?"

"No," he said, belatedly spotting the steel in her hand. "Er . . ."

It was in all fairness now hard for him to miss the hatchet, since she had spun it into the air and caught it by the handle without looking at it.

"Because if I hadn't opened it, you'd still be denting my shiny paint and putting your smudgy fingermarks all over my nice clean knocker, wouldn't you?" she smiled.

"Um, yes," he said, gulping as he now saw matching steel in her eye.

"So, constable, now we've cleared that up, how may we help you?" said Mr Sharp, who seemed to have appeared from nowhere and was smiling pleasantly over Cook's shoulder.

"Where is the owner of the house?" said Bidgood from behind the constables.

"Did someone say something?" said Cook, looking from one constable to the other. "Only I didn't see your lips move."

"Excuse me," said Bidgood, pushing the constables aside. "I have a warrant to search this premises."

"Premises," sniffed Cook looking down at him and then at Mr Sharp. "The gentleman thinks these are 'premises'."

She looked back at Bidgood.

"This is a home. And a law-abiding one. This is not *premises*."

"And I am a magistrate. I have it on good authority that there is a girl here, an abducted girl being held against her will," blustered Bidgood. He looked back at Mountfellon's carriage, and seemed to gain confidence through his connection with the unseen aristocrat who was watching from the shadows within. Mr Sharp saw the direction in which his eyes flickered and nudged Cook. They both looked at the carriage.

"And there may also be stolen property. We will search the house."

He held out the hurriedly drafted warrant. Cook and Mr Sharp looked at it.

"It is the Law," said Mr Sharp.

"Indeed," said Cook.

"We are sworn to uphold it," he said under his breath.

"Yes," she replied. "That's the trouble with swearing. Never ends well."

"I must insist," said Bidgood. "Or you will be arrested."

"There is no girl in this house, and no stolen property," said Mr Sharp, looking deeply into the magistrate's eyes. "You have my word."

"And mine," said Cook.

"Well," said Bidgood, wavering as he began to fall under the spell of the warmth tumbling in Mr Sharp's eyes. "Well . . ."

"We will find that out for ourselves," said an icy voice.

Mountfellon, apparently frustrated by the delay, emerged from his coach. He wore dark-lensed spectacles which he adjusted as he strode up the steps.

"And you are?" said Cook.

"Unaccustomed to introducing myself to other people's domestics," he replied.

Cook tensed. Mr Sharp quietly reached down and removed the hatchet from her hand.

She exhaled.

"The aggrieved party," said Bidgood, regaining his momentum.

"No, he's not," said Cook under her breath. "He's trouble."

"I'm sorry," said Bidgood. "I didn't catch that."

"I said you may have a warrant but you forgot something," said Cook, seeming to swell like a wind-freshened sail and filling the doorway.

"The document is legal," he said.

"Yes," said Cook. "But you forgot to say please."

"I don't have to," blustered Bidgood. "I am an officer of the court . . ."

"Please," said Mountfellon, though the frost crackling in his voice made it sound more like a threat than a request.

"Miss Falk is the owner of this house. She is currently quite severely indisposed," said Mr Sharp. "You will make your search quietly."

"But we will have to search her room too," said Bidgood, pushing past them. "We must be most thorough."

The search was indeed thorough, beginning in the cellars and missing nothing except the very well-hidden door to the passage which went to the Privy Cells and the Tower beyond. The kitchen was searched as Cook simmered by the range, looking as if she might boil over and grab the blunderbuss at any moment. The formal rooms on the ground floor were examined, floors and walls tapped for hidden entrances or hideaways, and then the searchers moved to the first floor.

Mountfellon stalked impatiently behind the knot of constables as they moved through the house, his eyes tracking and scanning everything they passed, recording everything for later appraisal, but when they reached the landing and he saw the great doors to the library, he stiffened and was still.

"Ah," said Mr Sharp, who had appeared behind him. "That's what you want."

Mountfellon turned a little. Their eyes met.

"Who are you?" said Mr Sharp very quietly, so quietly that no one but Mountfellon noticed.

"You may try as hard as you like to turn my brain to your way," said Mountfellon, "but as you see I wear smoked glass and I should warn you, if you do not already sense it, I wear cold iron."

He flicked his waistcoat back a little to reveal a thin metal corset beneath it.

Mr Sharp's eyes widened and glittered in amusement.

"Cold iron!" he said, pantomiming a step backwards. "Why, I see you have the measure of me . . ."

"I do. I am a man of science and have provided myself with an antidote to your powers," said Mountfellon, matching Mr Sharp's whisper, and then, in a loud, public voice, "And you have what is mine, by God, and I will have it returned. Open that door!"

"It is locked," said Mr Sharp.

"Then BREAK IT DOWN!" bellowed Mountfellon.

One of the constables looked at Bidgood, who nodded. He raised a crowbar and then felt his hands lighten as it was taken from his hands by Mr Sharp, who had appeared at his side very suddenly.

"Oi!" he began.

"My apologies," said Mr Sharp. "It is a library full of very valuable old things, and so we keep it safe. But if you wish to enter" – he reached into his pocket – "you will do less damage to Miss Falk's doors if you use the key."

He handed one over. The constable looked at it, then at the door and shrugged. "Fair enough," he said and reached for the lock.

"Wait!" shouted a strangled voice, and before he knew what was happening he was again looking in surprise at an empty hand.

Bidgood had sprung forward and snatched the key. The magistrate was suddenly humming with energy as he reached excitedly inside his coat and pulled out his glasses.

"My lord," he said. "My lord, we have it!"

"Have what?" said Mr Sharp, looking at Bidgood hopping from one foot to the other in excitement.

"St Vitus's Dance, by the look of it," said Cook. "Or maybe a general pruritic discomfort of the nether extremities."

Bidgood held up the key.

"My lord!" he said. "Your drawing, if you please!"

Mountfellon stared at the key in Bidgood's hand and slowly pulled his papers from his own coat. As if unable to credit what he was seeing he unfolded them, revealing the detailed sketch of the cobra-headed key.

The same key that Bidgood held so excitedly in the air.

"By God and Newton, you have it, sir!" he breathed, and the papers slipped forgotten from his grip as he stepped across the landing and took it in his fingers.

"And now I do," he whispered.

"Have what?" said Cook. "It's just a key . . ."

He looked at her for a brief irritated moment, and then his eyes were drawn back to the key in his hand.

"A very poor stratagem," he smiled. "Very poor indeed to try and hide it in plain sight."

"He wasn't hiding it," said a voice from above.

Sara Falk stood on the stairs in a long silk robe, holding on to the rail for balance, white as ash, her mutilated wrist hidden in a sling of scarlet silk holding her arm tightly across her body.

"He gave it to you," she said.

"And well he might, for it is mine," said Mountfellon. "And mine alone. You stole it from me."

"What do you think it is?" she said as Cook hurried up the stairs to steady her. "It is just an old key, but I assure you that you are mistaken, for it is mine."

"It is priceless," he hissed. "And it is not yours. It is unique and more valuable than anything a normal man might imagine!"

He looked at Bidgood, his eyes hot and hungry.

"We must search the house, for they will have more stolen items, I am sure."

"Unique?" said Cook. "As in only one?"

"Yes," said Mountfellon. "As you well know."

"Oh," she replied. "Only if that's unique, what are these?"

And she held up the bunch of keys normally chained to her apron.

Every one had a cobra head.

"Or indeed those?" said Mr Sharp, pointing to the door on the opposite side of the landing, a door with a cobra-headed key sticking out of the lock.

"All the keys in this house are like that," said Sara. "My grandfather, who built the house, revered the cobra as a symbolic and ancient guardian of secrets. He was a fanciful man. Please feel free to check the truth of what I say."

"But," said Mountfellon, a vein bumping ominously on his temple as his face began to purple. "But . . ."

"But if you want one of your own, you might try Mr Chenevix, the locksmith on Ratcliffe Highway," said Sara. "He makes all our keys."

"Ah!" said the constable who'd tried to crowbar the library. "That's right. I knew I'd seen one like that before. Old Chenevix does do keys like this, and ones with little brass suns on the end, and horse's heads and shells, right pretty they is! I knew I'd seen 'em before."

"But the girl!" exploded Mountfellon. "The girl may be behind those doors. Why, this is a palpable ruse—!"

"Open it," said Sara. "There is no girl. Search the house from cellar to chimneys. You are mistaken."

And with that her legs gave way. Cook caught her and lowered her to sit on the steps.

Mr Sharp waved at the door.

"As Miss Falk says, go where you will. You will find no occupants of this house save the three of us."

Mountfellon stepped forward with the key, but Mr Sharp stepped in front of him and spoke quietly again.

"I do not know who you are, but if your irruption into this home has caused Miss Falk any damage whatsoever, I warn you openly that I will find you and demand satisfaction."

Mountfellon sneered back at him.

"How quaint and antiquated of you. Now let me pass."

Mr Sharp took the key from his hand and opened the door himself.

"Be careful," he said. "There is a snake loose in there."

Mountfellon stopped on the threshold, whereas the constables all took three steps backwards as if they were being choreographed.

"A snake?" squeaked Bidgood.

"Mr Sharp," said Sara. "Do not tease them, pray."

"There is a cobra in the glass cabinet," he said. "It escaped its cage which is being repaired."

"And not just the cage," said Mountfellon, stepping into the library, his eyes again hot with anticipation. "You appear to have had an accident."

The largest table in the centre of the room had been cleared of its customary clutter of books and papers, and instead a scrabble of broken mirror shards had been laid out at one end like a giant jigsaw puzzle waiting to be made from the tiny sharp-edged pieces.

"Seven years bad luck," he smiled.

"A baseless superstition," replied Mr Sharp.

"Or in your case, an underestimation, I fear," said Mountfellon, turning up the gas lamps and feasting his eyes on the library and its many treasures. He saw the black obsidian block that had held the cobra and the key, and noted the shards of steel that had been woven into the cage neatly piled beside it. He walked to the bookshelves and the cabinets piled with curiosities and gazed at them with a naked greed which he didn't try to hide. He ran his hand over a carving of a Green Man's face which looked as if it had been hacked from the wall of some long-forgotten church roof, and then he reached for a book on the shelf above. His eyes drank everything in, recording it all. With his back to the room his face relaxed and something close to a smile fleetingly played across his lips.

"How big is the girl?" asked Cook.

He turned. Mr Sharp was gone.

"A normal-sized girl," he said. "With reddish hair."

"So not small enough to hide in that book," Sara said, walking unsteadily into the room and waving off Cook's disapproving cluck. She sat on a hard upright chair by the door and drew herself straight. "Be kind enough not to touch anything you do not need to."

As she spoke, Mr Sharp was moving with unnatural speed through the house.

He entered the secret passage and sped down it without bothering to take a light to guide him through the long black tunnel beneath the city. He passed the door to the Privy Cells and felt the ground beneath him rise slightly as he approached the door beneath the wall on Tower Hill.

Mountfellon stood in the centre of the library under Sara's watchful eye. She saw his hands flex with greed and the almost ungovernable desire to touch or take the objects ranged around the room, and she saw how he controlled the urge by gripping one in the other and thrusting them behind his back and holding them there. She saw from the muscles clenching on either side of his jaw and the prominent vein bumping in his temple that the restraint cost him a great deal of effort. But she also noted that his eyes never stopped moving as he applied the proto-photographic quality of his mind to the array, storing it all in his head for future unpacking and mental perusal. The rabid hunger in his eyes may not have been actual theft, but was quite enough of a violation in itself to feel most uncomfortable, not to say dangerous.

By the time the constables had carefully but politely searched

Sara Falk's room, Mr Sharp had raised Hodge from his bed in the kennel house and told him in the shortest terms about what was happening. By the time the constables had decided the attic held nothing living beyond a possible mouse, Mr Sharp was running back downhill in the dark, and Hodge, acting on Mr Sharp's instructions, had found the Raven beneath the south wall of the White Tower and was communicating them to it. By the time Mr Sharp was back in the kitchen in the basement, the Raven was carving an invisible tunnel through the morning air which roughly matched the trajectory of the underground passage the man had just twice run the length of.

The search proceeded with speed and thoroughness, and once the constables had returned to the library and reported that no girl was to be found in the house, and been sent to look again, there remained only one possible place unsearched.

"Then she must be in the glass cabinet," said Mountfellon. "The snake story is another lie to prevent us finding her."

"You are free to open it," said Cook. "But I'm going outside and closing the door before you do. Snakes give me the screaming abdabs."

The constables looked nervously at Bidgood.

"Open it," he said. "But carefully."

"I'll open it," said Mr Sharp, who was suddenly there as if he had never left, although only Mountfellon noticed this.

Mr Sharp walked to the cabinet, yanked the door open and caught the snake as it lunged into the air, aimed like a javelin, straight at Mountfellon.

For an instant it remained rigid, like an accusing finger, and then Mr Sharp shifted his grip and held it behind the head, whispering something into the depression in the side of its skull where ears would be if cobras had ears. The snake's mouth stretched wide and pink, its angry ruby eyes glittering, and then it flopped as limp as a rag in his hand.

"Interesting," said Mr Sharp. "He doesn't seem to like you."

Mountfellon pushed past and opened the double doors of the cabinet wide. There was nothing but four mirrored walls and doors, with one wall conspicuously bare where the broken mirror shards had been removed.

Mountfellon turned with a convulsive snarl, that vein again bumping in his temple.

"I want everything in this house seized," he spat. "There is trickery here."

"The only trickery," said Cook, "is the pretence which you have used to gain entry to a private house."

She held out the papers he had dropped on the floor outside.

Mr Sharp smiled at Bidgood.

"I think if you are satisfied that nothing illegal has occurred here, we must not detain you any longer, Mr Bidgood."

"No . . . no . . . perhaps," stuttered the unfortunate magistrate, caught between Mountfellon's power and Mr Sharp's persuasively warm eyes. "Perhaps."

"Perhaps indeed," said Mr Sharp, steering him to the door. "Perhaps this has all been a great misunderstanding. Perhaps someone wishes Miss Falk harm and has libelled her with some false evidence."

He looked back at Mountfellon.

"Indeed perhaps someone has worked on your friend here too."

"I am not his friend," barked the noble lord, unable to tear himself from a room whose every object his fingers itched to possess. "Nor am I yours, I assure you."

And with a further visible convulsion, as if his mind had to struggle with his body, he tore himself away from the room and stumbled towards the door.

"Until we meet again then, Mr——? I did not catch your name . . ." smiled Mr Sharp as he passed.

"I did not give it and I do not, damn your eyes!" hissed Mountfellon. "But meet again we will, and you shall not best me a second time."

Cook and Mr Sharp watched the constables and Bidgood follow him out into the street. They saw him enter his coach and saw the coachman whip the horses into a fast trot which took them out of the square as fast as possible.

"Who is he?" said Cook.

"An enemy," said Mr Sharp. "But perhaps not *the* enemy."

"You should follow him," said Cook.

"We are," said Mr Sharp, and pointed to the sky, where a raven wheeled in the morning sunlight and set off in the direction the coach had taken.

CHAPTER 33

A Pyefinch for Breakfast

Lucy woke in the first light of dawn, drawn from sleep by the smell of frying bacon and the sound of a muttered conversation somewhere outside her field of vision. She was lying beneath a canvas roof, on a bed of dried bracken stuffed inside an old miller's flour-sack. The blanket covering her kept some warmth beneath it, and her exposed nose was quite cold enough to make her lie still and enjoy it while she thought about what to do next.

She would have to run, that much was clear.

She always had to run.

But her head was not quite as clear. One of the few fragmentary memories of her life which survived since losing her mother in Paris was of a time many years later, drinking brandy: it had been fiery stuff which she'd stolen from a lecherous farrier in Etaples who had been so intent on drunkenly trying to fumble her dress open that he had not noticed her picking the bottle out of his coat pocket and then hitting him with it. The bottle had been of thick enough glass not to break, though the crack she had heard as it connected with the side of his head suggested that his skull was not so lucky. She had kept the bottle as she fled through the night and the town until she hit the sand-dunes and then the moonlit sea beyond. When she had stopped running, she'd drunk the contents to try and stop the trembling and erase the memory of his hot breath on her neck and his hands on her body. The brandy had made her throat raw and her head spin. It was the only time she had ever been drunk, and the next morning she had spewed into the sand on the cold beach where she had passed out and spent the night. Spewing seemed to cure the hangover, but only for a treacherous few minutes, and she had spent the rest of the day recovering, lying in the long grass atop the dunes as the sun slowly warmed things up, watching the fishermen coming and going and wanting to die.

That's what her head felt like now: hungover. One other thing that having got herself drunk had done was to give her worrying blanks in her memory, lost hours that she could never recall no matter how hard she tried. She had had no idea how she had got from the farrier's to the beach, or how long she had been lying there. Similarly she realised she still had holes in her memory about the recent past. They were disconcertingly large ones, too large for her to concentrate on right now.

Of last night she remembered the sack and Ketch and all the events which had taken place in the house on Wellclose Square, though she didn't quite remember the bit between drinking warm milk and being put to bed and then waking to find herself holding a snake and having to hide in a hurry. With a shudder she remembered tumbling through the mirror without breaking it and the pig-headed woman in the circus tent and the confusion and the clown, and above all the hand, the black hand crabbing towards her like vengeance. It had been a nightmare.

The impact of this recollection bounced her to her feet and she made her way towards the light at the end of the low tent, ignoring the grunts of protest from the sleeping people she trod on as she went.

She stumbled into the new day and stared about her.

It was not a nightmare. It was a water meadow laid out in the early morning light, the pale sun beginning to drive away the dawn mist. There was a small cooking fire right in front of her at which a youth of about her own age was sitting and steering rashers of streaky bacon around a blackened cast-iron frying pan. His face turned to look at her and cracked into a guileless and appealingly lopsided smile.

"Why, *bong-joower* again, *mamzel*," he said. "And *common tally-voo*, if I might make so bold?"

"I '*allez*' very bloody well, thanks," she said after a pause.

His smile grew and evened out.

"You're not a Frenchy."

"No," she said. "Not exactly. You're the clown."

"No," he said. "At least not when I get the blessed greasepaint washed off of me I ain't a clown: I'm just Charlie."

His smile was frankly irresistible, and thus dangerous. She knew she should start running, but there was the smell of the bacon sizzling in the pan, and she couldn't help but notice that her feet were bare and getting cold and wet in the dew-drenched grass. She shivered.

"Stick your feet by the fire," said Charlie, who had quick eyes that noticed everything. "Watch that bacon don't burn and I'll get you boots and a blanket."

He sprang to his feet with a wink, and handed her the stick he had been using to steer the rashers with.

He disappeared back into the tent.

She thought of running now, but he looked fast, and also there was the matter of boots and the prospect of bacon and, if the basket by the stump he had been sitting on didn't lie, eggs too. So she poked and flipped the bacon, by which time he was back at her side: she'd been right in her assessment – he was fast.

"Boots," he said, holding them out. "Blanket."

"Thanks," she said, exchanging them for the cooking stick. Meeting his eyes was suddenly disturbing; she covered up her discomfort with a question.

"Charlie who?"

"Pyefinch," he said, and then put on a mock-serious face and bent forward in a half bow. "That is, Mr Charles Allflatt Pyefinch, at your service. But everyone calls me Charlie. And what's yours?"

"Falk," she said, without a flicker of a pause. "Sara Falk."

Lucy survived by her own rules: there was bacon; there might even be eggs. But breakfast and a nice smile did not entitle anyone to the truth, even if she could have got the contradictory snarl of her own story straight in her head.

He stuck out a hand and they shook.

"Hello, Falk," he said. "Pleased to meet you."

"I fainted," she said.

"Either that or took a knock to the head, that's what they thought," he agreed.

"They?" she said.

"Ma and Pa," he replied, hooking his head towards the tent from which she'd just emerged. "Ma, she said they couldn't just leave you there, and no one from the town knew you, so once things had calmed down a bit she had us carry you back here, and here you are indeed. They're sleeping late because it took so long to clear up the mess."

She wanted to ask where "here" was more than almost anything else in the world, but didn't want to reveal she didn't know.

As they'd been talking, her eyes had been doing a fast tour of the area. There were other tents and wagons and carts, and on the other side of a small stand of willows was a large tent of the kind used for circuses, festooned in limp but still colourful flags of bunting. Some of the tents around the larger one had garish paint on their façades. She could read one announcing a "House of Marvels" and another advertising "Lady Sowerby, Porcine Prodigy! – The One and Only Educated Pig!"

"What mess?" she asked.

He pointed to the big tent and told her how yesterday's fair had gone well and the townspeople and villagers had enjoyed themselves, spent freely and gone home happy and tipsy with all the fun of the fair, after which the various showmen had closed up shop and settled back to count the takings and eat round their own fires with their families. Then he explained how the satisfactory calm of the night had been riven by shouts and crashes from the big tent, and how by the time they had all run there "Big Nellie" had got loose and lanterns had been kicked over and there was a real danger of fire burning down the whole thing. He explained how the showpeople – ever resourceful as was their nature – had distracted the by now highly agitated Big Nellie and put out the small fires before they could grow into a large conflagration, and generally minimised the damage, the only irreplaceable item being a large mirror used in a magic act belonging to one Na-Barno Eagle.

"And anyway, Nellie calmed down in the end, so no great mischief," he said, looking down at the pan. "And that's that. Well, Falk, you fancy an egg?"

She nodded and he broke two into the pan, keeping the bacon clear of them as they cooked.

"And that's where we found you all asleep on the ground, like a regular babe in the wood," he added. "Or stunned, more like."

He let the unasked question hang in the air, but she didn't catch at it. He shrugged and carried on with his cooking. Lucy was busy stitching what he'd told her into the fabric of her own recollections: it was clear that somehow she'd fallen through a mirror in the house in London into the middle of a circus, which was itself in the grip of a momentary panic and emergency. She was beginning to feel more comfortable, but then she remembered the hand crabbing towards her across the floor again: she shivered and looked instinctively around her as if suddenly expecting to find it creeping up on her. The thought of it made her skin crawl, and reminded her not to relax as she had been doing with both the comforting heat of the fire playing on her legs and the equally warm smile and ease of her companion.

"You ain't from round here, are you?" he said, interrupting the narrative she had been running in her head.

"No," she replied.

This was the point where people usually asked where she was from. This was where she began building the wall of lies which cut her off from those she met, a wall necessary for survival. But Pyefinch just nodded as if that was quite enough of an explanation, and slid an egg onto her plate.

"Join the club," he said, nodding round at the campsite. "Loveliest thing about being a showman is none of us is ever from where we are, most of the time. Hey-ho for the open road, eh?"

And he grinned at her and then dug into his own egg and bacon as if she wasn't there at all.

Lucy relaxed. The smell of the bacon was making her stomach gurgle in rude anticipation, so she followed his cue and dug in herself. She chewed slowly because having her head down over the plate let her think and meant she didn't have to talk. She ate some of the bacon and used the fried bread to scoop up the egg and then mopped the broken yolk out of the bottom of the tin plate.

"Here," said Charlie. "Mind your fingers – that cup'll burn you if you don't use the handle."

She looked up to see he was offering her a battered tin cup of tea. She took it and sipped, watching him pour his own cup from the black kettle hanging over the fire. He sat back and pulled a stubby clay pipe from his waistcoat.

"Smoke?" he said.

She shook her head as he lit it from a twig pulled out of the coals.

"Best bit of the day," said Charlie, drawing on the pipe and coughing a little as he did so. "Before the others is up and making their racket. Before they all start sending me on errands and suchlike. Be busy today and all, since we're striking camp and heading west."

And he closed his eyes and smoked his pipe with so great an air of contentment and – most importantly for Lucy – casual disinterest in her that she allowed herself to sit by the fire for a few more warm minutes as she tried to plan her next move. She began to see the shape of it, of a way to be for a few days that might not involve her running, but she liked to examine possibilities from all angles, and to know as much as possible about anything before she made decisions. That was how she stayed safe.

"Who's this Big Nellie?" she said after a while.

"Nellie Sowerby," he said, pointing at the sign on the distant wagon. "The Educated Pig . . ."

He paused to relight his pipe. She realised as he did so that there were now sounds of movement all around them as people were waking and getting ready for the day. In the distance she saw a man emerge from his wagon and stand there on the backboard, unconcernedly pissing off it into a nearby patch of brambles. Closer to, a young girl stumbled towards the canal, a bucket clanking emptily at her side. She still looked more than half asleep.

"Who's Na-Barno?" said Lucy. Charlie spluttered in amusement.

"Na-Barno? Who's Na-Barno? Na-Barno Eagle, the Great Wizard of the South? Don't let him hear you asking that, not after he's paid a small fortune to put posters up all over the county!"

"He's a . . . wizard?" said Lucy.

"Course he is," said Charlie, dropping an eyelid in a slow wink. "Leastways he's a wizard same as I'm a clown, once I got the greasepaint on."

He ran his finger behind his neck, close to the hairline and showed her the white smudge on it.

"Na-Barno ain't a real wizard, cos there ain't such a thing: that's 'is stage name. Off the boards he's plain old Barney Eagle, a conjurer. Does magic tricks. He's a character too, and no mistake. Don't let him play cards with you though or he'll have your arm . . ."

"Charlie Pyefinch, how can you speak of Father like that? He's the kindest man in the world."

Lucy looked round at this spirited interruption to find herself looking into the enraged face of the prettiest girl she had ever seen.

"Now Georgie—" he began.

"Don't 'Now Georgie' me," spat the girl, stamping her foot. "After everything he's done for you!"

Lucy had never seen anyone actually stamp their feet in frustration before, but then nothing about the girl was normal: rather she was an exaggeration of all the finer points of beauty in one person. Her pale skin was almost translucent in its delicacy, daintily offset by the pretty rose highlights which her current outrage had flushed across it, pinking both her cheekbones and the very tip of her elegant nose. Her blue eyes, which flashed angrily at the unfortunate Pyefinch, were not the more everyday washed-out blue but the most uncommonly deep sapphire. The hair framing her face was a gilded mass of ringlets and curlicues which shook and quivered in sympathetic outrage. She held an empty bowl in her hand, a thin cracked china thing covered in faded roses.

Standing there in the early morning light, surrounded by the ramshackle disarray of the showpeople's camp, Lucy thought she looked as out of place as a princess in a pigsty.

"Who's this?" she said, turning on Lucy.

"She's Falk," he said. "Banged her head in the hurly-burly last night. Ma took her in."

"She isn't one of us," said the girl.

"I don't know what she's one of," he replied. "Only just met her."

"I mean she's not show-folk," said the girl. "And yet you choose to gossip with her and laugh about my father."

"I wasn't laughing; I just—"

Whatever he just never got said because the girl threw the bowl at him and turned away before seeing him snatch it out of the air an inch from his face.

Lucy watched her hair bounce out of sight among the other tents.

Then she turned and looked at Pyefinch, who was looking at the bowl with a rueful smile.

"Your friend seems upset," she said.

"That's just Georgie. Georgiana Eagle. Na-Barno's daughter. Proud as cockerels the Eagles, but you see this bowl? Haven't got enough to buy sugar for their tea. She come to borrow some off us, and now she's got to go back and tell Barney there's none to be had. That'll make her twice as angry!" He said this with a mixture of glee and pride, as if the ability to enrage Georgiana Eagle was something he revelled in. "You better watch out for her if you're going to stick around."

"What makes you think I'm going to stick around?" said Lucy, looking at the canal. It was time to go, and the canal was as good a road as any if she could slip onto a passing barge.

"I think you're going to stick around because it'll suit you for a bit," he said. "Thing about show-folk is no one asks any questions, except can you earn your keep?"

He looked at her and though his smile was unchanged, his eyes were, for a moment, a lot older than his face. It made her uncomfortable again, not because he was suspicious of her, but because he was understanding. That was a knife which got a lot closer in under her guard, and she feared it. He was dangerously friendly, but maybe he was also right: maybe staying with a group of people who were all from somewhere else and who spent a lot of their time pretending to be something they weren't and who didn't ask questions might be exactly the kind of thing that would suit her very well indeed.

CHAPTER 34

AN ENGAGEMENT TO HUNT

"You. Failed. Me."

Mountfellon's voice was tight with barely contained rage. Issachar Templebane stood in front of him, curiously unflinching.

"The ruse failed, my lord."

"You were engaged to make it work."

"And no one could have done more than I. If it failed, it failed because of something you did not factor into your calculations."

Mountfellon stepped closer to Templebane, who did not move backwards. Instead he smiled and waved a hand around the long room they were now standing in.

"We gave you the full assistance of our house, an assistance that is still yours to command, should you wish it."

It was a cavernous office lined with bookshelves and racks, piled with ledgers and deed-boxes. A long clerk's desk ran the length of the room with sloping lecterns and stools to accommodate ten clerks on each side. Candles were lit along the table for, although the room was lit by windows along both sides, the dark oak of the shelves and desk and perhaps the ancient ink-splattered floor somehow sucked the light from the space and left the well-lit room with a sense of brooding darkness.

"The game still runs, my lord," he continued, "and nothing is lost until it is over."

Mountfellon stared at him, nostrils flaring in outrage.

"Do you think I am a callow schoolboy, sir? A booby to be fobbed off with trite inanities like that?"

"No," said Templebane calmly. "I think you are the most dangerous man outside London."

"I can assure you that I am the most dangerous man in London too, sir," snarled Mountfellon, spittle flying from his mouth and landing on Templebane's still unflinching face. "Indeed I can assure you that I am the most dangerous man in this room. You have betrayed me!"

"We have done no such thing," said Templebane, impassively producing a handkerchief and wiping his face. "Our word is our bond."

"Disappointment and failure are betrayals and you, sir, have this day served me a foul breakfast made from *both* of those things," spat Mountfellon.

His bunched hand flexed open and slid inside his coat.

"Do you know what happens to those who betray me? I think not. I think you would not stand so insolently unmoving and unrepentant if you did—"

"You kill them and dissect them in the interests of what you see as natural science," smiled Templebane. "Usually but not, I believe, always in that order."

Mountfellon froze, looking as if Templebane had slapped him.

"I understand you have resorted to vivisection, that is you have cut into the living flesh of those you deem to be unnatural in order to anatomise them and determine if they are made like normal people."

Mountfellon started to interject but Templebane waved a hand airily, as if dismissing a charge no one had voiced.

"I understand your reasoning, indeed I do, though I am

not a man of science but a mere creature of the law. You are not, my lord, any kind of monster, whatever others might say were this habit more widely known. I am aware you have been known to flay the cadavers to see if the blue markings and scarification on their skins come from within or are mere tattoos and indignities applied to them from outside. I know you have put the anatomised cadavers in a boiler and seethed the flesh off their bones, bones which you have then painstakingly varnished and arranged in cabinets and added to your already extensive collection of skeletons and other natural historical specimens."

"Knowledge is a very dangerous thing, Mr Templebane," said Mountfellon.

"I know that. I know all that, my lord, and more. I know you carry a folding surgeon's scalpel in the right hand pocket of your waistcoat, and I know you carry one of Nock's overcoat pistols in the skirt of your coat, just below where your hand is at the moment resting a little uncertainly."

"And that does not give you pause, lawyer? To know what I am capable of?"

Templebane just smiled wider.

"No, my lord. Those are just mildly dangerous weapons. I, as you have just intimated, have a very dangerous weapon. I have knowledge."

"Do you think to blackmail me, sir?"

"No more than you think to slash my neck with your scalpel or pistol me on the floor of my own counting house," said Templebane.

Mountfellon's right hand twitched and clawed at the air, and then disappeared behind his back where it was gripped by the other hand as he drew himself to his full height, visibly containing the great rage coursing through his veins. The smile he mustered in response to Templebane's was thin as a paper cut.

"Not blackmail, then, but insurance," he said. "You are indeed a cunning man, Mr Templebane."

"Thank you, my lord."

"And what does the cunning man suggest we do now?"

"We? Jointly? Nothing. Separately I suggest you go to your London house with all dispatch and clear your head of the reasonable cloud of disappointment that at present may be fogging your faculties."

Mountfellon's right hand broke free of his left for an instant but he quickly regained control both of it and his temper.

"My head is always clear, Mr Templebane, I assure you. To see the world with full clarity is my guiding principle. And it is clear to me that the next logical step for us is to find the girl."

"The girl? Is she not a mere dupe, a cat's paw used in a ruse which has sadly failed? Or is she something more to you . . . ?"

"What she is or is not to me is not a scintilla of your concern," snapped Mountfellon. "And it is not clear to me that the ruse failed entirely: the occupants of the house were obviously shaken by more than just our arrival. The Falk girl was in visible distress and the man Sharp was highly exercised. It may be that the girl *did* manage to steal the key, and this is why their feathers are so ruffled. It may be that she succeeded, but herself and it are now lost to both our knowledge and theirs. So we must scour London and find her."

"To find the key?"

"At the very least to eliminate the possibility that she has it from the list of probabilities. It is only scientific to do so," said Mountfellon.

Issachar Templebane nodded.

"If she is in London, our sons will find her. If she is outside London, then those we have already engaged must work a little harder for the flag you have promised them."

"The Shadowgangers," said Mountfellon.

"The Sluagh," agreed Templebane. "They have a web of contact one to the other which stretches across the countryside like a fine mesh in which we shall catch her, for wherever the darkness falls at the end of the day, they have eyes."

"And how will they watch for someone they have never seen?" said Mountfellon. "She is as nondescriptly well formed as any young person, with no particular oddity of hair colour or feature."

"She has a resonance," said Templebane. "As a gaze-hound hunts by sight and a scent-hound by its nose, the Sluagh are attuned to resonances, and that girl has a very strong one, I am told, connected with the ring she carries. A piece of which you retain . . ."

He looked expectantly at Mountfellon, who nodded slowly and dipped into his pocket, retrieving the square of paper in which he had wrapped the fragment of unicorn-engraved bloodstone.

"Resonances," he said with interest. "I have not heard of this before."

"Like giving a hound a scent of the fugitive's clothing, they will follow it, but better than that, they can pass the description of that resonance one to the other so that as fast as word can travel, faster than any hound, the Sluagh will be attuned to her wherever she will go."

Mountfellon passed the piece of bloodstone to him, and immediately delved back into his pocket for a peculiar notepad made from four thin wafers of ivory about the shape and size of a visiting card held together by a silver rivet through the top left-hand corner so that they could be fanned out like playing cards. He produced a graphite pencil and proceeded to write quickly across the topmost. His writing was small and precise enough for Templebane to read "Resonance" and "Web" before the notebook disappeared again.

"It would, one day, please me to speak with any of these Shadowgangers you might find me," he said. "This matter of resonances is full of interest to me."

"No doubt," said Templebane. "And no doubt the Sluagh would like to converse with your Lordship. Though on their part the conversation would be highly distressing to yourself since it would undoubtedly turn on the matter of your cutting and flaying one of their number in the name of science."

"They know?" said Mountfellon, for the first time displaying an unguarded emotion other than anger. "But how?"

"How they know, I do not know," said Templebane. "Their ways are largely outside my ken, but I do know that they know, for that is how I came by the knowledge."

Mountfellon stared at him in shock.

"My house is bound against them, my rooms warded in cold iron: they cannot . . . !"

"I find that 'cannot' is a perilous word to use when talking of the Sluagh," said Templebane.

Three minutes later, Templebane was seeing Mountfellon's coach off into the teeming thoroughfare beyond his premises with a polite bow and the still unbreakable half smile. His face remained that way until the coach had turned the corner, and then it dropped into something much more serious as he scanned the immediate vicinity, his eyes scouring the faces of passers-by and loiterers. Having satisfied himself that all was as it ever was on the street he knew so well, he looked up at the sky, squinting at the pale sun partially hidden by the thin clouds overhead.

Because he was squinting, he missed the flutter of wings on the roofline opposite as a large black bird launched itself off a chimneystack and began to glide north-west, following the track of the noble lord's carriage through the city.

"You're displeased, Father," said Coram, materialising at

his shoulder as if from nowhere, an ability that Templebane normally admired. This time he shivered in irritation.

"Announce yourself with a cough, boy," he said.

"Sorry, Father," said Coram. "The Lordship's disappointment has cast a pall on the day."

"That man is a dangerous fool," said Templebane. "Dangerous because he is powerful and toys with things he does not understand: a fool because he came straight to us from the Jew's house."

"He wasn't followed," said Coram. "We kept close and watched our back."

Templebane looked out at the busy street.

"Maybe," he said. "Maybe. I hope you're right, boy, because though they may be on their last legs, there's a legion of very disappointed and dead men who got to be that way by underestimating The Oversight and trying to kick them when they were down."

"Question, Father: how did the Sluagh know about his anatomising? You have told me his house is all but bound in iron?"

Templebane did not reply. Coram knew that this was an answer, however, and that he was meant to infer something from the silence.

"They don't know," he said. "His Lordship can bribe and frighten his servants better than any man living, but every secret is just a betrayal waiting to happen.

"And by making him believe the Sluagh know of his atrocities, you ensure your position as intermediary, since he believes they will not speak to him directly," continued Coram. "And your source, his servant, is not suspected and thus will continue to be an asset to us in the future."

Templebane's face gave nothing away bar a small twitch of a suppressed smile of approval at the corner of his mouth. For Coram it was as good as a pat on the back.

"What would you have us do now, Father?" he said.

"Put the word out for the girl if she's still in London. You saw her: describe her well, especially the wrapped hands, and keep the eye on the Jew's house. If you have not found her by sunset, my brother will have to be abroad and treating with the Night Walkers. Tell Bassetshaw he will accompany him, and that they shall require firearms. We will need iron and luck if we are to stay in this game, boy, for the Sluagh will be expecting their prize and disappointment sits ill on their stomachs. There may be dark deeds at the crossroads before the coming night is out."

CHAPTER 35

EELS FOR BREAKFAST

The Smith arrived too late for breakfast, but he brought eels, a great basket of them which he dumped on the kitchen table with a smile.

"Eels, Cook, my dear," he said. "I know you like them, and my traps out on the marsh are fairly humming with them at the moment. Something's got 'em agitated."

Cook looked into the basket and saw the serpentine jumble of bodies coiled within.

"Fat ones," she said approvingly. "Why, those two must be more than three foot each!"

"Good eating," said Hodge, who walked in behind The Smith. "But bad omens."

"You're right at that," said The Smith. "When the eels run like this, means something bad's got them stirred up."

"Old wives' tale," snorted Cook, hefting the basket to a sideboard. "And I'm an old wife so I should know. Only thing that's going to be stirring this lot up is my big spoon, soon as I got them rinsed and cut up and seething in the vinegar water."

Hodge and The Smith exchanged a look that said they didn't agree with her but knew better than to argue when she had the bit between her teeth. Indeed it was more than that, for Cook's kitchen was her precinct and manners dictated she should be deferred to when visiting, the same unspoken species of professional courtesy applying to those who visited The Smith in his workshop or Hodge in his kennels.

"Besides," she said grimly. "The bad's happened, worse than you know. The girl's gone and Sara Falk has lost her hand."

They both opened their mouths and started asking questions at the same time.

"Quiet and I'll tell you," she said warningly. "That's just the start of it. Now don't clamour at me or you'll wake her, and I've just got her to lie down again."

Neither Hodge nor The Smith were given to panic, and both knew Cook would tell them more quickly if they let her do it her own way, so they each took a seat at the table and waited, though The Smith's eyes kept straying to the door as if he wanted to burst through it and go to Sara's side to see for himself.

Cook poured tea for the two of them, and as they sat watching her dispatch the eels and chunk them into bite-sized cylinders, she explained all that had befallen since the arrival of Lucy Harker. The Smith did not interrupt once, but he leant forward when she told of Lucy seeming to be only able to speak French, and again when hearing of how Sara's hand had been lost as she had reached into the mirror to try and save the girl just as it smashed. He exhaled like a steam-train easing a pressure valve, and bit his lip to keep it shut as Cook went on to outline the visit from Mountfellon and Bidgood.

When she had finished, he looked at the scrubbed tabletop for a long time.

"Well, Hodge," he said eventually. "And you were thinking my lead caskets were a little premature."

"Caskets?" said a voice from the door, and they all turned

and rose as one at the sight of Sara Falk leaning on the door-jamb for support. "Has it come to that?"

She was pale to the point of transparency, and Hodge and The Smith made her sit by the stove and fussed over her until Cook growled and they gave her some space. Sara drew her silk robe around her neck, as if warding off a chill though the heat from the Dreadnought was positively dragon-like.

"You have prepared lead coffers?" she said.

The Smith nodded.

"Hodge was right in thinking you somewhat premature, Wayland," she said. "We have plenty of resources at our disposal, and an enemy, if not *the* enemy, has indeed made himself apparent only this morning by bursting in here and showing his hand in a way which weakens him. We have not yet begun to fight back."

The Smith shook his head and pulled up a chair so that he could sit with his eyes at the same level as hers.

"No, Sara," he said. "The end always happens faster than you think. Our strength is going. And when there is no strength, there is gravity."

He looked deep into her eyes to make sure she understood.

"And when there is no strength, there is gravity," she repeated, like a child in a classroom. He didn't smile. He just nodded.

"Strength fails and has to be regained. Gravity never tires. It pulls everything down in the end. So the coffers are ready because the wolves are circling, and what we can no longer protect here we must hide in safety."

Her eyes moved to Cook's, looking for support.

"It is *not* the end. While there are five, it is not the end," Sara said. "I am not frightened of anything much, Smith, but you of all people saying that this is the end makes me tremble . . ."

She put a brave smile on it as if making a half-joke but

got no answering smile from him. If anything, the protective rage banked up in his eyes glowed stronger. He shook his head.

"An end is nothing to be scared of, though in this case it is also profoundly not something to be wished for. However, ends are not always what they seem. The rings you all wear were not born as circles. They were cut from rods of straight metal, and at that point had not one but two ends. I bent and hammered those rods into rings and joined them. Now you look at them. I'll guarantee you cannot see the ends any more, for my joins are good. But the ends are there, hidden in the circle. And where two ends meet in a circle, who's to say whether or not one remains an end and the other becomes a beginning?"

"Those are just words—" began Sara, and then stopped as he banged the table hard enough to make everything on it bounce into the air.

"I'm sorry," he said. "But they are *not* words and we *must* act. I make the rings. And not all the rings are small. Not all the rings are gold. Not all the rings are even visible. But I ensure the circle continues. Even when we come to an end, The Smith always ensures The Oversight can revive when the wheel turns and time moves on. That is why I am The Smith. I make the rings and I hide the joins. Now excuse me. I must speak to Sharp. Where is he?"

"He went north with the Raven," said Sara.

"Can you find your bird?" said The Smith, looking at Hodge.

"He's not my bird," said Hodge. "But yes. We can go and find them."

The Smith stood, then surprised Sara by leaning over her and hugging her, before leaving wordlessly. Hodge raised an eyebrow at her and followed. Cook chose to ignore the wetness that The Smith's unaccustomed show of affection had brought to Sara's eyes, and busied herself putting a bowl and a spoon on the table.

"Soup," she said gruffly. "Nothing in the world that can't be made worse by facing it on an empty stomach. Even if the end's coming, there's always time to eat. And you're drawn thin as a rasher of wind. I could read a newspaper through you."

CHAPTER 36

RAZORS AND RABBITS

The showmen's camp was waking up all round them, and the easeful quiet of the early morning, which Georgiana had shattered with her temper tantrum, had not returned. Lucy watched Charlie scoop up the breakfast plates and put another log on the fire. He picked up a bucket.

"I'm going to shave and fill this," said Charlie, hand scratching his chin as he nodded towards the canal. "You can have a wash-up too if you like. Canal's good clean water."

Lucy stretched her legs and then stood up and followed him, still thinking. He seemed happy enough not to talk or ask questions as they threaded through the other tents and wagons. At the water's edge she watched him pull a straight razor from his pocket and swiftly work a nub of soap into a thin lather which he applied to his face before shaving it off with a minimal number of deft strokes. He grinned at her as he did so, and she had the strong impression that – given his age – he was newly enough come to the necessity of shaving for it still to be something of a badge of pride for him. But she also noticed how deftly he worked the blade.

"So," she said after he had finished and she had washed

her face in the water he pulled up from the canal in the bucket, "Georgiana is your sweetheart, yes?"

Charlie snorted a laugh at her and rolled his eyes, flicking the last of the soap from the edge of his razor into the canal.

"Sweetheart? Some chance!" he said. "We've known each other since we was little nippers is all."

Lucy snorted right back at him. "So why'd she throw the bowl at you? You don't just do that kind of thing at anyone. That's an angry sweetheart kind of a thing to do."

"No, that's just Georgie," he said, "always wanting her pudding *and* her pie. Her mum spoiled her, and since she went, her dad spoils her twice as much; least he does when he's sober."

"He drinks?" said Lucy.

"Like the Pope," said Charlie.

Lucy was about to ask what the Pope drank like, but he ploughed on.

"See, the Eagles is under pressure. Na-Barno may call himself the Great Wizard of the South but he's got a rival, Hector Anderson, the Great Wizard of the North. He's got his nose out of joint about Na-Barno copying him, because he was the Great Wizard long before Na-Barno decided to be the Wizard of the South."

"I see," said Lucy.

"Now normally the fact they hate each other's not a problem, because it's a big country and there's fairs and shows enough for all. In fact there's a Northern Circuit, which is what Anderson travels, and why he's the Wizard of the North, and there's the circuit we're on, the Southern, and almost ne'er the twain do meet!"

"Almost?" said Lucy, who had an eye and an ear for the clues as to where trouble lay.

"This far into the season, we come far enough up the country to run into the northern lot who are on their southernmost loop. It's always been a bit of a tinderbox – no one agrees as to who owns the territory as it were – so both circuits meet up. Luckily the fair's a big enough thing for everyone to make money, so no real harm, not normally . . ."

"But this isn't normal," prompted Lucy.

"Anderson has an automaton. Like a real person but run on clockwork and levers and such. People love it. So Na-Barno, last winter, while we was overwintering in Clerkenwell, he got a watchmaker chappie there to make him an automaton of his own." He grinned at her and whispered, "Like I said, it's not a complete lie about Na-Barno being a bit sticky-fingered when it comes to ideas that make money. Trouble is Na-Barno's automaton looks lovely but it's broke, and he don't know how to fix it. And cos – Na-Barno being Na-Barno – he only went and gypped the watchmaker of the final payment so he can't send it back to be repaired. Now Anderson has challenged him to appear at the fair, same as him, and put this to an end, head to head, like. He wants a contest."

"A contest?"

"He says let the people decide who's the best, and the loser has to stop calling himself the Great Wizard of anything. He's papered the county with posters saying as much. Drums up interest for the fair, which is good for us all, but it's bad for Na-Barno because the truth is Anderson's the better conjurer, and with the automaton broken, he's going to look very shoddy by comparison."

The voice that came from behind startled her.

"Charlie!" it shouted. "Charlie Pyefinch."

"Uh-oh," said Charlie.

"What?" said Lucy, turning to follow his eye.

"My ma, and she don't look happy," he said.

Mrs Pyefinch strode through the tall cow-parsley like an avenging angel, if avenging angels brandished cast-iron frying pans instead of flaming swords. She was a tall woman with high cheekbones which were at this moment flushed with irritation. She was lean and muscular and wore a man's shirt tucked into her skirt. Her hair was tied off her face with a spotted kerchief whose green matched her eyes.

"You're a selfish young pig!" she roared at him. "Your dad's got nothing for his breakfast except tea!"

"What?" said Charlie. "I done nothing!"

Lucy noticed he was keeping her and the bucket between him and his mother. She didn't blame him. Mrs Pyefinch held the iron pan cocked and ready to fling, and her overall air of competence made it look like she'd be a good shot.

"You ate all the bacon and eggs," she retorted. "Unthinking hoggishness is what that is, come here!"

"No fear," said Charlie with a smile. "I'm staying here. Besides, we didn't eat it all. There was plenty left in the basket."

"The basket's empty!" she said, her eyes seeming to see Lucy for the first time. "Good morning," she said, more like a threat than a greeting.

"Hello," said Lucy.

"We've already met," said Mrs Pyefinch. "You trod on my arm on the way out of the tent this morning."

"Sorry," said Lucy.

"Yes, well," said Mrs Pyefinch. "You have to be careful in tents. I thought you were French."

"Well, she isn't," said Charlie. "No more than I'm hoggish. There was bacon and there was eggs left enough for a breakfast for you and Dad, and that's a fact."

"It is a fact," said Lucy.

Mrs Pyefinch looked from Lucy to Charlie and shook her head sadly.

"Fact or no fact, there's no bacon and your dad's striking camp on an empty stomach. Now hop to and give your dad a hand. You know the drill," she said, turning away. Lucy looked at Charlie.

"You can come with us, I expect," he said cheerily.

"No useless mouths, Charlie," said his mother without looking back.

"She'll be useful at something," he shot back, winking at Lucy. "Won't you?"

Mrs Pyefinch turned and looked at them.

"You a show-person?" she asked. "Gymnast? Horse rider? Patterer? Sing-a-bit-dance-a-bit girl?"

"No," said Lucy.

"Any skills at all?"

Lucy shrugged. Mrs Pyefinch shrugged back at her.

"Then sorry, my dear, it's harsh, but it's been a year of short rations and less money jingling in everyone's pockets. But look on the bright side – a night's shelter and egg and bacon for breakfast isn't a bad bargain for nothing, is it?"

"No," said Lucy. "And thank you for it."

Mrs Pyefinch looked like she wanted to say more, but she just nodded and turned away with a wave.

"Come on, Charlie, daylight's a-burning and we need to be gone."

"Don't worry," said Charlie. "She's just always worried about money and things have been a bit tight. She'll change her mind."

"No," said Lucy, looking at the woods beyond the encampment. "It's all right."

Lucy watched Charlie shrug and walk away with a smile and a wave of his own, and then turned away into the cool shadows of the wood.

She was gone for maybe twenty minutes but by the time she emerged the camp was reduced by at least half. All the tents were down and the wagons were bumping over the hummocked grass out onto the smoother going of the high road. There was already a good line of them dwindling into the distance away from the campsite. It was, in its own way, a kind of race. She saw some wagons bouncing along the grass beside the road, trying to get ahead of slower carts which had struck tents earlier, and the sounds of whips cracking and good-natured railing between carters, who clearly knew this game and enjoyed it, filled the air.

When Lucy got to where the Pyefinches' tent had been, there was nothing but crushed grass and a lump in the turf where the square, which had been lifted to build the fire in, had been replaced and stamped down. Wagon tracks led towards the road, and Lucy followed them, weaving a path through the remnants of the camp. An old man who was tying his tent onto the back of a dilapidated cart turned and watched her as she went.

"How much?" he said, pointing at what she carried in her hands.

"They're not for sale," she said, and walked on. "They're payment."

Once on the road she saw that all the wagons were different, but she had no idea what the Pyefinches' looked like, so she jogged past each one, turning to look at the drivers and families sitting on the driving bench as she went.

Tired faces looked back at her with no recognition and not much interest, except for a couple who again offered to buy what she had in her hands. Then she came round to the front of a particularly weather-worn wagon and saw a tall man hunched in a blanket that hooded his head sitting next to a girl who was flicking a whip at the rear of a horse with a frustrated snap. The girl looked at her and nudged the man.

"There, Father. That's the girl. That's the one the Pyefinches found."

It was Georgiana, and her beautiful eyes looked coolly at Lucy in a way that made her feel clumsy and awkward. She was conscious of her muddy boots and the blood on her hands. This made her angry, because she was not used to worrying about her appearance. She didn't like the way Georgiana, who was sitting on a wagon that looked as if it still carried the dirt of every thoroughfare it had ever travelled on its sides, still managed to appear somehow regally above and beyond the grubbiness of the road she was sharing.

The man's eyes looked out from beneath the cowl of the blanket: they were blue, like Georgiana's, but watery and sad. His face was partly hidden, but didn't look like a wizard of any kind, thought Lucy, certainly not a "Great" one. He looked beaten, and his hand, which emerged to point at her, shook. Lucy saw the other hand held a green bottle which she took to contain the liquid that was the cause of the rheumy eye and the trembling hand.

"She has rabbits," he said in a voice that was doubly surprising. It was a deep and gentle voice, and it was also a cultured one.

"Yes, Father," said Georgiana. "Fat ones."

Her eyes had dismissed Lucy and returned to the road.

"Perhaps she would give us one. I am very fond of rabbit stew," he said.

"No, Father. We want nothing of her. You have already had good bacon and eggs for your breakfast," said Georgiana, cracking the whip.

Lucy looked at her, but got no more than the side of her face. So she jogged on. Nine wagons onwards, she saw Charlie sitting on the back of a cart, his legs dangling over the bumpy road. His face split in a grin and he called over his shoulder.

"Ma. Look what we got for dinner!"

The gap in the canvas behind him opened and Mrs Pyefinch looked out. Lucy trotted behind the wagon, holding both hands up, showing the four fat rabbits she had taken in the wood.

"For the breakfast," she said.

Mrs Pyefinch looked at her for a long beat, then her face cracked in a smile which was the mirror of her son's.

"Where'd you get 'em?" she said.

"Took them in the wood," said Lucy.

"And there was you saying you had no skills!" said Mrs Pyefinch. "Well, pull her aboard, Charlie; don't just leave our new friend in the road!"

And with that she disappeared back into the wagon.

Lucy tossed the rabbits onto the tailgate, and then took Charlie's hand and jumped aboard.

"Well," said Charlie. "Now you done it, girl."

"Done what?" she said, getting comfortable next to him.

"Run clean off and joined the circus," he grinned. "No telling what'll happen to you now!"

CHAPTER 37

THE DROPPED MASK AND THE DEAD CITIZEN

It was a good thing for Issachar Templebane's digestion that he had not been able to see Mountfellon in his carriage as he drove away from their meeting: the moment the door was clapped shut and he was alone, he had discarded the anger that had clouded his face as easily as a carnival-goer drops a mask, stretched back in the seat and smiled.

He was still smiling as he exited his carriage and entered his house on Chandos Place in the west of the city, a handsome Georgian building whose windows were glazed in opaque milk-glass for privacy. He did not notice the Raven finding a perch on the crest of the roof of the house opposite. It had followed the coach easily as it had wound its way west through the City and on past the dangerous jumble of Seven Dials and the equally ill-favoured rookeries of St Giles until it had turned north into the more civilised streets of Marylebone.

Mountfellon walked through the hall and on through the long ballroom behind it. He descended the stone stairs to the basement and knocked on a door.

"*Entrez, Milord,*" said a voice from within, faint and scratchy as a dry nib on parchment.

Mountfellon entered another long room, at the end of which was a very old man in a sea-green coat sitting at a desk snowed under with papers and books. The collar of the coat was tall enough to brush his ears, and his face was lined and twisted like a walnut. But the eyes which looked back at Mountfellon were made young by the incorruptible thirst for knowledge that blazed out of them.

Behind him was a cage.

"Good day, Citizen," said Mountfellon.

It was a peculiarity of their relationship, which was one of equals, that the old Frenchman called Mountfellon "Milord" whereas Mountfellon called him "Citizen", the peculiarity being that though both used the words in irony, neither resented it.

"Well?" said The Citizen. "Do we have the key?"

Mountfellon was a man of many secrets but his partner, the hidden resident of Chandos Place, was the deepest secret of all: The Citizen was the reason all the windows were opaque, for he was not just old – nearly ninety by Mountfellon's reckoning – but he was also dead. He was not dead in the sense of being a mysteriously reanimated corpse, he was merely dead in the eyes and mind of the outer world. That world was convinced that he had died a long time ago, publicly and incontrovertibly separated from his head by a guillotine, itself an ironic fate for a former Jacobin and beheader of kings and aristocrats.

Mountfellon never called him by his real name. He was just The Citizen.

"The key is a stratagem for the foolish by which they seek to draw out those who covet their secrets," said Mountfellon. "It was a lure, as you conjectured. The key is not a key, I am almost certain of it."

"And the girl?"

"The girl is gone. She did not succeed."

The Citizen betrayed no interest in the fate of Lucy. He just shrugged his shoulders.

"*Tant pis*. And were you sufficiently foolish?"

Mountfellon smiled.

"I was very foolish and very haughty and very convincingly angry. Issachar Templebane thinks me a perfect *aristo*, blinded by arrogance and a so thoroughgoing dupe, and The Oversight is now, I would say, aware of me."

"Good," said The Citizen. "We shall teach them a thing or two about luring and the long game. And now what shall you do?"

Mountfellon was collecting paper and pens and brushes from a bureau.

"And now I shall be very industrious for the next few days. We may not have grasped the Blood Key but all was not a failure, for I walked into the great treasure house of The Oversight with my eyes open, did I not?"

"Indeed. You may have seen things of great power whose purpose we do not yet understand," said the Citizen. Mountfellon nodded.

"It would be a crime against science and rational thought were I not to catalogue them while they sit clear in my head before the freshness of recollection passes. And you, my friend, your strength is still on the wane?"

The Citizen shrugged.

"I have an arrangement for the full moon, the same I engaged in before I came to this country. If the rendezvous is kept, my vigour shall be quite recruited as before. I shall then make the creature an offer to remain here permanently."

"A wise precaution," said Mountfellon, smiling without mirth. "And your studies are deep enough to keep your mind from the pain, I trust?"

The Citizen tapped a book in front of him and jerked his thumb back towards the cage. On closer inspection it appeared to contain a naked man whose skin was green. His mouth was gagged and he lay curled like a dog on the floor.

"I have been reading Denys's monograph on blood transfusion again," said The Citizen. "I would still be interested to see what would happen were we to swap blood with one of them one day . . ."

Mountfellon took his equipment and headed for the stairs.

"One day, Citizen, one day. And we will get to that day one plan at a time. I must go and work."

And with a half bow he closed the door behind him, leaving the dead man to his studies.

CHAPTER 38

TWO CROOKED HOUSES

Mr Sharp did not seem surprised when Hodge and The Smith appeared at his shoulder in the dripping shadows of the alley in which he was sheltering from fine drizzle while observing the Templebanes' house. He had heard the creak and clatter of Hodge's dog cart drawing up at the rear of the alley behind him, and he knew that Hodge was able to talk to the Raven over long distances. It was an unusual ability which he took quite as much for granted as he did his own capacity to turn people's minds or move exceptionally fast and unnoticed through the world. He was relieved to hear the noise because he wanted, more than anything, to get back to Wellclose Square and see how things lay with Sara. The double shock of losing her hand and having strangers force their way into the Safe House under cover of Law was insupportable, and he felt a cold mixture of anger and concern in his gut that he was wholly unused to.

"You took your time," he said shortly. "How is Sara Falk?"

"As well as one could hope, considering," said The Smith. "Whose house is this?"

"A lawyer," said Mr Sharp. "The man who came into the house with the magistrate came here directly, and then, after a short interview, left in a hurry. The Raven followed him. I stayed here."

"The Raven is outside a large house in Chandos Place," said Hodge. "The man has gone in and not emerged. The windows are shuttered and barred."

"Then you find out who he is and watch him," said Mr Sharp. "I must go back to the house. I do not like the idea of leaving Sara and Cook undefended."

"Cook is never undefended," said The Smith. "And you'd do well not to ever let her suspect you think that you're defending her. Who is the lawyer?"

"I was just going to find out," said Mr Sharp, "before leaving."

"I will do it," said The Smith. "I can see you wish to be elsewhere."

Mr Sharp nodded and turned to Hodge.

"You went to The Three Cripples?"

Hodge nodded.

"And Ketch?" said Mr Sharp.

"From what I gathered from the tapster, he's a regular and a sot — and here's where it gets strange — never had a child or a woman, not like he said he had."

Mr Sharp looked at The Smith.

"The man Ketch—" he began.

"I was told all about him," said The Smith. "If Sluagh were abroad in the city, who's to say that his mind had not been worked on?"

"So the girl was planted on us," said Mr Sharp. "So there is a plot."

"There's a something," said The Smith. "My eels are disturbed. As I said to Sara and Cook, the wolves are circling."

He looked across the street.

"Lawyers are kin to wolves, I hear. You go back to Sara. I think I shall go and see who we have here. Hodge—"

"Chandos Place," said Hodge. "I'm on my way."

Mr Sharp nodded at them both once more and sped off towards the river.

"I do not envy whoever is responsible for injuring Sara," said The Smith. "But I do not like the heat in his eyes. He has a capacity for violence which he has always kept strongly under control. Keeping it under control, indeed, is what has made him a valuable member of The Oversight. Were he to unlatch that control, I do not know if he would be able to come back to us. Nor whether we should want him."

"I'd trust him with my life, and Jed's," said Hodge. "Cold and haughty as he can seem when he's preoccupied-like. Trust him with any of our lives, come to that."

"Yes," said The Smith. "But can we trust him with his own?"

Hodge shrugged, whistled Jed to his heels and jumped back in the dog cart.

"Too deep for me, Wayland," he said, cracking the whip lightly and jolting into motion. "You fathom it if you can."

Coram heard the knocking on the main door of the building, and hurried to answer it before it became so loud and persistent that it woke his Night Father.

He opened the door to find The Smith standing there, a somewhat unexpectedly rural figure in the midst of the city in his caped oilskin coat and high, heavy boots. A farmer, perhaps, thought Coram, and then found himself stepping back reflexively to avoid being barged to the floor as The Smith stepped out of the rain inside the shelter of the hall without being asked. Definitely a farmer or some species of rustic, for he had outdoor manners, Coram concluded.

"Help you, sir?" he said with a superficially engaging smile.

"Sorry to trouble, but I understand this is a lawyer's office," said The Smith in an uncharacteristically querulous voice, as if unsure of his status and right to be knocking on so fine a front door. "I am in need of a man of legal knowledge."

"Ah," said Coram, his smile impregnable. "I'm afraid my fathers do not take approaches from prospective clients at this time, being more than oversubscribed."

"But I had been assured that this was the office of Mr George Chapman Esquire, Attorney at Law, and that he was highly amenable," said The Smith in confusion.

"Ah," said Coram, looking distastefully at the small pools of rainwater collecting on the hall floor as The Smith's oilskin shed the share of the external deluge that it had brought in with it. He would get Amos to mop it up, he thought, and then remembered Amos was still abroad. His smile curdled into a scowl. He would have to get the mop himself. "And therein lies the hinge on which the misunderstanding turns, my dear sir. These premises are not Mr Chapman's house, nor have they ever been."

"But I assure you they are," spluttered The Smith. "The driver of the Hackney that brought me here was quite definite on the matter."

"I am afraid you have been worked on," said Coram, drawing himself a prideful inch taller. "This is the house of Templebane & Templebane."

A sharp eye would have seen The Smith drop his bumbling look for an instant as the name hit him, but Coram was reaching past him to open the street door and so missed it.

"Who and who?" said The Smith.

"Mr Issachar and Mr Zebulon Templebane, Attorneys at Law," said Coram with a hint of pride. "My fathers."

"Templebane," said The Smith. "An interesting name."

"But not the one you were seeking, I am afraid," said Coram, pushing him politely back out into the street.

"I have one question," said The Smith, putting his foot in the door as Coram tried to close it.

Coram rolled his eyes.

"I am sorry," he said, the smile wearing thin now. "I do not know where Chapman's chambers are. I have never heard of him."

"That wasn't my question," said The Smith, who suddenly, to Coram's surprise, did not look so bucolic and doddery as he had seemed a moment ago.

"My question is: are you expecting sunshine?"

And he looked up into the drizzle.

"Sorry?" said Coram.

The Smith pointed to the smoked-glass pince-nez hanging from the ribbon around his neck.

"I think you're not going to need those today, are you?"

Coram fumbled his fingers towards the glasses, and then let them fall limply to his side as The Smith's eyes bored into his.

"I am The Smith. You will forget that when I am gone, but if anyone should come to you and say that The Smith sent them, you will accommodate them. And if you happen to be wearing those glasses when they come, you will take them off and look directly into their eyes, do you understand?"

"Yes, sir," said Coram, looking slightly puzzled.

"Good," said The Smith. "And as a last parting gift, would you be so kind as to tell me the name of the man who came here in a black coach earlier, and left looking a little exercised?"

"Viscount Mountfellon?" said Coram dully. "You mean him?"

"I didn't," said The Smith. "But now I do." And hearing footsteps approaching from behind Coram, he turned and walked off into the passing crowd.

Coram sneezed three times and then jumped as Issachar tapped him on the shoulder.

"Who was that, boy?" he said, peering into the street.

"Just someone, no one, Father," said Coram, shaking his head to clear it. "Wrong address."

"Well, stop standing there in a dwam and close the door. We don't need the weather inside," said Templebane. "And mop that up."

The Raven was still perched patiently on the roof overlooking the house at the end of Chandos Place. Its black and lively eyes were fixed on the contrastingly opaque milk-glass windows opposite, windows that kept whatever happened within the building entirely invisible from the outside. It was a peculiar arrangement: when seen in conjunction with the main door which was offset and not in the centre of the façade, as might have been expected from the otherwise symmetrical Georgian proportions, it gave the building a wall-eyed, crippled look, as if it were blind and tilting to one side.

If the Raven had been a fanciful bird, it might have thought it an unlucky building.

"A crooked man in a crooked house," said Hodge, five floors below in the dog cart. "Have a closer look, shall we?"

Jed trotted across the street and began to sniff his way around the perimeter of Mountfellon's house as if in search of rats.

The rain squalled into a greater fury, and Hodge pulled his coat tighter round his neck as big drops spattered the street around him.

The Raven fluttered over the road, somehow unbothered by the water pouring out of the sky at right angles to its slow trajectory. It landed on the top of the portico and tapped at the glazing bars which divided each sash into six panes of glass.

"Iron," said Hodge in surprise. "Now that's something you don't see."

The raven dropped to the front step and hopped up to the door, rapping its beak against it once.

"And an iron door," said Hodge. "Well. Someone's protecting himself."

The Raven curved round the side of the house to where Jed had smelled a rat and was forcing his head down a drain-hole in order to smell it better. Jed and the Raven had an unspoken agreement. Whenever Jed killed a rat, which he did on strict principle and not out of any desire to eat them, the Raven got to pick at the squishy bits, which he particularly enjoyed.

Hodge looked up at the milky-eyed house.

"I don't like this," he said. "Not much at all I don't like it."

It wasn't just the blank and well-protected face of the building. It was the rain-slick roof tiles above it. They pricked his memory like a twinge from a bad conscience and made him think of other roofs recently visited, and coops full of dead birds.

In the teeth of this new crisis, he was aware that he was perhaps dangerously ignoring the day-to-day duties of The Oversight entirely.

CHAPTER 39

ILL-MET

Zebulon Templebane travelled north through Bethnal Green, secure in his night carriage, which was driven by his son Bassetshaw, who rode with two blunderbusses hanging in coaching holsters on either side of his narrow seat. Bassetshaw spat out his chewing tobacco as they crested the narrow bridge over the Regent's Canal, and had the satisfaction of seeing the wad break the calm crescent of the reflected moon into rippled shards beneath them. At the bottom of Mutton Lane, Zebulon banged sharply on the roof and Bassetshaw stopped the coach abruptly, with little regard for the mouths of the two horses as he tugged on the bits and yanked the brake with his other hand.

For a moment they sat there in the quiet of the street, the only movement being the steam coming off the horses' backs in the chill of the night, backlit by the half-moon.

A trap slid open behind Bassetshaw's shoulder.

"You have the guns?"

"Loaded with iron nails, Father, as you said," said Bassetshaw. "I don't need to be told twice. Especially on a night like this."

"When we next stop, cock them both and be ready when

I am talking to them. At all times be alert. You know what to look for."

"You could stay in the coach, Father," said Bassetshaw.

"I won't show fear to them, boy. We never have, not us nor our father nor his grandfather and all the way back. Show them fear and you open a door into your mind that they will happily exploit. Have you your spectacles?"

"Father . . ."

"Put them on. I do not want them working on your mind while your finger is on the trigger. Now mind me: if you have to shoot, shoot straight. Only shoot in extremis, only if it goes bad, then shoot straight, shoot fast and think of nothing but hitting those closest to me first."

"But, Father, what if I hit you?"

A grim laugh trickled out of the trap and Bassetshaw glanced back to see Zebulon attaching his own smoked-glass spectacles inside the darkness of the coach.

"If it goes wrong and I am still within their reach, better you *should* hit me than they take me off into the dark. But don't worry. I carry iron of my own. Now drive on and stop at the junction at the top of this street. There'll be a triangle of grass where three roads meet, and that's where we'll find them. Move now."

When they stopped a couple of minutes later, the grass was deserted. The travellers from the previous night had travelled on, leaving only the scorched patch where they had lit their camp-fire as a memorial. The grass was pale as frost in the moonlight, and Bassetshaw shivered at an unseasonal coldness borne towards him by the wind gently soughing through the leaves and shadows of the trees ahead. He had the strong sense of being on the edge of something, with the warmth of the known city huddled at his back and the chill of the unseen country ahead stretching away into a wilder world beyond his ken. He quickly cocked both blunderbusses and laid one across his knees while holding the other ready. He only realised he had forgotten to breathe when he exhaled involuntarily and sucked in a big breath to ease the ache in his lungs.

"Breathe steady, boy," said Zebulon from the trapdoor behind him. "This is no time to swoon."

"What do we do?" whispered Bassetshaw.

"Wait."

Time passed. A dog barked somewhere on the far side of the canal, but it was too late at night for any other dogs to join the chorus. An owl screeched in the woods ahead and something small and low to the ground rushed out of the undergrowth and disappeared into the ditch with a splash. Then there was more quiet for quite a long time.

"There's no one coming," whispered Bassetshaw.

"They're here," said Templebane and opened the coach door. As he eased his bulk onto the road, the springs squealed in relief and the coach bounced lightly. He stretched and pointed at the road.

"Mutton Lane. It's on a way-line, as is that road and that one. Where the old way-lines meet like this there's always more than a fair chance a watcher has been set."

"I don't see anyone," Bassetshaw whispered.

"Good . . ." said the darkness. And Bassetshaw forgot to breathe again. Nothing moved for another long time.

"Father . . ." he breathed.

"Don't whimper, boy," said Templebane.

"Where is our flag?" hissed a different bit of darkness. Bassetshaw whirled his blunderbuss in the direction it came from.

"It's safe," said Templebane, walking calmly into the centre of the grassy triangle.

"Safe?" said the darkness from the other side to which he had just spoken. "Safe?"

Bassetshaw had just turned to cover that particular bit of darkness when a voice came from right behind him.

"We had a bargain," it rasped.

Templebane was not reacting to the game of hide and seek. He just stood four-square and talked to the darkness straight ahead of him.

"The bargain was that you would turn the girl's mind so that she would follow our instructions once in the house."

"We did," said the darkness.

"She didn't," said Templebane.

"Impossible," snarled the darkness, suddenly making itself visible as the tall Sluagh with the billycock hat crowned with woodcock beaks detached from the shadows. He did so so suddenly that Bassetshaw nearly shot him, shocked by the fact that he had been looking at him for a good five minutes but had thought him part of the tree trunk.

"That is impossible," hissed the Sluagh.

"Well," shrugged Templebane. "There are those who would say the Sluagh are impossible, the stuff of nightmares, old wives' tales and fairy stories, but here you are . . ."

"What do you mean?" said the Sluagh, slowly circling round him.

"That the impossible happens," said Templebane. "The world is too various for it not to."

The Sluagh shook his head as if trying to rid himself of a troublesome horsefly instead of an unwelcome idea.

"We had a bargain," he repeated.

"No," said Templebane.

And before he could continue, and much faster than Bassetshaw could possibly react to, he had a bronze blade at Zebulon's throat and the Sluagh was behind him, his other hand twined in the man's hair and pulling his head back.

"No?" said the Sluagh. "No? I will skin you for that . . ."

Zebulon Templebane was a strong man. He kept his head straight.

"No," he said. "We *have* a bargain. It is just not yet fulfilled."

The Sluagh tugged at his head again.

"I should point out that my right hand holds a small pistol somewhat awkwardly pointed at your stomach, but pointed there none the less. The pistol is charged with iron filings. At this range you will enjoy it quite as little as I am enjoying your blade at my neck."

The Sluagh held him for a beat and then stepped away, disappearing the blade inside his long coat as if it had never been there.

"Where is our flag?" he growled.

"Your flag is out of your grasp but remains within your reach. If you still want it."

"Of course we still want it. It is ours."

"Then find the girl and it will be in your hands."

"Why should we find her? We gave her to you. We turned her mind, and that of the drinking man who carried her. You lost her . . ."

"No!" said Templebane, the syllable sharp as a whip-crack in the night quiet. "You did not bind her mind enough, and she has escaped."

"No, no . . ." said the Sluagh, waving a finger at Templebane as he began to pace round him again slowly, like a big cat circling its prey. "You want a new deal. You sent your son on an errand . . ."

And he tossed something onto the ground between them. It was a rectangle of brass with a recently broken leather strap: the words "Mute but Intelligent" clearly readable even at ten paces distance.

Templebane cocked his head, betraying surprise for an instant before covering it up with his impregnable smile.

"Yes, yes," continued the Sluagh. "We know who you serve, man-in-the-middle. We know where our flag must be. Here is a new bargain: your son for the flag. I can have him brought here tomorrow night. Bring the flag or I will cut his—"

Templebane broke the night with a bullet of dry laughter.

"Cut him where you will. That bargain is not to our taste or our interest."

The Sluagh stared at him. Templebane shrugged his great shoulders and smiled wider.

"We have many 'sons'. One more or less is not even an inconvenience. The poorhouses of London are full of replacements."

The Sluagh circled closer and peered into his eyes.

"You think to pitch your cruelty against mine? You think you can make your heart harder than one who has forsworn the ease of daylight and embraced the dark?"

"Forswearing the daylight does not impress me much," said the Night Father, holding his gaze. "We both know daylight is dilute, watery stuff when compared with the richness of the night."

The Sluagh shook his head.

"We Shadowgangers have dealt with your family for generations. If you do not know we will walk away from a broken bargain without a qualm, you have learned nothing of our ways or the strength of our will and our honour. You know less than nothing, for what you think you know is wrong—"

"I know you want the flag."

"WE HAVE WANTED OUR FLAG FOR CENTURIES!" shouted the Sluagh. "But we can wait. Maybe your son's sons will be better men to deal with."

And with that he spun on his heel, clattering the small bones hanging off his tattered coat, and walked away towards the darkness of the woods.

"The boy who does not speak, cunning man? Your son? Do not expect to see him again."

As he stepped into the darkness, Templebane spoke.

"I can offer you more than the flag."

There was a beat of silence and then the darkness spoke with a weary laugh.

"Go away. Our business is done. Your father's father was a better man than you or your brother, Zebulon Templebane."

"No," said Templebane. "No, he was not. Because he could never have offered you what we can: he could never have offered you the destruction of The Oversight and the end of Law and Lore."

The hiss that greeted this seemed to come from all around, and Bassetshaw was suddenly horrified to see how many of the innocent shadows and shapes around him stepped forward and revealed themselves to be Sluagh.

There were seven and they all looked into the darkness which had enveloped the tall one. After another moment he walked straight out of it and back towards Templebane.

"How?" he said.

Zebulon unwrapped the square of paper Mountfellon had given him earlier. He held it out, the fragment of bloodstone stark against the whiteness that held it.

The Sluagh stared at it, poking it with his finger.

"This is from her own ring," said Templebane.

"Unicorn," said the Sluagh, looking up at him. "She is one of The Oversight then?"

Templebane laughed.

"No. Not at all. Even she does not know what she is. But I know she is the means of their destruction."

The Sluagh picked up the bloodstone and put it in his mouth. He held his lips open and Templebane saw it vibrating between his teeth as he tasted its resonance. The Sluagh looked round at his blood brothers. All had the same expression: teeth clenched, lips drawn back, nostrils distended as if they too were tasting the stone. One by one they nodded and turned away. In a moment there was just the one with the woodcock crown. He spat the stone back into the paper in Templebane's hand.

"We have her taste. My brethren will pass her on one to

another. If she is abroad we will find her." And with that he turned and was, for the last time, part of the darkness again.

Two minutes passed and neither Zebulon Templebane nor Bassetshaw moved. Then Bassetshaw cleared his throat.

"Have they gone?" he whispered.

Templebane turned and walked back to the coach without meeting his eyes.

"They are always somewhere in the dark," he said. "Watching."

The coach tilted as he opened the door and hoisted himself on to the step.

"Amos . . ." said Bassetshaw.

The face Templebane turned suddenly up at him was terrible in the moonlight. There was no more emotion than an axe-head.

"Amos is dead. As you will be if you breathe a word of this to your brothers."

CHAPTER 40

THE ALP IN THE ATTIC

The breath-stealer had made a bad mistake. It knew it as soon as it saw the man with the terrier for the second time. It looked out of the narrow garret window, jammed in beneath the dripping eaves of the high building, and saw him in the flat space between the mismatched roofs of the buildings below, searching among the pigeon coops by the light of a lantern. The coops were empty now, only feathers showing where the dead pigeons had been.

It was the light moving among the wet roof tiles that had caught the breath-stealer's attention and raised it from the floor on which it had been resting as it listened to the sound of the woman breathing in her sleep and the baby gurgling in the cot across the room.

The breath-stealer should have moved further away: it knew that. It would have done so had it not been so weak on arrival in the city. It would not have been so enfeebled had it not been forced to take such a circuitous route to get there from its home in the high forests fringing the high karst plateau known to the local Austrian valley dwellers as *das Steinerne Meer*, the Stony Sea. Travelling from the Berchtesgaden mountains to the real sea had not been hard, but the boat it had hidden on had been held up for so long, first by contrary winds in the Kattegat and then by not one but two unseasonal storms in the North Sea, that by the time it entered the Pool of London and took its place amidst the bewildering multitude of other cargo ships, the Alp was exhausted.

"Alp" was the name given to its kind in the folklore of its native forests, Alp not only being a word for the adjacent limestone peaks, but also being the old word for the male variety of mara: like the mara it was a night-rider, an incubus who took the strength from sleeping beings by pressing on them.

It was not, however, the insubstantial spirit that folklore would have it: the Alp was flesh and blood and entirely human in shape if not habit. That shape was, like its face and hair, entirely unremarkable: in fact it was so unremarkable as to be instantly forgettable. It was of middling height, mild and regular featured, hair not quite dark and not especially fair. There was a faint greyness to its skin but nothing too striking, and its age was indeterminate, as was its sex. It could have been a youngish man or a slightly older woman. Though it was dressed in man's clothing, its hair was long enough to overhang its ears; it was what would have been called a "twixter" on the streets below, had anyone on those streets noticed or remembered it for long enough.

When weak and as debilitatingly reduced in power as it had been on arrival in London, it was its habit to recoup its vitality by preying on small animals and birds, building its strength by taking their breaths for its own before moving on to larger hosts. There was a particular intense, distilled quality in the final exhalation of a dying creature which it especially prized, which explained the coops full of dead pigeons. As the Alp watched Hodge and Jed move among the empty coops, it remembered the dry snap and pop of the pigeons' breastbones as it had pressed the life out of them, forcing the small lungs to empty their essence into its mouth between the lips it held clamped over their struggling beaks. It had glutted itself on last breaths, and should then have gone far away to rest and let their power restore it to its usual state of health.

Instead it had heard the baby cry in the attic opposite and seen the woman move across the window to comfort it, and so had decided to lie up with her. Waiting until the penny candle had been extinguished, it had used a fair portion of its newly acquired vitality to leap across the courtyard and swing itself up the building and into the room. It had sung quietly as it stepped over the window, a low wordless tune which was calming and soporific and unworldly in equal measures.

The woman had stirred a little in her sleep as it had climbed onto the horsehair mattress, but its hands had soothed her by stroking her face as it knelt carefully on her chest and concentrated on making itself heavier and heavier until her breath began to become ragged, at which point it had clamped its mouth over hers and inhaled. It freed her mouth to allow her to inhale, but bent and sucked every third exhalation. As it did so it felt strength returning, and though her eyes opened and stared sightlessly at it, like someone in a drug-fogged waking slumber, its own eyes were twisted sideways, fixed on the surprisingly plump baby in the cradle across the room.

Youngest breaths were the purest breaths, and it watched it with the greed of a gourmand at a feast, saving the most delicious sweetmeat until the end.

The woman had remained in a comatose state for two days, days during which the Alp had regained its strength from her exhalations, and stopped the baby from crying by taking it from the cot and allowing it to latch on to its mother's breast at the first sign of hunger. Like any parasite, the Alp knew its own survival relied on keeping its hosts healthy – at least until it was time to move on to new ones.

It had known it would have to move eventually, for it had not come to London unbidden or upon a whim. It had been sent for, but it would have failed in its purpose had it presented itself to its client in anything less than the full measure of its strength. But it had certainly made the mistake of sleeping too close to where it fed, and it would now have to move.

It began to sing its low lullaby under its breath as it turned back to the room. But this time its light steps did not take it to the bed.

It wetted its lips and walked towards the cot.

Hodge let Jed sniff his way around the perimeter of the roof. He could see the dog was on to something.

"Where'd it go, boy?" he said. "What you got?"

Jed scrabbled up the wet slope of the roof and stood with his front paws on the ridge, his nose searching the breeze.

"Stops there, does it?" said Hodge. "Can't be, 'less it flew off, whatever it was."

Jed's back suddenly stiffened and his tail went straight and quivery. Hodge lowered himself so he could follow the dog's eyeline towards the gaunt building overhanging the roof trough they were standing in.

He was still trying to make out what the dog was looking at in the small windows under the eaves when he heard the woman scream.

CHAPTER 41

Out of the Past

"Who this Mountfellon of Chandos Place is I do not know. But he and his house are warded against the supranatural so we must assume he is more than aware of us. Templebane is a surname which The Oversight has encountered in former times," said The Smith, and spat into the fire. "There were Templebane witchfinders in the fen country."

Hodge, Mr Sharp, Cook and Sara sat in a half-circle in front of the hearth at the centre of the Red Library. Hodge was grim-faced and visibly unsettled, the hand he rested on Jed's head at his knee was shaking with some kind of pent-up emotion which the others had all noticed but were studiously not commenting on. Emmet was quietly shuffling the glass shards of mirror from the Murano Cabinet, ordering and rearranging them on a tabletop cleared of books and other manuscripts.

Sara sat closest to the fire but looked wintry cold, her face a green only a few shades paler than her eyes, and from the shivers which sporadically racked her body it was clear that the blanket Cook had wrapped around her was not good for anything other than hiding the stump on the end of her arm.

"Witchfinders," she said, her voice barely more than a rasp.

"Men who made a living encouraging frightened and credulous folk to kill others weaker than themselves for being something that doesn't even exist."

"Not like they think it does at any rate," said Cook. "Not devils and black magic and all that carry-on invented by fat monks and priests to frighten the people into feeding them or giving them more silver."

The Smith nodded.

"Ordinary people have always known something other than themselves exists just beyond the beyond, but the witch-finders created a travesty of what actually does live on the far side of that threshold to feed off their fear."

"Do you think they'd be any happier knowing how the world really is?" said Mr Sharp, pointing at a large brass-bound book at the centre of the table behind them. It was as big as a church Bible, but it had a lock and was neatly parcelled with a thick red silk grosgrain ribbon, somewhat like a Christmas present. "Do you think that if they could read *The Great and Hidden History of the World* that they would sleep any better? There'd be witchfinders and worse on every street corner."

"Man's weakness in the face of uncertainty is to harness the powers of the mob by giving it a common enemy, real or imagined," said Sara, and then coughed so long and hard that Mr Sharp got to his feet and had to be waved back by Cook, who gave him a warning look. Sara eventually stopped coughing and looked up at them, her eyes red and watery from the hacking spasm. "That's one reason we exist: to hold the line."

Mr Sharp watched her with something like pain in his eyes.

"That's just it. We ain't holding the line," said Hodge in a burst. Perhaps because he said less than the others when in company they tended to listen whenever he did break his silence, and it was clear from his tremoring hand that he had a head of steam built up which needed to get out before he exploded. "We can't do our job right and that's a fact. Too few of us running round a city that's sprouting like ragweed, spreading everywhere. We miss stuff, or when we do spot it there's too much going on for us to do the right thing in time."

"Nonsense," said Cook.

"I wish it was nonsense," he snarled bitterly. "But it ain't. It's something else entirely. It's a woman in a garret gone clean mad with grief because her little babby's breath's been stolen. It's her feeling his little broken breastbones all jagged and wrong under the soft skin, skin that ain't hardly even seen sunlight it's so new to the world. It's that poor mind-turned woman thinking it must've been her that done it, in her sleep or some-like, because she's alone in the room and she's got no memory of the thing that did it."

They all stared at him.

"What happened?" said Mr Sharp.

"What happened was I listened to you and ignored what the Raven was telling me when it showed me them pigeons all dead in their coops. Warning that there was a breath-stealer abroad," said Hodge.

And with that he told them of the rooftop full of lifeless squabs and how he'd not had time to fully investigate, and then how he'd gone back and looked harder just too late to stop the Alp sucking the breath from the baby and making its escape. He choked as he told them of the horror that greeted him when he and Jed broke down the door and found the distraught mother slumped on the floor with the crushed child in her arms. And then he turned his eyes to Mr Sharp, eyes that were now haunted with what he'd seen and the knowledge that he might have stopped it.

"I'm sorry," began Mr Sharp. "But I still—"

Hodge shook his head with a bitter grunt.

"No. I ain't putting this on you, old mate, because what you told me was right. Sensible. Efficient. And I could have ignored what you said. This is a Free Company. But I didn't. I did what was sensible. And so the babby and the woman's on me. But the way I see it now is either I'm sworn to protect, or I'm sworn to be sensible and efficient: the two don't always run hand in hand. And I'm damn sure which oath I took."

"If there's a breath-stealer working the town we will find it," said The Smith.

Hodge shook his head,

"No. I shall find it myself. Jed has the scent of it; we will pick up its trail. And I shall track it above, on or under the ground, and I shall discover it. And then I shall kill it. It's taken life, and Lore and Law say the punishment must fit the crime."

It was, in its grim way, an oath, and as such they gave it the space of a moment's silence to honour it. And then Sara spoke up.

"That we are stretched is no new news. It does not mean this is the end; we have been stretched and yet have prevailed before . . ."

"No, Sara Falk," said Hodge, looking pointedly at The Smith. "Hear me out. Way I see it is: this is a day we've long known was coming. Letting that magistrate in with the Mountfellon fellow was bad, but it's not as if we don't have normal folk in the house often enough without them a-knowing what we do or why we're here. That's almost regular. What ain't normal is the girl smuggling herself into your good offices and then getting in here. And then trying to steal something. And then escaping into the mirrors. And taking your blessed hand with her. That's a sign. That's a sign of the time. And the time is come. The Smith knows it. He's been making lead boxes."

"That's a last resort," spluttered Cook. "We're not finished yet—"

"People who are finished never know it until it's too late," said The Smith. "It is a matter of safety. We seal the valuable, the powerful and the irreplaceable in the chests. And above all, we put the Wildfire in a double-sealed one. And then we put them all beyond reach."

"And where would that be?" said Cook.

"At the bottom of the Thames. Hidden from all eyes, chained to the riverbed under flowing water. Hide the Discriminator and put the Wildfire under the water," said The Smith.

"This is hysterical," said Cook, bridling. "Why it's—"

"No," said Sara. "It's the right thing to do. At the very least we must put them both out of harm's way."

"Mr Sharp," said Cook, turning for support, "tell them this is ridiculous—"

"It is not," said Mr Sharp. "It pains me to agree with the others, but it may well be necessary."

"But how will we do this without drawing attention?" said Cook. "It is impossible to move that much without doing so because we must now assume that the house is being watched by ill-wishers at all hours . . ."

"Come," said The Smith. "I will show you how."

They all followed him down the stairs and into the kitchen, Sara leaning heavily on Mr Sharp's arm as they brought up the rear. The Smith led them into the furthest pantry, where they were presented with a wall covered in shelves, all groaning under the weight of glass jars full of preserved fruits and jams.

"No," said Cook. "We do not open that door."

Sara put her hand on her arm, stilling her.

"In extremis," she said. "In extremis we do."

The Smith reached up and beneath the topmost shelf. There

was a metallic click, and then he slid the entire wall out on a hinge, revealing it to be a door into a dark passage.

"Light," he said, reaching back.

Mr Sharp produced a candle from inside his coat, and snapped his wrist. The candle flamed brightly as he handed it forward.

They followed The Smith down the passage silently, or as silently as a group could be that included someone like Cook, who could not keep herself from tutting in disapproval every few steps.

The ceiling above them was smeared with soot from the generations of candles and torches that had preceded them, and the soot was smeared where others had dragged their hands through it. The reason they had done this became apparent as the band of light from The Smith's candle reached the studded door at the end of the passage. The last fifteen yards or so of the wall were covered in sooty handprints of all shapes and sizes, and beneath each print an initial or a mark had been scratched into the plaster. The unavoidable impression created by all the handprints and initials was of a kind of informal memorial wall.

"Wait," said Sara, as The Smith was unlocking the door. Her eyes scanned the handprints until she came to a pair at shoulder height, bearing the initials RF and CF. Her hand reached gently towards them.

"No!" said Sharp, pulling her away, but a beat too late.

Her hand touched the smaller handprint and stuck to it.

To the others watching she appeared to go rigid with shock, and her head snapped back as she glinted, the tendons on her neck arching, her eyes wide open and unblinking as the past pent up in the wall slammed into her.

For Sara it was — as ever — as if it hit her in a series of jagged blows.

The tunnel was full of people.

Some walked past with weapons.

Some stopped and smeared their hands on the sooty ceiling.

Their clothes were those of a past generation.

Their faces were grim and determined.

There were women and men.

The women carried blades and pistols too.

They made handprints.

A tow-haired young man, almost a boy, scratched his name with the point of a seaman's dirk.

A dog barked close by.

Then the tunnel was emptier.

A woman stood with her hand in the same place as hers.

Face lit by a shuttered lantern held by a tall man at her side.

A woman with a face very like her own, but with unruly black curls escaping from beneath a sailor's stocking cap.

The woman seemed to look right into her eyes.

Then she was speaking.

"Goodbye, my strong girl. My brave little one."

The others who could not see what Sara was seeing saw her choke at this.

The woman smiled and cleared her throat.

"If all goes well, we shall be back before you wake. If mischance befalls us, you will have to be stronger still and take our place in the Hand. Cook and The Smith will guide you and young Jack Sharp has sworn to be your friend and guard you until you are grown into your power. Go easy on him, my child, for he has a wildness in him, and he struggles to master it. You will understand this, for you have a different kind of fierceness in you, and we have seen you learning to control it—"

The past jerked again.

The woman wiped her eyes and smiled bravely.

Tears leaked down Sara's cheek.

Again the past jerked forward, and she was looking at the woman again but now with the man beside her leaning down and smiling out at her in the warm light of the shuttered lantern. He was speaking, his voice deep and strong.

"—ever befalls us, good or ill, hold this one truth close to your heart, Sara: however much armour you have to put outside you to deal with the world that is coming, you have always been truly and most deeply loved. And whatever they tell you, child, we have always held that in both worlds, natural and supranatural, this one truth holds strongest in the end: love conquers all."

He kissed the tips of his fingers and held them out to her, and then, just as they nearly touched her, just as the others saw her strain her face forward towards something they could not see—

—the past snuffed out and Sara staggered away from the wall, her hand falling limply to her side.

Her eyes fluttered and she looked confusedly at Cook and Mr Sharp as she whispered hoarsely, "I thought I should draw strength from it. From them. I thought I would . . ."

And then her eyes rolled back in her head in a dead faint, and she would have dashed her brains out on the cobbles had Mr Sharp not caught her as she crumpled.

The others watched as he scooped her up and carried her away, back towards the light in the kitchen.

The Smith turned and unlocked the door at the end of the passage.

"No good has come of being down here," said Cook, her eyes still on Sara. "There's a good reason that door's been locked since the Disaster."

"There's no reason," said The Smith, stepping into the cellar beyond the door. "No reason other than sentiment. The Disaster happened because of the mirrors, and the Murano

Cabinet has been moved to the Red Library. As well say we should not go there!"

Cook still grumbled as she followed him inside to where Jed was already sniffing hopefully round the edge of the wall for any rats that might have chosen to hide there.

It was a bare cellar, with dry brick walls and stone flags. At the far end was a half-flight of steps leading to a double door studded with iron nails.

"There," said The Smith. "Emmet takes the caskets out through there. It leads to a Thameside culvert, close by Talleyman's Cut."

"I didn't know there was another tunnel," said Cook.

"Well, all the more reason not to let superstition and sentiment cloud your naturally enquiring mind," smiled The Smith. "If you'd come here you would have known."

Cook harrumphed and looked around.

"Could store my preserves in here," she allowed. "It's dry enough."

The Smith carried on, pointing at the doors.

"From the culvert we put them on a boat and take them midstream up by Blackwall Reach where it's deepest. Then we sink them. Far as any watchers see, we'll deliver caskets to the front door by cart, and they'll be waiting to follow the cart once the caskets come back out."

Cook looked at Hodge.

"I don't like it," she said.

"Don't have to like it," he said. "Just have to handle the boat."

There was a beat of silence as she absorbed the word "boat". A close observer might have seen a dreamy look pass over her eyes for an unguarded instant.

"Been a while since I was out on the water," she said.

"But I expect you'll remember the ropes," said The Smith. "Once you've done it, you never forget. It's just like riding a horse—"

"Don't ride horses," said Cook. "Horrible things. One end kicks and the other bites."

She shook herself and glared at them.

"I still don't like this," she said.

"Nor I," said Hodge. "Mind, I don't feel like I'll like much ever again after that babby's eyes a-staring at me."

"I don't like this either," said The Smith. "But it needs doing. Sara is dying. Or worse. And without her we lose the Last Hand."

CHAPTER 42

THE SHOWMEN'S DRUMHEAD

The long line of carts and wagons crawled across the landscape for two days in a snake which stretched as it went, those who travelled lighter moving to the head as they inexorably outstripped the lumbering wagons grinding heavily along in the dust-cloud at the tail.

"Them poor flats choking at the back will be wishing it would rain," said Charlie, looking up at the sky. "Then when it does they'll be axle-deep in mud and hoping the jolly old sun will pop along and dry it all out again."

He smiled with the assurance of one who knew everything and was lucky enough to travel at the front of the line.

Lucy didn't meet his father until they stopped to water the horses in the early afternoon of the first day. Then Charlie and she hopped down and helped him.

Mr Pyefinch was an energetic man of medium height who limped as he walked, but did so with such vigour and so nimbly that he seemed twice as able as most undamaged men. The damage had been acquired, Charlie confided to Lucy with some pride, fighting the French at the Battle of Waterloo, more than thirty years in the past.

"But don't worry," he said. "He don't bear a grudge. He

won't mind that you might be a Frog."

"Don't mind at all, girl," said Mr Pyefinch. "It was a long time ago, and I was no more than an eleven-year-old drummer boy minding my own business in the middle of a crowd of Guardsmen as Boney's cavalry rode round us trying to break our square. Fellow who shot me was as English as me, a big fumble-fingered Kentishman he was, dropped his musket as he was reloading and it landed just clever enough to put a ball through my shin, it did!"

He held out a hand and shook hers with a nod.

"Frenchies never touched me, though one of them Imperial Guard put a bayonet through the Kentishman later in the day – nasty-looking bloke he was with a big bushy moustache. Thank you for the rabbits."

"Thank you for looking after me when I passed out," said Lucy.

"Wasn't me," he said. "Thank Rose for that."

Rose, it transpired, was his wife. They returned to the road, and this time Lucy was invited to sit at the front. It was a situation she would normally have avoided if she could because she was sure that she was going to be plied with questions about how she'd appeared in the big tent last night, and where she came from. Strangely they didn't ask her any of those sort of questions at all, not even why she wore gloves at all times, something people usually remarked on, and as the afternoon progressed and the warmth of the sun worked with the rhythmic sway of the cart, she relaxed and listened to them talk instead. The particular "show" that they travelled the country exhibiting was a series of "Historical and Infamous Tableaux" which, she gathered, were glass-fronted cases behind which were tiny models of places and people that were made, by a well-blacked-out tent and a clever use of lighting, to appear all the more real as Mr Pyefinch gave a reading or narration to add to the drama.

"We've been doing the Battle of Waterloo since the beginning, and very profitable it is too," he said. "Being ever so patriotic, you see. People come to the fair in a holiday mood and gets some holiday ale in them, and that produces an excess of the sentimental humours, and there's nothing as sentimental as patriotism. It's been so nice an earner that I had a very talented maker in Clerkenwell do me up a diorama of the Battle of Trafalgar which we do on alternate nights."

"It's very cunning," said Mrs Pyefinch. "Almost like magic, for the ships are connected beneath the sea with wires—"

"The sea which is a cleverly contrived piece of shantung silk, dyed special," interrupted her husband, "in the hue known as *eau-de-nil*, which as I'm sure you know is French for Nile water, though I've never seen the Nile nor a pyramid neither, truth to tell . . ."

Mr Pyefinch had the habit of dreaming of things while he talked, and his eyes seemed to drift a long way off as if he was imagining desert sands and sphinxes all around them.

"The ships are connected with rods and piano wire, which enable us to move them as Mr Pyefinch tells the story of the battle," said his wife.

"Most effective, the illusion," said Pyefinch, his eyes coming back into focus. "The general public finds it highly gratifying."

"The general public likes an illusion, and pays well for it," grinned Charlie. "Which is just as well cos in our world nothing's what it seems. Everything's like Huffam's Educated Pig, if you know what I mean."

"I don't really," said Lucy.

"You see a pig in a dress?" he said. "Before you fainted?"

She was about to say she didn't faint and wasn't the sort of girl who did faint, but then she remembered two things: that she had, shamefully, done so, and before so doing had seen, amongst the other horrors, a woman with the head of a pig.

"Well Huffam's Educated Pig looks like a pig, but ain't," said Charlie. "I mean you could get a pig in a dress, but you couldn't get it to sit upright or walk on two legs, could you? So what they does is take a little bear and shave the poor thing. All its nice brown fur comes off, right down to the pink skin beneath, and what with its snout and its tusky teeth, it looks like a pig in a bonnet. They offered me thruppence a week to shave it for them, but I won't do it. I'll do most things for money, but I won't do that. Do that, you got to look in the poor creature's eyes, and they're so like a person's that it'd break your heart to see it."

That first night they camped on a rising slope of heathland beside a long stretch of the river which had been flirting with the dusty road all through the day's journey, sometimes kissing the edge, sometimes darting off through the fields to make hidden oxbows behind distant stands of willow before returning again. Lucy stood back and watched the neatness and speed with which the showmen turned their vehicles into homes, watering and feeding the horses, throwing up canvas shelters into which they decanted tables, chairs and lanterns from the wagons, and kindling fires on top of which soot-black kettles were soon steaming away all across the camp. They did all this with so little fuss and such economy of movement that Lucy thought they moved like sailors, at which point she sat down because she couldn't remember *how* she knew they were like sailors. She was sure she must have been on a ship, the feeling was so strong, but it was one of those memories that seemed to have fallen into a black hole in her head.

Remembering those black holes made her feel nauseous with vertigo. She was used to dealing with fear by moving away from it as fast as she could, but the worrying voids in her memory were travelling with her. At some point she hoped she'd start recalling how she got here, or at least begin to understand *why* if not *where* the memories had gone. Until then she knew she had to keep her hands busy to keep the sick feeling in her head at bay, so she borrowed a jack-knife from Charlie and skinned and jointed the rabbits, and by the time Rose had the tea made the meat was ready to go into a pot.

"You're a handy one," said Rose, nodding at Mr Pyefinch to draw his attention to Lucy's dexterity. "Though I've never seen anyone cook in gloves before."

Lucy had a practised answer to this and it rolled out with all the ease of an old untruth oft repeated.

"The skin on my hands is damaged," she said. "Sensitive. I worked in a soap factory. The stuff, the lye, burned me."

"Lye sounds about right," said Rose, casting a sharp eye at her husband behind Lucy's back. "Yes, lye would do that. Poor girl."

"We shall have to see what else you can do," said Mr Pyefinch with a smile. "I'd say you've got hidden talents, Miss Falk."

"Sara," said Lucy, beginning to wish she hadn't lied about her name, or at least, if she had lied, that she'd chosen a completely made-up one: the name Sara Falk seemed too weighty, too well known or too obviously belonging to someone who actually existed for her to carry it lightly, as if she'd called herself Jack Spratt or the Duke of Wellington.

"We'll leave this to simmer," said Rose after she'd added vegetables and herbs to the pot. "Have it after the Drumhead."

"Drumhead?" Lucy said to Charlie.

"Showmen's Drumhead," he said. "Like a town meeting. All the showmen come together to discuss what's fair when something's been done, or has to be done."

What had been done, it transpired, was the whole business of Nellie the Educated Pig going berserk and one very expensive mirror having been smashed. Lucy sat at the edge of a great circle of light as the showmen hunched round a fire discussing it, painfully aware that the mirror in question was the one through which she had fallen.

The aggrieved party was revealed to be Na-Barno Eagle, Georgiana's father, and as he spoke Lucy was able to see him properly for the first time. He was a tall clean-shaven man with sad eyes, long grey hair and a nose of the proud and upturned variety, criss-crossed with broken veins giving it the unmistakeable rosy glow of the tap-room. He wore a suit of darkest velvet that had evidently seen better days but was cleverly patched and mended. His energy rose and fell like a flame, sometimes flaring, sometimes guttering as he told his side of the events, and she saw that whenever he looked about to topple over Georgiana was always at his side, watching and ready to help. The gist of his complaint was that someone had broken his mirror and he should be reimbursed for its loss.

There seemed to be several problems attending his claim. The first was the cost he ascribed to the mirror, which was generally opined to be much too generous. Secondly was the reason why his mirror was in the big tent, which belonged, along with the Educated Pig, to a Mr Huffam, rather than within his own smaller establishment.

"The mirror," he said, "was in Mr Huffam's tent by a prior arrangement. It is no secret that I am engaged to perform my illusions in a contest with the imposter Anderson in the near future. My own modest Temple of Magic being inadequate in size, I wished to practise a new effect away from prying eyes, an effect necessitating the use of my large and expensive looking-glass."

"He's all mirrors and smoke," whispered a voice in Lucy's ear. The hairs on her neck stood up because she knew from long experience that her senses were too sharp and permanently on guard for anyone to be able to get close to her without her being aware of it. She turned. It was Charlie, who had appeared silently out of the dark. He grinned, unaware of how he had disconcerted her. "Only he's slowing up and fumbling things on stage now he's getting older, I reckon. That's why he bought himself an automaton he doesn't know how to use properly, so a machine could manage the illusion and he'd just have to do the patter. He's still a talker, ain't he?"

Eagle was holding forth at the centre of the circle of fire-light, listing the various oppressions and difficulties he was beset by.

"I ask for no more than what is due me," he said, sweeping his arm around the ring of faces. "Is not such open-handed fair-dealing as vital to our lives as the very water we drink?"

"The only water Na-Barno drinks is that what Georgiana dilutes his gin with when he ain't looking," whispered Charlie.

"That's all well and good," said one of the showmen, "but you ain't got a clue who broke the thing, and no more nor do we. You just got to take it on the chin as an accident and write it down to bad luck."

General nods and grunts of assent followed this, and it seemed the matter was over, but Na-Barno turned on the man who had spoken, a finger jabbing into his face.

"You say bad luck, but I say bad intent. I have been prac-tised on. Ill-wishers have sabotaged me. Sabotaged, I say. And it is not the first time. My Mechanical Moor has been damaged, and now my great mirror lies in shards. I see Anderson's hand in this!"

"Careful, Na-Barno," said a showman. "You're amongst friends here, but that's a slander and you wouldn't want it finding its way back to Anderson's ears."

"Anderson can go hang," said Eagle. "And if any of his lackeys are within earshot, you may tell him I said that too!"

And with that he sat down with an impressive bump, so impressive that his momentum (and the gin he may well have imbibed) conspired to tip the chair backwards and pitch him heels over head on to the grass.

It was such a sudden fall from dignity that Lucy snorted in laughter an instant before everyone else burst out in merriment. It was unfortunate that she was so quick to laugh, because Georgiana Eagle caught it and fired a look of pure hatred across the fire at her as she bent to lift her father onto his chair with the help of two of the acrobats.

"I am glad that my misstep affords you all such merriment," said Eagle stiffly. "But laugh as you will at an old man tumbling in the grass; I will still have justice. The mirror was in Huffam's care; I do not like to say it but—"

"No, Barney," said Mr Pyefinch, speaking for the first time. "That's too rich. Don't come that one. Can't make old Huffam pay for doing you a favour and letting you use his tent for your rehearsals."

The general grumble of agreement which met this seemed to hit Eagle like a slap. His eyes goggled and his mouth worked, but nothing came out. He looked round and found Georgiana.

"You see?" he said. "You see, my child, the unkindness with which we are beset?"

This signalled the end of Eagle's claim, and the crowd rose and turned their backs on the fire as they walked away to their tents and wagons: disgust at Eagle's attempt to extract money from Huffam, who they saw as having done him a favour, was part of the reason, but the main part was that it had been a long day on the road and they knew tomorrow would bring an early start and more of the same. They now wanted nothing more than hot food, a warm blanket and then a good night's sleep.

Eagle himself tried to keep going, clutching at sleeves with rising desperation, attempting to keep people interested, but other than a few mildly apologetic chuckles and some pats on the back, he got nothing. He slumped in his chair by the fire. Georgiana strode against the flow of the thinning crowd like an arrow aimed right at Lucy.

"Georgie," began Charlie with a half laugh. "What—?"

"She laughed at Father," said Georgiana.

"Everyone laughed—" said Charlie.

Georgiana didn't break step, just marched right up to Lucy.

"Nobody laughs at the Eagles!" she hissed and slapped her face, hard.

Lucy felt the red sting on her cheek and didn't even have time to think: on reflex her fist bunched into a hard knot and she punched straight back. There was a sharp crack as the blow landed and a gasp and then Georgiana was flat out on the grass.

"And nobody hits me," said Lucy.

Georgiana looked more stunned by the sheer outrage of the counter-punch than the fist that had solidly connected just below her eye. Lucy could feel the dull ache in her knuckles and a breeze on her skin which seemed to tell her that she'd split the seam on the old gloves. She wasn't going to give the other girl the satisfaction of seeing her look down to check.

They glared at each other, neither moving for a long moment. Lucy saw Georgiana was quivering like a wild animal, ready to spring, though whether to fight or flee she couldn't tell. Then Georgiana's perfect lips curled back into something close to a snarl, revealing similarly perfect teeth clenched in fury.

"You'll regret that," she hissed. "Oh my. You'll regret that a lot."

She tossed her curls and spun prettily on her heel, striding away towards the slumped figure of her father alone at the side of the fire.

"She does like the last word," said Charlie. He watched the retreating figure, and then turned to Lucy.

"What?" she said.

"You punch like a boy," he said. "Where'd you learn that?"

"I didn't," she said. "I just do it."

"Most girls slap," he said with a grin.

"Do they really?" she said, trying to remember who had taught her to punch and finding another of those vertigo-inducing holes. "Let's go and have some rabbit stew."

They walked together towards the Pyefinches' wagon. Lucy saw him sneak a look back to the Eagles, who were huddled together talking. Eagle raised a hand to Georgiana's face and turned it to the light of the fire so he could see where she'd been hit. He looked back at them, and then quickly away.

"Georgie-girl'll have a right old shiner in the morning," said Charlie, sucking his teeth. "I'd say you made yourself an enemy there."

CHAPTER 43

A CHAIN BROKEN

Amos Templebane, London-born and London-bred, thrived on his new life in the countryside. The open spaces were like his dreams but bigger and wider and – when he lay on his back and looked up at the sky – deeper. In London there was always a wall somewhere close, and beyond the walls, people. And where there were people there was noise – not just the sound of talking or shouting, there was the incessant sound of their thoughts. Most of the time he could fade them into the background of his mind, and though he'd got better and better at it as he got older, the noise from other people's heads was always there even if it was a very quiet but constant sound, like the hiss of fire in the grate or the wind in the trees. And the noise meant that he was never alone.

In the country there were fields and hills and woods, and Amos felt bathed in greenness and silence. He walked the less travelled ways, the drovers' paths and the sheep tracks, keeping clear of the turnpikes and the high roads. When the food in the tinker's pack ran out, he found his way to a farm and was given more provisions in exchange for sharpening all the knives and trading a pair of tin canisters.

The only time he walked the high road was on the first

day, and he stopped when he came to a crossroads and was faced with the choice of going home to London in the south, or turning east or west. The road west was the least frequented, and he took it. At the time he could not have explained why he did so, but as he walked the countryside and felt himself getting stronger he knew it was because all that waited for him in the south was more of the life he had been trapped in, whereas the other directions offered the hope of freedom. They also contained no Templebanes.

Something had broken inside Amos. At first he thought it was because he had run away, because he had killed the murderous tinker, because he now bore the mark of Cain. He sat for several nights over lonely fires looking at the flames and thinking about this after long footsore days on the road. And then he took the tinker's sharp knife, his "snickersnee" and threw it into a weedy dewpond and walked away.

He had decided that what had broken was not anything good, not something he should feel guilty about, nothing to be mourned, regretted or lamented: what had broken, as cleanly and suddenly as the strap which had once held the Templebanes' "Mute but Intelligent" label around his neck, was a chain. He was no longer a prisoner manacled to his past. He did not belong to anyone but himself. He was free and answerable only to the future. And whatever it held, he swore he would never be chained or imprisoned again.

CHAPTER 44

THE LONG HAND

Sara was sitting quietly by the range, contemplating the soup bowl in front of her and even remembering to take a spoonful every now and then. Cook matched her silence, and though the atmosphere remained charged, a companionable quiet enfolded them as she prepared the crust for a large pie.

Sara was eating when it happened.

The spoon was halfway to her mouth when she flinched and cried out in shock. She dropped the spoon and half rose, slamming her hand onto the table to brace herself. The heel of the hand hit the lip of the bowl and it overturned, splashing hot soup into her lap.

She stood up on reflex, gasping again as the liquid burned her leg, the spoon clattering unheeded to the floor at her feet.

"My hand—!" she choked.

Cook had a wet dish-rag in her hand and was at her side in an instant, pulling the dress away from her leg and sponging the soup off it.

"Are you burned?" she said.

"My hand . . ." Sara repeated queasily, looking as if she might be sick at any moment. "Someone is holding it."

The shutters to the caravan had been closed for privacy, the coal had been quietly moved, piece by piece, and the trapdoor opened. The box had been removed and opened, and Sara's hand was indeed being held and examined by the light of a lantern.

"Now," said the voice. "How *do* you work?"

Sara's hand was put back in the box, which was plunged back into shadow as the person redirected the bull's-eye lens of the lantern to help as they rummaged in a drawer for something.

When the lantern was redirected onto the hand, the flash of light steel announced that they had found the sharp bodkin needle they had been looking for. The point of the needle was slowly pushed towards the hand, and then stopped an inch from the flesh as the hand itself moved.

"Hello," breathed the person. "What's this?"

The hand was moving. Not trying to escape this time, but doing something else entirely. Instead of crabbing blindly about the tight confines of the box and finding nothing but insurmountable sides, it was moving with a different but very obvious purpose.

Three fingers curled under the palm, leaving the index finger sticking straight forward like a pointer. The thumb stuck straight out at right angles to it like an outrigger, providing balance and a kind of lever to raise the hand enough for the index finger to have room to manoeuvre, which it began to do. It flexed and bent and the tip of the finger began to trace a repeating pattern on the floor of the box.

"What are you up to?" said the person, holding the light closer and bending low to examine the pattern. "What are you a-drawing?"

The finger repeated the pattern, slower and slower, as if trying to help the viewer.

"Letters," said the viewer. "You can do letters, by God."
The moving finger wrote and moved on.

"P . . . H . . . C . . . L . . . another P . . . H . . . C again
. . . V or is that another L? . . . P . . . doesn't make sense, no
sense at all . . . that's definitely H again . . . C, no it's not a
C!" the viewer gasped. "It's an E! . . . L . . . P . . . H . . . E
. . . L P . . . Help! By heavens you are spelling, aren't you,
my beauty?"

And they leant forward and patted the hand as if it were
a dog or other small animal that had just successfully
completed a trick.

"Well," said the voice. "If we can't make a bucket of money
from you, we can't make money from anything. You shall
be The One and Only Hand of Glory, my friend, shan't you
just?"

Sara sat at the table, braced against it with her one hand as
if the stump on the end of her other arm, which was stretched
out in front of her, might at any moment try and hurl her
to the floor. Her face was beyond pale, distinctly green around
the edges, and sweat was dropping from her forehead onto
the scrubbed white floor below.

Cook sat opposite her, crouched low and peering into her
face with great concern.

"Sara, whatever you are doing . . ."

"I am writing," said Sara from between clenched teeth.

"You are harming yourself."

"I am doing what I can," she panted. And then her face
twitched and she gasped again in surprise, but this time the
expression which flooded her eyes was one of relief. She
breathed in and allowed half a smile to twitch the side of her
mouth.

"What?" said Cook. "What happened?"

"Water," said Sara, her mouth dry.

Cook spun to the sink, filled a glass and put it in front of her. Sara chugged it down in one draught and then looked up at her. Something like her old self kindled in her face.

"They patted my hand," she said. "Someone patted my hand."

"They patted your hand," said Cook. "What does that mean?"

"It means they read my message. It means we can communicate!"

Before Cook could ask another question she took a deep breath and concentrated on her stump again. This time Cook could see it twitch and move in tiny increments as if Sara was sending nerve pulses out into the air.

"What are you writing?" she said.

"Don't talk," said Sara sharply. Then she smiled an apology. "This is hard. It feels like my hand is made of lead."

She concentrated for a minute and then exhaled. "I'm asking who they are."

"Who . . . are . . . you . . . ?" whispered the voice. "Who am I indeed? And who are you?"

The index finger on the hand stopped writing and tapped on the bottom of the box, as if demanding attention. After a pause it did it again, more insistently.

"Ah," breathed the voice. "Ah, no. I don't think we can have that. I don't think we can have that at all . . ."

With one hand they gently grasped the wrist of Sara's hand, stilling it, and with the other they reached for the bodkin.

Sara inhaled sharply and bit off a yelp of pain.

"What?" cried Cook. "What, girl? What happened?"

"Hurt," said Sara. Staring at her stump as if it had betrayed her. "Hurt."

"Come to bed, child," said Cook, reaching for her.

"I am not a child," snapped Sara. "And you are not my bloody nursemaid!"

Cook looked as if she'd been slapped. Indeed Sara had never in her life spoken to her in this sharp and unfeeling manner. She had certainly never heard her utter even the mildest swear-word, swear-words being as much Cook's particular and distinctively delimited preserve as her kitchen was.

"Well," she said. "Well. You are out of sorts. Sail your own course then."

Sara would not meet her eyes, perhaps because she knew there would be something close to tears in them, perhaps because she was still angry.

After a long silence, Cook sniffed and Sara spoke down into the table, very quietly.

"They are writing on my hand. I must concentrate."

Cook stared at the top of her head and saw Sara was quivering with the tension involved in focusing on what was happening to the absent hand.

Being a sensible if piratical Cook, she reached for the teapot and slid two cups onto the table between them. She poured them each a measure of tea and lightened it with some milk. Then she reached behind a crock of wooden spoons and spirtles and retrieved a black bottle out of which she glugged a large measure of whisky into each cup.

"Don't tell Mr Sharp," she grunted, and put the bottle back. When she turned and reached for her cup she was surprised to find Sara's hand waiting to take her own.

Sara's eyes were wide and apologetic, and in them Cook could see the heartbreaking shadow of the younger Sara, terrified by the Green Man she had found in her room almost a lifetime before.

"They wrote on my hand," she said. "I wrote, 'Who are

you?' and then they pricked me badly and then wrote, 'Your master.'"

"Sara," said Cook gruffly, squeezing the hand in hers.

Sara squeezed back and then let go in order to sit back and breathe deeply. She wiped something out of her eye and found a smile that was, in Cook's heart, even more heart-breaking than the ghost of the young girl she'd just glimpsed again. Sara took the teacup and took a good swig.

"I had hoped to tell them my name and ask them to come. I had hoped to offer a reward," she said. "But I do not think my hand is safe. I think it has fallen among evil people."

CHAPTER 45

THE ALP LOOKS AT THE MOON

The naked Alp looked up at the night sky, or what it could see of it through the dirty window. The pale wash of moonlight falling across its face flattened its habitually blank expression and made it seem even more than normally like a harmless and forgettable mask, a face devoid of everything except symmetry, lifeless and joyless – and guiltless. It was a face which few registered, and one that had the strange quality of erasing itself from the memories of those acute enough to notice it almost as immediately as it passed beyond their immediate vision.

It was naked because it drew calm from bathing in the moon's rays. The woman upon whose breastbone it was kneeling was not naked since the Alp's needs were not sexual. Her eyes were cloudy with gin and the influence the Alp had worked upon her, and her breathing was stertorous. The Alp noted with satisfaction that the waxing moon was a fraction off full. It had a rendezvous contracted for the night of the full moon, a contract that had brought it to this teeming city from the mountainous heart of Europe across the grey and contrary sea, and it did not intend to break that appointment since the consequences of so doing would be disastrous for the family it sprang from.

Satisfied that it had kept a good track of passing time, it looked down at the woman upon whom it knelt and concentrated. Pound by pound it made itself heavier by will alone so that it pressed more and more strongly on the thin ribs below its bony knees, licking its lips and preparing to lock its mouth over the woman's. It was no longer a hungry gesture since the Alp was no longer stealing breath for itself. Rather it was a business-like matter since the vigour it was storing up was for another.

It would have been less content had it known that half a mile away Hodge and Jed were patiently casting round in ever expanding circles as the terrier tried to recapture the distinctive scent of the Alp that it had memorised amongst the pigeon coops. They had been doing it almost without pause for more than three days, moving from rooftops to sewers in their methodical quartering of the city, Hodge's jaw set in a murderous clench of determination, while Jed and the Raven worked above and below him with no sign of tiring.

CHAPTER 46

ON WITH THE SHOW

The rhythm of life on the road suited Lucy well. The wagons and carts travelled from town to town and fair to fair, sometimes en masse, sometimes splitting off from one another as they diverted to smaller villages and hamlets along the road. From listening to the Pyefinches she learned that this progress around the country was an annual routine, and was in its own way as inflexible and predictable as the seasons themselves: just as spring led to summer and then winter, so the circuit that began the touring season at Reading led eventually to Lansdowne Fair at Bath, which in turn led to Bristol and Devizes and so on. They talked of this as a "circuit" because most of the showpeople overwintered in London and attempted to head back there before the bad weather and the snows made the journey treacherous.

She learned from Charlie that in the winter months the Pyefinches put up in a big yard attached to the "King Harry" public house in the Mile End Road and turned traders and costermongers until spring, repairing and improving their "show" in the long evenings, repainting their wagon and hoardings and planning new draws to attract the next year's customers. In the touring season, the big fairs were the main events where every showman would attempt to attend and pitch his tent, but between the hiring fairs at the start of the farming year and the harvest fairs at the end, there was plenty of time and space for individual showmen to branch off to try their luck at smaller opportunities like market days and local galas.

It was at one of these lesser festivals where Lucy got her first taste of the Pyefinches' show. After three nights on the road they arrived at a cheery little town tucked in a fold in the heathland at a point where the river they'd been following acquired a tributary. They arrived late, having spent all of a long and tiresome day on the road. They found a spot on the centre of a wedge of empty common bounded by river on two sides and the town on the third, and barely had time to water the horses before everyone was asleep.

When she woke in the morning, Lucy found that the field had sprouted tents and wagons while she slept, so that what had been a patch of bare land was now a canvas village all a-flutter with bright flags and pennants and gaudily painted frontages promising all the unimagined wonders of the world for a ha'penny.

It was a sight to make anyone smile, and Charlie told her to have a walk round "before the flats get here". Charlie divided the world into "flats", who were unwary simpletons or sheep to be shorn, and the enterprising "sharps" (in whose number he counted himself as one of the very keenest), who did the shearing. Lucy looked at Pyefinch and Rose, conscious that although she had provided rabbits on her first night, they had been feeding her ever since.

"Let me help you set up," she said.

"We can set up in a jiffy," said Pyefinch. "You can help later."

"You can help Charlie sell the rock," said Rose. "People'd rather buy from a pretty young lady than a half-washed raga-muffin."

"I have washed!" protested Charlie.

"Maybe," said his mother, pointing at his neck, "but you didn't stand very close to the soap."

Lucy left them to argue about Charlie's washing habits and walked through the small fair which had sprung up as she slept. She wondered if she might find a stall selling gloves as she had indeed split Sara Falk's when she had hit Georgiana, and though she had stitched them up they were old and already beginning to fall apart again. She did not want to find herself glinting by mistake and revealing herself to her new companions.

It was not only the sights and the colours and the variety of the attractions on offer that pleased the senses as she threaded her way through the temporary lanes bordered by wagons and tents, it was the smells: after three days on the road Lucy felt as if all the open air had washed through her and left her empty and ready to be filled with this new rich assault on her nose: underlying the clean smell of wood-smoke which always attended the camp there was the smell of new ale and cakes and boiling sugar and pies and cinnamon and roasting meat and spices whose names she did not know. It was a heady, holiday smell, and as with all holiday things it made her feel a little bit happy, which was not a normal state for her. A harassed latecomer was edging a wagon through the fair looking for a pitch and she stepped out of the thoroughfare into the gap between two tent sides to let him pass.

Alone and unseen among the guy-ropes, she allowed herself to pause in the middle of everything and stop, just closing her eyes so she could concentrate on drinking in the smells and the rising noise all round her as the first fair-goers were spotted by the barkers and patterers, who began pitching and counter-pitching the attractions of their rival shows.

It was an unguarded moment, and one she regretted the moment she opened her eyes.

Georgiana Eagle stood right in front of her, her eye still

blackened from Lucy's punch. Her face was unreadable. For a moment Lucy thought she was going to slap her again, and bunched her fist to retaliate.

Then Georgiana's face changed in an instant, like a lamp igniting.

"I'm sorry I slapped you," she said with a bright smile. "I find it so very hard when people laugh at Father, and you laughed first. I have a terrible temper."

She held out her hand.

"If you can forgive me, let us be friends."

She was, despite the black eye, which was now fading to mauve, perilously beautiful when she grinned. Her smile and her eyes seemed to dazzle Lucy and fill her head with such delight that there was almost no room for any other thought than just wanting to reach out and shake her hand and start a friendship.

Something stopped her and kept her hands at her sides.

It was her sense of self-preservation, and it was telling her to cancel the unbidden smile, which was even now trying to twitch up the edges of her mouth, and think.

"Why?" she said.

"Why?" echoed Georgiana. "Does there have to be a why? Is not friendship a good thing all by itself?"

"No," said Lucy. "It is dangerous. It is not something to be given unthinkingly."

Georgiana's brow crinkled, and she looked so suddenly hurt and betrayed that Lucy's fist twitched open and almost reached out of its own volition. She took a breath.

"But I am sorry for the shiner."

"Shiner?"

"It's Charlie's word for it. For the black eye."

Again Georgiana looked hurt and unsure of herself. Her hand fluttered up and smoothed the hair around her bruised cheek.

"You and Charlie have been talking about me?"

"No," said Lucy. "Yes. Just about me hitting you."

"Did you laugh about it?"

"No," said Lucy.

"You laugh at my father," said Georgiana, her face curdling back towards something cold and proud.

"No," said Lucy. "Why would we?"

"Because people do. You all do. But he is a genius and a good man," she said. "He is a kind man. He told me to seek you out and apologise for striking you. He said it was no way to treat a newcomer and a stranger."

Lucy didn't know what to say.

"Well," said Georgiana. "I have apologised. And Father says you are welcome to visit. Rabbits or no rabbits."

And with that, she turned an elegant heel and stepped quickly and daintily away down the canvas passage between the two tents, never looking down but still managing not to trip on any of the criss-crossed guy-ropes. Lucy watched her go, and when Georgiana turned the corner she felt as if something good had been taken out of the day.

"Rabbits or no rabbits, indeed!" snorted Rose later as she was filling Lucy's basket with rock for the third time since the pleasure-seekers had begun to pour into the fairground in serious numbers. Rose had made the rock the previous two evenings, boiling up damp sugar and peppermint oil over the camp-fire. Lucy had a lump of it in her mouth and didn't want to risk her teeth by trying to crunch it, so she just nodded. She hadn't found any new gloves but had decided to pocket the ones she did have and not wear them out whilst in the country so as to keep them as much as possible for villages and towns. There were certainly advantages to this new world of canvas and wood that she had fallen into, one being that the past didn't seem to lurk in wood or canvas the way it did in stone walls, and so she felt freer and more relaxed.

"That Barney Eagle don't miss a trick, for all that he's trying to drown himself in a sea of gin and tinctures," said Rose. "You get nothing from an Eagle that doesn't come at a price."

Lucy sucked on the rock and raised an eyebrow.

"Oh, I'm not saying Georgiana doesn't want to be your friend — I've never seen a girl who likes to be liked so much as she does — but the bit about the rabbits is the tell," said Rose.

"What's a tell?" said Lucy, transferring the minty lump to her cheek.

"It's a clue. Watch people close and they all got a tell, something they do when they're lying, or when they're uncomfortable, or when they're trying not to show they've been sneaking peppermint rock instead of selling it," grinned Rose, sticking her tongue inside her cheek and bulging it out in mimicry of Lucy. "Now get along and sell another basket. Barney Eagle's too lazy to trap his own rabbits and too keen to spend his money on drink to buy enough food for the pair of them. He was hinting that you should bring them some supper one of these nights. He's always used that poor girl like a bright little lure to draw people in. Same as he did with her mother, may she rest in peace. She had the dazzle and something of the glamour too, did Sally Eagle . . . and it's her passing that turned Na-Barno to the drink."

Her eyes had gone away into the past for a moment, and when they came back they saw Lucy looking at her.

"The glamour?" said Lucy.

Rose rubbed her hand over her face as if to clear her head. Lucy wondered if that was a tell, and if so what it meant. Rose shrugged as if it was nothing.

"Oh, glamour . . . glamour's just another word for beauty. Beautiful people catch the eye, and it's easy to lead others once you've caught them by the eyes," she said. "The rest of

us have to work for a living. Go sell some more lovely pepper-
mints!"

As she walked back into the open, which was now teeming
with people, Lucy thought about what Rose had said. She
was sure of two things: firstly, Rose had just lied about something to her, and though she wasn't sure what it was, it was
important. And then she thought about Mr Sharp's eyes and
the way the brown flecks in them seemed to tumble like
autumn leaves—

—and then a drunken ploughboy caught at her arm and
asked to buy some rock for his girl, and she put both thoughts
away in the back of her head and took his money with a
smile.

CHAPTER 47

THE HUNTER HUNTED

There is a phenomenon that all hunters of dangerous prey who stay long in the field become aware of eventually: a vague unease creeps in and – prompted perhaps by some horripilant tingling in the triangle between the shoulder-blades and the back of the neck – the hunter wonders if at some stage the roles have been reversed, and the prey he seeks has doubled back and is perhaps even now stalking him.

Hodge got this feeling as he walked carefully along the ridge of a roof above one of the nastier rookeries on the westernmost limits of the City. Even at this height, the smell was so bad that he wondered how Jed could possibly distinguish anything useful from the rich and varied stink, a noisome concoction of damp coal fires, rotting vegetables and raw sewage bound together by the underlying accreted funk of the hundreds of unwashed occupants of the ramshackle mess of dwellings below.

This jerry-built hotchpotch of buildings was crowded so close around the maze of alleys that at certain points they seemed to lean over them and drunkenly support one another. This kept light and fresh air out, and ensured that life at ground level took place in a permanently crepuscular miasma of shadows and stench which made it dangerous and unhealthy in equal degree, though the sullen and usually gin-soaked knots of corner-men lurking in the gloom contributed an extra level of threat to the unwary.

Jed worked the alleys, keeping his nose down and his head low to the ground. Hodge took the high ground, walking the roof ridges and gable ends with the ease of a practised urban mountaineer. He carried a small grappling hook which swung easily from his hand as he moved, and which was attached to a strong length of Manila rope. On the steeper pitches, he would lob the hook ahead, secure it and then pull himself onwards and upwards. He was sure-footed but he was not reckless, rather relying on the methodical and practical side of his nature, the one that balanced the berserker streak that also ran through him.

It was his methodical approach that kept him so relentlessly on the trail of the breath-stealer even though the scent was still lost to him and Jed. He had begun by circling the building the Alp had been in at a ten-yard radius, hoping to cross the trail. When that failed, he had painstakingly widened the circle and tried again and again. Failure had not dented his determination; rather it had bedded it in and strengthened his resolve.

Now he was patrolling a circle whose radius was almost a full mile and a half from the room in which he had discovered the dead baby, a wide sweep that brought him to both the roof ridge upon which he now stood, and the moment when he became aware that something or someone might be watching and following him.

He squatted in the lee of a crumbling chimneystack and made himself as still and as calm as he could. He wished the Raven was with him, but it had been decided to leave it watching the house on Chandos Place. If he had been able to use the Raven's eyes as it circled above, it would have been easier to spot if there was another person moving in tandem with him, keeping pace or perhaps closing in.

He slowed his breathing and let his eyes meander across the surrounding roofscape. He knew the easiest way to catch sight of something was not to look for it with the eye direct, but to allow attention to drift across a scene and catch any anomaly with the tail of the eye as it passed.

The irregularity of his current perch and the nearby slates and gables spread away on all sides before flattening out into more recognisable and uniform formations hinting at the wider streets and orderly squares beyond. Here and there, church spires jabbed through and pointed hopefully at the louring sky above, and far in the distance he saw the comforting swell of St Paul's dome. He did not see anyone following him or watching him.

"You're there though," he growled. "I can feel your damn eyes on me."

CHAPTER 48

THE MECHANICAL MOOR AND THE READER OF MINDS

When she had emptied her basket of peppermint rock, Lucy stuck her head into the tent where Mr Pyefinch was leading an enthralled crowd of rustic ladies and gentlemen through the heroic intricacies of the Battle of Waterloo while Charlie used a pointing stick and a cunningly rigged lantern to highlight the important points on the battlefield as he spoke.

It was Lucy's way not to look at what people wanted her to see, so she watched the audience instead, noting how Mr Pyefinch's words held their attention and how they all moved their heads in time with the insistent pointing of Charlie's stick, as if they were all on a string. They were deeply enthralled by the spectacle, and she decided to leave them to it and see what else the fair held by way of attractions. She'd kept a piece of peppermint rock in her pocket, and slipped it inside her cheek as she ducked out of the tent into what was now twilight.

She wandered between the attractions and the tents as if she didn't know where she was going, but her feet took themselves to Na-Barno's pitch as surely as if Georgiana Eagle had given her an invitation and then dragged her there. She saw a bright naphtha lamp throwing stark shadows across the façade, a cleverly painted canvas screen that was part pyramid, part Grecian temple and had a big eye in the centre from which radiated beams of light picked out in silver paint which sparkled in the lamplight. "THE TEMPLE OF MAGIC" was written across the foot of the pyramid, cleverly painted to look like it was incised in stone. At the doorway, which was closed by a crimson curtain, stood Na-Barno. He was wearing his suit of black velvet and a cape lined in scarlet satin, which he twitched and swirled as he encouraged the fair-goers into his entrance.

"Roll up, roll up, ladies and gentlemen! Do not tarry at the door, for while you make up your minds, others may step ahead of you and gain your valuable place in the Temple of Magic! Come and see the wondrous feats of your most humble servant and present interlocutor, Na-Barno Eagle, the Great Wizard of the South! Not to be confused with my pale imitator, the imposter Anderson, who calls himself the Great Wizard of the North, wretched fellow . . ."

The idea of his rival seemed to drain Na-Barno of some energy, but Lucy saw someone poke him in the back through the canvas walls of the tent, and he shook himself and rekindled the fire in his voice, launching into a practised avalanche of words as he addressed the passing crowd in a deep ringing baritone.

"Roll up and enter the Temple of Magic! Leave your preconceptions at the door, for once within you will see untold wonders and marvels, things you will be proud to tell your grandchildren about in the years to come: you will see a prodigious panoply of persiflage and prestidigitation! A chimerical conquering cornucopia of conjuration! An immense inchoate itinerary of illusion and impossibility! And you will be made mute, marvelling at the magnificent mind-reading mentalism masterfully manifested by my magically Mechanical Moor who will answer questions about the other world, the realm beyond the veil of life, questions only you and he know the answers to!"

The tent poked Eagle again, and he coughed and looked a little lost until he remembered something in his pocket which he reached for and then flung into the air.

There was a bang and a flash and a cloud of blue and red smoke, which jolted the crowd and allowed him to start declaiming again at the top of his voice.

"No matter how far you have travelled in the realms of gold, my good friends, or how many goodly states and kingdoms have you seen, never will you feel a wonderment so serene as when you see the Great Wizard of the South conjure silver to gold! Then you, pretty madam, And you, tall sir, will feel like some watcher of the skies when a new planet swims into your ken, or like stout Cortez when with eagle eyes . . ."

"Who's stout Cortez?" shouted a man standing by Lucy. "Who's stout Cortez when he's at home then?"

"He's a fat dago, don't be ignorant," said his wife, pulling him away into the entrance. "It's a poem."

Lucy walked beside them, going fast-but-slow as she did so, so that she entered the passage into the tent without really being seen and certainly not noticed enough to have to pay an entrance fee at the small window. She could hear Na-Barno, muffled now as he picked up the thread and carried on outside.

"Like fat— I mean like stout Cortez," he roared. "You will be like stout Cortez when he stared at the Pacific with a wild surmise, silent, upon a peak in Darien."

"What's a wild surmise?" mumbled the man beside Lucy as his wife rattled coins onto the narrow wooden ledge of the window.

"It's like a tame one, only not house-trained," said a man in front of him in the queue, and for a moment Na-Barno's pitch was drowned by the rumble of laughter in the narrow canvas corridor.

"Can't we go in?" said a voice. "I feel like a sheep in a fold, just before shearing."

"Been shorn already," said another. "Ha'pence to stand in a dark passage? I can do that at home!"

"Oooh, fancy!" said another voice. "Hark at her! She's got a passage. Must live in a palace!"

More happy rumblings, and as the crowd shifted in the dark, Lucy saw the shutter come down at the payment window. From its position, she realised that whoever had been sitting there taking the money was also the person who had been poking Na-Barno in the back and keeping him going. She assumed it had been Georgiana.

That assumption was quickly confirmed as she heard the sound of small bells being shaken close by. The crowd quietened itself to listen as the noise passed up and down the passage on the other side of the canvas.

"Ladies and gentlemen," said a deep woman's voice, somehow Georgiana's but lower. "Thank you for your patience in waiting here for one more minute. No one may enter the inner room of the Temple of Magic without the Great Wizard being in attendance to control the powerful forces penned within it. This is for your protection."

The crowd rumbled agreeably, rather liking the frisson of danger the voice was alluding to.

"As you wait, anyone wishing to ask a question of the Mechanical Moor should think of who they wish to contact and attempt to get a seat close to the stage. We would not like you to miss your chance of having your question answered, and a good seat will assure you of the Great Wizard's attention. We will open the doors to the inner sanctum in one minute exactly."

The crowd began to whisper to itself: Lucy heard people discussing with their friends or spouses in quiet voices whether they should dare to try and contact someone in the spirit

realm. "Ow about Grandmother? . . . What about our Jessie?
. . . Ask Jethro who he lent the good scythe to? . . . Don't
get Grandpa Watkins; he hated magic shows . . ." the various
voices said, some laughing nervously in the gloom.

The passage was ill-lit but not entirely dark, and as she
stood there, unnoticed, Lucy saw a brief shiny reflection of
one of the boxed candles on the other wall, and realised she
was looking at an eyeball peering at the crowd through a
small hole in the canvas.

She smiled at it, thinking it must be Georgiana, but at that
moment the doors at the end of the passage flung open to
reveal the brightly lit inner sanctum. The people flowed happily
from the dim tunnel into the auditorium, which was little
more than a small stage hung with black velvet curtains looking
out over ranks of thin benches arranged in front of it.

By the time Lucy got into the place, the seats had all been
taken and she had to find a space against one of the walls,
squashed between a fat boy who smelled of cabbage and a fatter
woman who breathed entirely through her nose in a series of
excited nasal wheezes, close-set eyes bright with anticipation.

"I hope he cuts someone in half," she said to the fat boy.
"I do so like it when they cuts a pretty lady in bits, though
they always have to go and put her together again . . ."

The lights dimmed suddenly, and the flares in front of the
stage brightened. Georgiana pirouetted on and swept her hand
towards the wings. She looked glorious, thought Lucy, her
bruising hidden by cunningly applied powder, her heart-
breakingly pale face and perfect eyes offset by a deep green
silk costume which showed off both her colouring and her
body to great effect.

"Whoar!" said the fat boy. "Whoar! If she ain't a pippin!"

The fatter woman reached behind Lucy and smacked his
head sharply.

"Shush now!" she hissed. "He's coming . . ."

"My lords, my ladies and my most welcome gentlemen," said Georgiana in a voice clear and sharp as cut crystal. "I give you Na-Barno Eagle, not just the Great Wizard of the South, but the greatest wizard in Great Britain itself!"

The crowd roared in good-natured approval, entering into the spirit of the thing, and began stamping their feet and clapping their hands in a rhythm that got slowly faster and faster and louder and louder until – at the very moment Lucy knew the rhythm would break – there was a bright magnesium flash and an explosion of white smoke revealing Na-Barno where a moment before Georgiana had been. It was quite as if she had instantly changed into him, for she was nowhere to be seen.

The crowd roared even louder and the show began.

Querulous and odd though he might have been at the Showmen's Drumhead, Lucy had to admit he was very different on-stage as he ran effortlessly through a series of tricks and turns. He made coins appear and disappear. He filled cups with water and then showed that they were empty. Then he made them rise into the air unaided. Then he poured water from an empty cup and filled a jug. Then he upended the jug and showed it was still empty. Then he made the jug turn into a pink sugar mouse which he gave to a little girl on the front row. He did not cut anyone in half, but he did lay Georgiana on a plank between two sawhorses, and then remove sawhorses and plank, leaving her floating in the air, so wholly that he was able to demonstrate the fact she was not supported by anything other than his "power" by passing one of his juggling rings round her from feet to head and back.

In fact it all went superbly until he reached behind himself and whipped the cover off the magical Moor and commanded him to "Wake and hold open the veil between this world and the next!"

For a moment nothing happened, and the crowd stared at the torso and head which Eagle had revealed. The Moor wore a sky-blue turban with a large spangled brooch on it and a crimson jacket, brocaded in gold and sewn with brilliants which sparkled in the glow of the footlights. He bent forward as if looking at his hands resting on a board in front of him.

The board was angled so that the crowd could see it, and inscribed with the letters of the alphabet, in gold against a black background. Additionally the words "YES", "NO" and "IT IS HIDDEN" and "I MUST REST" were written around the edge of the alphabet. The Moor's hand pointed at "I MUST REST".

"AWAKE, MIGHTY ONE!" shouted Eagle, putting his hand on the Moor's shoulder.

There was a slight metallic click, and then, as he removed his hand, the Moor's wooden head slowly began to tilt backwards so that it was looking at the audience, or would have been if its eyes weren't still shut. It was a black face, cunningly sculpted to give a sense of haughty power, totally unrelieved by colour except for the lips, which were a startling crimson.

"AWAKE!" bellowed Eagle.

The room was silent, everyone holding their breath. The Moor's head came to a stuttering halt, seemingly stuck as it kept ticking back and then meeting some resistance and dropping a fraction forward again.

"He's resting," whispered a voice in the crowd. "Just like my broken mangle's resting."

And just as a suppressed titter began to spread out in the darkness, Eagle touched the shoulder of the Moor once again, and the head jerked and the eyes flew open revealing a flash of white as the jaw flopped, revealing lifelike teeth, made from bone, and the shiny red cavern of the mouth beyond.

The audience gasped.

The Moor's finger moved jerkily and rested on the "NO".

"No!" cried Eagle with what Lucy thought was an overly naked show of relief. "He is not resting! See, he has said so, and his eyes are open! Who has a question to tax the ancient wisdom and unparalleled perception of my friend?"

Before anyone could answer, the Moor started to judder, his eye blinking faster and faster in counterpoint to his mouth, which began to open and close with increasingly loud snapping noises.

Someone sniggered, and Eagle waved his hands and gamely made as if this was an expected part of the show.

"He senses a presence!"

The head now began to rock backward and forward, and the whole effect would have been tragically like someone having a fit had it not been for the growingly humorous spectacle of the large turban slowly slipping drunkenly over the Moor's face. Eagle's hand darted out and caught it before it fell to the ground.

"A . . . er, an oppressive presence," he cried. "The Moor is reacting to the presence of an ill-wisher who is upsetting the mystic balance in the room! Who is it? We must ask you to leave . . ."

At that, there was a snapping noise and the head of the Moor swivelled sideways, the eyes stuck wide open and the mouth snapped shut.

To Lucy's horror, the Moor's finger rose off the table and pointed inexorably at her.

A cold shudder went down her back as the wooden face stared in unblinking, silent accusation.

Lucy was a survivor, and what she did next she did on instinct, without conscious thought: as heads turned and eyes started trying to pierce the gloom and see what or who the automaton was pointing at in the shadows at the edge of the tent, she went slow-but-fast and slipped behind the backs of the crowd and moved a good ten feet away before stopping.

And so it was that the crowd focused its displeasure on the fat boy who had been standing next to her.

"Oi, fatty!" shouted a cheery voice from the darkness. "What's your game?"

"It's not me," he squawked. "I done nothing!"

"He looks like an ill-wisher!" shouted another. "Wishes ill to every pie he meets!"

The crowd laughed and hooted as the boy's face reddened into a pretty exact impression of a beetroot. Lucy, with her habit of looking in the direction other people weren't, saw Eagle take advantage of the distraction to throw the cover back over the Moor and look beseechingly off to the side of the stage.

In a moment it was clear that he had been looking for Georgiana to rescue him, for she appeared from the wings, walking solemnly, as if in church, with her eyes shut. The crowd hushed itself, drawn by her blind silence as she moved inexorably to the edge of the stage.

"She's gonna fall off!" whispered a woman beside Lucy. But she didn't. She stopped with her foot hovering over the drop, and then, without opening her eyes, stepped back and stood quite still.

"Quiet please, ladies and gentlemen," said Eagle in an urgent voice. "The spirit of the Moor has taken refuge in this, the frail vessel of my only daughter. It has done so to protect itself against ill-wishers as it has done before . . . but my friends, if you will ask your questions, perhaps the Moor will speak through her!"

Georgiana's eyes began to agitate behind her closed lids and her head began to wobble slightly. Eagle leapt forward and placed his hand on her head.

"Oh great mage!" he cried. "Will you speak through this fair girl?"

The fair girl's eyes opened and stared at Eagle. Her mouth

opened and out of it came a deep, guttural man's voice wholly at odds with her delicate looks.

"*Vaig a parlar amb vostè, fort mag,*" she rumbled, the voice seeming to come from the bowels of the earth, "*a través d'aquest bonic vaixell!*"

"I will speak for you, mighty wizard," translated Eagle, his eyes wide with excitement as he looked out at the crowd. "Through this beautiful vessel!"

The crowd oohed appreciatively. Eagle turned back to Georgiana.

"And will you let her speak in her own voice?" he asked. "So the ladies and gentlemen here assembled can partake of your great wisdom?"

Georgiana's eyes raked the crowd haughtily, and then she gave one decisive nod.

"*Si!*" she boomed. "*Deixi que és així!* Let it be so."

The contrast between the rough man's voice and her gentle tones could not have been greater, or delighted the audience more. Lucy saw them nodding and leaning forward in their seats.

"Who has a question?" said Eagle.

No one wanted to be the first to raise their hand, though there was a good deal of muttering and nudging. Eagle pointed at a man in the audience.

"You, sir – do you have a question?"

It was the man who had been encouraged to enquire about the whereabouts of a scythe. His wife giggled and nudged him.

"You have lost something perhaps?" said Georgiana, her blindfolded head casting about, as if trying to catch a scent.

"Er, well," mumbled the man, clearly unhappy at being the centre of attention.

"Don't say anything!" commanded Eagle. "The Moor will tell you what you have lost, and where it is!"

Eagle turned to Georgiana and gently pointed her towards the man.

"Great Moor, can you tell him exactly what he has lost?"

The tent was quiet as Georgiana reached an open hand out towards the man, as if feeling for him in the air.

"It is a tool," she said.

The man nodded.

The crowd saw this and murmured appreciatively.

"It is a sharp tool. I see a blade which has been honed many times," said Georgiana.

The crowd looked at the man, who nodded again. The crowd murmured more loudly and looked back to Georgiana.

"It is a not a knife," she said.

The man shook his head. The crowd held its breath.

"It is not an axe," she said.

Again he shook his head. The crowd held on.

"It is . . ." she said. "It is . . ."

Her hand kneaded the air once again.

"It is a scythe," she said.

"Yes!" said the man, and the crowd roared with appreciation. Hands slapped him on the back as if it was he who had got something right, and others applauded Georgiana.

Lucy could not work out how Georgiana had done it. Even if she had overheard the man's wife in the passage before the show began, how had she identified him in the dark both then and now, when she was blindfolded? It didn't make sense.

"Your scythe was not lent. Your scythe was stolen by a tinker who came past your house while you were away seeing someone called Jed. No. Jethro. You were seeing someone called Jethro and the tinker saw your scythe and took it," said Georgiana. "Am I right?"

The man looked at his wife, mouth open in shock.

"How'd she know about Jethro?" he said wonderingly.

"Bloody tinkers," said his wife.

"Am I right?" repeated Georgiana more insistently.

"Yes," said the man, "I lost my scythe and thought it was Jethro who had lent it to someone, but he died afore I could ask. But I got no blessed idea how you know that!"

The crowd burst into a round of spontaneous applause. Lucy agreed with the man: she had no idea how Georgiana had known all that either unless she really could read minds.

Which was impossible.

But only impossible in the way that her glinting was impossible. So perhaps Georgiana had a similar ability which she used to help her father pull off these mind-reading tricks, the trick of course being that it wasn't a trick. Only impossibility. Or rather, only an impossibility for a natural person. For someone with what Sara Falk had called supranatural powers, perhaps not so very hard at all . . .

And this, she thought, might be the reason she had such a strange feeling when she was around Georgiana. Perhaps the frisson she had felt, the strange mixture of excitement and caution, was simply the result of like calling to like, blood to blood, a conversation taking place beneath the level of actual thought.

And if she could read minds, Lucy wondered, would she perhaps be able to read hers? Because if she could and would, and if Lucy could trust her enough to let her in – another big question – then could she perhaps help her fill in the worrying blank spots in her memory? With that in mind, Lucy settled back into the shadows and watched closely as Georgiana proceeded to read more minds and bring more messages from the other side.

CHAPTER 49

A MOSAIC OF DESPAIR

Mr Sharp stared down at hundreds of shards of broken glass. In them, as in a fractured mosaic, he saw pieces of himself looking back, haloed by the bright gas lamps of the Red Library. He looked tired. He looked worried. He looked, in fact, exactly what he felt like – fractured, damaged and not entirely himself.

Emmet's dark head swung into view over his shoulder, multiplied in a hundred miniature reflections. Mr Sharp turned and saw that the clay man was holding another tiny sliver of glass, and was looking for somewhere to place it.

They had finished cleaning the room, collecting all the fragments of the broken mirror from inside the Murano Cabinet, and had begun painstakingly to grade them by size and shape, laying them out on the newly cleared tables in the centre of the library. Mr Sharp intended to order the splinters in such a way that it would be easier to reconstitute the broken mirror piece by piece.

That was the plan.

Looking down at the assorted shards, he wondered, not for the first time since they had begun, if he was becoming as distracted as Sara. Perhaps, he thought, this was a kind of madness.

Emmet laid his jag of mirror on the table and went to fetch another piece. Mr Sharp knew Emmet never needed to sleep or rest, and somehow the thought of the golem working slowly and methodically until the job was done gave him hope.

The door creaked, and Cook looked in. Her eyes widened as she took in the nature and scale of the project they were involved in.

"What *exactly*," she said with a dangerous pause in the middle of the phrase, like someone carefully cocking the hammer on a perilously hair-triggered gun, "are you doing?"

"What you see," replied Mr Sharp shortly.

"This is no time to be playing at jigsaws," Cook said.

Mr Sharp and Emmet carried on with their painstaking sorting of the shards.

"You cannot mend glass," said Cook, an edge creeping into her voice.

Mr Sharp would have much rather she had not burst in on him while his project was so close to its infancy and looked so obviously unfinishable. He would have preferred it if it hadn't been so obvious what he was planning to do. Her disapproval was not going to change his mind, but it would lend a strain to the next few days that he and the whole house could have done much better without.

"You cannot mend a broken mirror," she insisted. "No more than you can unroast a chicken. When a chicken is roasted, it's roasted. When a mirror is broken, it's done for. You may as well go to the glazier and order new glass, though why you see fit to mend the cabinet when there is so much else that is more pressing and demanding of our time, I do not know."

He pointed at the interior of the cabinet, one side silvered with the surviving mirror, the other showing the wood where the glass on the table had once been intact.

"If I put a new mirror in there, it will not hold the pathway that Lucy took out of here," he said. "This old glass holds the resonance of that."

Cook shook her head slowly at him.

"You cannot do what you are planning. Since the Disaster we have forbidden it, and for good cause."

He said nothing. There was little reason to engage in an argument when his mind was fixed.

Cook's eyes had been judging tough characters from before he had been born, and the look she scoured over him told him that and much else besides, little of it at that moment to his credit.

"Well. You are stone mad," she said decisively. "And I won't have it."

"And I won't discuss it," he said.

They stared at each other.

"All right," she said. "We'll see what the others have to say about that."

The door bounced on its hinges as she stormed out.

Emmet carried on methodically sorting the glass. Mr Sharp continued for a few minutes, until the uncharacteristic flush of colour had left his cheeks and his breathing had calmed to normal. Then he stepped away from the table.

"I will return soon," he said. Emmet nodded slightly, so slightly that even one as keen-eyed as Mr Sharp wondered if he'd imagined it.

He found Cook in the kitchen, furiously stabbing the range with a poker, riddling the coals in the grate back to fiery life.

"If there's another way," he said, "tell me and I will gladly follow it. But there isn't."

She continued to gore the fire with the poker. Her face was red in the glow from the blaze she had reignited, and her eyes were bright. Mr Sharp reached in and gently removed the poker from her hand.

"She's dying," he said quietly.

Cook shook her head violently.

"She's strong," she said. "She's always been strong, even when she was little . . ."

"She's strong, but she's dying," said Mr Sharp loudly, as if the only way he could express such a painful thought was to get it out in a burst. "You heard Wayland say it. And losing her hand has somehow accelerated it. Without her heart-stone she dies inside . . ."

". . . a little more each day . . ." said a voice from behind them.

It was a quiet interruption but it silenced them both. They turned as one to see Sara Falk standing in the door behind them. Her lips, usually healthily red against the pale cream of her skin, were now bloodless and white. In contrast, her normally flawless complexion was now bruised with dark half-moons beneath her eyes. She was holding on to the door-handle with her remaining hand, just as an invalid might lean lopsidedly on a cane, one shoulder hunched higher than the other. It gave her the look of a broken marionette, or someone expecting a blow from above. Her stump was bound across her front in a scarlet shawl fastened like a sling. Her smile was so clearly an act of will that it hurt to see it.

"And then one day she'll be hollowed out, and whoever she is won't be her any more," she continued. "Oh, she'll walk and talk and may indeed cry and gibber, she may sit in the corner dribbling for decades, but she won't be Sara Falk ever again. She'll just be the madness that echoes round the void inside her."

"Miss Falk," said Mr Sharp stepping forward, feeling he had to stop her, had to say something or else himself cry out in wordless pain. She waved him back, as if all this was nothing, as if her bravado came at no cost.

Her smile was replaced by a grim seriousness as she looked at them both.

"The truth is that my heart may pump for years. But I, as I, as Sara, will be dead. And if you do not face up to that and act on it, The Oversight itself will fail. You know that."

"Sara," said Cook, pulling out a chair. "Sit down."

Sara stepped away from the door and stumbled. Mr Sharp moved fast to catch her and led her by the elbow to the chair. She nodded her thanks, for a moment unable to speak. She wiped her eyes and took a deep breath.

"We are the Last Hand: The Smith, Hodge, you two and I," she said as if explaining things to a child. "If I cannot be myself the five of us become the four of you, and four is not enough for a Hand."

"Stop," said Mr Sharp. "Please."

"No. Let me finish. I have to say this and if you keep fussing over me I shall not be able to," she said. "Without a Hand, the Wildfire cannot be contained and The Oversight must be disbanded and the remains of you dispersed to the four corners of the wind to search for recruits to form a new Hand. Maybe that has to happen. It has happened before. Or maybe our time is finally come; maybe the darkness bleeds in from the edge of the world and wins. But if it does, it will not be because we were stupid, or weak, or sentimental about the truth. I am dying, dying as a useful member of the Free Company if nothing else, and I must be replaced . . ."

"You know that The Smith could not find any willing to join our ranks," said Mr Sharp.

"We are tainted by the Disaster," said Cook. "A generation later and no one forgives us for those who were lost."

"Betrayed," said Mr Sharp.

"Betrayed and lost," said Cook.

"Killed," said Sara. "Use a plain word for a plain deed. They were betrayed and killed. And no. That is not what they do not forgive us for. They do not forgive us for surviving."

She started pushing herself to her feet, waving off the hands reaching out to help.

"I do not regret surviving," she continued. "And I feel no guilt. We survived through luck. That is all. Fate dealt us better cards than our friends and forebears, and in their memory I will play them as well as I can."

She stood straight and stretched, scowling at the effort it took. A tear had leaked from one eye, and she reached for it with her stump, forgetting she had no fingers there to brush it away quickly and hide it. She stopped and used the other hand. It was an uncharacteristically clumsy gesture, her body's memory of itself fooling her conscious knowledge of her injury. Mr Sharp winced at it.

"Why the loss of a hand should make all my bones ache I do not know," she said through a tight smile. "I am going to lie down for a while."

"Let me help," said Mr Sharp.

"No," she said. "I do not need help moving around my own house. Not yet."

They let her sway unaided to the backstairs, the ones down which she had once fallen running away from a Green Man who had stepped out of a child's nightmare, and silently watched her hoist herself back up towards her bedroom by the banisters, her back stiff with the effort of not making it look hard.

When she had gone, Cook took the bottle from behind the spoons, placed two glasses on the deal table and poured them both a jolt of amber liquid. She drank hers in one, grimacing at the warm burn as it went down her throat. Mr Sharp drank half of his and looked at the remnant as if he expected to see an answer to his dilemma swimming in the depths.

"More?" asked Cook, pointing the bottle at him.

"No, thank you," he said. "I'm still assessing the damage of that last mouthful. What was it?"

"Medicinal waters," she said. "Waters of life."

"Whisky," he scowled, and finished his dram with a decisive movement. "No wonder almost so many Scots come south to escape it. Thank you."

He handed back the glass.

"I have never seen her cry before," he said.

"She is flesh and blood," she said.

"I do know that, my dear Cook, I assure you."

"And yet . . . ?" she said, watching the tight stretch of his coat across his shoulders.

"And yet. I do not choose to see her . . . dwindle in this excess of distress," he said. "I will not see her diminished so in her own eyes. I will not . . . allow it."

"She wants you to find a replacement for her. She wants you to keep The Oversight alive."

"We agree on the need to protect The Oversight. Where we disagree is on method."

"We need another member, Mr Sharp. For the Hand. We need many more members for other Hands. But we must at least have the Last Hand intact," she said.

"Not if Sara Falk is healed," he said. "Then the Last Hand will survive and we can build on that."

"Her hand and ring are gone," she said.

"Then I shall find them."

Her eyes rolled to the ceiling, where there happened to be a cutlass hanging from a hook next to a milk pan. She looked as if she wanted to grab it and start flailing around with it in frustration: instead, she stabbed a blunt finger at him.

"In this of all moments, when reality needs to be faced, you the ever careful, the ever cautious choose to be fanciful and quixotic! It is not enough that Hodge seems consumed by a death-wish, out in all weathers, hunting this breath-stealer he has become obsessed with, and so all but lost to us as a useful member of The Oversight! Sara's poor hand is lost in the mirrors. It could be anywhere in the world where two mirrors face each other. It could be in Manchester or Munich or Macau! You'd have an easier time finding a needle in a thousand haystacks."

"Finding a needle in a thousand haystacks is not impossible. It is merely very, very hard," he said with a thoroughly provoking display of calmness under fire.

"And time-consuming!" she roared, slamming the palm of her hand onto the scrubbed pine with enough force to make the glasses jump in the air and fall on their sides. Mr Sharp caught one as it went over the edge.

"And while I know you think you can do very, very hard things, Mr Sharp, even you cannot make more time!"

He placed the glass he had caught carefully back on the table and straightened it.

"I am sworn to protect her. I swore that before I was admitted into the Free Company. I cannot do otherwise. If I break my honour to save the Hand, then I am as useless to it as if I were an enemy. I would be creating a false Hand, with rot at its core. And that would lead to another Disaster, worse than the one that nearly destroyed us last time. I will go into the mirrors."

She shook her head.

"You will die in the mirrors."

He shrugged.

"You must all follow The Smith's plan and bury the Wildfire and the treasures beneath the Thames. And I can do nothing other than what I must, old friend. If I am not true as my blade is true, I am nothing. Might as well be a Sluagh . . ."

CHAPTER 50

NA-BARNO'S HAND REVEALED

The crowds had melted away, and the showmen had shut up their stalls for the night. Those who had not gone to bed, wearied at the long day they had passed entertaining the public and lightening their pockets and purses, sat around camp-fires passing bottles between them and amusing themselves by telling old stories and new lies to each other.

Na-Barno Eagle did not join any of these fire-lit pools of conviviality. He sat in the cramped quarters of his own cart, warmed by the meagre glow from the small travelling stove in the corner. He was staring out of the door at the Temple of Magic. Georgiana sat on the narrow bed holding the moneybox with the day's takings on her lap. She watched him turning the bottle in his hand as he stared murderously at the tent which hid the treacherously broken automaton that had so nearly spoiled his show and damaged his reputation.

"Father—" she began.

"No," he said decisively. "No, my angel, it's no good. It's broken. The damned mechanism is broken. I was told it was robust, by God I was, but it is not robust. It is skittish and over-delicate and wholly unsuitable for transportation. I was sold it in the clear understanding that it would exceed the abilities of the damned imposter Anderson's automaton, but all I have beggared myself to acquire is a frozen piece of useless clockwork which is wilfully unmoving. I have been betrayed yet again."

"The people enjoyed my mind-reading, Father," said Georgiana. "And the communication with the spirits went off very prettily . . ."

"You seek to ease the pain of disappointment in my heart, dear child, but there is only one kind of spirit that can give me solace and that is within this bottle," he said, holding up the green flask. "And it will only numb me for the night. Tomorrow I shall wake and still be beset by all my enemies and betrayers. And I will still have the prospect of facing the braggart Anderson and being grossly humiliated in public for what will no doubt be the last and fatal time, for who could endure such public ignominy and still perform? And if I do not perform we shall not eat, and if we do not eat, well, it is sure that we will waste away and die . . ."

He threw himself back in his chair and swigged a great mouthful of tincture, eyes wet with self-pity.

"But, Father," said Georgiana, smiling brightly. "All is not lost. What need we with an automaton when I can perform our mind-reading? For am I not more pleasing to look at than any old wooden effigy? Do I not have vivid charm and a bright and compelling presence? All is not lost!"

"Our mind-reading?" said Eagle, lip curling bitterly. "Our mind-reading is a trick that happily bedazzles and amazes dull rustic minds who exercise their thinking capacity little more than watching one foot follow the other behind a plough. Anderson spends his days thinking and concocting illusions of his own. His mind is not dull. It is like a scimitar! It is sharper than a Turk's razor. He is the very devil incarnate, but he is no fool!"

"But you are clever too, Father, as am I!" Georgiana cried. "We can polish and extend my mind-reading . . ."

His hand snapped out and grabbed her wrist. She gasped at the unexpected fierceness of his grasp.

"Your mind-reading?" he spat. "What makes you think it is yours? It was your mother's first, and before that . . ."

He looked away.

"Father?" she said.

"Before that it was someone else's."

"Whose?" she said.

He exhaled slowly.

"When I rescued your dear dead mother from her previous life of bondage and abuse, she did not come empty-handed."

"But whose trick was it?" said Georgiana, her eyes bright.

"It was . . . some other magician. She was his assistant. Her family travelled the same circuit as he did, and when his wife became dropsical, he arranged for your mother to assist him in her stead for a season."

"So . . ." began Georgiana.

"So it is a known routine amongst the fraternity. So imagine if we were to have done the act tonight in front of Anderson, as I shall have to face him in two weeks' time. When the flats and yokels marvelled so that you knew the clod had lost his scythe, up he would have jumped and with his look of bumptious conceit he would have cried out to the crowd, 'Stop! Let me show that the only true illusion here is that Eagle and his daughter have any powers, for this is but a cheap and easy trick to pull off! When you were penned in the passage muttering to one another, you were being listened to! And you, sir, did you not perhaps mention a scythe?' And when the clod concurs, someone still favourably disposed to us might pipe up quickly, 'But she can still not have known who the talker was!' and then he will stand even taller, positively about to burst with self-satisfaction and explain our code: 'Did the imposter Eagle not say, "Great Moor, so can you tell him exactly what he has lost?"' he will boom, and they will nod and agree, and then he will say, 'Observe the first letters in the phrase following "Great Moor" – "so can you tell him exactly": "so" is S, "can" is C, "you" is Y, "tell" is T, "him" is H, "exactly" is E, spelling what word?' And then he will have them in the palm of his hands and they will roar the answer 'SCYTHE' and we will be exposed and objects of ridicule. Ridicule I say, and I will brook no man laughing at me!"

He threw himself back in his seat with such a velocity of despair that it cracked ominously as he stared at the ceiling of his wagon.

"Nor I, Father," said Georgiana, sitting down, her face pale. "Nor I."

He dropped his eyes and found hers, and for a long moment they both stared at each other as if they had noticed something for the first time. Eagle broke the gaze and looked away first.

"So we are to be ruined?" said Georgiana. "You accepted this duel with Anderson thinking you had the better weapon, and now know that to be false."

He nodded and took another murderous swig from his bottle.

"Well," she said, shaking the moneybox. "We have tonight's money so we may eat a while longer. And where there's life, there's always hope."

"And where there's hope, there's always a great candle-snuffer hovering over it ready to extinguish it just as it flares brightest," he sighed.

Georgiana slapped him.

He was so shocked that he froze completely, not even having the wit to resist, and she leant in and took the green flask from his hands. "You struck me," he said, his lip quivering like a child's.

"No, Father. You were befuddled," she said. "I struck the fuddle, not the man. If we are to avoid ruin, we must be clear-headed."

"I do not wish to be clear-headed," he sobbed.

"And I will not have you fuddled," she said, keeping the bottle out of reach. "You do not talk when the bottle is on you, and you do not answer anything."

"I am answering for everything," he wept. "I am answering for my life with my life."

"And mine?" she asked. "Must I answer for your life too?"

"No, child," he whispered hoarsely. "No, you should be spared that unnatural punishment at least."

The fire crackled weakly and for a while was the only sound in the narrow space as they both contemplated their joint and separate futures.

"What else have you not told me?" she said.

"About your mother?" he asked. "About Anderson?"

"That's dead news and the past won't help us," she said. "What have you found?"

"What, my child?"

"You have found something you have not told me about. I have heard you talking to it. I have heard you weep and call it our salvation. If it is salvation, I should like to see it," she said.

He shook his head wildly.

"I cannot tell you. I must not. I cannot—"

"Why?"

"Because . . . because it is something I do not understand. I found it on the night my beautiful mirror was broken. I found it scuttling blindly across the floor."

"It," she said. "It is an animal?"

"No," he said, his mouth opening and shutting as if he were a frog and the words he could not find were flies he was trying to pluck out of the air.

"What is it?"

Eagle shook his head and stood abruptly. He rubbed his face and grimaced.

"I call myself a magician . . ." he began.

"A wizard," she said. "A great wizard."

He nodded appreciatively.

"But you, my beautiful child, know I am merely a conjurer. An illusionist."

"Merely the best in the country," she said.

He smiled weakly and felt his cheek where she had slapped him.

"You are a loyal girl, even when you strike your own flesh and blood."

"It was necessary," she said.

He nodded.

"I have travelled the length and breadth of this island for two decades, and I have seen things. More than seen: I have sometimes felt things, sensed them."

"Things?" she said.

"An edge. A pit. A darkness. A shadow," he said.

She looked deep into his wet eyes.

"I think you are still befuddled."

He shook his head again, and then, as if the effort of talking and standing at the same time were suddenly too much for him, he sat back down and looked at his boots.

"What I mean is that though I face the crowd and perform in the bright glimmer of our footlights, I have sometimes felt I was alone and performing with my back to a great void, and that the void contained things that I knew nothing of other than the clear sense that they were watching me and laughing. They were laughing because they controlled the real magic which I was merely counterfeiting."

He looked up at her.

"I am the clearest-eyed man alive when it comes to spotting

the mechanics of an illusion. Even the fastest and most limber-fingered card conjurer cannot elude me. But sometimes I have caught things with the tail of my eye that I cannot explain. What I found in that tent, what I found then . . ."

"You cannot explain," she said.

"I think it comes from that darkness. And no, I cannot explain it." He was racked by another sob. "Unless I am run mad . . ."

She put her hand on his shoulder and leant forward until barely a foot separated their eyes, his wet, hers dry and unblinking.

"Am I mad, Father?"

"No."

She stood back.

"Then show me. And I will be the judge."

He pointed quaveringly at the coal box.

"It is under the coal. In the secret place. In a casket."

"What is it?" she said, beginning to move the coal out of the way.

"It is a hand," he said. "I have been trying to see how it works."

"A hand?" she said.

"A *Manus Gloriae*. A Hand of Glory. A hand with a mind of its own, that moves as if alive."

She looked back at him as she moved the coal.

"And would that not be a greater trick than a wooden automaton?" she said. "Anderson does not have a Hand of Glory!"

She revealed the false bottom to the box and removed the casket. She held her hand out for the key without looking back, and he slipped it into her hand.

A moment later they were both hanging over the casket as he opened the top.

"Your hand is shaking, Father," she said.

"I am . . . scared," he said. She reached past him and pulled the top open.

Sara Falk's hand lay in the bottom of the box, unmoving. They both stared at the black leather of the glove and the two rings that caught the firelight and reflected it back at them. Georgiana looked less than impressed.

"Are the rings gold?" she said.

"I had not wondered," he replied.

"Well," she said, "the rings have value. We can sell them. I do not know for the life of me why you did not wonder . . ."

"I did not wonder because the rings were quite the least remarkable thing about the hand," he said.

"It is just a cadaver's hand," she said with a shrug, clearly believing her father to have imagined anything more than that while in a "fuddle". "It is gruesome enough, but—"

"You have not seen it move," he said.

And he leant past her and jabbed the hand. It spasmed and flopped, then tried to scuttle into the corner of the box, where it scrabbled at the walls. Georgiana stared at it, eyes wide.

"Is it some kind of ingenious clockwork?" she breathed.

He grasped the hand and unbuttoned the glove at the wrist, displaying the pale skin beneath.

"Feel it," he said.

She reached her fingertips forward and touched the skin, tentatively at first, then – when the hand didn't try and grab at her – more boldly.

"It's flesh," she whispered. "Warm flesh . . ."

He stabbed a pin neatly into it, and held it tight as it convulsed in protest. He pointed at the red bead that appeared at the puncture point.

". . . and blood," he smiled.

Georgiana was breathing slowly, as if trying to control a rising excitement.

"It feels pain," she said.

"It does."

Now she looked at him, a slow smile edging across her face.

"Then we can train it," she said.

He shook his head at her in slow wonderment.

"Child," he said. "The hand moves independently of any connection to the body it came from. Does it not fill your mind with terror at the unknown world which it evidences?"

"No, Father," she said. "What terrifies me is penury and ugliness."

She took the hatpin from his hand, a hungry look coming over her as she leant over the box.

"Let's see what it does . . ."

And she jabbed the pin into the hand and watched it flinch.

THIRD PART

THE BROKEN HAND

THE COMPANY OF HANDS

. . . take your hand and put the tips of your fingers and thumbs on a piece of parchment, keeping your palm a good thumb's height from the surface. Take a quill, dip it in the ink and make a mark at the end of each one, and then join each mark to the others with a straight line. You have just drawn an irregular pentagram, or a five-pointed star, inside an outer boundary. The star is for power. The boundary is for protection. It keeps the power within, and stops it spilling out into the world unchecked.

The ignorant, or those who would chain you to a superstition cloaked as a religion, will tell you a pentagram is a thing of darkness, a tool of black magic, the sign of any number of devils.

It is precisely the opposite. It contains and protects the light, and it does so within a symbol based on the earthly, upon the human hand – not on something unearthly and superstitious. A pentagram says humankind has the ability to contain power and not be consumed or corrupted by it . . .

. . . Gawain, one of the most virtuous of Arthur's knights, carried the pentagram on his shield, not only representing duty but also generosity, fellowship, honesty and compassion.

These same virtues inform the Free Company for The Oversight of London, who arrange themselves in "Hands" of five in memory of this . . .

Extract from *The Great and Hidden History of the World* by the Rabbi Dr Hayyim Samuel Falk

INTERLUDE

The Andover Workhouse was in uproar.

Mrs M'Gregor was outraged.

M'Gregor himself was conducting a thorough search of all the grounds, rooms, chattels and persons within the misery-dulled precincts of that grey and thankless institution. Beds were upended, cupboards rifled and even the ominous piles of bones awaiting grinding in the work-yard were being picked over by the smallest and most nimble-fingered of the inmate children.

All the men were lined up and stripped, their clothes checked and then returned by the male under-wardens. The women suffered the same indignity with the female under-wardens, this time assisted by their male counterparts whose presence infinitely deepened the humili-ation. It was perhaps only because they were already so ground down, ground finer than the bones in the work-yard, that there was no boisterous rebellion at this, but other than mumbling and whispered curses, the search went on without obstruction or objection.

It also continued without result.

This made Mrs M'Gregor's outrage burst its banks, and she, one of the least ground down and most sharp-edged of women, unleashed her invective on the assembled ranks of inmates. She enumerated the many kindnesses she and her husband had lavished on them, how nutritious the gruel was, how hard-wearing their blankets were, how sturdy the wooden clogs with which they were furnished at no extra charge! She extolled the virtues of the regimen under which they lived, praised the modernity of the system of daily work and the avoidance of that notorious free time in which the devil might otherwise find work for their idle hands. She lauded the warmth of the one sea-coal fire they provided in the winter and generally launched herself on a wide-ranging panegyric on the virtues of fresh air (in the dormitories) and the high walls with which they were surrounded, as being necessary to protect them from the shame of being viewed by those worthy and munificent parishioners whose hard labour furnished the funds with which she and her husband — a brass-bound saint of a man — were charged with paying for their board and lodging. Charity, she said, began at home, but this home, their home, had been outrageously and burglariously predated upon. In short, someone had stolen her hand mirror, and since charity provided the most admirable and nutritious gruel (known to the inmates, but not to her, as "old sweat and bone") the same gruel would be withdrawn from their board of fare and replaced with stale bread and water as their only sustenance until it was returned.

Mrs M'Gregor could not abide the thought of a thief in their midst. Her hand mirror had a silver clasp on its handle.

It had belonged to her mother.

This was not true.

Her mother had handed it over on her death-bed.

This was only true in Mrs M'Gregor's mind.

It was her most precious possession.

This was only true if you did not count the strong-box in which the money she and M'Gregor had not spent on the inmates of the workhouse was hidden. It was of course easy not to count this money because it had already been officially if only theoretically counted in the yearly accounts of the institution where it publicly appeared to have paid for necessary meat and medicines, things which the M'Gregors had privately considered less necessary than the need to provide for their retirement.

And so it was that the greatest thief in the establishment harangued the innocent poor unfortunates who had been left in her and her husband's care on the subject of their rank ingratitude and unforgiveable dishonesty. She shouted and spat at them in a most unladylike way until she was unattractively red in the face, her double chins wobbling furiously like the wattles of an especially discommoded turkey.

The other smaller thief sat abstractedly at the back of the room, head bent to the thin light filtering in the windows high above, her fingers endlessly moving in her lap, as if sewing something invisible.

She knew in a moment someone would rush in, having found the mirror handle in the bone piles.

She knew there would be a moment's celebration.

And she knew this would turn to consternation as they saw the handle was blind, that the mirror it had contained was gone from the frame.

She knew they would then fear someone had taken the shards to fashion a knife.

She knew some of the least-liked under-wardens would tread carefully for the next few weeks, worried about someone rushing upon them to revenge any of a score of past unkindnesses and humiliations.

She thought that was no bad thing.

She also knew the mirror lay at the bottom of the water butt in the vegetable garden, and that it would not be found.

She knew the next hand that would touch it was at present making a daisy chain in her lap.

And though her mind was too wrapped in fog to know how precisely it was that she knew, she was also sure it would soon be time to escape.

CHAPTER 51

WHAT HAPPENED ON WYCH STREET

Jed got the scent of the Alp as he passed an offal pedlar's stall in Clare Market, and it was greatly to his credit that he did so since his attention was more than half distracted by a brimming crock full of old bone ends and butcher's discards sending invisible tendrils of rank temptation across the alley at precisely the level of his nose.

Hodge heard him bark and caught the urgency in the dog's tone. He was three floors above the street, which was a crowded and unsavoury mixture of meat sellers' shops and greengrocers' stalls so higgled in beneath ancient over-hung gables and sagging casement windows that there was barely room to breathe, let alone pass through with any degree of ease or dispatch. Hodge immediately slung his hook across a narrow side alley and tugged it secure against the lip of brick it had found, and then with no hesitation swung across the short gap and walked himself down the crumbling wall, nimble as a salty topsail man coming down the foremast on a flat calm. He reached the ground and shook a curve back up the rope, freeing the grapple with a practised tug and catching it as it fell out of the sky.

He jogged out into the bustle of the market, still looping the cord in his hands, eyes searching for the dog.

He caught sight of the brindled tail disappearing in the direction of Wych Street and ran after it, buffeting shoppers and traders who were unwary enough to get in his way or deaf enough to ignore his shouted entreaties to,

"Make a hole there!"

There was no question that Jed had the scent. He was humming with tension, his whole body vibrating with it, tense as a bowstring. Wych Street was a lot less crowded than the market and Hodge caught up with him halfway down from St Clement Danes.

"Where?" he said.

Jed mounted the step and entered a dingy shop-front beneath a sign reading "M. A. Ormes – Dealer in Coal". Hodge followed him into a dark space which was as quiet, sooty and light-starved as any mine. An elderly man was propped between two piles of sacks, tallying an account book by the glimmer of a single candle.

"Do you have rooms?" said Hodge, gesturing at the stair at the back of the shop.

"Who's asking?" said the proprietor.

"The Law," said Hodge, and showed him a badge which he pocketed before the man had time to look closely at it. "Any new tenants?"

"No," said the man. "Just the missis and myself on the next floor and then a nice young couple, no trouble, on the top. Been here three years, never a peep out of 'em. What kind of law are you . . . ?"

"The busy kind," said Hodge. "You stay put."

Hodge took the stairs three at a time, Jed bounding ahead of him. At the top of the house was a closed door. By the time Hodge got to the landing, Jed had his nose to the crack under it and was inhaling noisily, as if trying to suck the contents of the room on the other side bodily across the floor.

Hodge did not stop. His blackthorn stick was in one hand and a knife in the other as he went through the door boot first. The cheap wood splintered as the lock tore free, and he leapt inside.

The room was clean but meanly furnished. There was a small grate with cooking paraphernalia ranged around it, a deal table with two mismatched chairs and an oilcloth tacked to it on which were laid place settings for two; there was one moderately easy chair leaking horsehair from a split covering of threadbare velveteen, and behind a thin curtain of cheapest cotton, much laundered so that the original sprigged roses which had once splashed cheerfully across it were now more like the faded ghosts of flowers past, was a bed.

"Come out, I say; by oak, ash and thorn I shall have you, you bastard!"

And he ripped the curtain aside.

There was no Alp.

But there had been.

The dead woman was proof of that.

And the Alp was long gone, at least half a day from the look of her. She lay on her back in a rumpled shift which was more than half off her body, her mouth open and white-lipped as if she had died between one breath and another, her eyes open and unseeing in a face already showing the beeswax pallor of the long dead. Because her shift was rucked up, he could see the blood in her body had given way to the insistent pull of gravity so that the underside of her limbs were a mottled bluey-purple against the grey sheets, a startling imperfection when compared with the idealised pale marble quality that death had brought to her skyward features, a paleness caused by the draining of that very blood from even the smallest capillaries of her skin.

Even though she bore all the signs of a none too recent death, Hodge still unaccountably found his hands on her shoulders shaking her, trying to wake her.

He heard himself saying "No, no" repeatedly, all trace of exultation gone from his voice. He felt the sting in his eyes and the catch in his throat, and he knew that somehow something had broken inside him. In a long and steadfast life of adventure and service he had certainly met failure before, and he had seen death in mind-scarringly worse guises than this case. There was no reason he could have given for why something cracked deep within him, why failing to catch this particular breath-stealer was so insupportable, but maybe it had something to do with the long and painstaking search, the lack of sleep, the slow and unmarked erosion of his vital energy which resulted from following his tireless dog. Maybe it is not the last straw which breaks backs, but all the ones that went before it. Whatever it was, Hodge broke.

"Annie?" said a voice behind him. "Oh my God!"

He turned to see a youngish man in a clerk's tight jacket standing in the doorway with a piece of wet fish wrapped in a damp twist of newspaper in his hand.

The hand opened in shock and the fish slapped to the floor.

"What have you done?" yelled the man as he launched himself across the room. "Murder! MURDER!"

The clerk wrenched Hodge off the bed and threw him into the wall. Hodge did not defend himself. Jed snarled into the attack, but Hodge waved his hand.

"No, Jed! Stay."

The clerk stared in horror at his wife's lifeless body.

Hodge said nothing. He felt quite exhausted by the three words with which he'd stilled the dog. For the first time in his life, he could not think what to do next, nor could he bring himself to care much about it.

The clerk was six inches shorter than Hodge, and half as

wide. He was thin as a pen. He came at him in a fury, snatching up the poker as he did so.

He caught Hodge a glancing blow on the side of the head, and then another less well-placed one on the neck.

Hodge did not defend himself.

The clerk kicked Hodge's legs out from under him, and was about to hit him again when the coal seller and his son came through the door. They took in the ghastly scene with horrified indrawn breaths, and then came across the room in a flurry of oaths and boots and set about kicking the life out of the fallen Terrier Man.

Hodge lay there, one eye disappearing behind a bloodied swelling, feeling the blows as if they were happening to someone a long way off. Someone who deserved them. Someone who welcomed the oblivion they would inevitably bring.

Jed whined and snarled, and pawed at the floor, but Hodge held him with the remaining power of his eye. "No," he croaked. "Go."

He could stop Jed attacking, but persuading the terrier to leave him was beyond his powers.

"Stomp him," shouted the coal-man's son enthusiastically. "Stomp the life out of the murdering bastard!"

Hodge turned halfway round, and even managed a kind of weak smile through his split lips as he saw the hobnailed boot rising above his eye.

The boot never landed. A whirlwind entered the room and grabbed the son by the collar, tossing him across the room into the wall. The coal merchant turned and met a fist like a hammer that dropped him on the spot, and in the next instant the clerk found his throat gripped so tight that he could not breathe as Hodge's rescuer lifted him bodily off the ground and held him there, his boots kicking air as he took in the scene.

Hodge looked up at The Smith.

"Too late," he said thickly, looking at the dead woman's feet, which were all he could see sticking over the edge of the mattress from where he lay, mashed into the angle where the floorboards met the wall.

The Smith looked down at him like a thundercloud.

"Just in time, I'd say," he growled.

He let the clerk go and looked at him. The clerk's frenzied grief drained from his face as he met the banked-up fire in The Smith's eyes.

"This was your wife?" said The Smith.

The clerk nodded.

"Then my sorrow for your loss," said The Smith. "You will remember how happy she was, and that you parted on loving terms. You will believe she died without pain, sleeping, and that she always told you to find another and make her as happy as you made her should she die before you. You will mourn the year out and, come next summer, will feel that she has let you go and now watches over you with joy. You will not be diminished by her death, but strengthened by the happy memory of her. You will forget I or my friend or his dog were ever here. And now you will sleep for ten minutes."

The Smith waited as the man sneezed, and then led him to the easy chair and lowered him into it.

"What are you?" said a voice hoarse with dread.

The Smith turned and saw the coal-man's son cowering against the wall.

"What do you see here?" said The Smith pointing at his eyes. The son looked into them and after a spasm of choking, relaxed.

"Downstairs you go," The Smith said. "And you too forget us."

The young man sneezed and stumbled out of the room like a man sleepwalking.

The coal seller stirred and found his chin held by The Smith.

"And you fell on the stairs running up them when you heard the poor gentleman here call for help. Which he will do in eight minutes or so. Go and sit on the landing. And again, forget us entirely."

The Smith watched him stumble away. Then he crossed to the dead woman and felt her chest.

"Broken ribs," he said. "You found your Alp."

"Not in time," said Hodge, who had not moved.

The Smith straightened the girl's shift and made her look a little more decent. He sighed. Then he turned and looked at Hodge.

"Can you stand?"

Hodge shook his head.

"I've half a mind to leave you here with your self-pity," said The Smith. "Only we don't have men to spare."

He picked up Hodge's knife and stuck his cudgel in his belt. Then he bent, grabbed the Terrier Man around the middle and walked over to the window. He peered out and saw the flat roof beyond. He nodded at Jed.

"We'll come back and pick up the trail later." And with a disgusted snort, he carried Hodge out of the room and past two sets of now unseeing eyes, back into the anonymity of the street below.

CHAPTER 52

A DRINK AFTER DARK

Two days before the big fair at which the two Great Wizards were to have their much-advertised confrontation, Lucy found herself sitting with Georgiana and Charlie against the side-wall of a low-built public house overlooking a green which was now covered in all the paraphernalia of the coming gala. It was more crowded than usual because the showmen from the northern circuit were here also, and it was a festive atmosphere as old friends and rivals met and weighed up the past year's effects on each other.

The publican was an old friend of the showmen, happy to have them come annually and set up on the common land midway between the village and the nearby town since their presence there brought customers from all over the county streaming along the road, which ensured he sold a prodigious amount of beer and cider as they passed. They had travelled into cider country in the past week, and Lucy, courtesy of Charlie, had decided she preferred it to beer.

Charlie had climbed the thatch on the roof of the tavern and garlanded it with flags and a big sign reading BEER BY THE JUG, and as a result had been given a flagon of the stronger cider called scrumpy. Lucy hadn't drunk much of it, disliking the astringent taste and finding it lacked the sweetness of the cider she had enjoyed up to now. Georgiana had surprisingly matched Charlie drink for drink as they sat and watched the older showmen go in and out of the pub, carrying jugs and pitchers of their own.

No one noticed them in the lee of the building. Lucy was quiet and thoughtful and Charlie was saying less than normal because Georgiana was doing enough talking for them all: Georgiana had a strong opinion about everything, and an only child's sense of entitlement in believing everyone should be glad to hear her pass them on: she had opinions about whether drinking cider on an empty stomach would give them colic (she was sure it would, but drank on anyway). She had opinions about cuckoos, cow-parsley, hurdy-gurdys, portable soup, canned meats and dresses suitable for dancing in. She knew what colours suited her by sunlight and by candle-light, and what colours would not suit Lucy in any light at all. She had good opinions about hairstyles, moustaches and her ability to hold an audience in the palm of her hand, and poor opinions about dogs, tight boots and gypsies.

Had she not been so compellingly beautiful, Lucy might have found the deluge of her observations grating, but as it was she was happy to sit against a wall which still retained the day's warmth, sharing the jug and listening to her new friend – as she was invited to consider her – babbling away as inconsequentially and charmingly as any sunlit brook.

There was something about Georgiana, some alchemy of looks and voice and delicacy of movement that was irresistibly engaging, and it was easy to be in her company without thinking too much.

Lucy had travelled the countryside bare-handed, unafraid as she was of touching natural things, saving the deteriorating gloves for the villages and towns where every innocent stone or brick could be a trap ready to spring open like a hellish

Jack-in-a-box and spill the recorded horrors of the past straight into her brain. She wore the gloves again now as the pub looked old enough to have seen dark deeds and sadnesses in its long past. She picked at them, worrying the fraying threads and seeing that they really were on the point of falling completely to bits. She'd tried to sew them again, but the leather just gave way as soon as there was any tension put on the thread. Tonight she decided just to be careful and not worry about them until tomorrow.

Charlie drained the jug and looked disappointed.

"All gone," he said sadly. "Must be someone drank it. Excuse me."

Lucy watched him stumble off round the edge of a tall nettle patch, fumbling with his trousers. When she turned back she caught Georgiana looking at her.

"What?" she said.

"Exactly," smiled Georgiana. "What?"

And she reached over and brushed her hand on Lucy's cheek.

"In this low light, the flames catch the light in your hair. You're really quite pretty. Why are you wearing gloves?"

A shiver ran through Lucy, though whether it was from the fingertips just barely touching the fine hairs on her face or from the question she didn't know.

"What?" she repeated, feeling quite as sluggish as if she'd also had her share of the scrumpy. Which she hadn't. She was playing for time. She was saved by Charlie stumbling back and slumping down the wall at her side.

"Careful," he said. "Georgie's a mind-reader, remember!"

The way he said it said he knew she wasn't. Georgiana bridled and pulled away, looking outraged.

"I am!" she said.

"Of course you are," said Charlie. "What was I thinking?"

He grinned at Lucy.

"You're thinking of getting us some more scrumpy," said Georgiana. "Be a gentleman."

"My head's just fuzzy and warm enough as it is," he said. "Any more apple juice and tomorrow will be hard pounding."

Georgiana fluttered her eyes at him.

"I'd be ever so grateful if you'd see if they would give us even a half jug more," she said. "Father would like it so."

"Come off it, Georgie," he said, "I'm not a flat; Na-Barno can buy his own drink!"

She looked down, half proud, half tragic.

"He can't," she said quietly. "We're on our uppers until things get better. And he's working so hard on his new illusion . . ."

"That's an old song," said Charlie.

She looked up at him, a tear quivering on one of her lovely eyelashes.

"Oh, spare the pump-handle and don't turn on the waterworks," he sighed, rolling to his feet. "I'll see how charitable the proprietor's feeling."

And he scooped the jug off the ground and walked into the tavern.

"Sara," said Georgiana, and Lucy looked round for a moment, forgetting she was pretending to be someone called Sara Falk.

"Yes," she said.

"You're a strange one," said Georgiana. "I can see why Charlie likes you. He likes odd things. Like that shaved old bear."

"He likes you," said Lucy.

Georgiana threw her head back and laughed, full-throated, the tear of a moment ago quite forgotten.

"Charlie doesn't like me! I mean he does, but not like that. He's known me for ever. We've just rubbed along so long growing up that we tease each other to stop getting bored."

She looked round at the tented village which had sprouted on the green. "I could get bored of all this quite easily. I will, I expect, one day when Father's illusions make us rich. Then I shall live in a brick house without wheels and never go anywhere again except to pay visits, and shop, and attend balls."

Her eyes were dreamy now.

"I should look very good at a ball," she continued. "I should have beaux lining up to dance with me. I shall like that. And I shall treat them all quite horribly and they shall line up all the more. Men like to be treated badly. It adds drama to their lives. I think being a man should be a very humdrum thing without a bit of drama to give it colour."

Her eyes rose to the stars and Lucy was able to look at the uncanny regularity of her profile without being observed. If Georgiana had an imperfection, she decided, it was perhaps that very lack of fault, the astonishing symmetry of her features in repose – but then she had to admit the way one corner of her mouth hoisted into a smile a fraction before the other did broke that balance and made the expression of her pleasure all the more beguiling.

"Can you really read minds?" she said without meaning to.

Georgiana's gaze dropped from the heavens and met hers full on.

"Do you want me to try?" she said, that smile skewing into life.

They could hear the revelry inside the tavern, and see the busy camp around them, but here, in the shadow of the wall, they were in a pool of solitude.

"Yes," said Lucy, her voice catching. She cleared her throat. She was nervous because the idea had come to her slowly, but had been voiced before she meant to. The idea was this: if Georgiana could really read minds, she might be able to see things in Lucy's head which she couldn't conjure up for herself. She might be able to fill in the alarming holes in her memory. She might even be able to furnish clues as to how and why those holes got there. It was a strange plan, but the world was stranger than she had thought before she saw Sara's Green Man and her golem, and had fallen out of a London library into a travelling circus. A beautiful girl who could read minds was a small thing in comparison with all that.

"Yes," she repeated. "I would like that."

"You must be very still and quiet then," said Georgiana.

And she put her hands on either side of Lucy's head and closed her eyes.

"Close yours too or I shall just see you looking at me," she said.

So Lucy closed her eyes and tried to think of nothing in particular. It was hard because she was very conscious of the warmth and pressure of Georgiana's hands on her temples. Then it was harder still as Georgiana began to move the hands gently through her hair.

"I—" said Lucy.

"Shhh," said Georgiana. "You're hard enough without distraction."

She gripped her head tighter and then she leant her own head into Lucy's and sat there, unmoving, forehead to forehead. Lucy could feel the heat of her breath on her cheek. It was disturbing. It was almost more intoxicating, in its way, than the scrumpy.

"Apples," she breathed.

Georgiana's hands dropped and she pulled away.

"What?" she said.

"Apples," said Lucy. "You smell of apples."

"Oh, Sara!" cried Georgiana. "I just don't think I can read you. You wriggle so in your head. Like a child with worms that can't sit still."

"I can," said Lucy. "Sorry. Try again – I won't move."

Georgiana shook her head decisively.

"No. It's no good. It's not your body. It's your mind. It's different to others. Hard to read. It's like there are depths where I cannot see . . ."

"Holes?" said Lucy, a sudden coldness making her voice crack. Georgiana caught the change and nodded enthusiastically.

"Yes, holes! Holes. That's it. That's the very word . . ."

Lucy felt kicked in the stomach. Georgiana could see she was damaged so it was somehow even more real. She didn't have a memory like other people. She had pieces of a patchwork, but no clue to the overall pattern.

"Oh, thank you, Charlie," laughed Georgiana, somehow relieved at his return. "I must take this to Father directly. Goodnight, goodnight."

"She was in a sudden hurry to go," said Charlie as they watched her flit towards the tents balancing the cider jug in both hands.

"She was reading my mind," said Lucy dully.

He looked at her with his head cocked.

"Was she now? And you believed her?"

"She saw it right," she said.

She stared murderously at the ground, clenching her teeth.

"She can't read minds," said Charlie after a bit. "It's a trick. So don't be blown so flat by whatever she said."

"It was true," she insisted.

"No," he said. "Not if it made you sad. You're a good 'un, Falk. Don't let her play games. It's what she does: keeps people off balance."

"It wasn't a game," she said. "She did."

"Sara," he said. "You've been with us long enough to see how the show world works, but I'll tell you this for nothing. It's all about what people expect, and how you play with that. You know how you make a trick work best? By making the person you're tricking want it not to be a trick at all."

She stayed staring at the ground.

"You coming?" he said. "Early start tomorrow. We'll get there long before lunchtime and start to set up."

She looked at her hands. Sara's hand-me-down-gloves really were coming to bits: her skin showed pink through holes in each one.

"You think there'll be a glove shop?" she said. She needed gloves.

"There's any number of shops, but you won't like the place. It's a sad little town, really. You coming?"

"I'll come in a moment," she said.

"Fair enough," he said, and walked off towards the wagon. "Sweet dreams, and don't trip over Mum again when you get in the tent."

She closed her eyes and ground the back of her head against the rough plaster on the wall, trying to clear the cider fog from her brain. When that failed, she got to her feet and wove back to her bed at the Pyefinches' wagon.

Because she came back by herself she heard the talking before they heard her, and stopped to listen.

She heard Charlie speaking quietly to his father.

"She was asking about gloves," he said.

"She's a strange one. Hobb told me there was someone in the shadows in the pub last night asking to see if anyone had seen a girl who sounded like it might have been her: a girl who kept her hands covered."

"Someone in the shadows with what looked like tattoos on his face," said Rose, her voice heavy with a meaning Lucy couldn't follow.

"He was offering gold," said Pyefinch. "But don't worry. Hobb knows the ropes. Kept mum."

"Hmmm," said Rose. "There's gold and then there's gold."

"She don't seem like harm," said Charlie.

"Well, there's harm and there's harm, and all," said Mr Pyefinch. "Best keep on keeping an eye on her, Charlie boy."

Then they stopped talking and she heard them getting to bed.

She waited for a minute, and then made more noise than she would have done entering the wagon. Charlie grinned goodnight at her and turned down the lamp at his end.

She got under her blanket and lay in the dark looking at the shapes of the pots on the hooks in the roof of the wagon, feeling weak and wondering what exactly Rose's last observation had meant.

She wondered if the stranger had been looking for her, maybe sent by the real Sara Falk. Or maybe just looking for someone who looked like her.

And now she would always wonder if Charlie's cheerfulness was a cloak for something else.

He had gone from a friend to a watcher.

She was tired and felt cider-sick. She closed her eyes.

She wouldn't sleep. She wouldn't dream. She'd be too busy planning how to leave.

It was nearly time to go again.

CHAPTER 53

THE COBURG IVORIES

Mr Sharp stooped over a table in front of the glass cabinet, stripped to his waistcoat with his sleeves rolled up. His coat was neatly folded on the chair at his side, and he was honing his blade on an oiled whetstone with long precise strokes. He was quietly whistling a melancholy tune which anyone listening would have identified as an old ballad known as "The Parting Glass".

Emmet stood beside him, not looking like he was listening, or indeed looking at anything in particular. He had mended the mirror, working without a break for days, painstakingly sticking the pieces back to the frame with a fish glue that was still adding its unpleasant odour to the shuttered room despite a fire he had kindled in the grate to draw the air up the chimney.

"You will please be so kind as to guard the house especially vigilantly when I am gone," said Mr Sharp. "And I would be greatly obliged if you made sure no harm comes to Miss Falk, whether by the agency of others or by her own hand should her mind become sufficiently unstable as to make that a possibility, which I greatly fear it may."

Emmet nodded.

"Thank you, my old friend," said Mr Sharp, testing the blade with his thumb. Satisfied, he slid it into the left-hand sheath hanging from a leather harness looped flat around his shoulders. A matching knife hung on the right. He ignored that blade and reached down to his boot from which he extracted a third blade which he began to sharpen with the same deliberation as the other.

"Do you know how the Murano Cabinet came to be here?" said a voice from the doorway.

Mr Sharp turned his head without breaking rhythm with the knife on the stone. The Smith was standing with a leather-wrapped package in his hands, watching him.

"No," said Mr Sharp, turning back to his honing. "And I had hoped they would not try and get you to persuade me not to go into the mirrors. I assure you my mind is made up, and my resolve adamantine."

"Well, Jack," said The Smith. "Adamantine, eh? You're quite the poet these days."

"I cannot be cajoled out of this," said Mr Sharp, aware that The Smith, and indeed no one else, had called him by his true first name since he was a child.

"I shouldn't dream of it," said The Smith. "I think you're right."

The rhythmic sound of steel on stone stopped abruptly.

"You think I'm right?" Mr Sharp said, voice hollow with surprise.

"Desperate measures for desperate times," said The Smith cheerily. "Go down fighting. It's what we always do, if you think about it. It's not as if The Oversight hasn't dwindled to less than a full Hand before. I remember thinking the same thing the last time . . ."

"The last time?" said Mr Sharp.

"In the old premises. On Pudding Lane."

"Before the fire?" said Mr Sharp. "Before the Great Fire?"

"That's the one," said The Smith. "About half a minute before the damn thing started, as a matter of fact."

He beamed at the younger man.

"Nice knife," he said.

"Wayland," said Mr Sharp slowly. "How old are you?"

"Older than most, younger than some," said The Smith.

"And why haven't I asked you this before?" said Mr Sharp, looking as though he had just found something unexpected and unwelcome at the back of his mind. "Why has this not . . . occurred to me?"

"People don't and it doesn't: ask and occur, I mean," said The Smith. "You're not the only one who gets into folks' minds and draws a veil over some things . . ."

Mr Sharp slid the knife back into his boot thoughtfully.

"Then I must really be in great peril," he said, "if you're revealing this to me now. You must think I really am not coming back to talk about that with the others. I mean I know there's always been a smith in The Oversight. I just hadn't thought it was the same smith . . ."

"When things are calm, I go away for years at a time, travel the highways and byways, a traveller, the wayland smith. People forget and then welcome me back. It just needs a little thought adjustment and it works well enough," said The Smith with a self-deprecating shrug. "But we're not here to talk about that."

"Why drop the veil now then?" said Mr Sharp.

"Because you need to know that I know what I'm talking about, and do what I tell you," said The Smith. "I'd much rather you came back, and came back the way you left. Seems I'm fond of you, for all your stiff, proud ways. And just coming back's hard enough. You need to come back to the right here, the right now, and you need to come back as the right you."

"I . . ." said Mr Sharp.

"No, you don't," said The Smith. "Sit down and listen."

Mr Sharp sat. The Smith opened the doors of the cabinet.

"I asked if you knew how this blessed Discriminator cabinet got here," he said. "Any idea?"

"No," said Mr Sharp.

"It was a gift from one of the Rabbi Falk's friends. A fellow freemason and Kabbalist and what-not," said The Smith. "All that stuff and nonsense by which clever men miss the truth. Anyway, he was a Venetian, hence it's Murano glass, and he certainly was clever. He was called Giacomo Girolamo Casanova de Seingalt, and as much of a mouthful as his name was, he was more than twice the handful. Never could keep his fingers off anything he took a fancy to, always picking up the tools and such in my workshop and putting them back wrong. Anyway, water under the bridge; he's dead and gone now. Thing of it is, he knew this cabinet here was powerful, but didn't know how to use it. Lost a woman he loved in it once, hiding from her husband who surprised them up to no good, and never got her back."

He reached out and touched the candlestick on the back wall of the cabinet. The wick lit instantly and the light which blazed from it was stronger than anyone would have expected from a single flame.

"The Discriminator," he said. "The Blood Key, the flame that only kindles for those with enough of the old supranatural blood in them to give them more than normal powers. Because only those with enough of the blood can travel into the mirrors."

"I do know that, Wayland," said Mr Sharp.

The Smith smiled at him.

"You know the esoteric power of the thing, but its practical application is more mundane but equally important. It sheds a light."

He plucked the candle from the holder. It immediately extinguished.

"If you're in the cabinet and the doors are closed, then you need a light to see the reflections in the mirrors. So without the candle, and any old dip will do, the cabinet won't work. The Key is the holder, not the candle. That said, your travels may take you into other dark cabinets or rooms. So always travel with a candle somewhere about your person."

He pointed to the mosaics on the floor and ceiling of the cupboard: the tesserae which made them were black and white and brown, strangely dull and at odds with the freshness of the pale glass swags and twisted pillars that adorned the outside of the cabinet.

"There's a cathedral in Venice, though it's not as Christian a place as you might think. These are the same mosaic tiles as they have on the floor there. It's not a flat floor like you might find in our St Paul's; it's a rolling floor, hummocked like the swell of the very sea that Venice sits on. And these compass roses, they're to guide your travels as you set off on your voyage into the glass."

He pointed at the floor.

"That one sets where."

He pointed at the ceiling.

"That one sets when."

"When? I think I'm lost," said Mr Sharp.

"You won't be if you do as I say," said The Smith, unwrapping the rawhide lace that kept his leather package tied up. "Long as no one changes those mosaic dials, you have a chance of coming back to the right place and time."

"But the mirrors," said Mr Sharp. "I thought the mirrors just opened into a series of tunnels between different places where mirrors were set up facing each other."

"That they are," said The Smith. "But that's just the smallest part of it. You can move along the tunnel of mirrors and choose the one to step out of, but you can also stop between mirrors and look at right angles to the tunnel you're in."

"What do you see?"

"Another infinite tunnel of mirrors," said The Smith. "It's a web of shortcuts behind the world's scenery — that's the way I think about it — or a grid. Or a maze. More like a maze really, because the trick is not getting lost."

He dropped the leather wrapping onto the table and placed the object it had hidden in front of Mr Sharp.

"Don't lose it, and it won't lose you," he said.

"It" was an object that looked at first sight to be an ivory ball about the size of an ostrich egg perched on top of a long stand, somewhat like a candlestick. The stand was elaborately turned, with a spiral-fluted column and a flared base, itself highly decorated with concentric ridges and pierced holes which gave it the look of lacework.

The ball was pierced with large circular holes, each about the size of a plum. Through those holes, on closer inspection, Mr Sharp could see that the ball contained, seemingly impossibly, a whole diminishing series of other ivory balls, each with their own holes bored into them; each of these balls seemed to have a thickness little greater than watercolour paper.

"Know what it is?" said The Smith, watching Mr Sharp examine the intricate object. "You can pick it up. The handle comes out of the stand."

Mr Sharp lifted it out of the base and felt the nested balls shift as he moved it.

"It looks like the Chinese balls that the tea clippers sometimes bring back," said Mr Sharp. "Except those are thicker and crudely carved with dragons and such."

"I suspect that if we were to find others like us among the Chinese, we'd find these balls serve the same purpose," said The Smith. "It's a get-you-home."

"A what?"

"A get-you-home," repeated The Smith. "Made by a

German called Eisenberg, a long time ago. You line the holes up to start, and then as you enter the mirror tunnels, each time you step out of a mirror, one sphere rotates. Step into another mirror? Next sphere rotates. When you want to come back, the holes turn and guide you home. Seven spheres, seven hops. More than that, you're on your own."

Mr Sharp took a tighter grip on the fluted handle.

"Thank you," he said.

"Thank the Venetian," said The Smith. "He ended his days in Bohemia as court librarian. When he was cataloguing some oddments he came across two of these. They were known as the Coburg Ivories. He sent them to Rabbi Falk, with his suspicions as to how they were to be used."

"Where's the other one?" said Mr Sharp.

The Smith looked a little uncomfortable.

"The Disaster," he said. "They took it with them. It never came back."

CHAPTER 54

BURNT AS A WITCH

It was, as Charlie had said, a sad town. The buildings weren't especially mean, and it didn't seem more afflicted by poverty than any other place they had visited, but it did have a heavy air of melancholy which bore down on everything within it: dark gabled buildings jutted over the pavement like stormclouds, and the trees lining the wide main street were sickly and beginning to lose their prematurely yellow leaves even though it was not yet autumn. The people who walked beneath them all had faces like closed doors, faces that gave nothing away, neither a smile nor a scowl, and the shopkeepers watched passers-by as if they were something to be defended against rather than welcomed as potential customers. The smell of the local brewery was equally oppressive and entirely unavoidable to anyone possessing a functioning nose: its musty sourness mixed with a heavy sweetness was so thick it seemed to stick to your skin.

Maybe that was it, thought Lucy, maybe the smell is why they all look so miserable. Maybe they need the money from the brewery and just have to bear it; maybe their faces are so blank and shut because they're trying to seal out this horrible and invisible malty cloud they're living in.

She felt the money in her pocket and looked at the signs jutting from the louring buildings in the hope of finding a shop selling gloves. She threaded her way between the trees all the way to the town hall at the end of the street, and then retraced her steps up the other side in case she'd missed something, but there seemed to be no haberdashers or clothes shop of any sort. She went into an ironmonger in case they had any work gloves, but all she was shown – grudgingly, by a suspicious-looking shopkeeper – was a thick pair of rough suede blacksmith's gloves. She might as well have tied flour-sacks to her hands, she thought. She asked if there was a more suitable lady's shop somewhere off the main thoroughfare and he admitted there was, without offering to tell her where it might be. When she asked for directions he bristled as if spotting a ruse, perhaps one by which she was trying to lure him into the street to point the way while she darted back in and stole a barrel of penny nails or a bundle of mattock handles. With a knowing sigh, he stamped on the floor, which produced – with startling rapidity – a small defeated-looking boy who he directed pointedly to "watch the blessed shop" while he stepped out from behind the counter, shooing Lucy ahead of him as he leant into the street and grudgingly pointed her on her way.

She thanked him and walked into the narrow side-street he had indicated. She was so busy trying to remember the intricate sequence of lefts and rights he had fired at her that she stopped watching where she was going. Her foot hit something and she stumbled forward, going down hard on one knee before bracing herself with her hand to stop pitching all the way onto the ground. She winced and stayed down for a moment, rubbing the pain away.

It was because she was hunkered down that Georgiana Eagle didn't see her. Georgiana was standing in front of a shop and rattling the door-handle, evidently frustrated that it was closed. She stood back, clearly hoping to see someone moving inside. Frustrated, she turned away from the locked door, looked quickly up and down the dim alley and then hurried off without a backward glance. Lucy was a connoisseur of furtive glances, having spent much of her life hiding and watching people who didn't think themselves observed, and there was something in the hot immediacy of Georgiana's look that piqued her interest so sharply that she forgot, for the moment, all thoughts of gloves and began to follow her.

Lucy stayed far enough back not to be seen, but just close enough not to lose her. This worked well enough until the narrow alley they were walking down ended in a small open square with a tall crumbling stone cross in its centre, overlooked at one side by a squat ill-favoured church, and on the other by a low bow-fronted shop whose double windows advertised "Finest Wines" in flaking gold leaf on one side of the narrow door, and "Remedies and Cure-Alls" on the other. It was into this establishment that Georgiana disappeared, with a cheery tinkle of the bell on the shop door. Lucy thought she saw her flinch at the bright tell-tale noise, but that might have been just her fancy. From the glimpse of bottles and jars stacked within, she could see it was an apothecary shop. Why Georgiana was being so circumspect, when all the show-people drank freely, was another mystery to her. In order that she wasn't discovered when her quarry retraced her steps, Lucy slid into the square and walked along the side towards the church with the intention of sheltering in the mouldering shadows of the lych-gate until Georgiana emerged with whatever it was she was so keen not to be seen buying.

It was that cheery bell that almost saved her. She heard it ring behind her, and without needing to think or turn, stepped quickly sideways into the nearest doorway. It was the door to some kind of shop because she saw a thin mirror on the side lintel with lettering on it, but she did not read what it said at first, instead using it to observe Georgiana's progress across the square over her shoulder without having to expose her own face.

She saw her gripping a small blue bottle, a squat thing, not a wine bottle at all but the kind of thing used for potions or medicines. It was quickly disappeared beneath her cloak and stowed somewhere safe. Again Georgiana checked the ground around her for observers, and then she suddenly felt something in her dress, squirming as though a mouse or some other unwelcome creature had just announced its presence in her underclothes. She gasped and reached within her garments and removed the offending object.

It was Lucy's turn to gasp. Held in Georgiana's open palm was a piece of liquid fire, the grey-green colour of a midwinter wave: it blazed light across the dim square for an instant before Georgiana clamped her fist shut on it, but in that moment Lucy not only knew exactly what it was, but felt the answering heat in her pocket. She looked down and saw the amber light of her own heart-stone flash an answering warning. She closed her hand over it on reflex but there was no doubt in her mind, though the fact of it hit her like a poleaxe, stunning her for a moment: Georgiana Eagle also had a heart-stone.

This must explain the connection she felt towards her. It was not just the common or garden attraction to a superbly beautiful person that anyone of either sex might feel.

It was more.

It was that Georgiana was also a Glint.

She saw Georgiana turn towards her and realised she must have betrayed herself with a gasp. She flattened herself further into the dark alcove of the shop door, and in so doing reached back with her hand and felt the narrow, twisted pillar behind her through the hole in her gloves, rough stone worn by the passage of weather and time. It was clammy with damp, but it was not that that made her shiver and give herself away.

What did that was the old thing, the bad thing, the blood-curse she always tried to guard against, the treachery of her ungovernable ability to touch the past hidden in stone and have it rear up and bite her.

She stiffened and felt her face jolt into a stiff rictus of anticipation before the pain itself hit as the past slammed into her in the familiar, hated series of shards and slices. Her neck jerked painfully as she saw—

The same church –

But the stone lighter

Less aged

Emptier churchyard

Wider spaced graves

No lych-gate

The same square –

But younger

Fewer houses

Built lower, built differently and thatched.

In the middle of the square –

No ancient stone cross. Instead a pile of sticks and branches

Lashed into faggots

Piled up like a bonfire.

It was not a cold day.

It was summer, and flowers bloomed around the bottom of the houses in the sunlight.

A sweating man was unloading another bundle of sticks from an ox-cart and laughing with a young boy who stood at the foot of the pile, catching the bundles and piling them up on the fire.

A woman walked straight through Lucy and offered them each a leather tankard of ale.

The man drank all of his and half the boy's share.

They all laughed and nodded to the priest who emerged from the church.

Then time lurched again with a sickening thump in the pit of Lucy's stomach

and there was a sudden crowd

and much more noise

and in the square the pretty flowers were being trampled as more and more people mobbed in.

Carts had been pulled up so that those at the back of the crowd could stand on them and see over the heads of those in front of them.

The man and boy upending wicker-wrapped demijohns of oil

Soaking the waiting pile

The hungry wood

The priest stood on the now empty ox-cart at the centre of the square, in a crisp white surplice with a garland of bright cornflowers round his neck, as if the day were a holiday.

The man beside him was, in contrast, dressed in black leather, scuffed dull with long use, as was the sword handle that hung on his hip.

The priest looked at the man in black

"Finder – if you please . . ."

The witchfinder raised a hand and pointed at Lucy.

And his voice cut through the hubbub of the crowd like a hatchet:

"Bring her."

And again someone went through Lucy.

Not the serving girl

Another girl

Pulled by her arms

Her bare feet skidding on the ground

Her body scarcely covered in a rough linen shift

Her face not quite right

Not quite adult

Not yet a child
Not all there
Simple
Unguarded
Screaming
Stumbling
Caught up by the men on either side of her
Carried through the crowd
The mob silent now
As if holding its tongue so as to hear her shrieks all the more clearly
"Please!" she cries raggedly. "Mercy!"
A gloved fist rises
Falls through the sky
A shriek cut off in a thwack of leather on bone
Lucy tries to close her eyes.
Can't close them
Can't even wince
The mouth of the man in leather
Wet and red
Fragments of words spilling from behind his white teeth
"—most abhorred and unnatural creature—"
"—abnormal and detestable powers—"
"—affront to the godly—"
"—friend of shadows—"
"—damnable witch, condemned by statute, punished by custom—"
Tongue darting forth to wet his lips
Snake-like
Hungry for the last
"—most blessed and purifying fire—"
Time slices again
She fights the urge to vomit
As everything goes slow.

So slow she sees it all
A branch
In silence
Dipped in pitch
A torch now
Now afire
A flame
Cartwheeling through the air
A child's eyes follow it above the crowd
The only sound the no-noise of one giant held breath
So slow she can see the torch's smoke-trail leave a smear
on the world
Heading for the ladder in the woodpile
The girl tied to it
Arms above her head
Mouth slack
One eye bruised shut
Leaking blood thinned pink with tears
The other bright with the incoming fire
The torch lands in a shower of sparks
as
The oil-soaked faggots
WHUMP
Ablaze
The sound dam bursts
The crowd yells
An animal roar
A holiday roar
The man in black leather whoops and lifts his hand to the
sky
Conducting, exulting
The impresario of incineration
The priest softer-eyed, shudders, turns away, clutching his
throat

The cornflower garland breaking
Falling
As the girl on the ladder bucks and shrieks
Time slices
Out of the fire and the thick oil smoke a reaching hand
Already a black claw
And with it
In terror, pure as silver
The voice of any girl
Any boy
One thing from the fire
One last word-bullet that hits the hidden everychild in each man and woman in the crowd
Killing the holy roar dead in their throats.
"Mummy!"
Faces flinch
Turn away
And the world kicks again
And Lucy drops to her knees, held upright only by her hand, still stuck to the pillar by the past flowing from it, like a magnet.
It's dark.
The square is almost empty
There is light from the tavern at the far end, the end where one day an apothecary's shop will stand, and from it leaks the growl of men drinking and arguing.
It isn't a happy sound
The fire is gone
A hummock of ash sits in the centre of the square.
The priest sits awkwardly in front of it
Legs akimbo
A bottle clutched to his chest
The witchfinder walks across the square
His son at his side.

They reach down to help the priest to his feet.

He waves them off.

Mumbles something. The witchfinder says,

"It was God's work, Father"

The drunk priest chokes out a bitter laugh and shakes his head.

"No, my child –"

He is pulled to his feet.

He sways.

" – it was man's."

He tries to drink

The bottle is empty

He tosses it.

"We have cursed ourselves, Finder Templebane. We have cursed ourselves."

The bottle shatters on the ground, splashing sharp fragments into the ash and breaking the connection with the past.

Lucy's hand came unstuck from the pillar and she knelt there, head down, panting, looking at the ground until her stomach rebelled at what she had seen and she convulsed, retching her lunch onto the cobbles.

"Sara," said a voice.

For a moment she forgot her name was meant to be Sara, and just stayed where she was, on all fours, waiting to see if her stomach was going to turn any more somersaults. Then she heard the voice again and looked up.

Georgiana was looking down at her with a mixture of shock and something close to disgust.

"What is it?" she said. "My heavens! Are you ill?"

Lucy spat a thin ribbon of sour bile into the gutter and shook her head.

"Why are you here?" said Georgiana, a flicker of suspicion overriding the distaste in her voice.

"I shouldn't be," said Lucy. Now the past had gone and

she was getting control of her own head back, she remembered the heart-stone she had seen in the other girl's hand what seemed like centuries before, but was in fact only seconds ago. She pulled the stone out of her own pocket.

Georgiana's eyes widened in shock, and Lucy saw her instinctively tighten her fist over the stone she knew she held there.

"What," said Georgiana. "What—?"

"I shouldn't be here," said Lucy, as the shadows bounced around them. She pocketed her stone. "And neither should you."

The light around them was not coming from either of their stones. It was coming out of the mirror on the side of the doorpost. Lucy saw it faced a matching mirror on the other side, a mirror reflecting a parallel world of infinitely receding images of itself like a tunnel. And, just as she had seen in the Murano Cabinet, the otherwise unbroken repetitiveness of those images was being walked through by a dark figure holding a bright torch in its hand as it seemed to step effortlessly from reflection to reflection, as simply as a man stepping through a door.

"What is—?" began Georgiana, seeing the fear in Lucy's face, but not what was provoking it.

Lucy stared at the relentlessly approaching figure for one more breath, just long enough to see the unmistakeable shape, and then the light flared off the blade held in the man's hand, and she was suddenly convinced it would be very bad if he was to reach the front panel of the reflections and step out into this world.

So she tore her eyes away and did the only thing she could think of.

She raised her leg and hacked her heel into the mirror, shattering it.

"Sara!" yelped Georgiana. "What—?"

"Just run!" gritted Lucy, dragging her by the arm as she ran for the narrow alley leading out of the hateful square.

They ran.

CHAPTER 55

THE INVISIBLE THREAD

Amos had walked towards the setting sun for so many days that the tinker's pack he carried was no longer burdened with the jangling festoons of tinware and implements that it had been. He still had several knives and had kept one lidded canister in which to carry any milk that he might trade for along the way, but now the heaviest part of his burden was the knife-grinding wheel strapped to the pack. Because he was getting stronger every day he walked, it was less of a weight to him than it had been, but on the steepest uphill portions of his journeyings he did still wonder about leaving it behind, or better, trading it.

There was still enough of the Templebanes' upbringing left in him to make him see the folly in that, because however irksome a load it might be, making the straps of the pack itch and chafe at his shoulders, it was a source of regular food, and occasionally – amongst the more well-to-do cottagers whose cutlery he honed and cleaned – income.

Having begun his travels with no plan other than to keep moving away from London and the House of Templebane's wide sphere of contacts, on the road he had developed an ambition. It seemed a lofty one to him, and all but unattainable without considerable hard work or cunning, but it was one of the characteristics – he felt – of a truly worthy ambition that it should be so.

What he wanted was a horse.

He had developed a frank envy for the confident characters who passed him on horseback, and he coveted both the speed of their passage across the landscape and the elevated viewpoint that they had of it from the high saddle. He had developed, in addition to stronger muscles and healthier lungs, a great hunger for the countryside, and a horse seemed like a good means of ranging farther and seeing more of it.

He had once overheard a distant connection of the Templebanes' who had come to the city from the depths of the West Country talking in an almost indecipherable rural burr about what sounded like the "vreedoms of the New Varest", and of how there were wild ponies there. Amos knew the New Forest was in the west and so perhaps that, he decided, was what drew him so strongly in that direction. Maybe he was on his way to enjoy that "vreedom" and catch a horse for himself.

It must be that, he thought as he lay on his back at dusk, swaddled and alone in the tinker's blanket, looking up at the emerging immensity of stars overhead, because there was certainly *something* calling him westward: he felt it like a tug on an invisible thread which had been laced through his heartstrings.

How he knew it he did not know, but he was convinced that his destiny lay somewhere over the distant horizon, where the sun had set.

CHAPTER 56

TOO CLOSE FOR COMFORT

Since it was after dusk and the streets of the melancholy town had emptied, they were not stopped and asked why they ran as young girls might otherwise expect to be in the circumstances, but Lucy was still circumspect enough to know they must not draw attention to themselves, so whenever they saw groups of people she slowed down and they walked slowly, heads down, until they were past. Because of this they had to walk for most of the High Street as the shopmen were on the pavements packing up and shuttering their unwelcoming establishments for the night, but once they reached the road beyond the lights of the town she gripped Georgiana's arm and sped into the darkness towards the camp.

"What?" gasped Georgiana. "What is it? I can't run as well as you! What are we running from?"

"Something bad," Lucy said. "And yes, you can."

So they did. And though for the longest time the only sounds around them were the slap of their feet on the road, the distant murmur from the canal and the occasional shriek from an early owl out hunting, Lucy felt like she was running from two things – the walker in the mirror and the final scream of the burning girl.

Georgiana allowed herself to be swept along by Lucy's urgency until they were about two-thirds of the way to the camp, and then she stopped without warning and folded, bending double in the middle of the road, her wind blown.

"I cannot," she puffed. "I have a pain – in my side – as if I have been – pierced by a hat – by a hat-pin, I swear—"

As she bent over, something slipped from within her cloak and broke at her feet.

"No!" she gasped. It was the bottle from the apothecary shop. She instantly bent and tried to scoop it up, saving any liquid that might remain cupped in any intact section, but there was none. She stared at the dark stain on the road.

"Father," she whispered. "Father will be— I must go back . . ."

"The shop will be closed," said Lucy, looking back down the way they had just come. The moon was already up and a nail-paring off full so she could see that no one else was on the road running after them. She pointed to a stile a few yards further on.

"Sit," she said. "Compose yourself. We're safe, I think."

Georgiana stumbled to the rough wooden seat and flopped down on it. Lucy sat next to her. For a while they both sat there in the moonlight as Lucy got her breath back. She thought Georgiana was still breathing hard, but then realised that she was sobbing.

"What?" she said tentatively.

Georgiana shook her head, gulping awkwardly.

Lucy knew what it was. Or at least she guessed it was one of two things – either Georgiana was ashamed at being found out as a fellow Glint or else, being a fellow Glint, she had also seen the girl being burned. That agonised scream for a mother who couldn't come and wouldn't rescue her from the fire, that last shout of panic and horror still rang in her own head.

She put a careful hand on the heaving shoulders next to her.

"It's all right," she said.

And to her surprise, Georgiana, the icy and aloof Miss Eagle, choked out a deep sob and melted into a warm tear-racked bundle in her arms.

Lucy didn't know what to do, so she just held her and stroked her back comfortingly, trying to calm her, as if she were a horse which had been spooked.

"I didn't know you were one," she said.

She felt the girl stiffen beneath her hand.

"But it's all right," she said. "Really. It's all right. I'm one too."

There was a tremor and she was sure the girl relaxed just a fraction. She could feel the other heart thrumming beneath Georgiana's ribcage, right against her own.

Lucy remembered how strange it had been when Sara Falk – the real Sara – had shown her her own heart-stone. It seemed so long ago now, but she felt she understood exactly what was going on in the other girl's head: thinking you were the only person who could suck the past from the stones you touched was one thing – discovering there were others like you, finding out there was a name for it, that other people had found their own heart-stone that gave them strength and glowed when danger was abroad, that was a whole other thing. That was both a great relief and a terrible shock.

She felt the dangerous rightness of this moment, this unexpected intimacy with the trembling girl in her arms and gave her a comforting squeeze.

Georgiana pushed herself gently back a few inches as she raised her head to look at her with an expression she couldn't read.

"You're a what?" she whispered with a catch in her voice.

In the clean moonlight that illuminated the exquisite planes of her face but allowed no colour to intrude, she looked like a perfect, marble statue.

"I'm a Glint."

"A . . . Glint?"

Lucy nodded.

Georgiana pushed back another inch.

"I don't know what a 'Glint' is," she said carefully.

Lucy had not known what she was had a name either so she saw no trap here. She tightened her grip on Georgiana's shoulders and smiled.

"It's nothing to be scared of. It just happens. I mean it's not pleasant, but it's just in the mind, though it feels real at the time, so real that you saw me retch. But it passes."

"What passes?" said Georgiana, pushing further away, and getting to her feet. Suddenly her whole demeanour had changed: where she had melted and been warm she was now freezing up, nervy again like a deer about to flee from an unwelcome noise in the forest. "Why should you want it to pass . . . ?"

"Glinting," said Lucy. "Wait . . ."

She laughed. Georgiana took another step away from her.

"Wait. It's all right. Glinting, touching stone, seeing the past as if it's real. Feeling it—"

Georgiana stared at her.

"What did you think I meant?" said Lucy.

"I thought you meant you . . . liked me. In a special way," said Georgiana, uncharacteristically stumbling over the words.

"But did you not see the poor burning girl?" Lucy asked, trying a different tack.

"Burning girl?" said Georgiana. And then she cleared her throat and tossed her head as if shaking the instant of unguarded awkwardness away. "No. I did not see a burning girl."

"Fine," said Lucy. "Doesn't matter. In fact, lucky you. But you know what I mean."

"No," said Georgiana. "No, I don't. Not at all. Are you drunk?"

"Drunk?" said Lucy. "No. I'm not drunk. Why do you—?"

"Because you were sick and you're behaving very oddly," said Georgiana.

All at once Lucy realised that the reason Georgiana was being so strange was because she didn't know how Lucy knew her secret: she didn't know she'd been seen with the sea-glass.

"I saw the glass, your heart-stone – I saw you take it out of your pocket and then hide it when it flashed," she said.

"When it flashed?" said Georgiana. "It didn't flash. It's just a bit of glass." Her tone shifted. "Wait. Were you following me?"

"No," said Lucy. "No, it doesn't matter; I just saw you when you came out of the apothecary shop . . ."

"It's medicine," said Georgiana sharply. "It's special tonic. Father has nerves. It isn't what people say. It's just a soothing draught—"

The intensity of her tone and the speed with which she leapt to the defence of Na-Barno, even if he wasn't being attacked, was striking. Lucy swallowed and regrouped.

"I have one too," she said, and pulled her stone from her pocket. "See? We're safe."

Georgiana looked at her and at the stone, and then pulled the ring with the stone from her pocket, and in that moment, seeing the pale flash of the skin at her wrists, Lucy understood in an instant that she had made a terrible mistake.

Georgiana's hands were bare. They were always bare. She had never resorted to gloves or even rags to protect her from inadvertently touching a loaded stone and glinting the past. She had not covered her hands for the simplest of reasons: she was not a Glint after all, and when she said she had not seen the glass ignite and blaze a warning about the approaching walker in the glass, she was doing no more than telling her own truth. For had Sara Falk not said that the rest of the world saw the heart-stones as mere sea-glass, and that only a Glint could see the light it shone when peril approached?

This shocking fact that Georgiana had no idea what she was talking about hit her with almost the same stunning effect as when she had earlier seen the sea-glass in her hand and assumed that she too was a Glint. And what was worse was her stupidity: like any flat at the fair she had fallen under Georgiana's spell and drifted into a kind of infatuation that made her not think about something so very obvious.

"Where did you get it then?" she said.

"Get what?" said Georgiana.

"The heart-st— The sea-glass," she said, correcting herself and pointing. "That ring?"

Georgiana looked at the thing in her hand.

"This old ring?" She looked away to her left. "Charlie gave it to me."

"Charlie?" said Lucy.

"Yes," said Georgiana, looking back at her, eyes wide and composed again.

This information took the wind out of Lucy's sails, and she took a breath and slowed down.

"Why did Charlie have it?" she asked, the words out of her mouth before her cleverer self could tell her that there was no reason for Georgiana to know this. "I mean, why did he give it to you?"

Georgiana's mouth made a perfect moue, a slow-motion pout of flawless innocence so perfect it was almost pantomime.

"He gives me things because he likes me, I think. I don't know why he gave me this . . ." Her eyes sharpened as she looked at the now dull piece of glass in her hand. "It's not valuable, is it? I thought it was just some pretty coloured piece of old glass . . ."

"Yes," lied Lucy.

But the sharp eyes had snagged the truth.

"What's the trick of it?" said Georgiana. "There's a trick to it, and I'll wager something to do with the mirror that you smashed too."

She giggled and twined a finger in one of the ringlets cascading down on either side of her face.

Lucy was glad she giggled at that point. Lucy hated girls who giggled, and she needed something to push her away from the unconscious magnetism of Georgiana and let her think straight.

"It was quite a thing, smashing that mirror. I shouldn't be surprised if there's not a constable coming after us as I speak," said Georgiana, craning her head down the dusty road towards the town. "If you won't tell me what the trick of the glass lumps is, tell me why you did it?"

"I just lashed out," said Lucy, aware how weak her reply was: she felt too worn out by the glinting and seeing the girl burned, and then running the mile or so from the town to think in her normal straight line and produce a better lie.

"No," said Georgiana, taking her arm gently. "No, you don't want to tell me. I upset you by not understanding about this glistering thing you were talking about . . ."

"Glinting," said Lucy despite herself.

"Glinting," said Georgiana, twining an arm back around Lucy's waist. "There, I have it right now. And so you must tell me all about it, and we shall be friends again."

Lucy shrugged out of her grasp and began to walk towards the camp.

"Maybe later," she lied. "I feel too ill to talk now. I must lie down. It may be that I have a fever coming."

CHAPTER 57

PACKING UP

The arrival of the lead caskets in the Red Library was a strange thing for the whole house. The already oppressive atmosphere, occasioned by Sara's injury and all that surrounded it, became successively heavier with each muffled thump made by Emmet laying the metal boxes on the floor of the room as he brought them up from the secret passage to the river.

Of course, he was tireless and strong enough to carry two of the boxes at a time, but Hodge and Mr Sharp helped, managing to bring up a single box between the two of them for every four that Emmet brought up the stairs. Hodge was limping and his side still clearly hurt from the boot-storm it had absorbed, but no one commented, nor mentioned the black eye, which was still swollen to a slit and gone all the colours of the rainbow, mauve and indigo in the ascendant. The Smith and Cook busied themselves in the library, packing the books and objects in muslin and straw.

The Smith had a good blaze going in the cavernous marble fireplace and he kept a salamander crucible filled with molten lead in the heart of the fire. Whenever they had packed a casket and could fit no more inside, they put the close-fitting lid on it, and he took long-handled tongs and thick leather gloves and gripped the salamander, lifting it out of the fire. He then poured lead into the waiting runnels around the lid with unwavering hands to make a waterproof seal.

The first thing that had been sealed in the only casket which was double-walled, and lined with both fire-clay and chalk, was the innocent-looking single candle that always burned at the centre of the kitchen table. They carefully seated it in the middle of the casket and took care to transfer the five leafy twigs surrounding it without disturbing the star shape made by the oak, ash and thorn interlaced through the apple and hazel.

The Smith then carefully unscrewed the candle-sconce from inside the Murano Cabinet, wrapped it in red silk and sealed it in the same box.

"Wildfire and Discriminator can sleep safely together beneath the water," he said.

"You'd know if any of us would," said Cook. "Though why anyone would call a candlestick a key is beyond me. It's just confusing."

"Nothing wrong with a little confusion when you're hiding something," said Hodge, puffing past them carrying a smaller lead box.

"Look who's cheered himself up," said Cook.

"He still has hopes of the Alp," said Mr Sharp quietly. "The Raven is abroad and Jed is still casting about for the trail. Think the beating he took knocked a sense of proportion back into him."

"Good," said Cook. "Because I was worried you were *all* going hysterical on me."

They worked quietly and efficiently, and part of the silence between them was due to the fact that none of them felt good about what they were doing, or what it signified. The Smith had been right when he had told them that ends of things come quicker than most people realise, and they were each in his or her own way absorbing this new and bitter truth.

The only item which was not due to be casketed was the Murano Cabinet itself. Mr Sharp had insisted, and since it was the biggest object anyway, it had been decided to carry it down and put it in the brick arched room at the end of the secret passage lined with the handprints of the doomed victims of the Disaster.

"It's where it used to be anyway," said Mr Sharp. "That's where they went into the mirrors, and it'll stay well enough hidden there for now."

They agreed more easily than he'd expected because they knew why he wanted it kept above water. They had each talked about it with The Smith and had agreed that, since they were a Free Company, he should be allowed the liberty of leaving of his own volition, and leaving in the way he thought most fit.

"And if it's off on a wild goose chase into the mirrors. Well, good luck to him," Hodge had said. "He's an obdurate fellow, and we won't argue him out of it."

"Said the pot about the kettle," said Cook darkly.

The other thing they agreed was not to tell Sara. She had been declining so rapidly that she had stopped coming out of her room and was now only capable of making the short journey from her bed to a table by the fire where she insisted on eating her meals, although "eating" was a euphemism for "leaving most of it on the plate" in Cook's view. Cook had suggested that she take a tray in bed to save her the evident exhaustion of walking shakily across the carpet, but a spark of her old fire had kindled in her eyes as she announced that "only invalids eat in bed, and I haven't given up yet".

At the end of the day, Cook brought a tray of hot broth and two poached eggs on toast up the stairs. She stopped in the doorway, for there was someone else in the room.

Sara was asleep, her face slack and her breathing so light as to be almost unnoticeable. Cook saw Mr Sharp lean in and check that Sara was actually inhaling and exhaling by holding the back of his hand close to her nose. His other hand gently held hers, an intimacy Cook had never seen before.

She was about to clear her throat and give him a moment to compose himself before she entered, when he reached down and back into his coat and drew a blade that caught the candle-light in a short flat flash of highly sharpened metal.

Cook breathed in in shock, and was about to cry out, but stopped as she saw him gently take the end of Sara's hair, which was loose and tumbled around her head on the pillows, and cut a short length from it. The knife disappeared and he pulled a length of dark ribbon from his pocket, and quickly bound the stolen lock together.

Cook took a quiet step backward. Then another. Unfortunately there was a loose floorboard and it creaked loudly. She harrumphed and walked forward, eyes on the tray, and entered the room.

"Oh," she said, "there you are."

Mr Sharp was standing by the bed, no hint that he had ever been holding Sara's hand, the tell-tale lock of hair nowhere to be seen.

"She is no better," he said.

"She looks no worse," she replied.

"No better, no worse is not acceptable," he said. "I just came to bid her farewell. If you would be so kind as to tell her I came, and that I . . . wish her the very best of everything."

He stopped with his hand on Cook's shoulder.

"As I do you, my dearest old friend. As I do you all."

He shocked her by taking her hand and kissing it, and then walked stiffly out of the room without a backward glance. She put the tray down and wiped her eye.

"Bloody dust," she said to no one in particular. "Gets everywhere."

And she reached into her sleeve, fetched out her sail-sized handkerchief and blew a brisk cannonade into it.

Sara stirred but did not wake, even at that.

CHAPTER 58

A DECISION DEFERRED

On the morning of the day when Na-Barno Eagle (the self-styled Great Wizard of the South) was due to have his long-awaited and much-advertised contest with his arch-rival Anderson (the likewise self-styled Great Wizard of the North) Lucy woke late with a sick feeling in the pit of her stomach.

She lay with her eyes closed, listening to the sound of the showmen all around her getting their attractions ready for the holiday crowds, and tried to think why she should be feeling such a strong urge to run. She had certainly been feeling too happy and secure travelling with the Pyefinches, and having overheard them the night before last she was more than suspicious about their motives for being so kind and accommodating. Rose in particular seemed able to fire the most innocent-seeming yet pointed questions at her when she was off her guard, and Charlie definitely kept an eye on her, even when he thought she wasn't noticing. But it was more than that: something of what had passed between her and Georgiana on the previous night stayed with her. Although she knew Georgiana was a sharp and calculating girl and had been wary of her, all it had taken was a tearful appearance of vulnerability and the disconcerting warmth

and closeness of her body to make Lucy open up so perilously. It was almost as if Georgiana had feigned weakness to
pierce her well-placed defences.

And once that thought had occurred to her, she knew it
was so: Georgiana was good at reading people and using what
she read to manipulate them. Lucy had seen her do that in
the mind-reading show, and she had seen her do it around
the camp.

The sickness in her stomach was partly disgust at herself
for being needy enough to respond to Georgiana's pretended
weakness. She had wanted Georgiana to be something she
was not just because she, Lucy, was alone; that the Georgiana
sobbing so artlessly in her arms might be a fellow Glint had
been enough to make her betray herself. Softness and warmth
had undone her.

She opened her eyes and looked at the ceiling.

She was done with softness. She had no need of warmth.

And the only thing that stopped her leaving immediately
was the matter of the heart-stone in Georgiana's possession.

She did not quite want to believe that Charlie had given
it to Georgiana. The girl had looked to her left as she had
said it, fluttering her eyes in a way that made Lucy think it
was a lie. But she wanted to know how she had got it, and
why she had lied. So Lucy ignored the voice telling her to
run, and run right there and then, and instead remained at
the fair for one more fateful night. Her innate curiosity, and
something she couldn't quite put her finger on about the
specific stone in Georgiana's possession, overrode her natural
caution. If she ran now, she reasoned, she would never know
what it was. If she stayed just one more night, she might be
able to put her finger on it – indeed, by the time she had
washed her face and gone to find the Pyefinches she had
decided to do more than that. She had decided that since
Georgiana had no need of the heart-stone ring, and since it

was only the third that Lucy had ever seen, she would steal it before she left.

If one heart-stone was good, two would be better, and she would be insured against the frightening possibility that one day she might lose her own.

She rose quickly and rolled her blanket around a small bag of food she had been storing up for this very moment, and then walked out into the pre-dawn and hid them both behind the water butt on the side of the wagon in case she needed to make a fast getaway.

So as the day broke and she hunkered down next to Charlie at the camp-fire and asked for an egg with her bacon, Lucy had already determined to turn thief again, though by the time the day ended, the fruits and object of her larcenous impulse would turn out to be much darker and more perilous than she could possibly have imagined.

The day passed quickly as all fair days did, and she was so busy selling baskets of peppermint rock that she had little chance to do anything but take the money, smile at the customers and shuttle back and forth to Rose Pyefinch for new supplies each time she sold out. Rose thrust a piece of bacon sandwiched between two pieces of crusty bread into her hand at one stage and told her to sit down and take ten minutes' break, but Lucy smiled it off and said she was much happier eating as she went. Rose watched her dart back into the crowd with the basket crooked in one elbow, the other hand holding the sandwich as she bit chunks out of it, then turned to Charlie who had just come in the other side of the tent, looking for his and his father's lunch.

"She's got something on her mind," said Rose, nodding after Lucy.

"Nothing fresh there then," said Charlie with a smile. "I think she's just got that sort of mind."

"No," said Rose. "She's itchy about something new."

"Think she knows she's being asked after?" he said.

"Maybe," she said. "She's got keen ears as well as sharp eyes."

"Then maybe we should bundle her before she takes fright and does a runner," he said.

"We can bundle her any time we like," said Rose. "That's not the problem. It's how we keep the package safe once it's bundled. Lose the package and no one wins."

"I thought Pa had that in hand," said Charlie.

"I do," said his father, ducking his head under the flap in the tent. "Where's my sandwich?"

"You got it in hand?" said Rose. "Since when?"

"Since Hobb told me of the tattooed man asking questions in the shadows. I sent word up and down the water," he replied. "Well, word's come back. We have friends going east and west after the fair."

"Maybe that's it then," said Rose, looking at Charlie. "Maybe it is soon."

"She'll fight like a hellcat," said Charlie. "I ain't looking forward to it."

"Don't worry about that," said Rose, tapping her herb bag. "I'll give her something for it before we do it. She won't know a thing until they've got her miles from here."

Lucy, while unaware of this conversation, was not so caught up in selling peppermint that she closed her eyes and ears to the other business of the fair: this particular one had a different undercurrent to the others, and it all flowed one way, pulling the talk and the fair-goers towards Huffam's big top, for it was there that the great "Battle of the Wizards" was due to take place at dusk. It was to be the great finale to the day's revels, and from the number of people who flowed into the fair grounds, it was clear that the weeks of advertising and playbills which had been distributed ahead of the fair advertising the "magical duel" had done their work well.

She heard people talking excitedly about it, some who remembered Na-Barno's earlier tours through the area taking his side, others excited by what they had seen or heard of Anderson. Even the clench-faced citizens of the nearby town seemed to loosen up and become a little brighter-eyed at the forthcoming contest, especially as the day progressed and the sales at the beer tents began to have an effect on the general level of cheeriness.

The one strange thing which she noticed at the centre of the fairground was an ancient apple tree heavy with tawny russets glowing gold in the sunlight. What was strange was that each time she passed the tree, the apples were still on it: given it was a fair day and crowds were milling, she would have thought there were enough enterprising young boys to have stripped the thing by midday. Only when she finally got very close did she understand: there were two enormous mastiffs chained to the tree, growling if anyone came too near.

She did not have a chance to talk to Georgiana, who was busy selling tickets to the battle. She had come up with the novel scheme of giving away ribbons as well as tickets, all of a yellow colour. She herself was bedecked with them, twined in her ringlets, worn round her neck as a choker, and covering her dress so thickly that it appeared to be made entirely out of yellow bows.

"These ribbons and bows are favours, such as in olden times a fair lady might have worn for her gallant knight!" she cried. "Wear them to show which party you support in the coming contest! And when we win I shall kiss each and every one who wears the yellow!"

She was bright-eyed and at her most beautiful, and Lucy saw young men lining up to buy the tickets and ribbons in droves, and even their female companions, who Lucy would have thought might resent this, were themselves charmed and happy to bedeck themselves in the yellow favours.

By the time the sun had sunk behind the long palisade of willows, which marched across the landscape in company with the distant canal, the crowd pressing to get into Huffam's big top was so large that an announcement had to be made that due to the *excessive* interest in the duel, the show would be enacted twice, and only after a tally had been taken from each audience as to who had done better would the announcement be made as to which of the two magicians would henceforth be allowed to style themselves as "Great Wizard of North and South".

"Two shows?" said Lucy to Georgiana, who was hurrying past as the announcement was made.

"I know," said Georgiana, leaning in to whisper excitedly in her ear. "Two shows is twice the money. Father is beside himself with pleasure."

And she skipped off to tempt a group of farm boys who were eyeing her slyly from the shadows.

"Twice the money to be lost and all," said Charlie from behind Lucy.

"What do you mean?" she said.

"It's the bet," he said. "Na-Barno or Anderson, whoever wins the duel, they get to keep the takings. Loser gets nothing and agrees not to call himself wizard of anything. Dad's shutting up the stall early, special-like. It'll be a corker! You coming to watch?"

"I don't know," said Lucy, knowing she would and that it would be the very last time she saw him or Georgiana again.

CHAPTER 59

SAFE HOME

Mr Sharp did not linger on the matter of his departure: he took the Coburg Ivory from the empty shelf in the Red Library and walked down to the kitchen. Hodge and The Smith were sitting at the table, working on their pipes, adding a tobaccoey fug of their own to the steam from the burbling pudding-boiler on the range.

Jed sat up from where he was stretched out in front of the range and allowed Mr Sharp to scratch his head. The other two pointedly ignored the tell-tale ivory ball in Mr Sharp's hand.

"Got your knives?" said The Smith.

"Yes," he replied.

The Smith pulled a small thin-bladed dagger in a scabbard from his waistcoat and held it up without turning to look at him.

"Always room for one more."

Mr Sharp took it and drew it out of the shagreen sheath.

"Beautiful work," he said.

"Thank you," said The Smith. "Meteorite iron went into that, and that wavy line down the blood groove is purest silver I could find. Handle's made of oak, ash and thorn."

"So I see," said Mr Sharp. "Thank you, Wayland. I am most obliged."

"May help you more than a normal blade against some comers," said Hodge. "I made the sheath. Lined in red silk inside, it is."

"Thank you, both," said Mr Sharp.

They did not comment on the fact that he took his free hand and wiped it on the mixture of chimney soot and grease lining the brass catch-all above the range. He crossed to the door to the secret passage and opened it.

"I have been honoured that you all . . ." And here he coughed, cleared his throat and scratched Jed's head again, including him in what he was saying. "I have been deeply honoured that you all have done me the great kindness of being my friends since first I came here as a child. It has changed my life, and only for the better. I hope to see you again soon."

And with no more ceremony than the hint of a bow, he went into the passage and closed the door behind him.

"What did you say?" said Hodge, sure he had heard The Smith muttering something.

There was a pause.

"I said, 'Safe home' if it's any of your damned business," said The Smith eventually, puffing furiously at his pipe.

They both sat there for a while, watching the smoke eddy.

"Sorry," said The Smith.

Hodge waved the apology away as if it had been nothing, and then stopped.

"What's that noise?"

"Can't hear it," said The Smith.

Hodge shrugged.

"Thought I heard singing."

The Smith snorted.

"Have you ever heard him sing?"

"No," admitted Hodge. "He whistles sometimes."

And they left it at that.

And later, when they went into the passage to turn off the lanterns and snuff the candle in the Murano Cabinet, Mr Sharp was gone. All that remained was one new handprint on the wall by the door with his initials scratched below it.

CHAPTER 60

THE BATTLE OF THE WIZARDS

Lucy insinuated herself into the crowd as it wedged itself excitedly into Huffam's big tent for the first showing.

She wove her way through the crush, all the way to the front, and made herself unnoticeable against the canvas wall separating the crowd from the wings of the stage. She could hear voices on the other side, but before she could quite make them out there was a drum roll and a bright explosion of flash powder, and Huffam himself was on stage.

"Friends!" he roared. "Most esteemed friends and patrons, welcome to my humble auditorium, where we have the honour, nay, the distinction of presenting to you the two greatest magicians in the land! On my right, the esteemed Hector Anderson, the Great Wizard of the North—"

Anderson was a little older than Na-Barno, and a little shorter than Huffam, but there was a dark intensity to his eyes that held the audience until he dropped in a simple bow, at which point they cheered and whooped their approval. He was dressed in dark broadcloth and this, along with the way he held himself with a sober dignity, gave him the air of a senior member of the church rather than a showman. In fact the only strikingly showy aspect to his look was the startling contrast between his beetle-black eyebrows and the snowy white hair he wore brushed straight back from an impressively high forehead.

"—and on my left," continued Huffam, voice beginning to get hoarse from shouting, "is Na-Barno Eagle, the Great Wizard of the South!"

Na-Barno strode out from the wings to another good-natured roar of approval. His more theatrical rig of navy velvet was somehow rendered a little cheap-looking by the unshowy costume worn by his nemesis, and made all the more frivolous by the addition of a large yellow rosette he wore on his arm, fashioned from the yellow ribbons Lucy had seen Georgiana handing out throughout the day. Indeed, much more than half the crowd were waving yellow ribbons in the air as they cheered him. He smiled appreciatively and waved back.

Huffam wasted no time in getting to the nub of the event. He explained what the stakes of the battle were, that the winner would be allowed to call himself the Great Wizard of North and South in perpetuity, and the loser agreed not to call himself the Great Wizard of anything at all, ever again. He didn't mention the financial side to the wager. But he did explain he was going to toss a coin, and that if it came up tails, Na-Barno would perform first, if heads, Anderson.

Every head in the crowd tilted as they watched the gold coin spin up into the darkness and then fall back into the gleam of the smoking footlights, hitting the wooden stage with a satisfying clunk. Huffam quickly stamped his shiny riding boot on the coin to prevent it rolling away, and then stepped back to read the result.

"Heads!" he shouted, and the crowd roared again.

Lucy saw Na-Barno's face twitch with something like disappointment, but by the time she'd named the emotion for herself it was gone and he was smiling gracefully, bowing to Anderson and walking off the stage to more cheers.

Anderson watched him go with an answering smile, but it was one in which Lucy thought she saw more than a little satisfaction.

The reason became apparent as soon as he began his act. He explained that he was "interested" to be sharing a stage with the esteemed Mr Eagle (he would not call him a "Great Wizard", since that name was to be granted by the crowd later, though he was, he averred with a raised eyebrow, undoubtedly a Great *Something*. What that something might be he forbore to enlarge on, but his very public display of restraint on the matter cleverly led people immediately to the thought that it must be something highly discreditable). He would not say more, he explained, because he believed actions spoke louder than words, and so he would begin his performance forthwith.

Lucy was jammed at the front of the stage, close enough to risk getting both singed and asphyxiated by the smoking oil lamps lining the platform as footlights. She was wedged hard against the right-hand wing, and with her ear to the thin canvas she could also hear a sudden shocked inrush of breath on the other side of the canvas wing.

"My God – my God – my God!" whispered Na-Barno, panic rising with each repetition. "The wretch – surely he cannot—"

"He is, Father," replied Georgiana flatly. "He most certainly is. We're dished. How simple. How elegantly simple, and how damnably clever of him to do it."

What Anderson was doing, the "it" which had dished Georgiana and Na-Barno, was nothing more or less than their very own act.

Or rather Anderson was not only doing their act in perfect mimicry but also improving on it, since he performed each illusion and trick precisely as Na-Barno did it, but then added an embellishment on the end, topping him. The crowd enjoyed the spectacle for what it was, particularly the mind-reading portion, but Lucy could hear a building chatter spreading through the spectators around her as those who knew Na-Barno's routines from previous tours in the area began to chortle and tell those around them what Anderson was up to. This itself added an extra frisson of delight, and each trick attracted greater applause than the last.

Na-Barno was done for: to come on after this performance and do the very routines which Anderson had now done with such extra flourishes and enhancements would be as excruciating as repeating a joke someone had just told, and repeating it with less coherence and with worse timing.

But it turned out that Anderson was not merely ruthless and clever: he was implacable in his destruction of Na-Barno. After he had performed a mind-reading act with an automaton just like Na-Barno's, he did something that made the two watchers on the other side of the canvas wing gasp again. He reversed the cabinet with the automaton in it, and lifted the turban from the finely crafted papier-mâché head. He then showed with forensic exactness precisely how the levers and wires worked, proclaiming it a miracle, certainly, but one of artifice and engineering, and not, and he was very definite on this, absolutely not of magic. Too much of what passed for "magic", he explained, was mere smoke and mirrors, and the clever advances in machinery and engineering powering the new manufactories and mills across this proud nation were also being used by those performers who lacked real ability, and who used automata, clockwork and the like to counterfeit it.

"But, ladies and gentlemen, we just have time for one more thing," he announced with a knowing smile. "And with it I will not trouble you with mirrors, vapours, gimmicked boxes or even a clockworked automaton as cunningly crafted to confuse as this one. I shall instead do one more thing only. A simple thing but, I think you will agree, a wholly impossible thing!"

The crowd growled happily with approval.

"And the only way to do the impossible is, of course, to use real magic!"

The crowd aahed, which sounded like a big happy purr of anticipation. He leapt to the front of the stage, looming out over the lights, his up-lit face suddenly both affable and vaguely diabolical.

"And not only that! But I shall give you, my friends, the choice of what instrument I shall use to do it with: balls, rings, cups or cards. For the plain simplicity of the tools, the very basics of the conjuror's art will only emphasise the impossibility of the feat! For, gentlemen, I think you will agree, there is no woman so beautiful that is not made all the more so when seen without the impediments of clothing or artifice. This, my friends, is the real magic, the natural magic, the thing itself! And what is more, I shall give one thousand guineas in gold coin to anyone who can now or within the next twelve months show how I did the trick in a way that was not magical!"

This offer delighted the crowd, who cheered and roared its approval.

Anderson stepped back and whipped a scarf off the small table in the centre of the stage. There were three blue beakers on it, next to five small yellow balls, and then there was a pack of playing cards in a red box. Lucy, who had sampled all the shows and booths that she had come across on the showmen's circuit, thought it looked one of the least promising set of props she'd ever seen. And that was, as it turned out, just another part of Anderson's genius.

"They'll choose the damned cards," she heard Na-Barno say behind the canvas wall at her ear.

"Obviously," said Georgiana. "There's not a flat born that won't choose red, unless they're an Irish crowd."

The crowd, by a rowdy show of hands, proved that they were not Irish.

"Cards it is!" cried Anderson, picking up the pack and casually tossing it into the crowd, where a young farmer snatched it out of the air. "Well caught, sir! Now if you would show it to those around you, any who wish to see, and ascertain that this is a normal pack of cards, all present and correct, no absences, duplications or tell-tales marked anywhere . . ."

The pack was opened and passed around, and after much prodding and poking, riffling and shuffling, measuring and feeling, and even some sniffing and one – loudly prevented – attempt to bite it, it was agreed to be as standard and complete a pack as ever was.

"Then shuffle it!" cried Anderson. "Shuffle it and pass it on and shuffle again, as much as you like, then throw it back to me!"

The crowd liked about three people shuffling the pack, tolerated a fourth, after which they grew restive and called for the pack to be returned and tossed back on stage so the "magic" could commence.

The pack was lobbed to Anderson, who nimbly stuck his hands in his pockets and leapt backward so the box of cards landed at his feet, untouched.

"I will not touch the cards. But the pack must be cut," he cried. "Who has a knife?"

It was a largely rural town, and a great many of the men in the crowd had blades, most of which were now scooped from pockets, belts or boot-tops and waved in the air.

"I need a strong man who you all know to be local," announced Anderson. "Someone many of you know and can assure the others is not a plant of my own, for it is at this point that a mere prestidigitator would seek to insert a confederate to aid in the trick. But since this is no trick, but the real magic, I need no such assistance."

After a great deal of pushing and shoving, and shouting

and counter-shouting a burly man in carter's boots was propelled up on stage. He stood grinning at his friends in the crowd, who whooped and whistled at him.

"Now, my friend," said Anderson. "Please take the cards out of the box again, and put the deck on this table."

The carter did so and stood back.

"Now take your knife and stab through the pack, as far as you like. Do not worry about how hard you strike, for the table is sturdy, but try not to go all the way through the pack, for we shall pick the card in this way."

The carter raised his knife and stabbed the pack as hard as he could. The knife went a little more than halfway through. Some of the younger members of the crowd jeered him for a weak stroke, but Anderson waved them quiet.

"A single card is easy to puncture, but fifty-two layered together? Why, I knew a soldier saved by a small Bible in his waistcoat pocket which stopped a musket ball. There is strength in numbers, do not forget. Now, sir, lift the point of the knife and show the ladies and gentlemen the card!"

Anderson turned away, his back to the audience so as not to be able to see the card and the carter raised his knife, leaving behind the unpierced slab of cards and showing the face of the last one he had stabbed to the crowd.

"Make sure I do not see the card, but ensure everyone else sees it."

The carter waved the impaled cards from left to right, slowly, so that all could see the seven of diamonds.

"Now, sir, behind you on the table are the three cups. In one is a pencil. In the other a pair of sugar tongs. Please write your name on the card and show it to the crowd. If you do not wish to write your name, make a mark."

It being the way of crowds to enjoy a joke at someone else's expense, there was certain amount of coarse suggestions as to whether the carter knew how to write, but write he did, and showed the card to the audience with the word "JOAD" scratched boldly across it.

"Thank you," continued Anderson. "Now please fold the card in two, then grip it with the sugar tongs and hold it in the candle flame until it is entirely alight. Let it burn to nothing and then drop the ashes to the floor and stamp them into dust."

The carter did as he was asked, burning the card and scrubbing the black residue across the floor with his boots.

At this point Anderson whirled on the crowd, shook the carter by the hand and helped him return to the crowded murk beyond the footlight.

"Now you all saw that the cards were not gimmicked. That they were shuffled, not by me, but by you. And then you saw I had no control over how deeply the knife penetrated the deck, and that there was no way that I could know which card Mr Joad there would show you."

There was a rumble in the crowd.

"Oh yes!" he continued. "I know the name that he wrote on the card, though I have never met him before in my life. I know it just as sure as I know the card itself was the seven!"

The rumble from the crowd became appreciative.

"Not just the seven but the red seven, and not the heart, for anyone's knife may pierce a heart, but the seven of diamonds, yes, diamonds, I say, for the knife is not made that could cut through a diamond! The card was the seven of diamonds!"

The crowd cheered happily, impressed. Some were astonished, others began telling each other that they knew the trick – Lucy heard the man beside her admit that it was well enough done, but of course Anderson had rigged a mirror and seen the front of the card without having to look backwards.

Anderson smiled and waved the crowd to silence.

"Impressive, I hear you say. But not, perhaps . . . magic? Well, you are a hard crowd to please, wise and suspicious, just as you should be. So far, so difficult, but not, I fear, enough to convince you?"

"Show us more!" shouted a woman at the back.

"Show you I shall!" he shouted. "But real magic must be unconstrained, so if you all follow me outside into the night air, and keep absolutely silent, I swear to you on my life that you will see the impossible, for the deed is but half done! I swear that you will see no sleight of hand, no conjurer's legerdemain; I swear you will see real magic! But only if you keep absolutely silent and do as I say. Will you trust me?"

The crowd roared an agreement, and then remembered he'd asked them to be silent, which reduced the noise to an apologetic mumble, which in turn dwindled to silence as he stood in front of them with his fingers to his lips.

Once he was satisfied, he took a torch and lit it from the flame of one of the footlights, then made a gesture like Moses dividing the Red Sea and jumped into the crowd, which obediently parted, leaving a corridor through which he led the onlookers to the front of the tent and out into the night.

Lucy was swept out in his wake by the press of eager watchers. It was a very eerie thing to be part of, as the silent mass of people formed a column snaking through the bright lights and flares rigging the rest of the fair. The fair-goers who had not come to see the show saw this silent crocodile of earnest faces and became so intrigued by such an odd spectacle that by the time Anderson came to a halt the crowd was about six hundred people.

He stopped at the apple tree guarded by the two brindled mastiffs, who broke the quiet by beginning to bay and snarl at him as he used his torch to light five flares stuck in the paling erected around the tree, and then climbed over the fence.

"Mind the dogs! They're vicious—" shouted someone, who was then silenced by the hisses of the crowd.

The dogs barked furiously at Anderson, flinging themselves towards him, their chains snapping tight.

He merely raised a hand. They stopped. He turned his hand. They dropped to the ground. He waved. They rolled on their backs. The crowd sighed approvingly.

He climbed on an apple box and looked round at them.

"You saw the card picked at random? You saw the name written on it? And then you saw it consumed by fire? Yes?"

The crowd nodded.

"You may shout the answer to my next question: is it truly IMPOSSIBLE that the card you chose still exists?"

"YES!" bellowed the crowd, the pent-up noise breaking like a thunderous wave.

"NO!" roared Anderson right back at them. "NOT IF MAGIC IS REAL! If magic is real ANYTHING is possible!"

And suddenly he was all action. He shot a pointing finger to the heart of the crowd.

"Miss Georgiana Eagle! Would you be so kind, so very kind as to come and take this long walking stick I have here, and pull any one of these apples off the tree? The choice as to which is entirely yours!"

Georgiana was pushed and jostled to the paling, looking decidedly unhappy about being chosen, but when she was helped over the fence she settled herself in her ribboned dress and turned a professional smile back to the crowd.

"I do not need your stick," she said. "I choose this apple."

And she plucked one from a low branch and held it out to him. Lucy could see she had afforded herself some small satisfaction by not following his instructions quite as indicated. Anderson was not perturbed, nor did he take the apple. Instead he put his hands in his pocket again.

"Mr Joad!" he shouted. "Come forward!"

Joad the carter came to the front again.

"Both of you look and tell us what you see," said Anderson.

"An apple," said Georgiana.

"'S 'right," admitted Joad.

"Any distinguishing marks?"

"No."

"Any nicks or cuts or signs it has been tampered with?"

"No," said Joad, squinting at it. "It's perfect."

"Show the ladies and gentlemen," ordered Anderson, and Lucy saw Georgiana bridle again at the way he had suborned her, his rival, into acting as his assistant. Georgiana won another small victory by handing the apple to Joad, who showed it to the nearby crowd.

"One apple, ladies and gentlemen, nature's everyday miracle!" he said with a final flourish. "Real magic, I think you'll agree!"

The crowd didn't agree. It was confused. Then nonplussed. Then certainly and increasingly noisily very disappointed indeed.

"Oh," cried Anderson. "Oh. You were expecting something more?"

The crowd growled in agreement.

"THEN BE SILENT AND YOU SHALL SEE SOMETHING YOUR GRANDCHILDREN WILL TELL THEIR GRANDCHILDREN THAT YOU SAW!" he roared, and so loud was his voice that the crowd followed his instructions and quietened down into one giant held breath.

"Mr Joad," he said. "Be so kind as to cut the apple in half with your fine knife, but gently does it and do it in plain sight so there is no hint of trickery."

Joad unclasped his knife, the torchlight flashing off the steel as he locked the blade in place. Then he made a shallow circumference of the apple and then looked puzzled.

"Split it, Mr Joad," said Anderson, hands still in his pockets. "Split it so that all can see."

Joad gingerly prised the apple apart. There was an intake of breath, for in doing so he revealed a folded rectangle of red in the very centre.

"Take it out gently," encouraged Anderson.

Georgiana's face was tight as she watched Joad do so.

"Unfold it," said Anderson.

Joad did so. His face went white.

"But . . ." he said in shock. "But . . ."

"Exactly," smiled Anderson. "It is inconceivable, unbelievable, beating the very bounds of possibility! But not if you believe in REAL MAGIC! Show them, man!" Joad held the card up to the crowd as Anderson continued. "Ladies and gentlemen – for your delectation and amazement – I give you . . . THE IMPOSSIBLE!"

Lucy knew what it was before she could see it clearly from the rapturous response of the crowd.

It was the seven of diamonds – pierced by a knife, with Joad's name in his writing scrawled across it in thick pencil. There was no doubt. It was the destroyed card, hidden in a perfect apple.

It was, it must, it could surely be – she and the entire crowd agreed – Real Magic.

She glimpsed Georgiana, her face yellow as the ribbons on her dress, searching for her father's eyes in the crowd. She looked like she was drowning.

"Now, my friends, an intermission!" shouted Anderson, who was being hoisted on the shoulders of the crowd. "And back to the tent in a quarter of an hour for my friends the Eagles! But first, I think, a drink!"

Lucy watched the crowd, uproariously noisy and happy now, carrying him off to the beer tents. She saw Georgiana dart forward and grab her father's arm, leading him into an alley between two tents, whispering furiously into his ear. He walked like a broken man. Lucy followed at a distance, keeping herself in the deep shadows cast by the full moon in the clear sky above them, her fascination with Georgiana leading her onwards.

She had seen how little the girl liked being used by Anderson as his assistant, and could understand it. Anderson had undoubtedly poured salt in the wound he had inflicted on his rival by using his daughter as an unwitting collaborator. Lucy stayed in the shadows as they re-entered Huffam's marquee, which was now empty while the audience was making use of the intermission to enjoy the beer and cider being sold in the adjoining refreshment tents. Because of this she was able to hear what was going on backstage, even if she couldn't see it.

Na-Barno sounded hoarse and bewildered.

"He's done our act and then shown them how we do it. He exposed the secret of my automaton. And then, to top it and bury us five fathoms deep, he performed a truly impossible trick. I do not know what to do."

"Father, it is simple: if you know how he did the trick, we are rich. If not, we must change our plan. And do it fast!"

Georgiana's voice was tense and emphatic, as if trying to wake her father out of a stupor.

"I can't believe how he knew how exactly to mimic our act . . ."

"That I do know," sighed Na-Barno. "Because I stole it from him, child, or your mother did."

There was a cold moment of silence. Georgiana's voice frosted over, and became icily deliberate.

"And you did not tell me this?"

"I saw no need."

"No need? If you had told me we could have foreseen his stratagem! We could have planned to counter it. Now you have no choice left to you except to—"

"I know, child: to leave quickly while it is still dark and there is a crowd to confuse."

Lucy heard the slap as it landed, and the shocked silence that followed it was like punctuation.

"I am not fuddled, child," Na-Barno's voice quavered, close to tears.

"I was not slapping the fuddle, Father. I was striking *you*!" hissed Georgiana.

"But—" choked Na-Barno, the tears coming now.

Georgiana's interruption was brutal as another slap.

"Fetch the hand."

"But . . . but I have not mastered it," blubbered Na-Barno. "We have not built an act round it."

His voice choked off as if he was being gripped round the neck, but it was clearly Georgiana's intensity of purpose that was acting on him as she carried on, her voice unstoppable as the logic she proceeded to steamroller him with.

"Can you not see what has happened? Anderson has changed the rules. It's not about an act, Father. It's now down to two things: our survival and the impossible. And that hand is the most impossible thing I have ever seen."

"But his card trick was impossible—"

"But it was a *card trick*. Even if it was impossible, even if that itself is true, even if, God and all the little devils help us, it was real magic, it was still a card trick. And that is the only chink in his armour. If we are to gut him back, the way he has filleted us, then that is the only place we can stick the knife. Because people will always suspect a card trick as working by a sleight of hand or a misdirection of some sort, even if they are too slow to see it happening, because they *know* that is how card tricks work. A card trick itself is stale. The hand is something truly out of the ordinary."

"But, child, I do not know—"

"I do, and one of us must make the decision or we shall

both surely starve and end in the poorhouse. Get the hand. Ask it questions. It won't matter if the presentation is a little unpractised; what will matter is that you are not only topping Anderson's impossible thing, you are showing them something truly novel. Do it! They will be back and stomping on the floor in five minutes if we are not ready, and they will all have drunk two more pints apiece as well."

"You're right, child. It's a long shot, but by God we'll take it."

She heard Na-Barno run off the stage, and then heard a rustling noise as Georgiana did something to her costume.

Lucy, overhearing all this, realised she had witnessed a second secret performance, for Georgiana had not only picked her father up and revived him, but set him to do her will quite as if he were an automaton himself, she manipulating him as easily as a child jerking a marionette around by its strings. The other thing that impressed Lucy was Georgiana's sharp intelligence. While her father was still reeling from the effects of Anderson's clinical double blow, she had already both analysed exactly how he had done so and come up with a counter-move. Though what this "hand" was she had no idea. All she knew was that it was going to be worth seeing, even if it did not out-impossible Anderson.

CHAPTER 61

DEAD AWAY

Sara moaned in her sleep and tried to get up. She managed to raise herself onto her elbows, but then hung there, exhausted, staring at the guttering fire at the end of her bed. Then she dropped back into the pillows and stared at the shapes and shadows the flames were casting across the ceiling, exhausted by the effort.

"Thought I heard music," she muttered.

A hand reached out from the chair and patted her hand reassuringly.

"Mr Sharp?" she said, tilting her head towards the figure sitting patiently in the dark.

It was Emmet.

She stared at him, her face slack against the pillow. And then a growing horror began to widen her eyes.

"What has he done?"

Emmet pointed at her dressing table.

"What?" she said, voice catching. "Emmet! What has he done?"

Emmet got to his feet and crossed to the table. He tapped the mirror.

Cook heard the frenzied jangling and looked up to the

bell-board on reflex although she was already on her feet, knowing it was the bell from Sara's room that had roused her from her doze.

She burst out of the door and took the stairs three at a time, like a girl half her age and size. She opened the door to see Sara sitting bolt upright in her bed, staring at Emmet in horror.

"What—?" began Cook.

"What is Emmet trying to say?" said Sara.

Emmet tapped the mirror helpfully.

"What has happened to Mr Sharp?"

Cook scowled at Emmet.

"You talk too much," she said.

"WHAT?" said Sara.

Cook came and sat on the bed. She took Sara's hand.

"He's gone to look for your hand."

Sara shook her head, first slower, then faster,

"No," she said. "No no no no no NO!"

Cook tried to stop her but she shrugged out of her grip and threw herself on her side, nose to the wall.

"Not into the mirrors," she said in a voice that was so small that Cook could have been sitting beside a ten-year-old Sara.

"Was no stopping him," she said.

Sara began to bang her head slowly on the wall.

"No, Sara," said Cook, holding her back. "That won't help. That won't—"

Sara pushed her violently away and carried on banging.

"No," she said as she carried on banging her head. "No. No. No."

Emmet stepped over Cook's shoulder and gently but firmly held her head still. Then he reached a hand back to help Cook to her feet.

Cook pulled herself upright with difficulty and looked at him.

"Sometimes I think Mr Sharp might have been right about you," she puffed. "Keep her still if you can. I shall go and get something to help her sleep."

Emmet might have nodded. The movement, if movement there was, was so slight as to be almost unnoticeable. His attention was focused on Sara, who lay there, eyes screwed shut, tears leaking from them, face twisted in mute despair.

Cook looked back from the door. Sara's back curved away towards the wall, face hidden, Emmet hanging over her like a flying buttress, a single candle barely piercing the darkness sending his shadow ominously arching across the ceiling.

This is it, she thought. This is what the end looks like.

CHAPTER 62

THE EAGLES FIGHT BACK

The audience filtered back in from the beer tents and cider stalls. Lucy saw that there were now fewer people sporting yellow ribbons than before. It felt both more crowded and more boisterous as the spectators began to stomp and clap and call for Na-Barno.

"Things look a little soupy for the Eagles," said a voice in her ear, and she turned to find that Charlie had done his unsettling thing and turned up at her shoulder without her realising it.

"Don't count your chickens," she retorted. "They're not done yet. They've got something up their sleeve—"

"Wouldn't be magicians if they didn't," grinned Charlie. "But I don't know how they can top that last trick. Walking back in here, the ground's carpeted in them yellow rosettes. Crowd's an ugly thing when it turns. Poor old Georgie-girl."

At that point Georgiana stepped onto the stage, and the crowd simmered to a mutter and then complete silence. It became clear what all that rustling noise had been. Georgiana had taken off the beribboned costume and all the flashy stage jewellery and stood in front of them in a white under-dress, the shift that she had worn beneath her finery. More than that, she had scrubbed the make-up off her face so that she looked pale and defenceless, which Lucy saw as a second masterstroke, not just because the stratagem matched Anderson's determinedly unadorned style, but because removing the finery and the make-up allowed the audience to focus entirely on Georgiana alone, and Georgiana alone and unadorned was infinitely more compelling and – the word popped into Lucy's head unbidden – genuine.

The shift dress was both virginal and pure in itself, yet almost indecent in the way it allowed the curves and prom-inences of Georgiana's body to reveal themselves without any restraining stays or corsetry – not that she had any need of their gravity-defying aid from what Lucy could see. Georgiana's body was clearly well developed, thin-waisted and flat-stomached. But the lack of flash in the costume also allowed the girl's extraordinary face to shine, her eyes glimmering brighter than any of the paste jewels she had discarded. Her demeanour, when she began to address the crowd, was a similarly compelling mix of the demure and the provocative.

"Ladies and gents," she said, and Lucy noted that she had subtly altered her accent to appear less lofty than she normally did, adding a cheeky, almost cockney lilt to her voice. "Gents and ladies, my father will be with us in a moment. After such a memorable and impressive illusion as we have just witnessed he was bowled over, as you might imagine! He was so very deeply affected by the skill and grace of Mr Anderson's achievement that he decided on the very spur of the moment to show you something more than he had at first intended."

"I bet he did!" cried a woman from the back. "Anderson ate your lunch, and showed us how you cooked it and all!"

There was laughter at this, but also some men who shouted that the heckler should keep a lid on it and let the little lady have her say in the name of fair play.

Georgiana did not bridle at this, instead she laughed gaily and shrugged like the best of sorts.

"I cannot deny that Mr Anderson has seen our old act and reproduced it perfectly with considerable vim and added spice, so well did he anatomise it . . ."

"Anatomise?" shouted the woman from the back. "He pulverised you!"

Less laughter this time, and more shushing from the men in the crowd who were, for differing reasons, becoming rather entranced by Georgiana and her visible attractions.

"Yes," she laughed. "Yes, he did. For those of you who have been lucky enough to see my father's act, it will be obvious that Anderson has stolen our wind, so that for us to offer you our normal show would prey on your indulgence. It is because of that that we will today perform for the first time ever a feat which stretches the very definition of the impossible far beyond the already extraordinary sleight of hand that we have seen tonight."

At this point she turned and led a fresh round of applause for Anderson, who was standing in the crowd just in front of the stage on the other side from Lucy. This was clever since she acknowledged the rival and flattered him, which had the result of getting the crowd to like her for the guileless magnanimity of her gesture. Yes, thought Lucy as she watched, entranced: Georgie was something.

"Ladies and gentlemen, two days ago my father received a letter from Buckingham Palace itself, requesting that what we are about to show you be displayed to a certain crowned personage whom I will not be so indelicate as to name. We were asked to conduct a private performance at Christmas time. But now my father feels that this very night, this very minute, is the right time to show you the quintessential impossibility of impossibilities, the *Manus Gloriae* itself, the one, the only Hand of Glory!"

And with that she swept her hand toward the wings where a black-gloved hand emerged into the light. The audience was quiet for a moment, and then the fingers flexed and Na-Barno stepped out, revealing that the moving hand was detached from a body, and carefully held in his own fingers. At this point there was a settling noise in the crowd – not quite an intake of breath, but a shared sense of "now this might be very interesting".

"That girl can lie as easy as water flows," whispered Charlie admiringly. "Letter from the palace, my arse."

Na-Barno placed the hand on the table at the centre of the stage. As he explained what he was about to do, Lucy stared at it with growing unease. When he announced that he would choose someone from the audience to come up and verify that it was a real hand, flesh and blood and not clock-work, Anderson shook his head at his boots and mumbled something. Fast as a snake, Georgiana pointed at him and hushed the crowd.

"Mr Anderson!" she cried. "I detect an objection! If you would be kind enough to share it with the rest of the audience, I am sure we would all be much obliged."

Her question led to more head-shaking and then Anderson cleared his throat and, with the encouragement of others in the audience who shouted things like "Go on then, matey!" and "Spit it out, man," he averred that the method of choosing a seemingly random tester to verify the hand was fatally flawed, as she had called for volunteers but had then herself selected the tester from the hands that had gone up. He was sure, very sure, he was almost entirely sure that the delightful Miss Eagle was beyond reproach, but he merely wanted to point out that a strictly critical viewer might suspect that she had picked a, er, planted confederate out of the crowd.

"Mr Anderson is RIGHT!" shouted Georgiana, and turned

to look at her father. Only Lucy and perhaps Charlie had the angle on them to see that she winked in triumph before turning back to the crowd.

"If Mr Anderson suspects us of such a cheap and obvious trick, perhaps he could suggest a foolproof method of choosing a tester?"

The crowd grumbled approval, liking her open-hearted offer.

"Or . . ." she continued, waving them to silence, "or indeed, who could be a more critical or qualified tester and examiner than the very person who has most to gain by proving us false in our assertion that this Hand of Glory is a REAL HAND! Who but Mr Anderson himself?"

The crowd loved it and Anderson found himself man-handled up onto the stage by a posse of sturdy farmers.

His eyes told Lucy that he knew he had lost the unstoppable momentum he had seemed to possess at the end of his own portion of the show, but was not yet clear how or to what purpose.

"She done that well," breathed Charlie. "Played him at his own game, like he used her. And turnabout is fair play. Style in plenty, that girl has."

Anderson climbed up on the stage, a slight sickness in his professional smile revealing that he was aware he was being paid back in kind.

Georgiana passed him the hand. He opened the buttons at the wrist and peeled the black leather to reveal the pink skin beneath. The crowd murmured in approval. He pinched the flesh and looked puzzled.

"It is warm," he said despite himself.

"Of course," said Na-Barno. "I told you. It is alive."

Anderson pinched the skin again. The hand spasmed and he almost dropped it in surprise. The reaction was so real, so genuine that the audience jumped too, and from that moment on were convinced something magical was afoot.

"That's just a—" said Anderson, trying to compose himself. "That's just a trick."

Georgiana reached into the bundle of hair artlessly piled up behind her head, and retrieved a sharp hat-pin. As she did so her hair fell around her shoulders in a shining curtain.

"Prick it," she said, holding out the pin. "Did not the immortal Shakespeare describe what it is to be alive when he said, 'If you prick us, do we not bleed? If you tickle us, do we not laugh?'"

"Perhaps I should tickle it, then?" suggested Anderson, trying hard not to be led by this unexpectedly formidable young girl.

"It has no mouth to laugh," she said. "It is just a hand. But it will bleed."

The crowd began to chant "Prick it! Prick it!" with such gusto that Anderson had no choice. He held the hand up and jabbed the needle into the thumb.

Sara Falk woke with a cry and folded in over the stump of her hand. Emmet stood beside her and Cook was sitting by the small fire at the end of her bedroom looking up from the book she had been reading.

"Sara?" she said.

Sara did not look at her. Her voice was sluggish and distant.

"My thumb. They pricked my thumb again."

A small bead of red trickled down the thumb of the hand in Anderson's grip.

"Blood!" cried a girl at the front of the crowd.

"Jab it some more!" shouted a nasty voice from the darkness. "Give it what-for! Make it dance again!"

Anderson turned to Na-Barno and looked at him, his back to the crowd. His face lost the patina of professional bonhomie as he whispered, "This is not something for show, Eagle! It is something you cannot explain or control! You have never understood; you do not know what you are playing at. It is real . . ."

"Mr Anderson has told my father that the hand is REAL," shouted Georgiana. "Is that not so, sir?"

And so Anderson had to turn back to the crowd and aver, with a sickly smile of forced good grace, that the hand was real.

A shiver of dark delight went through the crowd at this, a sense that now they were to see something truly forbidden. Lucy, however, felt something entirely different.

As she watched Na-Barno set up the stage for the next part of his performance, she looked at the hand, a pale crab-like thing with the leather peeled back at the wrist, and she knew what it was. And she knew whose it was, even before Georgiana made a great show of removing the rings from her fingers and placing them on the hand.

"The *Manus Gloriae* is a powerful thing, ladies and gentlemen, but to keep it safe we do not allow it to wear the magical rings that truly awaken its dark power until we need to make it work for us," explained Na-Barno. "The rings are a safety feature. But now the hand is beringed and we will, in a moment, see the spirit awake and the hand be ready to communicate with us!"

Georgiana held the hand by the wrist as Na-Barno angled a large mirror over the table at forty-five degrees so that the crowd could see the tabletop. He then lit a candle lamp and directed the beam onto the hand which everyone could now see was not just resting on the table, but on a sheet of white paper.

He held up his own hand and magicked a pencil out of thin air to a mild smatter of applause, and then put it between the fingers and thumb of the hand.

He walked to the front of the stage and calmly closed the shutters on the footlights until all that remained by way of light was the lamp on the table and the mirror reflecting the hand beneath it out into the audience.

The tabletop appeared to float in the dark. His face and that of Georgiana hovered on either side, like disembodied heads on the edge of the candlelight. It was an eerie and effective illusion, and the audience grunted in satisfaction.

"And now, ladies and gentlemen, silence please as I wake the hand and ask it my name. I do this by tracing the words 'WHO AM I?' on the back of the hand, like so."

And he used the hat-pin to write the question carefully on the skin.

The hand did not move. He smiled.

"The spirit is willing, but the hand is still weak with sleep," he said, and jabbed it.

Sara Falk gasped again and then gritted her teeth.

"It's asking me who it is," she said. "If I do not write 'THE GREAT WIZARD' it will hurt me again."

"Then do so," said Cook. "Why give it cause to give you more pain?"

The hand twitched. And then, to the audience's great approval, began to write.

It wrote:

$$I. \ AM. \ SARA.$$

Na-Barno shook the hand and pinched it with a smile at the audience to hide his irritation.

"It is sometimes hard to make the spirit wake and do our bidding."

He wrote the question again.

The hand replied in bigger letters.

$$I. \ AM. \ SARA.$$

Georgiana cleared her throat and widened her eyes at her father.

Sara gasped.

"Sara!" said Cook. "What do you gain by defying it?"

Sara looked at Cook, her red-rimmed eyes glowing like coals in the pale snow-field of her face.

"What do I gain by defying a cruel oppressor?" she growled quietly. "Everything. I gain myself."

Out of sight of the audience Na-Barno had palmed the hat-pin and jabbed the hand, holding it steady as it twitched and flinched in pain.

"We will try again! Perhaps an easier question, one which will tax its will a little less," he said, and he said the words as he wrote on the hand, "What colour is the sky?"

The hand gripped the pencil and wrote again.

I. AM. SARA.

Lucy was getting a sick feeling in the depth of her stomach as her brain played tricks on her and made her remember the smell of baking Eccles cakes and the kind eyes that had looked into hers as Cook had gently sponged the hessian gag from her mouth, the same grey-green as the stone on the disembodied hand.

Lucy was used to doing bad things. She was used to lying and cheating and stealing and running away. These were all the tools by which she survived. And though she could only remember her past in dribs and drabs, she could not remember this feeling, this sense that she had done something worse than just bad or criminal, that she had done something fundamentally wrong.

The crowd around her was silently staring at Na-Barno,

and she was aware that she had stopped listening for a moment. He was holding the hand, stump down, over the flame of the candle lamp.

Lucy heard herself gasp "Don't!" without knowing she'd said it, but the rumble of the crowd drowned her out.

"Sometimes we must warm her up!" cried Na-Barno.

Sara cried out and writhed in her bed, clasping at the mirrored end to her arm. She gritted her teeth and tried to keep silent, her jaw clenched shut, her eyes wide, and she tried until Cook was sure that the veins standing out on her temples would burst.

"Child!" she said, unable to watch any more.

As she reached out to her, Sara choked out a despairing gasp, tears streaming from her eyes.

"Hot," she sobbed. "Burning!"

"Sara—" said Cook.

"Enough," said Sara, falling back on the pillows. "Enough. It has won."

The hand flopped in Na-Barno's grip as he pulled it away from the flame, which had also dulled the mirrored stump with candle soot.

"Now we shall see!" he cried. "Now the spirit is AWAKE!"

He propped the hand onto a clean sheet of paper and put a pencil between its fingers.

"Another question!" he called. "Perhaps a simple mathematical one?"

A loud voice at the back enquired as to what three times six was. Na-Barno traced the sum on the hand and stepped back. The angled mirror showed the hand scratching out a number 18.

The crowd applauded.

"Another!" shouted Na-Barno.

Someone asked what seven times ten was, and the hand scratched out a large 70.

The crowd applauded even louder.

"A more general question, perhaps?" cried Na-Barno, elation pinking his cheeks. "Now the spirit seems to be so amenable!"

"What drink is made from apples?" shouted a woman near Lucy.

Na-Barno traced the question with his hat-pin. And the hand flexed and wrote "CIDER".

Now the crowd was baying its approval.

"Let us ask again if it knows who I am, shall we?" asked Na-Barno. The crowd roared a thunderous YES.

He wrote the question with the hat-pin.

The hand didn't move.

He prodded it with the point of the pin. It winced, and then began to write.

THE ENEMY.

The crowd gasped.

He smiled tightly and exchanged a look with Georgiana. She nodded at the pin. He jabbed a little harder.

The crowd oohed, this time catching the gesture and the bead of blood that dropped onto the paper.

"It cannot feel pain," cried Na-Barno quickly. "Not as you or I do. It only needs a little . . . gingering up!"

Lucy felt sick.

"Who—?" began Na-Barno, but the hand spasmed and began to slash letters before he could finish tracing the question.

I. AM. SAR. FALK.

The hand missed an A, but something broke inside Lucy, so suddenly and sharply that she felt it like a crack.

And so, without planning to, she moved.

As she moved she knew she had two things in her favour: Na-Barno had shuttered the footlights to give the single lamp on the table greater dramatic effect in showing what was being written on the paper. And secondly, the crowd was already confused and mostly drunk.

She snatched the hat off the man in front of her and skimmed it hard across the front of the stage. The hat hit the candlestick and toppled it. The flame went out, and for a moment the tent was plunged into darkness. Before the crowd could react, before it worked out that this was not some surprising part of the act, Lucy was in motion, going fast, vaulting over the shuttered footlights. She hit Na-Barno in his midriff with her shoulder and felt him grunt in surprise as he toppled backwards. She scrabbled for the hand and for a horrific moment couldn't find it.

Then, as she heard Georgiana shout "LIGHTS!" her hand closed on the gloved hand and she gripped it to her chest and ran for the rear flap of the tent. She tripped and stumbled as the noise of the audience rose in uproar behind her, and then she felt Georgiana's fingers grasping blindly for her, nails raking painfully across her cheek, narrowly missing her eye, and then she was free again, bursting out of the flap into the narrow tented back alley.

She heard Georgiana shouting after her, and saw a flare of light from within as someone unshuttered the footlights.

Knowing it would take time for the crowd to realise what was happening, she stopped and waited as Georgiana pushed through the gap, close on her tail.

"You?" screamed Georgiana. "You—"

Lucy hit her. The first punch stunned her to silence. The

second punch, harder and more measured, knocked her clean out.

And then Lucy sprinted away into the night, secure in the knowledge that her one immediate pursuer was out for the count. She jinked and dodged guy-ropes and tent pegs, zigzagging across the still crowded fairground, heading for the Pyefinches' wagon.

She fully expected to spend a few nights in the open, which was why she had hidden the blanket and food, and now she was not just running away but expected to be chased, she thought it even more important she take to the countryside and avoid the open road for as long as possible.

She felt the hand jerk and twist in her grip, and clutched it close to her chest.

"Shhh," she said. And then wondered why she'd spoken.

Behind her, several tents away now, she heard the hubbub of the crowd emerging from Huffam's tent, a noise punctuated by a piercing cry of "Stop, thief!"

She skidded beneath two wagons on the edge of the fair and then found the Pyefinches'. She hurdled the carriage shaft and felt her way to the barrel lashed to the side. She reached behind it, pleased to note that the hue and cry seemed to be moving away from her. She was experienced enough at disappearing to know that now she was going to be able to slip into the darkness and put many miles between her and anyone who knew her by dawn.

The metal shackle which dropped round her wrist, and the click as it locked, was thus more than a disappointment.

She tied to rip her hand free, but it was caught.

"Go easy on that, girlie," said a familiar voice.

She turned to see Charlie behind her, a strange look in his eye.

Before she could say anything, two more figures appeared from behind the barrel. It was his father and mother.

"Don't yank your hand; you'll just hurt yourself. You're caught and you're not going anywhere," said Mr Pyefinch.

What was even more of a shock was the fact that Rose and Charlie carried long knives, and Mr Pyefinch was hefting a short blunderbuss in his hands.

"Wherever you thought you was a-sneaking off to with my good food and blanket, you're not," said Rose. "You ain't who you say you are, and there's interested folk doing the rounds offering good money for someone who sounds just like you."

They looked at her. She was aware she was panting like an animal at bay.

"Face it, missy," said Charlie. "You been bundled."

CHAPTER 63

AN ILL MET BY MOONLIGHT

Ravens are not usually nocturnal, but the Raven was the least conventional of birds and this, among a host of other avian norms, was a rule it pointedly ignored. It perched on the roof of a house opposite Mountfellon's property on Chandos Place and watched. It watched by daylight, in rain and sun, and it watched in the moonlight. At present it stood in the night-shadow of a chimneystack enjoying the clear view afforded by the light of a new moon that rendered the street in an eerily precise grisaille, one in which detail was clearly visible although it was nearly midnight, but from which all semblance of colour was absent.

The Citizen slipped from house to shuttered coach almost without disturbing the stillness of the scene. The Raven caught the flash of motion in the narrow space between door and door, and saw the springs of the coach flex minimally as they took on the desiccated, almost negligible weight of the very old man. The coachman flicked the tip of his whip over the rear of the horses, and the coach eased into the street and headed east. The Raven stretched its wings and stepped up into the air, following silently from above.

* * *

The Alp had presented itself, as arranged, at a house in Golden Square. The doorman had not asked for a name and the Alp had not given one. No words were spoken at all. The doorman showed it up the stairs into what had once been the grand salon of a smart mansion. The damask wallpaper had begun to rot and peel off the walls in patches, and the chandelier above was bagged in muslin spotted with the droppings of birds that had evidently become trapped in the great room at various times in the past, on the rare occasions when the shutters had been opened and fresh air let in. From the musty smell, that had been a long time ago. The carpets had been removed and the parquet flooring, once elaborate and polished, had warped and sprung. What furniture there was had been pushed to the sides of the room and covered in dust cloths, similarly bespattered with droppings. A chaise-longue and a card table with two chairs stood in the centre of the room. A board about three feet by four was propped against the chaise, and on the floor next to it was a set of large stone weights with iron rings in the top, of the kind used for weighing corn sacks.

The doorman put a lit candle on the table next to a small summoning bell and left the Alp to enjoy the rapidly fading grandeur of the room by itself.

The Alp looked round the room once, pushed its hair behind its ears and settled down to wait, facing the door, face as blank as ever.

It waited calmly as time passed and little else moved in the dusty house.

It did not hear the secret door in the panelling open behind it, but it did not jump or show surprise as The Citizen creaked across the parquet and spoke.

"You are prompt."

The Citizen spoke in German with an Austrian inflection. The Alp turned to look at him, something almost like interest appearing in its face before vanishing behind the mask of impenetrable blandness it habitually affected.

"You are surprised I speak your language so well?" said The Citizen, walking around him slowly like a buyer assessing a brood mare.

The Alp did not react.

"I should do. I was given pointers by a very beautiful woman," smiled The Citizen. "A regally beautiful one. She helped me master the ugly gutterals of your tongue, and more than that . . ."

He traced the smooth skin of the Alp's chin with a trailing finger.

"More than that: she made a deal with me. For her life, she gave me my life. She gave me your secret, your family's secret. Lie on the chaise."

The Alp got up obediently, went to the couch and lay flat on its back. It reached over and pulled the board on top of itself up to the chin but leaving its face free. Its face gave no indication that this was anything other than unremarkable, and its eyes lost themselves in the intricacies of the peeling plasterwork above as The Citizen climbed carefully on top of the board, his knees drawn up so that he knelt on the Alp's chest in exactly the same way that the Alp had knelt on the breasts of its victims.

"She thought she was buying her life and that of her family, the Otherbitch," said The Citizen. "That's what we called her, you know. In French it is more amusing: 'l'Autrichienne' means 'Austrian woman', which she was, but it also sounds like 'la autre chienne' which means 'the other bitch'. Anyway, the Otherbitch got a life for a life, no more no less. And here I am. And there, no doubt she is, in hiding, forgotten somewhere, unless she tired of life without her luxuries and titles – in which case she no doubt let herself die, though I doubt she had the will to end her own existence. And here you are. Her family's great secret."

He stared down at the Alp, the greed in his eyes a stark contrast with the breath-stealer's studied blankness. His lip curled.

"Everything is a trade, all is commerce. Your family survive unmolested because you do service to the great and powerful who protect you. Your coming to me in this new city is a favour redeemed, like a token. What I propose is a new deal, which is as follows: you stay in the city in these apartments at my expense. You are discreet. You are available. I in turn provide you with young women, women who no one will miss. You recruit their strength within yourself in safety and comfort, with no fear of discovery or alarm, and in turn pass the vitality you harvest on to me. Do this for two years and your family's debts are paid. Do it for five and, if my plans and those of my confederate come to fruition, your entire family can escape the forests and mountains in which they have hidden for so long and walk London's streets as lords of a new order, lauded and not feared. What do you say?"

The Alp said nothing. It looked at The Citizen's tight parchment face and – after a moment – nodded.

"A deal then," said The Citizen. "We need not clasp hands on it for we shall presently seal it with a kiss."

He reached over to the table and lifted the bell. From the speed with which the door opened when he rang it was clear that the doorman had been waiting for his summons on the landing outside.

He faltered at the sight which greeted him, but recovered as he walked over in response to The Citizen's beckoning hand.

"Do you know who I am?" rasped The Citizen.

"No, sir. Never seen you before in all my born days," replied the doorman, evidently having decided that the best way to deal with the oddity of the tableau was by ignoring it and fixing his eye a foot above The Citizen's head.

"Good," smiled The Citizen. "If you'd be so kind as to lift those weights onto the board here, I'd be most grateful. I am too enfeebled to do so myself."

The doorman nodded and then grunted as he lifted the heavy weights as directed.

The Alp took a deep breath and held it as the pressure was increased, but even when the doorman fancied he heard a rib start to crack, it kept its breath behind a mouth which remained tightly closed. The doorman, now breathing hard himself, leant to pick up the last weight and The Citizen held out a hand in which there was a small doe-skin money-purse to still him.

"You told no one you came here tonight?"

"No, sir," said the doorman, eyes suddenly glued to the purse.

"You followed your instructions to the letter?"

"Yes, sir," gulped the doorman.

"And you will tell no one of what you have seen here tonight?"

"No, sir. Not a peep," affirmed the doorman, eyes fluttering as he said it. The Citizen graced him with a wintry smile made all the more like the grin of a death's head by the candle guttering in front of him.

"Then here. Your pay."

The doorman reached for the purse.

As he took it, The Citizen's free hand gripped his wrist and yanked him closer, while the other twisted and flicked a straight barber's razor out of its sleeve.

"Wh—?" the doorman began, but the rest of the word petered out in a damp gurgle as The Citizen slashed the finely honed blade across his throat, opening it to the night, cleanly separating the windpipe from the voice box and severing the great artery in one scything arc. He thrust him away immediately so that the doorman fell over a chair scrabbling bloody fingers at the great pumping wound beneath his chin.

The Alp's eyes followed the action but betrayed no emotion. The Citizen watched the doorman's heels drum and spasm on the parquet.

"He lied. All men lie. He would have told someone. This is too strange an occurrence for him to have bottled it up for ever," he said, flicking the blood off the razor with a practised snap of the wrist before folding it back into the handle and sliding it back into his sleeve.

"A pessimist would say I killed him. An optimist would agree that I enabled him to keep his word. And you, my friend, you say nothing, do you?"

The Alp looked back up at him, unblinking, its eyes beginning to bulge with the effort of not exhaling.

"Very well," said The Citizen. "I am quite exhausted. Bring me life."

And with that he lifted the final weight onto the board in front of his knees, and bent over the Alp, twisting his neck so that he could fasten his mouth over his mouth and nose at the same time, and began to inhale in as the Alp exhaled in a long and seemingly endless breath.

The Raven was outside in the mews behind the house.

The night was quiet.

But it was not so far from the great salon within that it did not hear a peal of laughter, strong and vigorous laughter, and a French voice, raised in delight as it announced,

"I am young! Again I am young!"

CHAPTER 64

AN EXCHANGE WITH THE SLUAGH

Lucy pulled hard at her hand but it was securely manacled to the water barrel. She was furious and scared. She decided to show none of that to the Pyefinches, who had clearly lived up to her very worst expectations and betrayed her. She cursed herself for having let her guard down so far as to like them. It just was the same kind of weakness that had led to her troubles with Georgiana. She wasn't normally this weak, this susceptible. She thought it was to do with the gaps in her memory. After all, if she could only remember half of her life, maybe she only had half the reserves of her normal strength to rely on.

"What are you doing?" she said, trying to sound very calm. "Why have you done this?"

"You're coming with us," said Charlie.

"I'll call for help," said Lucy. "Let me go."

"You won't call out," said Rose calmly, her eyes not on Lucy but scouring the blackness beyond the lights of the fair. "If you call out, the Eagles'll be here in a trice and they'll get their precious hand back."

Lucy laughed at her, a short bitter cough without a hint of good humour in it.

"Think I wouldn't swap the hand for my freedom?" She eyed the weapons. "For my life?" Rose stiffened, as if she had seen something in the night, and put the knife to Lucy's throat.

"Not another word," she whispered.

It took Lucy a moment to realise that they weren't looking at her. They were staring into the dark with an air of grim preparedness.

And then two bits of shadow shifted, and two Sluagh emerged from the blackness, almost as if the swirling tattoos on their faces were not inked but made out of the surrounding darkness, and were now bleeding them into the light from the heart of the night itself. As they advanced, she could see they were men whose clothes were patched together from animal skins and fastened with small bones. The tallest one carried an ugly bronze hook-backed blade which caught the reflections of the fair lights behind the Pyefinches. The other wore an old-fashioned bicorn hat, once black but now green with mildew and sporting a spiral fan of bird skulls where there had long ago been a silk cockade. It was hard to see if he was scowling because the tattoos on his face gave him a permanent snarl, but his voice was grim with malice.

"The girl," said Bicorn Hat, pointing at Lucy.

A nasty bullet of memory hit Lucy as she looked at him, a sharp, disjointed remembrance of someone similarly skin-dressed and bone-hung, talking to the man Ketch as he handed her over to him in London. The recollection came out of one of the dark holes in her mind. The Pyefinches now appeared to have captured her with the intention of handing her over to these tattooed men, who were not quite − or perhaps that was not *only* − men.

"And why do you want her?" said Mr Pyefinch, his blunderbuss swinging between the two of them.

"We will pay you for her," said the one with the blade,

and produced a jingling pouch from his pocket. He shook it noisily at him. "Gold."

"Why do you want her?" repeated Pyefinch.

Bicorn Hat moved towards him and looked him hard in the eyes. Then he turned his gaze on Rose. Rose met his stare, and Lucy saw something strange come across the older woman's face, first a flicker of concern, followed by a deadening of her look and a kind of sleepy dullness in her eyes. Before Lucy could even work out if it was in her interest to say anything, the Sluagh had moved to Charlie, whose head drooped in sleepiness even faster than his mother's. Lucy dropped her gaze and looked at her feet. She determined not to be practised on in whatever way the Sluagh had dealt with the others.

"Trade is trade. We have said we will pay you for her," said the one with the blade, stepping forward. "You daywalkers hunger for gold since it reminds you of the sun which lights and blights you, and we will give it to you. But if you want something from us—"

Pyefinch stopped him with a jab of his gun.

"Like an answer?" he suggested.

"Like an answer," sighed the Sluagh. "It is only fair you pay us. But in silver, mind, for silver is the moon's metal, and we go by night."

"Or if you have no moon-silver, give us that strange hand perhaps," said the other with a wheedling tone. "Give us the hand and then we'll tell you."

He smiled at Pyefinch, held his gaze, and after a moment stepped back, happy at the dull look that his eyes had produced in the other.

"That is all of them blunted and bent to our will," he said. "We should have waited to see if they had silver for us."

"We'll take the hand anyway," said the other.

"We do not need the hand."

"It is our enemy's hand. See the rings. We can burn it. Then the owner can never be healed, and The Oversight will be dealt another blow."

"Burning would be good," smiled the blade-holder. "Or flaying."

"Or both," agreed his companion. He nodded at the Pyefinches and Lucy. "What shall we do with them?"

"Take the girl who is listening to us while avoiding your eyes. We shall pass her to the Templebanes. Cut the others down. The rest of the daywalkers will think the girl did it and fled," said the one with the blade.

Lucy pulled against the shackle on her wrist but it was no use: she couldn't run. And now she was going to see the Pyefinches slaughtered. She didn't know why they had captured her, because it didn't quite feel right that they had done so to hand her over to these strange night men, though she could think of no other reason. She was confused and scared. She nudged Rose, who appeared not to feel it; her face was blank as if asleep on her feet.

"That is tidy," said Cocked Hat as he reached back into his tattered cloak and retrieved his own broken-backed blade. "Take the girl and leave the blame on her."

"Wait . . ." said the first.

His voice was sudden and puzzled.

"Wait?"

"There were four of them . . ."

Lucy looked round. Charlie had disappeared.

For the first time, the two Sluagh looked less than commanding as they peered about them, searching the shadows just as the Pyefinches had done a moment before they had walked out of the dark.

Rose looked up at them, the stupid look sliding off her face to be replaced by something chilling and tough.

"I expect you'll be feeling a little disappointed," she said.

"What?" said the first Sluagh, turning to his companion. "I thought you had bent her will."

"My will doesn't bend," said Rose. "I'm not built like that."

She turned to Lucy.

"Don't look," she said with great seriousness, and though Lucy normally made a point of not doing what people told her without first questioning it, this time she just closed her eyes.

Hearing it was almost worse, though it happened very quickly. There was a gasp and a rustle of clothing as someone turned very fast, and then a sound like a cabbage being chopped into with a knife, then a grunt of surprise and then she heard a Sluagh gasp—

"Bu . . ."

—and then a heavy meaty thump and another sound like something slicing through the air very quickly that ended in a snick and sudden wet gargle, and then there seemed to be a beat of absolute silence as no one moved, and then two bodies hit the grass, one slightly before the other.

"It's done," said Charlie. "But I shouldn't look too closely if you've got a weak stomach."

Lucy opened her eyes. Rose was bent over the body of one of the Sluagh, wiping her blade clean on his moleskin waistcoat. Lucy saw dark blood in the deep gash across his throat. Charlie was tugging a blade from the chest of the other Sluagh, whose heels were still drumming on the grass.

"Look away, girl," said Pyefinch, wiping something off the butt of his blunderbuss. "No need for your eyes to dwell on the butcher's bill."

The Pyefinches looked at each other.

"This is bad work," said Rose.

"Only bad if other Sluagh ever find out we did it," said Mr Pyefinch, slinging his blunderbuss over his shoulder by its strap, and then reaching down to grip one of the bodies by the collar of its jacket. "Come on. We'll put them in the canal while we wait."

Rose gripped the other Sluagh by the foot and the two adults dragged them off into the dark. Charlie looked at Lucy.

"Dunno what they had in mind for you or who these Templebanes is, but now you see why we had it in mind to bundle you."

"I thought you were going to hand me over," said Lucy, head reeling. "I thought you were going to take their gold."

"Their gold ain't ever gold," said Charlie. "They'd have handed over a bunch of pebbles or acorns or some such, and some poor flat would have thought they was gold coins for a while until the black glamour wore off their eyes again."

"They tried to fool your parents. I saw them pretending to . . ."

"We don't fool so easy. No time for a chat," said Charlie. "Eagles'll search their way here eventually and frightening as them Sluagh was, won't be nothing to what Georgie-girl will be if she catches hold of you. Now you can choose. I'm going to unshackle that hand. You can run, or you can come with me. Dad's got a plan for keeping you safe, see?"

And with no more than that he freed her wrist and stood back.

"If you're going to run, head that way and avoid the woods," he said. "Open fields until daylight, and watch the hedges. There'll be more Sluagh out there, I'm thinking, and they don't like open ground as much as something that can cast a nice shadow, like a copse or a spinney."

Lucy looked at him. He was smiling like the old Charlie she'd come to like so much, not like the new one with the knife.

"Fine," he said. "Reckon you can move as fast and quiet as me, so stay close."

She almost ran at that point because he was acting as if she'd made a decision to trust him, which she hadn't. But then he sped into the dark and she was following him, going fast-and-slow alongside him, and it was strange and unsettling for her for the first time in her life to be moving across the ground, jumping ditches and jinking through hedgerows with someone else who was going at her speed while the world around them appeared to have gone sluggish. It was also exhilarating.

They arrived at a low bridge spanning the canal just in time to see Rose tip the last Sluagh into the water. As the body slipped beneath the water there was a harsh sizzling sound and black steam came off the surface, and then the water flowed past and flattened out, reflecting the nearly full moon above them. For a short moment Lucy saw the steam make a shape against the silver of the moonlit bridge, as if the tattoos had been set free from the bodies in the canal, making a swirling, filigreed three-dimensional cage in the exact shape of a man, and then they lost their form and were gone in the wind.

"Night take them," said Rose quietly, and then turned to see Lucy and Charlie.

"Under the bridge," said Mr Pyefinch. "And we'll have us a little chat."

They ducked under the arch and found a log rolled up against the stonework. They sat on it in a line, and Mr Pyefinch stared up the river against the current, as if expecting something. The little chat began with a question that Lucy had been dreading.

"Who are you?" said Rose.

"Who are *you*?" countered Lucy.

"You're not Sara Falk," said Rose. "Never were, either, not in any of our minds. Not the real Sara. Though a name's like a coat, and if you've a need of stealing either, it's as well to take a good one, I'll grant you."

And though she too was scanning the darkness up the canal like her husband, she reached back and gripped Lucy's arm in a friendly way as if to say everything was all right. Lucy felt the grip on her arm, and the disembodied hand clutched to her chest. It was limp and lifeless now, though in the stillness she could feel it was alive, like the ghost of a pulse.

"I'm Lucy Harker," she said. And the whole story of her adventures since being taken to Wellclose Square poured out of her. She left it all in, even the fact she had big holes in her memory, even the fact that she had tried to steal from Sara Falk's library, and that somehow Sara's hand had been cut off trying to save her from being tugged into the mirrors. She told how she had mistaken it for a black crab on the floor of the circus tent in the pandemonium of her arrival. She told it all because once she started talking it was hard to stop the gush of words, and when she stopped she felt as if a great pressure had been relieved within the walls of her skull. And then when she finished they all sat there in silence as Mr Pyefinch busied himself with his pipe.

"May I see the hand?" said Rose.

Lucy let her take it, and watched as she stepped out from the cover of the bridge to examine it in the moonlight. She saw her look at the two rings for a long time, and then she ducked back beneath the brickwork and returned the hand.

"Lion and unicorn," she said to her husband. "And Sara Falk never goes ungloved."

"That's it then," he said, reaching into his waistcoat pocket for his matchbox. As he lit his pipe, he looked at his wife, and in the flare of the match Lucy saw his eyebrow raised in a question.

"It's not over, is it?" she said. "We've been right to stay clear of The Oversight all these years. In the old days, this girl would never have got within a mile of the Red Library, let alone steal from it. The Free Company's a danger to such as us, and not any kind of protection. Never has been, not since the Disaster."

"Nothing's been good since the Disaster and they brought that on themselves," said Pyefinch, sucking the smoke into his lungs and then blowing it out in a long sad sigh.

"What disaster?" said Lucy. "What was the Disaster?"

Pyefinch looked at his wife. Rose shrugged and carried on watching the darkness.

"No harm her knowing," she said. "Maybe she's got a right to, even though she's a thief. Maybe her story's wrapped up in it."

"Maybe it's why she's a thief," said Charlie. "Thieving's different if you're doing it to survive than if you're just greedy. I don't think she's greedy. She works 'ard enough."

"Well," said Pyefinch. "The short of it is this: about thirty years ago, when I was a nipper and the French were doing their best to kill me and my mates on the battlefields of Europe, things looked pretty bad. See, no one could understand how that Napoleon Boney-part come from almost nowhere to be such a blessed powerful leader of men and a fighter of wars. Because he was an ill-figured blighter and wasn't born to power or riches, see. And until he was twenty-three, he seemed a very ordinary man indeed, so they say. And then something changed, too fast for it to be quite normal. And it come to be noticed by those of them back here in London as watched events over the water, that he was perhaps not entirely natural in his powers. Indeed, it were clear to them as could read the signs that if he himself didn't have some powers, he was most certainly being helped by those that did. And using supranatural powers to prey on the natural world is forbidden, has been forbidden for centuries—"

"You haven't got time for a performance," said Rose. "Barge'll be along any moment. Give them the short version."

Pyefinch grunted ruefully, then tapped out his pipe on his boot.

"The cutty version of the tale is this: Frenchies done so well because their version of The Oversight, what they called the Paladin, was destroyed by the Revolution . . ."

He paused and spat on the ground, his face curdled in distaste, though whether at the pipe which wasn't drawing to his satisfaction or at the memory was unclear.

"Mind, there's some as say it caused the Revolution itself, though I shouldn't like to think it had become so corrupt as to cut all those poor people's heads off in the Terror. Anyway, what was left of the Paladin *was* corrupt enough to back Napoleon. Maybe they thought that breaking the Law Paramount, the rule about preying on the natural, just for a bit until they got their feet back under themselves again, was acceptable. So the French army and the French navy had people in it using supranatural skills to make them do so well. Which was bad. But what was worse was a plot to destroy London in one big stroke."

He sucked more flame into the tobacco, pulling at it until it was lit to his liking.

"The Oversight never ever got involved in Britain's wars. Was a point of honour, and a point of greater safety. Cos once you step over that line, you end up with something nasty like the Terror and them guillotines and old Boney hisself. The plan was exposed somehow, and it was clear that unless something was done to stop it, Britain was done for, and all our freedom gone for a ball of Dover chalk. So they held a vote. And they decided this was, just this once, the time for The Oversight to get involved in a war. Them as thought it was a good idea must have had some notion that because they would be fighting others with supranatural abilities, it was sort of fair, like. They must have sung themselves some such kind of song to do something so very wrong as break the Law Paramount themselves, because war's a messy thing and once you're in a fight it's hard enough staying alive, forget about working out who and how you can and can't kill."

"There was a spy," said Rose, watching the canal where a dark shape was beginning to come into view, floating towards them with one bull's-eye lantern on its stubby prow. "Our spy. He knew how to get The Oversight into the French ship."

"There was a ship, crewed by the Paladin and their type, heading across the channel. The plan was to appear suddenly by means of mirrors in the belly of the French and attack them from the last place they expected to be."

"Seventeen Hands went through the mirrors into that ship," said Rose. "That's eighty-five poor creatures that was never seen again."

"No one knew if they even got to the ship," said Pyefinch, right eye crinkled against the pall of pipe smoke he was creating around himself. "Because it was a trap."

"Were near as dammit the end of The Oversight," said Rose. "Five stayed because without a Last Hand there's no Oversight, and without an Oversight, there are certain things that get out of control a little too quickly."

"There were others, friends of The Oversight, if not actually members of hands, that spoke against it," said Pyefinch, "and when the Disaster became apparent, we decided to keep ourselves separate because the trust was gone and good women and men had been butchered."

"We?" said Lucy.

"My old dad had powers," said Pyefinch. "Me? Not so much. Just two things: I got a strong eye and can't be foozled by the likes of them Sluagh a-trying to put the black glamour on me, and I got a knack for making folk listen to my stories like they'd be missing something really important if they didn't."

"But the French never won," said Charlie. "And you never say why."

"Because I don't know," said Pyefinch. "No one knows. The seventeen Hands went, never come back, the French ship never snuck up the Thames into the centre of London and in the end there were those who thought it had never existed and that the spy was a double agent who trapped the eighty-five into going somewhere else entirely, into a killing ground like the bottom of a volcano, or in the deeps of the sea or something. And then I ended up a couple of years later getting shot through the ankle at the Battle of Waterloo, the battle that finally saw that bastard Boney off. No one knows the truth of any of it, but the lesson was clear: The Oversight overstepped itself and lost its way."

"And since then we have been staying away from them, and with good reason," said Rose. "They're unchancy and broken, even if they mean well. And there's those as think maybe they're corrupt and a crew of blackguards, though I don't."

Before Lucy could ask about Rose's powers, Charlie nudged her and pointed at what she was carrying.

"What were you going to do with the hand?"

"Take it back to Sara Falk," she said without thinking, and in that moment realised that was indeed what she was going to do.

Rose grasped her chin gently and turned her face to the moonlight, looking deeply into her eyes. As she did so Lucy saw two dimmer, yellower lights slowly approaching down the canal. It was the bow lantern on a barge, and a smaller bull's-eye lamp carried by a man leading the horse pulling it down the towpath.

Pyefinch stood and stretched out the stiffness in his legs.

"She's telling the truth," said Rose.

"Good," said Pyefinch. "She's trouble, but I took a liking to her first time I saw her."

He stepped out into the moonlight and waved at the barge. Lucy saw answering waves from a woman silhouetted at the back of the craft and the man leading the horse.

Rose turned back to her.

"This barge will not stop because there may be eyes watching the waterways as well as the road, and those lanterns are easily seen from a distance. You'll have to jump as it passes, but the bargee is a friend and will get you to where you need to go."

"But—" said Lucy, for whom things were going a little fast.

"Charlie will go with you," said Rose, pulling her to her feet. "You mean well, I think, but your head is muddied. Too muddied to be safe."

"Charlie has a gift too—" began Lucy.

"Oh yes," said Rose. "You'll have plenty of time to discuss it but we have none now. The countryside is death to you. The only things which can stop the Sluagh are cold iron and running water. Stay on the barge until you're within the city. They won't follow you inside the city – too many hidden waterways and underground rivers, and too much iron for them. Least I think so. I never heard of them in the big cities."

"We'll keep our guard up till we get to the Safe House," grinned Charlie. "Always wanted to see inside. All them stories."

The Barge was fewer than twenty-five yards away now.

"Well, son," said Pyefinch, handing over his blunderbuss. "You're going to be part of 'em now. Both of you. You're going to make a whole new story all on your own."

And without any more ceremony, he took Lucy's free hand and pulled her to the edge of the canal. As the man leading the horse passed, he just nodded and said, "Harry. Much obliged."

And then he helped her step from towpath to barge and then dropped back.

Harry did not break step but looked back and grinned at the Pyefinches.

"Rose, Barnaby. We'll look after 'em, worry not," he said, and then half raised a hand in farewell and led the horse onwards.

Charlie took a bundle from his mother and then leaped on beside Lucy.

And for the two of them, as simple as that, it was like the barge stopped moving and the moonlit landscape began to slide past them instead.

Rose walked beside them for a moment, keeping pace.

"Tell Sara Falk Rose Pyefinch bears her no grudge, as she can see from what you bring her. And mind you send word when you get there safe," she said, and blew Charlie a kiss.

"And if we don't see you before, we'll look for you at the King Harry down the Mile End Road come Michaelmas . . ." said his father, waving thanks to the silent woman bargee at the rear of the boat.

And with no more ceremony, they were sliding away into the unknown night, leaving the bridge, the Pyefinches and the distant lights of the fair far behind them.

"Well," said Lucy. "You never said your dad was called Barnaby."

"Not something he likes getting about," said Charlie, looking back at his parents, now just silhouettes framed by the arch of the bridge against the moonlit water behind them. "He's funny that way."

CHAPTER 65

THE WALKER BETWEEN THE WORLDS

Mr Sharp walked between the mirrors. Although it did not involve looking down, the first impression he got was a sickening kind of vertigo as he stared ahead and then behind himself to see the infinite disappearing line of matched reflections stretching away into the heart of forever.

Or that is what he called it in his head.

"I am walking into forever," he said, talking to the ivory balls he held ahead of himself like a lantern. They were the closest he had for company.

He had heard one click as he entered the mirrors, which he took to be the "home" ball at the centre of the nest registering his start point.

"That's good," he had told it. "You make sure you can get me home."

After that he had stopped talking to the balls because he heard the fear he was suppressing in his voice, and also because though there was nobody else to hear it and think him mad, he thought it of himself.

The first mirror he had looked out of was the one he felt Lucy would have walked into, from the limited understanding of how the mirrors worked as told him by The Smith. It was disappointingly black.

Unknown to him this was because the mirror she had been pulled out of had of course also broken, and the shards had been tossed into a midden and buried under succeeding dumps of night soil and other less noxious rubbish. So he resigned himself to taking the long way round, and carefully stepped from reflection to reflection, looking right and left and out of the mirrors on each side, in case there was something that would give him a clue.

One effect of walking in the mirrors was that time went very odd. He walked and walked but did not get tired. And because there was no night or day, he lost all track of the hours. The only other effect he began to notice was that he seemed to be getting thinner as he walked, not in the sense of his waist diminishing, but in the way he seemed to become less substantial, almost less dense, to the point where he held his hand up in front of himself and was sure that for a moment he could almost see through it.

"Perhaps I am becoming a ghost," he said. He walked on until he thought that maybe the further you got from your starting point, the more see-through you became.

Since he was not getting any sense of where to start looking, he took this as a cue to make his first turn. He heard the next ball in the Ivory click as he turned right, and stepped into a new passage.

It looked just like the one he had come from, and he saw how without the Ivories you would be lost for ever in a wilderness of reflections. He tried looking at his feet.

And that's where the vertigo really did kick in because the floor and the ceiling were also mirrors, reflecting him up and down to incalculable vanishing points.

He sat for a long time and closed his eyes. Cook had been right: it was a fool's errand. He should swallow his pride and go back. He should have gone back the moment he saw the mirror Lucy must have exited through was black and uncrossable. He was indeed a fool.

And then when he opened his eyes and stood he saw that something had changed. The light was different. The infinite passage was not static. It bounced a little.

And then he realised it wasn't bouncing, but that a light was approaching and the light was being carried, and the bouncing effect was made by the gait of the light bearer.

He spun and found he'd pulled the longest knife from his belt without conscious thought.

"Won't need that, friend," said a man's voice from behind the light. "Here. I'll put mine down."

And the indistinct figure bent and laid a small sword on the floor. When he stood, Mr Sharp saw a tall man with a jutting beard which sprouted horizontally off his chin like a goat's, deep-set intelligent eyes and a long dark robe. His hair was kept back with a long skull-cap with earflaps, and there was a chain round his neck with a jewel and a piece of nondescript rock attached to it.

"Who are you?" said Mr Sharp.

"Like you, I am a walker behind the worlds," said the man.

"What is your name?"

"What is yours?" The older man smiled a courtly smile and raised an eyebrow.

"Sharp."

"Like your blade."

"If you will."

"I will. And I shall similarly introduce myself as . . . Walker."

Mr Sharp was still on his guard. Smiles cost nothing and hid more than they revealed in his experience.

"Not your real name. Whereas mine is really Sharp. The blade is a mere coincidence."

The man bowed again and broadened his smile, eyes sparking with great good humour.

"My name is Dee."

He pointed at the ring on Mr Sharp's finger, and then showed him that what he had first taken to be a jewel on the chain round his neck was another ring, similarly but more crudely fashioned from gold and a carved bloodstone.

"But you may call me Brother John, brother."

Despite himself Mr Sharp lowered his knife a little and leant in to look at the lion and the unicorn insignia cut into the stone.

"Dee is dead," he breathed incredulously. John Dee had not only been Queen Elizabeth's mathematician and astronomer and much else besides; he had been a member of The Oversight from her reign until the Stuart king came south to succeed to her throne.

"Only in the past," grinned the other, and sat down on the mirrored floor as if exhausted.

Mr Sharp saw that the light he carried was a fine mesh bag in which were a lot of pieces of frosted glass like Sara's seaglass, but of all different colours and shining brightly. As he looked at it, he saw Dee was staring at his Ivory.

Dee saw him see that and laughed.

"What are you doing in the mirrors, brother?" he said. "And what is that preposterous rattle you are carrying?"

"I am looking for someone," said Mr Sharp stiffly.

"Not me, I hope," said Dee, looking pointedly at the blade in Mr Sharp's other hand.

"No," said Mr Sharp. "No. A girl. What are you doing?"

"Trying to find a way into a new layer," said Dee, and sat suddenly, looking tired and older. "It's been a long time."

He drew his knees up to his chin and leant back on his hands.

"Layer?" said Mr Sharp.

"Sit down," said Dee, patting the mirrored ground beside

him. "You don't know how this works, do you? Place to place is crude. Time to time is better. World to world is best, for there may be an infinity of worlds nested within each other, and in an infinity of worlds even a dead man may live for ever if he can step from one to the other fast enough."

And he threw the bag of stones to Mr Sharp, who caught them without dropping the knife.

"You want to examine them, go ahead. They help with the light and with the past," said Dee, rummaging in the inner recesses of his gown. "You can have a couple if you like. Do you like dried pear?"

Mr Sharp sat down opposite him and looked at the glasses in the fine metal net. They were just like Sara and Lucy's heart-stones, he thought—

—and then he didn't think anything else for a while because Dee lashed out with his boots, smashing them into his head, knocking him senseless.

When he awoke he was alone.

The Ivory get-you-home was gone.

As were all of his knives except the small one in his sleeve, the one The Smith had given him, which Dee must have missed. His boots were also missing. His head throbbed and his finger hurt and was chafed, from which he deduced Dee had tried to remove his ring too.

He stood and looked around him.

Everywhere looked like everywhere, all the way to forever and back.

"Stupid," he said. "Stupid."

Cook's prophecy and Sara's fears had come true.

He was well and truly lost in the mirrors.

CHAPTER 66

WATERBORNE

The bargee's name was Harry Stonex and his wife was Ruby, and apart from introducing themselves they didn't say much, other than that Lucy and Charlie were welcome aboard but should be so kind as to keep out of sight during the day. Ruby brought them food and hot tea whenever they made it for themselves, and Harry sat and had it with them in the space they found among the baulks of timber he was bringing to London.

"Hearts of oak," he said, patting the stacked wood. "Safe as old England you'll be in here. And you'll have noticed the iron."

Lucy had not noticed, but Charlie had. He pointed out an iron rubbing strake running around the entire boat like a belt.

"That's not just to protect the gunwale from scraping on the banks and lock-sides," he said. "That keeps the Shadowgangers away too."

Lucy didn't know what a gunwale was, and said so. Charlie's explanation was less exciting than she expected, being just the side of the boat. She didn't need to ask what Shadowgangers were. She had seen them appear out of the darkness and felt a cold chill of dread run through her guts at the memory.

She feared them even though she knew they were dead and all trace of them had been tipped into the water and was gone.

Except all trace of the Sluagh had not gone. The Sluagh's cocked hat had been knocked off in the short fight and fallen under the Pyefinches' wagon, where it lay unnoticed. Back at the fair, the enthusiasm for chasing after the thief who had snatched the *Manus Gloriae* had eventually worn off, and the crowd had evaporated into other booths and diversions. Because of the disruption, the great Battle of the Wizards was declared – unilaterally by Huffam – to be a draw, on the strict and financially advantageous understanding that battle would be rejoined next year at the same time and place. Huffam was a showman to his bones and knew that the stories about the night's marvels would only swell the crowd next time, so much so that he was already thinking of how to expand the capacity of his tent. Both Anderson and Na-Barno were privately relieved and did not contest this, so unnerved had each been by the other's performance, and were happy to split the take for the first showing.

Georgiana was not relieved, nor was she happy. She realised Na-Barno only planned his life from bottle to bottle. With money in his pocket, he was able to forget the uncomfortable fact that Anderson had destroyed their act, and that without the *Manus Gloriae* they had nothing to survive on in the long term.

"Something will turn up," said Na-Barno, waving her off as he hurried to the cider tent.

She wanted to slap him again, but instead decided to watch the Pyefinches' wagon in case the thief showed up in the night. So she sat in the shadows and watched Rose and Pyefinch return and close up, waiting for Charlie to appear. As the night drew on, the cold realisation that he had gone with the

Sara girl dawned on her. She kept herself awake by will-power alone, and by the time the early morning light began to re-appear she had crystalised her anger into something much closer to murderous hatred.

It was because of the light that she saw the cocked hat, and what drew her attention was the fact that it was moving. She slipped across to the Pyefinches' wagon and stared at it.

The bony cockade of bird's skulls were working together like the legs of a spider, crabbing the hat towards the deeper darkness below the wagon.

She was fascinated and horrified, but a girl who has handled a *Manus Gloriae* is already hardened to the uncanny. So she reached in and snatched it up, sprinting away through the dew towards her father's distant wagon, her heart suddenly lighter.

"I don't know what you are," she said to the hat with the writhing bird-skull cockade. "But if we can't build a turn around you, we deserve to starve."

Na-Barno had been right, against all experience: something had turned up.

What she could not know was that the cocked hat would lead her on a terrible journey – a journey that would one day help her revenge herself on her childhood friend and the girl she thought was called Sara Falk.

For the first night and day there was an awkwardness between Charlie and Lucy that had not been there when they had been together among the hurly-burly of the fair. This new uneasiness was partly because they were now alone together, but mainly it stemmed from what he had hidden from her.

"Why?" asked Lucy eventually, as they were lying on the front of the boat enjoying the last of the autumn sun on the second afternoon. "Why didn't you tell me what you all are?"

"It's not complicated," said Charlie. "Mainly cos why

would we? Same as you keeping it to yourself. Don't do much good strangers knowing our business, and it's not like Ma and Pa set much store by their powers, such as they have."

"But you do," said Lucy. "You can go fast and yet slow, you can sneak and not be seen. You're a . . . well, I don't know what you are but you remind me of a man called Mr Sharp who I saw in London . . ."

"Well, I'd like to see this Mr Sharp character too," said Charlie. "Cos I don't know what I am any more than you do. I'm just fast when I need to be, or maybe I just make everything else slow, I dunno. And as for sneaking around – look who's talking!"

And he grinned and held out his hand.

"None of us done you any harm, Lucy-if-that's-your-name-now."

"It's always been my name," she said. And shook his hand firmly. "Now tell me about the Shadowgangers."

In the daylight it was easier to talk about them. And since they were interested in her, she thought it only prudent to know as much as she could about them. So Charlie went aft and asked Mrs Stonex for a loan of her chart. It was a much-rolled thing, and he was careful not to add to the wear and tear as he laid it out on the deck. It was a crudely printed map of the lower half of the country, and had been clearly added to over time by Stonex drawing additional things on it in blue pencil, like spurs to existing canals, entirely new waterways and – criss-crossing the country, in black pencil – railway lines.

"That's England," he said. "Some of it anyway. Now how would you get from London to Birmingham?"

She studied the map for an instant and then traced the railway line.

"Right," he said. "Easy isn't it?"

"I thought you were going to tell me about the Shadowgangers," she said. "I want to know about the Sluagh."

"I'm showing you," he said. "At least I'm explaining what my dad says is why they are so riled up and angry nowadays."

And he pointed at the map again.

"Now try and get across the same bit of country without crossing water or an iron track."

Lucy snorted and said.

"Easy . . ."

But when she put her finger on the map and tried to trace a path avoiding the black and the blue lines, she found it was anything but. It was as if the whole landscape had been turned into an unwinnable child's game, a maze with no sane solution.

"They can't cross running water," said Charlie. "No more than they can abide cold iron. Before the canals they wove paths through the country, meandering in and out of the watercourses, which you can do easy enough if you have the stamina for making your night trails wind along the tops and the high ground, on the peak of the watershed, so to speak."

"What's a watershed?" said Lucy.

"It's like where the hills meet to form a ridge, like the roof of a shed and the rain drains off in one direction or the other depending which side it falls on. Water don't flow uphill, see? Walk the ridge, above where all the streams begin, and you don't ever cross flowing water."

She nodded.

"But then navvies began cutting canals across the old ways," he continued. "And that was like putting straight fences across open land to them, and then other men staked rails for the steam-trains criss-crossing it, and their old ways of moving across the land is ten times, no, a hundred times more complicated. It's like slipping through a net. And they have trooped the night freely for centuries. Can see why they're stirred up and turning nasty. Not that they've ever needed an excuse for that, from what I heard."

And then he went on to explain what he knew about them and their various other names, how abjuring the sun and embracing the night was their way, how everything they did and believed seemed like a world turned topsy-turvy. And he explained that they hated The Oversight.

"Why?" she said.

"Because running water has always been a bane to them, but cold iron, and what it does to them? That's down to something The Oversight did to them a long, long time ago. Like a punishment for something really horrible that they got caught doing."

"What?" said Lucy.

"Dunno," he said. "It was before the Tower of London got built, and that's the oldest thing I seen. Except Stonehenge . . ."

And that led to him explaining what Stonehenge was and drawing a picture of it and the talk meandered off into companionable silence, sitting and watching the world go past. Then he jumped off the barge and took Mr Stonex's place leading the horse, with a promise to wake him once it began to get dark.

"Ol' Barnaby'd skin me if he knew I let you be off the boat come dusk," he said. "Sun drops below the horizon, you jump on board and raise me sharpish, see?"

The Sluagh found them that evening.

Charlie was back on the boat and Mr Stonex, who carried a horseshoe in his belt out of superstition and self-protection, led the horse for another hour or two of darkness before they tied up for the night. "Led" was not quite the word, for the horse knew how to pull away along the clearly marked towpath quite as well as he did, and in fact he climbed up on its back and allowed himself to doze as it ambled along into the mirk.

Lucy was sitting with her knees drawn up to her chest, cradling the hand in its wrapping close to her, and not thinking about much in particular as her eyes watched the darkness drift by.

The Sluagh appeared on the bank so quietly that it took a moment or two for Lucy to realise that some of the darkness had detached from itself and was now keeping pace with her at a disturbingly leisurely pace, as if it were just out for a gentle stroll along the towpath only three perilous feet away.

She looked up to see a man with a face garlanded with ancient tattoos, wearing an animal-skin top-coat and a hat crowned with a coronet of woodcock skulls with all the beaks pointing to the sky.

"What is it you want, little girl?" he said calmly, his eyes open and guileless.

"Don't look at him," said Charlie. "Not in the eyes."

She kept her eyes on the Sluagh's hands instead.

"I have a proposition for you," he said calmly.

There was a solid click of metal ratcheting back against metal right by her ear as Charlie cocked the blunderbuss.

"And I have half a pound of cold iron nails in here for you if you try and warp her will," said Charlie. "Rusty ones."

"*Rusty* ones?" said the Sluagh, and there was a disconcertingly mocking tone to his voice. "Oh well then. That makes *all* the difference."

A second Sluagh appeared beside him, shorter, hunch-backed.

"You sound so confident – yet smell so very scared," the newcomer giggled.

Charlie jabbed the gun at them.

Lucy saw the first Sluagh's hands open and make a placating gesture.

"Just listen," he hissed softly. "Just words: I have a proposal. You are going to London?"

"We don't know where we're going," said Charlie.

"Will you let us have the girl?" said the hunchback.

"Why would I do that?" said Charlie.

"Gold," came the wheedling reply. "Gold which could change your life . . . make you rich, gold which would make you free . . ."

"Gold which would turn to acorns and beech-mast in my pocket as soon as your filthy glamour washed out of my eyes?" said Charlie. "No thanks."

"Real gold?" said the Sluagh wearing the woodcock crown.

"No," said Charlie.

"No?"

"No."

Lucy saw the Sluagh's hands fold round themselves and squeeze tight. He walked on with them clasped like that for several paces and when he spoke his voice was clenched as tight as the hands.

"There are men in London who would pay us well for her. Who have sent the word out. Powerful men."

"When did the Sluagh get interested in money?" said Charlie.

"It is not money they would pay us with. It is something much more precious. To us," said the first Sluagh.

"The answer's still no," said Charlie.

"I heard the answer. You haven't heard my counter-offer," said the Sluagh, a dangerous smoothness taking the edge off his voice in such a way that Lucy nearly involuntarily looked up into his eyes.

"You don't shut up and stop doing that thing with your voice, you'll bloody well hear mine: I'll sound like 'boom – splatter'," said Charlie sharply, poking the stubby gun in their direction. "This is the boom; your head'll be the splatter . . ."

The hunchback Sluagh growled in the back of his throat

and spat words back at Charlie in a snarl of barely controlled rage.

"Do you ever wonder what your skin looks like on the inside, boy? Step over the iron and say that. Then we could have a nice time showing you."

"What is your offer?" said Lucy. She was uncomfortable with several rather significant things about this conversation, first of which was who they were having it with, but the fact that she was being talked about as if she were just baggage with no will-power of her own was running it a close second.

"I offer you an uninterrupted passage if you will take a message to The Oversight," said the Sluagh in the woodcock crown.

"Who?" said Charlie.

"Don't play games, boy," said the Sluagh, irritated again. "We have been in her mind before, and we know where we sent her."

Lucy's stomach lurched.

"You couldn't interrupt our passage if you tried," said Charlie. "The boat's iron-bound, on flowing water you can't cross."

The Sluagh said nothing, but just walked on, its hands working against each other.

"If you are running to The Oversight, tell them we know they have betrayed us. We know they have given our most precious possession to a mere man. They have given him the thing they took from us when they laid the Iron Law across our shoulders. They have not only betrayed us, they have betrayed Law and Lore."

Lucy had the strong impression that the left hand was gripping the right hand to stop it flying across the narrow gap between them and grabbing her by the face, running water and cold iron be damned. She pushed back against the timber baulks behind her.

"I don't know what you're talking about," she said.

"But *they* will know," said the Sluagh with the woodcock crown. "And now they will know we know. And until they return what they took from us, and lift the Iron Law, we will work relentlessly to destroy them, even if it means working with men."

And he spat and stopped walking.

The barge passed under a bridge which neither Lucy nor Charlie had seen approaching, so concentrated had they been on the Sluagh.

"Phew," said Charlie. "Railway bridge. Cold iron for miles on either side. We're safe."

She felt strangely divided, a mix of relief and frustration. She knew she would sleep badly because the malice of the hunchback Sluagh would taint her dreams, but something else in her wished she'd had more time to talk to the other Sluagh. She might have had a chance at filling in some of the blanks in her memory.

"Safe as houses," said Charlie, as much to himself as her. "And old Harry says we should touch London tomorrow, and all your troubles will be over."

"For now," said Lucy, looking back at the darkness and wondering about the answers it held.

CHAPTER 67

SO-HO!

The Citizen had left it to the Alp to dispose of the corpse of the doorman, it being beneath his own dignity to do so, and in that way he was, perhaps, responsible for its ultimate fate.

The Alp trussed the doorman like a large turkey, a cord around his knees cinched tight round his neck, and then his ankles lashed in close to his buttocks, so that when the Alp had wrapped him in an old dust-sheet he looked more like a squarish parcel than a suspiciously body-shaped bundle.

The Alp hoisted the body onto its shoulder and set out into the cool early morning air an hour before sunrise, walking to a small leather manufactory close by the Pillars of Hercules tavern in Soho, where it dumped the body in a broken barrel which had been thrown into the adjacent alley. It then checked it was still unseen, and walked back to its new home in Golden Square.

It would not have trod so lightly had it known that five hours later Jed, still casting for its scent in ever wider circles, would be trotting alone and unnoticed through the now teeming street and would cut his trail and stiffen with recognition, nostrils quivering.

People had not hunted in Soho for generations, not since it was the open farmland known as St Giles Field attached to the leper hospital of the same name, but Henry VIII had often ridden to hounds across it, and it was the old hunting cry of "So-ho!" that had given it its name. So it was with a degree of appropriateness that Jed stuck his nose to the scent trail and careered off hot on the heels of the Alp.

Five minutes later he was circling the house on Golden Square, confirming that the trail went into the house and didn't leave it. Then he sat downwind beneath a wagon in the street and inhaled for a good ten minutes. The scent of the Alp was strong, and definitely coming from the house. Satisfied, he lay down and rested his chin on his front paws, watching the door to the house.

He would wait here without moving until Hodge arrived, which he knew would be soon. He had felt him in his head and told him what he had found.

The Alp knew nothing of this. It had cleaned the blood from the sprung parquet as best it could, and had looked at the money The Citizen had left it.

The Citizen had told it where it might find the kind of girls who would be willing to accompany a man for a price, and he had a mind to find one who might not be missed were she not to return. Giving The Citizen a new lease of life had left him flat and exhausted. He needed breath, and young breath at that.

And so the Alp prepared to stalk its prey, unaware of the hunter's eyes waiting patiently for him in the street outside.

CHAPTER 68

A LILY PLUCKED AND DISCARDED

Issachar and Zebulon Templebane had directed that the Safe
House be watched at all hours of the day and night, and from
all sides. This kept their adopted sons busy, sleepless and
consequently at increasingly short temper with each other.

The most annoyed of them was Garlickhythe, who had
been the youngest until the arrival of Amos into the cold
but extendable bosom of the family three years ago. As such
he had had to endure all the worst jobs for longer than he
liked to remember, and he had got used to enjoying his
freedom from them once the mute had been brought into
the house.

However, since Amos was not yet returned from his mission
to Rutlandshire, Garlickhythe had become the youngest again,
and thus the receiver of the short straw in all decisions. In
the matter of keeping the Safe House under surveillance it
was generally considered that the most uncomfortable post
was to the south, close by the river: it was windy, wet and
beset by the most startling and mephitic odours that the sewers,
emptying themselves freely into the Thames just below his
observation point, could provide.

He was not too upset by the smell, being a Londoner born,

but he was also a hypochondriac who spent much of the time worrying about his health. There was no question that his post, outside a most unappealing shop-front specialising in broken-backed chairs, scarred tables and all manner of second-hand bric-a-brac (including a rack of wooden legs which clattered ominously in the wind) was the most uncomfortable and exposed to the elements.

Worse than that, it was boring. It was so very boring that Garlickhythe decided to divert himself. Nothing other than the normal comings and goings of the fat cook, the thin man in midnight blue and a couple of tradesmen, a ratter and a blacksmith had been seen for days. He was sure he would miss nothing by a sporting encounter with one of the accommodating ladies from Neptune Street, and it would not take long.

He was, however, not willing to stray too far from his post in case he was whistled in by Coram or Bassetshaw or one of the other older "brothers". He knew they would have great glee in reporting his absence to Issachar. So he engaged with one of the girls to meet her outside the shop and then to repair to a less visible spot to conduct their business. The spot he chose was down some greasy steps that took them under the shadow of a disused jetty on the edge of the river.

Lily, for that was the girl's name, complained about the mud he was clearly intending her to walk through to get to his chosen private trysting place beneath the dank pilings and their ruined boardwalk. She was especially vocal on its pernicious effect on "her nice new shoes", shoes which were, as he pointed out, neither nice nor convincingly new. He suggested that she take them off, which she surprised him (since taking off clothing was something of a prerequisite of her chosen profession) by refusing to do.

"You can carry me," she said.

"Carry you, my arse!" he retorted.

"You'd carry me if you was half a gent," she pouted.

"If you was half the size you are I might give it a go," he said. "I ain't putting my back out trying to lift a dirty great plumper like you—"

And then he stopped.

In the shadows beneath the jetty there was a lighter or flat-bottomed barge moored in close in such a way that no one would notice it from the street above, and he saw The Smith disembark from it and cross the mud to the river wall where there was a barred culvert.

"You bast—" began Lily, outraged at the aspersions he had just cast as to her size.

His hand lashed out and grabbed her, yanking her down into the mud. She gasped and began to cry out again, but he was so acutely sensible of the need for silence that he mashed her face, mouth first, into the ooze at his feet and held her there as he watched what The Smith was about.

He was fascinated to see the culvert gate swing open and the fat cook emerge to look at the boat. There was a muttered conversation and in order to catch at least a few words he was obliged to push Lily's face deeper into the river mud so that the bubbles she was producing as she struggled and began to spasm did not distract him.

". . . load it up . . . turn of the tide tonight or tomorrow morning . . ." was all he could make out. Then they both disappeared back into the culvert and the gate was clanged shut and audibly locked behind them. He waited, frozen for a long while, until he was sure they were not going to return.

"Well," he said to Lily. "I think them has got themselves a secret tunnel to the river from that there 'ouse. What do you think the old fathers is going to give me for discovering that?"

Lily didn't answer, and when he stopped pressing down on the back of her neck she didn't get up either.

He looked down at the body with a cold disinterest, the excitement of what his fathers would do for him when he transmitted the intelligence having kindled a greater fire inside him than the lust he had intended to quench in the girl.

He looked around, especially watchful of the blank warehouse wall rising like a cliff above him, but no one was watching.

He sighed and bent to pick her feet up, dragged her to the edge of the mud bank and rolled her into the rising water. He looked down at his trousers.

"You were right about that mud," he said to the sad jumble of skirts that had been Lily. "It's ruined my bloody shoes."

And he walked gingerly back to the greasy steps and back up into the city, his pace quickening with excitement.

By the time he got to Issachar's and Zebulon's study, the Thames had risen enough to float the girl and start her on her journey around the great loop in the river pulling inexorably towards the darker expanses of Blackwall Reach.

From that point things moved fast: deducing that a lighter was engaged to carry something from the Safe House in secrecy, and further extrapolating that whatever – or whoever – it was that was to be the cargo must be something of rarity and value, Issachar went to see Mountfellon.

That interview was substantially more amicable than their last contact, although Issachar found the opaque windows that Mountfellon had glazed the house on Chandos Place with gave the interiors an unworldly and disconcerting feeling, as if one were trapped under ice.

A plan was agreed, which was as follows: Issachar would engage some biddable gentlemen who had no scruples about foul play.

"The Wipers will suit, I think," he said thoughtfully. "My brother or I, depending on time of day, will direct matters personally. This is too serious a business to delegate—"

"Exactly," said Mountfellon. "I will engage two boats, steam launches for speed. One can be crewed round the clock close by this hidden jetty, and when these damn people endeavour to make their escape with whatever it is they are trying to hide, the first boat will follow and effect an entirely justifiable act of appropriation as soon as they can. A reasonable act of piracy, if you will."

"And the second boat, my lord?" enquired Templebane.

"I shall pilot that myself. As soon as the hare is running, I am to be alerted and will embark in pursuit."

"But it will take a long time to get there from here," said Templebane.

"I do not intend to catch a chill sleeping on a boat," said Mountfellon. "And we do not know which of the two tides they will take. So I will stay at your house. It is close to the river. It looked clean enough, and I'm sure you can provide something approaching a comfortable bed."

And so the plan was made.

And all this before poor accommodating Lily had even been missed for her dinner.

CHAPTER 69

THE ALP SPEAKS TO A DOG
WITH NO BARK

The Alp had found its prey.

Jed had trailed it to the section of Haymarket known, because of the extraordinarily high density and brazenness of its prostitutes, as Hell Corner, and then trotted back with it to Golden Square, twenty paces behind, close to the wall, an unnoticed dog in a city full of strays.

The girl was gin-numbed and happy enough at the thought of the promised coins she would be going home with. She even liked the fact that the gentleman whose arm she was limpetted to appeared not to wish to speak: she favoured the shy ones because the business tended to be over quicker with them.

Hodge seemed to step out of thin air, straddling the pavement in front of them, a short man with a dog who circled in from behind and stood growling at his feet. Hodge held out a fist with a bloodstone ring on it, his eyes boring into the Alp's.

"By the Powers, and as a Free Companion of the London Oversight, I charge you that you allow yourself to be manacled and accompany me peaceably to the Privy Cells in the Sly House to await judgement."

The girl stared at him through a gin-fuelled haze.

The Alp's face retained its studied blankness.

Hodge raised the ring higher.

The Alp raised one eyebrow to match it. And then it just shrugged and tried to walk forward.

Hodge stepped in front of it, ring still raised. The Alp worked its mouth, as if moistening something that was desiccated from long disuse.

And then it spoke.

"Look like man but your stench is dog. Perhaps that is what you are: little dog with no bark . . ."

Its voice was rusty and disdainful, its lisping high German intonation adding an extra air of supercilious amusement to it.

"What can you do to me? Here? Now? In front of all these innocent, unaware people? All these . . . witnesses?"

The Alp smiled, a disturbing sight, not least because it had no teeth at all, just expanses of pink gum, so that the inside of its mouth was more like that of a fish or a baby than a grown human, a toothlessness which also explained the severity of its lisp.

"Out of the road, silly little doggie, or you shall have the kick you so richly deserve."

Hodge looked round at the crowded street, at the girl holding the Alp's arm, her eyebrows rising into a taut curve of incomprehension.

"See," said the Alp. "So much people. What can you do?"

"This," Hodge said, and raised his ring to his own forehead as if wiping his brow, and pressed the seal into his skin.

"*Ic adeorce*," he muttered, and then attacked without a hint of warning.

He didn't even lose his smile. In fact it widened as he leapt across the scant yard separating them and hit the Alp full in the throat with both of his hands, which closed like steel traps around it as he bulled it backwards across the road, heading for the mouth of an alley.

No one noticed. No one commented or raised their voice or pointed. No one *saw* them. It was not that Hodge had become invisible. It was not that kind of magic, which only exists in fairy-tales: it was the other real kind, the sort of workaday sleight which just makes coincidences happen at the right time. The simple thing which happened was that as soon as the old Anglo-Saxon words came out of Hodge's mouth, everyone in the immediate area had their attention taken by something else. They weren't all looking at the same other thing; they were each distracted by something different, the things which caught their eyes being as dissimilar as the eyes themselves. In fact the only thing that all these disparate momentary distractions had in common was that they were not Hodge.

The force of his attack tore the Alp from the girl's tight grasp and left her literally spinning in the middle of the street.

Hodge attacked like a terrier, straight in, no preamble, determined to be at it and done with it as fast as possible.

There was a horse trough in the alley and he ran the Alp back until the lip of the trough caught the breath-stealer behind the knees and it went over backwards.

Hodge went with it, shoving it under water and holding it there as the Alp's hands flailed at his face. Hodge bunched himself up and jammed a knee into its solar plexus, and was rewarded by a great bubble of air belching up from the gagging mouth below him.

"By the Powers," Hodge gritted. "By Law and Lore, for lives taken – your life."

The Alp stopped struggling.

After a clear minute, Hodge let go his grip on his throat and looked down at the motionless face beneath the water.

As the ripples stilled he peered down at it as if somehow the memory of it would obliterate the other memories of the two dead women in their beds.

The face below him did not move. The eyes stared back at him, unblinking.

Jed growled from the side of the trough. Hodge shook his head as if to clear it, then stood, knee-deep in the water, legs either side of the Alp's body.

"Your kind cannot die while there is a vestige of breath left in you. That I know," he said, and stepped up onto the Alp's chest.

There was a final stream of bubbles as he bore down on the breath-stealer, and then with a final convulsion the Alp truly began to expire, its hair going grey and lines appearing on its face as age claimed its true portion before death took it for ever. It aged twenty years in a moment.

Hodge stepped out of the trough and looked into the street. Without surprise he saw The Smith saying something to the girl, who sneezed and then just walked away, face blank with forgetting. The Smith walked into the alley, clapped a hand on Hodge's shoulder and looked down into the trough.

"He's gone," he said. "And so that's that."

"I'd thought he would wither and betray his great age once dead," said Hodge, sounding strangely hollow even to his own ears.

"He was a young 'un. That's all," said The Smith, taking a second look. "And you killed him, just as you said you would."

"He was a killer. And Law and Lore . . ." began Hodge.

"Killing him was right enough by Lore and Law," agreed The Smith, cutting him off. "Just might not have been the other thing you don't like."

Hodge met his eye.

"Sensible, you mean?"

The Smith shrugged and put an arm round his shoulder, leading him back out into the light.

"Well. It would have been nice to know how he got here, or what he was doing, since the Raven says there's a connection with the house on Chandos Place . . ."

They walked east for a while, through crowded streets that Hodge wasn't really seeing. Jed trotted beside him, looking up every now and then to check up on his friend.

"Better now?" said The Smith as they passed the City of York tavern. He jerked his head at the ancient door. "Better enough for a restorative ale? To celebrate?"

Hodge shook his head.

"Doesn't feel like a victory," he said.

"Death never does, old friend," said The Smith. "Death is no one's victory but its own."

FOURTH PART

THE FIVE PEBBLES

. . . *David* took just five pibbles out of the Brook against the
Pagan Champion
    from *The Garden of Cyrus* by Sir Thomas Browne (1658)

    This night is my departing night,
    For here no longer must I stay;
    There's neither friend nor foe of mine
     But wishes me away.
    What I have done through lack of wit,
    I never, never can recall,
    But know you're all my friends as yet,
    Goodnight. And joy be with you all.
  An additional verse to *The Parting Glass* (traditional song),
          known as *Armstrong's Farewell* (added c.1605)

INTERLUDE

She had screamed all afternoon, from lunchtime to supper. She had sat in the empty Itch Ward and hoarsened her voice with the screaming, listening to it echo off the scuffed plaster walls as she watched the dust motes drift through the sunlight. The M'Gregors had been ignorant of the noise for most of the afternoon since they had been about their business in Andover, but come teatime Mrs M'Gregor had returned and was being put off her crumpets and dainties by the keening coming across the yard to the Private Quarters, and had told her husband she must be allowed some peace.

M'Gregor had rung the bell for one of the under-wardens and explained that if he, M'Gregor, was to have any peace, Mrs M'Gregor must be given her own quiet, and directed that if the Ghost of the Itch Ward — as they all called her — was not amenable to reason or controllable by means of a belt or switch (which she never was), she must be taken to the Eel House on the other side of the water meadows and penned in for the night, this being the only way they had ever contrived to keep Mrs M'Gregor free from the infrequent but piercing screaming attacks the Ghost was prone to.

"Does her no harm, a night with the eels, but don't leave her with a blanket, mind, for 'tis my belief she benefits from the bracing chill and the turbulence of the stream. She always comes out subdued and tractable."

The under-warden was a kinder man than M'Gregor so did not lay about her with switch or belt, knowing that this occasioned nothing but doggedly endured cuts and bruises on the person of the Ghost. Instead he rounded up the sub-under-wardens and strapped her wrists together prior to leading her from the workhouse across the water meadows and into the small red-brick shed that was built straddling the chalk stream on the far side. The under-warden deputed the sub-under-wardens to escort her, and went in search of a hot sweet cup of tea of his own.

She screamed all the way across the meadow, the sound sending the normally lazy cows trotting off to the furthest corner beneath the elms, from whose deep shadows they watched with deep bovine suspicion as the procession jerked its way across the grass in the low evening sunlight.

The sub-under-wardens did not have the kindly streak of their immediate superior, and their progress was punctuated by several hard slaps across the face and repeated injunctions of the "shut up, you mad old bitch" variety.

Conscious that their tea was getting colder the longer the exiling of the Ghost took, they shoved her inside the Eel House with no more ceremony than roughly unstrapping her hands, and slamming the door on her.

Inside the house she stood in the gloom and looked around. And though she carried on screaming for form's sake, she smiled happily as she did so. And when she judged that the sub-under-wardens had walked out of earshot she stopped screaming and just carried on smiling.

The Eel House was built to catch eels as they moved downstream to the sea. There was a walkway over the stream and three arches on which the house sat. Each arch had a metal grille through which the river sieved itself, leaving the eels behind until someone came with a scoop to harvest them into the rush baskets hanging round the ceiling. The basket, once full of eels, would be put back in the stream on the other side of the walkway to keep the creatures fresh and alive until the carter came to take them up to London.

It was the time of year when the eels ran, and consequently the traps in front of the grilles were a seething mass of brown snake-like bodies. The Ghost looked down at them.

"Hello, my dears," she said, hitching her threadbare dress up and knotting it at her hip. "Hello, my dear ones."

And with that she stepped very daintily off the walkway, being sure not to tread on any of the creatures, slowly lowering her foot until it found the chalk bed of the stream below.

Then she just stood there, up to mid-thigh in the cold water as the eels roiled and tumbled round and around her legs, her fingers reaching down to let them brush against them as they passed in an increasing vortex that would certainly have led any watcher — had there been one — to think she stood in a small whirlpool of her own creation.

She closed her eyes.

"Now," she whispered, "where have you been and what have you seen?"

CHAPTER 70

CLOSE QUARTERS ON
BLACKWALL REACH

Cook clanked as she stepped from the culvert onto the boat. The Smith looked at her and held his finger to his mouth. The fog hiding the city and the river around them muffled everything but sound, somehow amplifying it, perhaps because the ears had to do double duty now that the eyes were handicapped by the viscid, almost semi-solid murk and the encroaching evening.

"Sorry," she whispered, putting her heavy canvas sea-bag on the deck. "Grappling hooks."

"Why did you bring *grappling hooks*?" hissed Hodge, who was holding the mooring rope with the look of a man who wanted to be about his business quickly. Which was the truth: Hodge was a man happiest with his feet on the ground, and least comfortable when afloat. He wanted this to be over soon so he could get back to the Tower with Jed and do a little light ratting to calm his nerves. Being afloat was the only thing he feared, perhaps because the little mongrel he had lost in the collapsed bank on the Isle of Dogs all those years ago had died struggling for air. Hodge was not especially frightened of dying, but did not want to drown.

"Grappling hooks are always useful," said Cook, pulling things out of the bag which were equally clanky but not the hooks in question. They watched her remove two cutlasses, a dirk and a boarding axe, which she stowed – respectively – in the red sash she was wearing as her belt, the top of her sea-boots and alongside her place at the tiller.

"We are just going to drop downriver on the tide and sink these caskets in the river, Cook," said The Smith quietly, watching her present her broad beam end again as she bent to pull more vicious-looking ironmongery from the sea-bag. "We're not going a-pirating."

"I know," she said, straightening and handing him a heavy metal sphere.

"What's this?" he said suspiciously.

"Cannon ball," she said. "It's my last one, so don't drop it."

"But we haven't got a cannon," said Hodge, looking at The Smith.

"Put it in the bows," said Cook to someone behind him. He turned to look.

Emmet stood in the culvert mouth, cradling what was, unmistakably, a smallish cannon in his arms. He seemed a little sheepish.

Cook felt the silence of the very pregnant look passing between The Smith and Hodge.

"It's not really a cannon," she said. "Not as such: more of a swivel-mounted carronade. I've been on the wrong end of enough privateering to know any lubber that goes to sea without protection's just asking to get a-pirated themselves."

She pulled two more cutlasses from her bag and held them out.

"Keep them handy and get ready to cast off." She sniffed the air. "Wind's changing and the tide's on the turn."

Hodge looked at The Smith.

"We're not going to sea," he said. "We're going for a short trip down the river, no further than Smith's Folley, where we'll tie this lighter up for the night, warm ourselves at the smithy fire and then come home by dog cart, on dry land, like normal folk."

Cook took a look back in the direction of Wellclose Square.

"Perhaps one of us should stay with Sara," she said. "I do not like leaving her alone in the house."

"Emmet can return the moment the caskets are safe on the bottom of the river," said The Smith. "We discussed this. He can run back. She will be alone for less than an hour, and what needs protecting most is in these caskets, not any one of us."

"Cast off then," grunted Cook with a look which said that though he might be right it was anything but fine with her.

As Hodge loosened the hawser attached to the mooring post, a gap widened between the boat and the land, and soon enough they were drifting with the tide into the centre of the river.

Unseen by them, as they moved away from the land, a thin length of tarred twine that Garlickhythe Templebane had attached to their boat stretched out and became taut.

Six hundred yards away, upriver, close to Traitor's Gate, a small paddle-wheel launch sat waiting. The three Templebane boys – Coram, Garlickhythe and Bassetshaw – had pride of place next to their Night Father, Zebulon, and were thus sitting closest to the fire-box. Around them, a crowd of toughs hunched in, trying to get some of the warmth into their bodies. They were a murderous-looking bunch, and had been recruited en masse from a drinking den in the darkest reaches of the Seven Dials rookery. They were known as the Wipers because they roamed after dark with spotted handkerchiefs ("wipers" in thieves' slang) pulled over the lower half of their faces to hide their identity as they robbed, beat and often as not dispatched their victims to the next world. Used to knives, razors and cudgels, they looked a little self-conscious with the guns and pistols they had been given for the day's work in their hands: self-conscious but not at all uncomfortable. They had been hired on the understanding that the job involved blood and plunder, and plunder and blood was their business.

Their leader, a sharp-eyed bruiser who went by the name of Magor, jerked in surprise as the twine looping out of the fog went suddenly taut and jangled the small bell Garlickhythe had attached to the funnel.

"Blimey!" he said, covering his surprise with a leer. "Shop!"

"Coram," said Zebulon. "Now."

Coram patted his brothers on the shoulder.

"Good hunting," he said as he jumped to the bank and untied the waiting horse. "I'll get Mountfellon, Father; don't you worry. You bag the boodle."

Zebulon let the familiarity pass and checked the blunder-buss he held across the blanket wrapping his knees. As Coram cantered off into the murk, the other brothers pushed off and the paddles began to churn. Magor sat on the bow, reeling in the tarry twine as they made way.

"Just like fishing, this is," he leered. "Only hope we don't catch us a measly little tiddler on the end of this here line."

"It's no tiddler," said Zebulon. "You get us what's on that boat and you'll be getting your just deserts, have no fear of that."

"We don't want just dessert," said Magor grimly. "We want the 'ole bleedin' banquet, from soup to nuts, as what you promised."

"Don't worry," said Garlickhythe, sharing a look with his brother. "You'll get what's coming to you. Never heard of anyone complaining about the Templebanes cheating anyone, have you?"

The look shared between the brothers and their Night Father was one of close understanding: once the deed was done and whatever was being shifted from the Safe House was in their possession, the Wipers would come to collect their pay: they would be shown the money and offered food and drink in celebration. They would eat, they would drink, they would not notice any strange flavours, because the Templebanes had learned well from the herbalists they had persecuted in the fens all those years ago, and then they would never be seen again. The money they had pocketed would never leave the premises, being reclaimed and returned to the Templebane vaults.

This had happened before. This would happen again.

This was the reason no one ever spread word about being short-changed by Issachar. It was also the reason the Templebane boys never, ever ate anything from the pie shop on the corner of their street. They knew where the filling came from and why the meat was of such a changeable quality.

Downriver, Cook held the tiller and peered into the fog.

"How am I meant to navigate in this soup?" she said.

The Smith pointed to the Raven, which was flapping with its eerie slowness just ahead of the bow. At this speed, it seemed to hang in the air in contravention of any of the more generally accepted laws of gravity, beating its wings out of form, rather than function.

"Follow the bird," he said. "He knows where we're going."

"Well, you just keep a sharp lookout forrard," she said. "And sing out if we look like hitting anything."

The plan, worked out in the warmth of the kitchen, was this: when they reached the spot, they would drop the first and most important casket, the double-walled one holding the Wildfire. It was attached by a chain which in turn was attached to a thick rope. They would let the casket hit the bottom, by which time the rope would be whipping out of its neat coils and paying out as they drifted beyond the spot. Emmet would grab the rope as his hands were immune to pain and thus not susceptible to rope burn and would slowly grip it, acting as a brake. Once the lighter was held against the tide by the unconventional anchor, they would all take hold of the line and help Emmet warp them back upstream to the spot directly above the first casket. They would know they were on top of it because The Smith had taken soundings and had made the length of the chain match the depth of the river, so when they reached the point where the chain came back out of the water on the end of the rope, they would know where they were.

And then they would drop the other caskets.

Emmet would sink down the chain and they would wait while he – as un-needful of air as he was un-heeding of pain – took the same chain and bundled all the caskets together with it. Then he would simply walk out of the river and hurry back to the Safe House to stand guard on Sara until they returned from mooring the boat at The Folley.

Plans made in warm kitchens are one thing; plans executed on something as wild and wilful as a great river in the thickest fog are another thing entirely.

The Smith and Hodge kept lookout forward, and Jed took up position next to Cook, his warmth leaning against her leg as he stood with his forepaws up on the steersman's thwart, looking aft into the blank miasma behind them.

Their progress was eerily silent since they had no need to make way against the river, going as fast as the tide and no quicker. They seemed to slide through a damp and dreamy half-world with little sound other than the gentle lap of water and the distant sound of church bells ringing. And as with all dreamy and unvaried experiences, there was a danger of being lulled into a kind of half-sleep. Cook shook herself and kept her eyes on the dark bird floating in mid-air just ahead of them, easing the tiller to keep the bows centred on its leisurely progress.

Time also seemed to be a little odd in the cotton-wool seclusion of the fog, for it seemed like hours but may only have been twenty minutes or even less when the bird flared its wings and dropped to perch on the bow post.

"Now!" said The Smith, and Emmet took the topmost lead casket and tipped it easily over the side. There was a deep gulping plop as the river slapped closed over the sudden hole it made in it, then a short sharp rattle as the chain followed it on down, followed by a softer hiss as it gave way to rope. Emmet stepped back and gripped the cable, slowly braking the boat against the urgent press of water heading towards the sea, and then The Smith and Hodge joined him as they hauled the rope back upstream.

"This would be the moment for one of your sea shanties," gritted Hodge.

"One of the clean ones," added The Smith quickly.

"Quiet!" hissed Cook, and looked down.

Jed's hackles were up and he was emitting a low growl that she felt vibrating against her leg.

"What's up, Jed?" said Cook.

"He smells something," said Hodge, peering back the way Jed was now looking, his tail straight out behind him, legs quivering in excitement, a hunter on point.

They heard a distant triple ring of a ship's bell.

The Raven hopped the length of the boat and stood next to Jed, head cocked on one side.

At that moment, the slight breeze freshened and cut a momentary gap in the fog. A hundred and fifty yards back they saw the outline of the paddle-launch and the small crowd standing on the deck, and heard the *chunka-chunk* of the steam piston turning the cam-shaft.

"Doesn't mean anything," said Hodge. "Not necessarily."

They heard the triple ring again.

"We could see what . . ." began Hodge, and then his words were cut off by a distant gunshot cracking across the gap between the two boats, followed by a smacking noise and yelp as the bullet scored a bloody furrow along the fur on Jed's side and hit Cook, spinning her round and toppling her into the water with a colossal splash.

The Smith sprang to the side, his eyes searching the water for her, but it was as if the river and the fog had swallowed every trace of her.

"Cook!" he roared into the blankness to no reply. He whirled on Emmet.

"Emmet—" he began. But in the moment that all this had taken, the golem had secured the anchor chain to a cleat, his hands blurring with speed, and was already stepping over the side. He hit the water and he too disappeared.

Hodge was at Jed's side, the dog trembling with shock, but still standing as Hodge quickly examined him.

"No bones broken," he said with relief, hands red with his friend's blood as he stroked his rough fur, calming him. "Good dog. Good man. You'll be fine . . ."

His eyes, when they looked up at The Smith, were like flint.

"Right then," he said. "Where's that damn cutlass?"

Coram rode pell-mell back to his father's establishment and alerted Mountfellon to the departure of the lighter. In short order Mountfellon had made his way to the second steam launch at St Katherine's Steps and they were on the water, heading downstream at great speed.

"You are sure they are on the move?"

"Oh yes, Milord," said Coram. "And my father will have them by now, or I'm a Chinaman. He's thought of everything, even this rotten weather and the darkness coming in. They'll ring the ship's bell every minute, three quick strikes so we shall find 'em in the fog, and we shall do the same as we approach."

"A sensible precaution," said Mountfellon approvingly. "And will there be unpleasantness?"

"Do you mind if there is, Milord?" said Coram.

"Not at all," condescended the noble lord. "In fact I should prefer it. Those people endeavoured to make me look a fool. I cannot tolerate that."

"No, Milord," said Coram, and peered forward into the fog.

In the distance he could swear he heard a gunshot, but it might as much have been someone dropping a piece of timber.

When the steam launch drew level with The Oversight's lighter, it appeared to have been abandoned. One of the Wipers clamped on with a boat hook, and looked to Bassetshaw for instructions.

It was a pregnant moment: a frozen tableau isolated in the fog, unworldly in its stillness, the only thing moving being the passing river kicking and gurgling beneath the hulls of the two craft and the gang, armed and ready, clamped onto a boat which appeared to be deserted but for a tall stack of lead caskets lashed on its deck, armed and ready, yet somehow unwilling to board the other vessel.

"They're behind the caskets," said Garlickhythe, shouting over the noise of the steam-engine and prodding one of the gang. "Go on then, you shy buggers, go get them out!"

As the man stepped forward, two heavy grappling hooks sailed into the air and dropped onto the deck of the launch. Immediately, the ropes were yanked taut, the hooks scraping across the deck, one catching Bassetshaw by the heel and tripping him as it passed. They crunched into the side of the launch, splintering wood as they bit in, the ropes twanging with tension while invisible hands behind the caskets dogged them tight.

"I told you they were behind the caskets!" shouted Garlickhythe. "Get over there and shoot the bastards."

"No," said a voice behind him. "We're here. And my parents were very happily married, thank you."

He spun to see a soaking Cook and a very large and equally wet Emmet step over the railing on the opposite side to the lighter. One of Cook's arms was dripping blood, but since the bullet had missed the bone she was ignoring it for the moment. She had her boarding axe in one hand and a cutlass in the other. And then – because Cook felt there was not much point talking if you were about to start a fight with people who have announced their intention of shooting your friends – the axe was spinning through the air towards a man who had had the misfortune to think faster than the others and turn his pistol towards her.

Things happened very swiftly after that.

Cook's now empty hand plucked the other cutlass from her belt even before the axe found its mark, and she and Emmet fell on the murderous gang. It was a peculiarity of the golem's make-up that he could not harm a human, but he could certainly protect Cook from any attack which meant that she could concentrate on dealing blows to left and right without worrying about parrying or defending herself, which the clay man did for her. Zebulon was the first casualty, Emmet just slapping him away so that he sprawled on the deck, twisted up in his carriage blanket, his blunderbuss skittering out of his grasp and across the deck.

As the broad-bosomed berserker fell on them on one side, The Smith and Hodge took advantage of the confusion to come at them over the caskets with a cold fury which matched hers in both speed and intensity.

The Wipers were used to weak and frightened victims – young women, or the elderly, or those with reactions muddled by drink – and the truth is they were predators and not fighters in the same mould as their opponents. Hodge, enraged by the wound to his dog, wielded his cutlass with a brutal severity rivalled only by that of Jed himself, who joined the boarding party in a snarling ball of fury, attacking at knee level.

The Smith hit the enemy like a battering ram, his hammer shattering weapons and bones with terrifying impartiality. The Oversight were outnumbered two to one, and surprise and speed will only get you so far, so there were some blows received as well as the many given. Hodge took several cuts across his body and one bad razor slash across his nose.

Magor lashed out with a heavy boot which sent Jed across the deck to slam against the side-rail with a loud yelp of pain.

Hodge looked round, grabbed the axe sticking out of Cook's first victim and took Magor's head off his neck in one vengeful sweep of steel.

The Wiper standing behind Magor froze at the red mist spraying out of his leader's still upright body, and then choked in horror as he saw Hodge come through it like a bloody whirlwind, swinging the axe in a double-handed back-swing his Viking forebears would have been proud of.

The rattled Wiper fired his gun too early and the bullet went wide, but before he could begin to register disappointment the scything axe blade had cut him off from this and any future cares.

Zebulon had regained the blunderbuss and smiled nastily as he swung it towards The Smith.

The Smith had nowhere to hide, nowhere he could reach in time given the blunderbuss's wide shot pattern.

Hodge saw the inevitability of what was going to happen and didn't think.

He just threw himself into the three feet separating them, and swung his axe in the same moment. He swung underhand because there was no time to do otherwise, but it was a good thing as the blade hit the muzzle of the gun and knocked it upwards just as Zebulon pulled the trigger.

The spread of shot blew a large hole in the smoke-stack instead of The Smith, but Hodge took the powder blast in his eyes at point-blank range.

He staggered backwards, silently grabbing at his face, and then Jed snarled over him and into Zebulon, latching onto his throat in a terrible snarling death grip.

Zebulon screamed and his eyes found The Smith's as his hands futilely tried to tear the implacable terrier from his throat.

"Please . . . !" he shrieked raggedly. "Mercy!"

"Certainly," said The Smith, and swung his hammer in a blow which made the deck bounce.

Then he bent and ruffled Jed's fur.

"Let go, boy," he said. "He's gone."

As fast as it had begun, it was over: the last Wiper standing dropped his weapon, retched at the sight of what had been Zebulon's face and tried to dive overboard, but he was too slow for The Smith, who snatched his foot as it flew past and swung him so that this head crunched decisively against the lead caskets.

The Smith dropped the foot and stood there, breathing hard but unscathed. Emmet was the most damaged and the least affected, having been shielding Cook and absorbing the cuts and blows intended for her.

"We shall have to get you a new coat," said Cook, breathing hard and leaning against the smoke-stack. "Thank you."

"Put the dead ones over the side," said The Smith.

"And what of the living?" said Cook.

Hodge said nothing. He was sitting holding a bunched

kerchief to his eyes, a curtain of blood seeping down his face, reddening it from the nose down.

"Hodge . . ." said Cook.

"Be fine in a moment," he said. Jed nuzzled up to him, making low whining noises of concern.

Emmet began tossing bodies into the river, two at a time.

Now it was over, Cook looked grey and tired. Her left arm was leaking blood in a wide scarlet ribbon dropping off her fingertips onto the deck.

Emmet dragged the last unmoving body to the side and tipped it into the passing tide. Cook watched it get swept away into the fog and shivered.

"That was a bloody bit of business," she said. "Tie this up for me, if you would be so kind . . ."

Emmet beat The Smith to her side and unwound his neckerchief to use as a bandage. The Smith looked at Bassetshaw Templebane, who had crawled backwards until he could go no further, jamming himself in the angle of the bows. His arm was broken and he was panting with shock. As The Smith approached him he scrabbled in his waistcoat pocket and tried to put on a pair of smoked-glass spectacles. The Smith batted them away.

"What . . . what . . . are you?" Bassetshaw gibbered.

The Smith made a fist and showed him the ring on it.

"We are The Oversight," he said, and pressed it to Bassetshaw's forehead. "And you will forget what happened today, and you will forget us. And then you are free to wander the country as you will, but returning to the city is forbidden you. You will seek out someone less fortunate than yourself, and you will dedicate your life to making him or her happier. But first you will tell us who sent you . . ."

"Father," said Bassetshaw. "The fathers sent me . . ."

"Cook," said The Smith. "We will help Emmet unload the caskets. Better for us all to be on dry land soon as we can. Listen to what he has to tell you, then we shall set him adrift in this boat."

"It's not a boat," said Cook. "It's a contraption."

And while she listened to what Bassetshaw said in answer to her questions, The Smith tied an impromptu bandage across Hodge's nose, holding the wadded handkerchief in place, clucking his teeth in concern at the damage.

"Just powder-flash," said Hodge, looking blindly up at him. "Wasn't shot. Eyes'll adjust in time, I'm sure – right?"

The Smith looked across at Cook and shook his head.

"You just rest," he said.

He went back to the lighter with a grim face and helped Emmet drop the heavy lead caskets down the anchor chain. It was hard work, and he was sweating despite the chill once it was done.

Emmet then dropped into the water and was gone for several minutes, taking the chain with him as he joined the caskets on the river bed together for safety.

As the weight came off the lighter, it rose higher and higher in the water on one side, kept low on the other side by the steam launch it was still grappled to, so that the deck tilted alarmingly.

Emmet resurfaced and nodded at The Smith, and then held the boats together while Cook freed her grappling hooks and tossed them back on the lighter. She looked back at Bassetshaw, who was sitting blankly on the deck of the launch, the impression made by The Smith's ring already fading on his forehead.

"Come," she said.

He shuffled to his feet and staggered over on to the lighter.

"We'll set his arm and cut him loose on the Isle of Dogs," she said. "If his punishment is to help another, we'd as best not send him to do it half crippled."

"And what of the other boat?" said The Smith.

"It's not a boat," repeated Cook, but he waved her down

before she could elaborate again on her dislike of steam navigation.

"Cut it loose and send it back the way it came," said Hodge, allowing them to lead him back across to their own boat.

At that moment they heard a distant triple bell. It was the same rhythm as the one they had heard from the launch, a signal Bassetshaw had warned them about. They looked at each other.

"Best be gone," said Cook. "Sounds like the confederates have arrived."

"A moment," said The Smith. "Emmet. Stay on this boat and answer the bell. Stoke this boiler as you wait. When they see you, push this—"

He looked closely at the pipes and gauges attached to the steam-engine.

"No, *this* lever, all the way over and swim to the shore. Then home as fast as you can, for Sara Falk is alone and in peril."

CHAPTER 71

REGENT'S BASIN

In her mind Lucy had anticipated arriving in London as a difficult thing, a sudden entanglement in a thicket of streets and alleys, complicated by a threatening press of people assailing them on all sides. She was girding herself for the jarring change of plunging back into the seething belly of the great metropolitan beast after the gentler rhythms of the road and the countryside. She had enjoyed that time, and though it was scarcely past she had begun to think of it as an almost idyllic interlude in a life normally spent feeling hunted. She had resigned herself to the prospect of them making their way through the mobbed labyrinth and probably getting lost several times on their way to Wellclose Square, despite Charlie's airy assertion that he knew the East End like the back of his hand.

But the great tiredness which had been creeping up on her had become too much to fight on the night after the Sluagh had walked beside them on the towpath, and so she slept long and deep. She didn't wake up as they made the change from the Grand Union Canal to the Regent's Canal at Bull's Bridge Junction, and so she slid into the city without noticing as the water took them from Paddington on the westernmost edge of the city all the way east. She only woke when Charlie shook her shoulder and grinned down at her.

"Wake up, sleepy-head," he said. "We're here."

"Where?" she said, still groggy and frustratingly not very refreshed despite the length and depth of her slumbers.

He pulled the tarpaulin back to reveal a sooty pigeon-torn sky hemmed in by masts, cranes and davits.

"Regent's Basin," he said with a proprietorial air. "And that over there's the Thames." He swept his arm and pointed towards the unmistakable silhouette of the Tower of London poking above the rooftops.

"And Wellclose Square's about halfway between us and the Tower. How's that for service?"

She scrambled upright and took the bundled hand from its place beneath the hay-stuffed flour-sack Mrs Stonex had given her as a pillow.

"Let's go," she said. "Right now. Fast as we can."

They thanked the Stonexes, who bid them as easy a farewell as they had given them a welcome, and undertook to send a message back up the line of the canal to the effect that they had both arrived in London without harm.

"Though in my experience," said Mrs Stonex, casting a jaundiced eye at her husband, "staying out of trouble on the way to London's not half as difficult *for some* as staying out of trouble once you're there."

The basin was so full and busy that their barge had had to moor next to another barge and not the dock itself, so Charlie and Lucy clambered over it and found their way ashore.

At this point, the assault on her senses which Lucy had anticipated began in earnest. Charlie evidently took her at her word and went as fast as he could so that she had to run to keep up with him as they buffeted past the bargees, stevedores and traders thronging the dockside. They kicked up flurries of pigeons pecking at spilt grain; they dodged handcarts and wagons, and stutter-stepped past men staggering beneath loads that looked as if they would have killed a horse.

The smells and noises all around them added to the sense she had of having been pitched pell-mell into a battle instead of a civilised city, quite as if she had woken to find herself in one of the great conflicts Barnaby Pyefinch described with his dioramas at the fairs. Faces, mouths, boots, knees and above all eyes were everywhere, blurring past her as she ran behind Charlie, taking care not to lose sight of his long coat or the flash of the tacks in the soles of his boots. The one thing she was thankful for was that people only seemed to notice them if they bumped or jostled against them: as long as they jinked and dodged their way without collisions, she and Charlie were as anonymous and unnoticed as the pigeons.

At least they seemed to be.

It took less than ten minutes for them to get to the quieter backstreet leading to Wellclose Square, and as soon as Charlie pointed out the single tall smoke-stack of the sugar refinery and the thin steeple of the church just beyond, she slowed.

It was Charlie's stopping and turning back to see what was up that caught the eye of the burly young man with no neck who was talking to someone inside a black carriage pulled up diagonally across from the Safe House. Though the burly young man had no neck to speak of, and so wore his head hunched down into the hump of muscle straining against the shoulders of his top-coat, he did have very sharp eyes, and he caught sight of the two because Charlie's sudden halting and reversal of movement broke the pattern and flow of a neighbourhood that he was wholly and unconsciously attuned to.

It was great bad luck for Lucy that the watcher was called Sherehog Templebane, and that he was talking to his father inside the coach.

"You are not attending me!" said Issachar testily. "I was just . . ."

"Hold up," said Sherehog, waving his father down in a gesture only he and perhaps Vintry, as the two oldest "sons", would dare attempt. "Ain't that the girl we put the pitch-plaster gag on?"

Issachar bit off the rebuke with which he had been about to savage Sherehog for his impudence and leant forward, squinting into the light.

"What is it?" said Charlie.

"I don't know how to do this," said Lucy, stopped dead outside a shop selling alarmingly lifelike glass eyes and less convincing false legs. "She might be dead. People die when their arms are cut off."

"And they also live," said Charlie.

"But if she's dead it's my fault," said Lucy. "The stone ring, the glass one gives her strength. I've got my own special bit of glass. I know how important it is. And I sort of stole that too, her one I mean. I mean I was taken to the house and I don't know quite how that happened, but they were kind to me, and I stole from them. And I don't know how to explain that to them because I don't know how I did that or why I tried it . . ."

"But she can't be dead, otherwise how could the hand be alive?" said Charlie. "We talked about this. She's communicating with the hand, ain't she?"

She nodded. She felt sick.

This was not a new conversation. They'd discussed this on the barge several times as they watched the countryside slip slowly past them. Lucy wished she were back on that simpler and more peaceful journey where decisions only had to be discussed, not acted on.

"We could always put it on the doorstep, ring the bell and run away," said Charlie with a grin.

"Be serious," she said. "This is hard."

He nodded and looked at the fog creeping into the square.

"You know the difference between you and Georgie Eagle?" he said.

She could think of a long list of answers, but she just looked at him.

"She'd do the easy thing, the thing that was best for her. In fact she wouldn't be having this conversation. She wouldn't be here. So why don't you think what she would do, and then do the opposite."

Lucy thought about it and then nodded decisively.

"Right. I can do that," she said. "Show me the house."

"I thought you'd been there before," he said.

"I was in a sack."

The Safe House looked blank and empty. The windows were shuttered and when they rang the doorbell the only sound was a distant jangle which died away to an echo, and then . . . nothing. No sound of feet approaching, no inner doors opening and closing, no movement of any kind.

"Ring it again," said Charlie after a couple of minutes had trickled past.

"There's no one in," she said, lead in her voice. This had been a stupid idea. And what was stupider was that she didn't know what to do if no one came to the door. So she pulled the handle again and listened to the noise startle into brassy life and then die once more.

"We can just sit here and wait," said Charlie. "Be fine unless it rains."

Lucy bit her lip and clutched Sara's hand to her chest as she looked at the worn stone around the door. It was an old house. And that stone wall looked just like the kind she spent her life avoiding touching for fear that the past locked inside it would reach back and bite at her. A house like this, with all the strange comings and goings it must have witnessed, was surely bursting with traumatic memories just hunched in the stones, waiting to spring back to life. She remembered Sara searching through her glove box, trying to find some for her to wear. No wonder she wore long black gloves herself.

Because they were looking up at the front of the house, searching for movement, they missed the sinister coach rolling slowly up to the gate behind them.

Three floors above there was someone in. And though it was recognisably Sara Falk, she herself was so weak and changed that she did not know who she was as the insistent bells woke her for a second time. She lay on the bed, as white and lifeless as the pillows around her.

"No," she said, and a tear runnelled out of her eye, unbidden and unnoticed. "No. No one home."

And she closed her eyes and sought the oblivion of sleep again.

Lucy was looking at the stone around the door, but she was thinking more about gloves when the voice from the street interrupted her.

"There's nobody in," it said. "Sadly. They have gone."

She turned and for a moment could not see who had spoken. Then she realised that the door to the coach was open and the voice came from the darkness within.

"Perhaps I can help?" said the voice.

"We're fine," said Charlie sharply. "Thank you."

Lucy knew they were suddenly not fine at all, and she knew that Charlie sensed it too, because he had instinctively stepped in front of her.

Since looking for the right direction to run in was second nature to her, she automatically checked the possible ways to flee, and in so doing discovered Sherehog leaning innocently against the side-gate. They would just have to run around the back of the house and hope there was a way out there . . .

"I was not talking to you, young man," said the voice,

honey over gravel. "I was talking to dear Miss Harker."

The words came out of nowhere and hooked her guts with such a strong and unexpected tug that she felt her heart bump up into her throat. So deep a sense of danger hit her that her stomach spasmed and turned to water. She clenched her teeth, controlling the terror rising in her gullet.

Charlie turned and looked at her.

"I don't know who that man is," she said very quietly, her pulse pounding.

"Then we're in trouble," he said.

Lucy knew that. But she also knew the worst of it was what she would now have to do. The man behind the voice knew her name. Which meant he knew other things. Things she needed to know.

"I have holes in my memory," she said.

Charlie nodded slowly as if he understood. Then he lifted his coat and showed her the blunderbuss hanging by its strap and the knife at his belt. Something about the cold way he raised an eyebrow reminded her of the man dressed in midnight blue who had cut her free of the sack in this very building.

She shook her head.

"I have to go," she said. "I have to."

She gave him Sara's hand and then leant in and, whilst appearing to kiss him goodbye, whispered something in his ear. Then she walked off the steps and peered into the carriage.

"How do you know my name, sir?" she said.

"What is the boy doing?" rasped the voice from within the dark carriage, frighteningly closer now that Lucy had walked down the front steps to stand in the gateway.

Charlie had his back to them, doing what she whispered in his ear: peeling the glove from Sara's hand so he could place it on the stone wall of the house. He was finding it hard to do, his fingers fumbling with the buttons and tight leather. He hoped that whatever piece of the past bit out would be felt by Sara wherever she was, and that she would recognise the house and realise her hand must be there.

Lucy prayed that if Sara was close she would return before it was too late because the pull of the dark voice and all the holes it promised to fill in her memory was very, very strong.

Charlie gave up on the buttons and stuck the tip of his knife under the leather and ripped outwards, revealing the palm of the hand.

He slapped it to the wall.

Sara Falk woke with a convulsive jerk, her knees jack-knifing towards her head as the past hit her in jagged slices as she glinted—

Wellclose Square

a minute ago

a girl

that girl

Lucy

yanks the bell

a young man turns, coat flaring

a blunderbuss hanging on a strap visible for a moment

"We can just sit here and wait," he says.

kind eyes.

Then a time jerk and the gate is blocked by a coach.

A voice comes out.

gravel and honey

"There's nobody in. Sadly. They have gone."

Lucy turns

time jerks

"I was talking to dear Miss Harker."

Lucy's face drains of colour

Sara felt the icy tug in the girl's guts as if in her own and tumbled out of her bed, retching. She hung over the Kashgai rug and panted, thin bile ribboning onto the brightly coloured wool below.

She had never felt this urgency.

She had never felt this weak.

She crawled and stumbled to her feet, tipping a chair onto the floor as she grabbed it to support herself.

She did not have the strength to walk down the stairs.

She fell back to her knees and dragged herself to the edge of the steps.

She remembered The Smith looking into her eyes, telling her it was all over.

There is strength.

And when there is no strength—

—there is gravity.

She grunted with the effort as she yanked awkwardly forward over the tipping point at the top of the steep slope of the stairs and tumbled herself downwards.

Lucy had to control her terror and step closer to the carriage to keep blocking the view of Charlie. The terror felt like vertigo because she was teetering on a razor's edge between the fear of asking the questions and the fear of what the answers might be. But she knew the even bigger fear was never knowing.

"Who are you?" she said, inching closer.

Something emerged from the gloom: a pale, pillowy hand holding what she first thought was a nut, but then saw was a stone. Or half a stone, mottled green and red.

"I am the man who has something you have lost, I think, and if you come in here, my dear, I can return it to you and take you back to the safety and riches you are heir to. I can return you—"

And at this point Issachar leant further forward so that his great slack-jowled face seemed for a moment to swim out of the gloom as a disembodied thing, before she saw the dark lawyer's clothes beneath. He smiled benignly at her.

"—I can return you, I say, and you would do me a great honour by allowing me so to do, to the very bosom of your warm and loving family."

She hesitated, trying to control the leaping sensations in her ribcage, trying to think straight.

"Look," he smiled. "Take it and look. It is the other half of your ring. Only a friend would have been vouchsafed it."

She reached for it and saw the animal engraved on it. Her fingers closed on it and in that moment Templebane's hand snaked out and grabbed her wrist, tugging her into the black maw of the carriage.

She tried to throw herself backwards, but he was strong and all she managed to do was brace herself against the door-frame with her feet and one free hand. She could tell this was a trial of strength she would not win, for if she released a hand or a foot to try and lash out at him, all her slim advantage would be lost in an instant and she would be tumbled inside the carriage with him, a fate she suddenly was terrified of.

"Sherehog!" he shouted. "Get her in and let's be away!"

As Sherehog lunged across the pavement the front door of the Safe House wrenched open with a bang.

"LET HER GO!"

Sara Falk hung in the doorway with one hand on the jamb, the stump hanging loose on the other side of her, white hair wild around her head, nightdress torn and whipping in the breeze, her knees and elbows grazed raw from her headlong tumbling crawl down the three flights of stairs.

Her voice was ragged, her body looked broken with exhaustion but her eyes were blazing.

Templebane's chuckle was deep and insulting as it rolled across the pavement and up the steps of the house.

"Or what, Miss Falk? Or what exactly?"

Lucy felt no let-up in his strength, and her muscles were screaming with the pain of resisting him. She craned her head back and saw with horror the wreck of Sara.

"I'm sorry," she choked.

"Sherehog!" shouted Templebane. "Get the bitch in!"

Sara looked at Charlie. He was holding her lost hand.

"Give me that," she said.

He held it out. She swayed dangerously as she let go of the door and took it, and so he grabbed her and kept her on her feet.

She looked at the hand. At the mirror on its stump. At the mirror on her own arm.

And then she just touched one to the other.

There was a click and a great jolt which Charlie felt go through her like an electric shock. She gasped in a great paroxysm of surprise and release.

Then he felt her straighten and push him away.

"Give me that too," she said in a wholly new voice, pointing to the blunderbuss under his coat.

Her face looked different. It was younger, more alive – and grim as cold death itself.

Without ceremony she yanked it so that the strap broke off his shoulder, and strode down the steps straight towards the carriage, blunderbuss aimed right at Templebane.

"Sherehog!" shouted Issachar, scrabbling a pair of smoked-glass spectacles out of his pocket with his free hand, and jamming them on his nose. "She won't fire; she'll hit the girl!"

Sherehog stepped in Sara's way and made the mistake of hesitating.

"Just a—" he began.

She didn't break step, just reversed the gun so fast that one second he was staring down its flared barrel, the next he caught the brass-bound stock under his chin and went down like a poleaxed steer.

Sara stepped right over him and pointed the gun past Lucy, into the carriage.

"Now I won't hit her, except with bits of you. And that'll wash off."

Templebane stared at her.

"Let her go," she said.

"You do not know who she is," he sneered. "You do not even—"

She reversed the gun again with eye-defying speed and broke his arm with a brutal jab of the butt-plate.

He gasped and yelped in shock. Lucy felt his hand release her. She stumbled backwards onto the pavement.

"In the house with the boy, *now*," said Sara without breaking eye contact with Templebane's shocked and hate-filled eyes.

"You—" he began.

"I don't know if Lucy is her real name. But I do know who she is. She is one of us. Not one of you, Mr Issachar or Mr Zebulon Templebane, for that is who you are, is it not? Not one of you." And she cocked the blunderbuss and aimed it at him, shaking with barely controlled fury.

He licked his lips and stared back at her, his arm clutched tight to his belly.

"You know my name," he said.

"Of course we do," she said. "We see everything. We are The Oversight."

And somehow saying that made her remember herself and she uncocked the gun and stepped back.

"And much as I would like to decorate the inside of this coach with you, it would be against the Law and the Lore."

There was a noise to her right, and she whirled.

Emmet stood there, dripping wet, his head cocked in a question.

She inclined her head at him.

"Better late than never. Put the unconscious one in the carriage with this one, and get them out of my damn square."

"Miss Falk," said Templebane.

She turned back and looked into the smoked-glass lenses hiding his eyes. He managed a very tight smile at her.

"I know where you live."

She matched his smile: winter for winter.

"And I you, cunning man. And I you."

And without another word she turned and walked up the steps into her house, and closed the door.

Lucy and Charlie stood in the hall, staring at her.

Sara sat on the nearest chair she could find, breathing hard.

"Well," she said. "My mother always said, if you're going to make an enemy, make a good one."

She tossed the gun to Charlie.

"You look like a Pyefinch."

"Charlie," he said.

"Your mother and I were friends once."

"That's what she said," he replied. "Still are, by her count. And no grudges borne, neither."

Sara nodded. She looked stronger now, at least in her body. Her eyes looked infinitely tired.

"And I expect you carry a blade," she said. "If blood runs true."

She looked at him but her eyes seemed to be seeing someone else.

She shook her head and looked down at her torn and dirty nightdress. She stood decisively.

"Right. Down those stairs is a kitchen. Lucy Harker knows the way."

"Even if she doesn't know who she is," muttered Lucy, looking at the floor, feeling somehow all the more wretched because of how easy Sara and Charlie seemed with each other.

"I know who you are," said Sara, voice again like a whip-crack. "I told that toad Templebane, and I'll tell you both now. You're one of us. You came back. That was brave. You have a true heart. That's all it takes; no magic to it, really. And that'll have to do for now. So you go and get some hot tea going and see if Cook left any soup or cake. I must tidy myself up and get ready. The others will be back before dark and we have much to talk about."

And as she walked past Lucy and stepped onto the stairs her hand reached out, and Lucy saw the flash of the join where it had been severed was now a thin silvery line, like a bracelet which had been tattooed into the flesh. Sara touched her arm for an instant.

"And thank you," she said. "This house is your home as long as you want it."

CHAPTER 72

THREE BELLS IN THE FOG

Mountfellon and Coram were navigating blind through the fog, Coram ringing the ship's bell three times every minute. It seemed to him that they must be far beyond Blackwall Reach when they finally heard the answering triple bell ahead of them in the fog. Mountfellon's smile was cold as ever, but it was an indication of eager anticipation.

"Close," he said. "I feared they would have gone further towards the estuary, and we might have lost them on the wide stretch of water . . ."

He leaned forward, alert and waiting for the next ring of the bells. When he heard it – closer now, he adjusted the wheel and aimed towards where the sound came from. This continued for fifteen minutes, slowly gliding blindly through the fog, and then, just as he was beginning to think the sound would never actually materialise into a solid boat, the unmistakable shape of the paddle-launch was revealed by a temporary eddy of air which rent a hole in the surrounding miasma.

"There," said Coram, but Mountfellon was already adjusting his steering. Though the fog swirled back and obscured the view, he had seen enough to ask a question.

"Where was the crew?"

"I didn't see them," admitted Coram.

The bell rang again.

"But they must be there, for who would be ringing the bell!" he said with relief.

There was the sound of a distant splash, like something large entering the water. And then, before they could comment on it, the fog whirled the boat up onto them at the last minute so that Mountfellon only had an instant to yank the tiller and meet the drifting launch side to side, instead of ramming it head on.

The boats creaked and crunched, and they had to hold on to anything they could grab hold of to stay on their feet. Unfortunately that meant, in Coram's case, Mountfellon himself. The noble lord looked down on the hands gripping his arm until Coram realised what he had done and dropped him like a hot coal.

Mountfellon pointed at the launch.

"Empty," he said. "Go and see what there is to see."

Coram made his way to the grinding intersection of the two boats.

"Tie her on," said Mountfellon, "or we shall drift apart."

Coram did so, lashing the painter of their boat around the low railing on the paddle-launch. Then he hoisted himself over the paddles and jumped onto the small deck area.

"Blood," he shouted. "Blood, by God!"

"Damn the blood," said Mountfellon, his head cocked. "What the blazes is that hissing?"

For an instant he tensed at the thought of the hissing snake that had leapt at his face in the Red Library and shuddered involuntarily, and then the hiss turned into a whistle which rose in pitch until it was painful to the ears.

On the deck of the launch, Coram looked apprehensively at the steam-engine. Even at two yards he could feel the heat coming off it in waves.

"It is the steam-engine!" he shouted. "I think—"

Mountfellon didn't wait to know what Coram thought, nor did he consider warning him as he sprang to the side of the boat, shucked a blade from the wrist scabbard beneath his coat, and slashed the painter in two.

"What are you doing?" yelled Coram in shock, seeing the boats part as Mountfellon jumped back to the controls and began to steer away.

And then the whistling became a shriek so high-pitched it hurt to hear, and some atavistic impulse of self-preservation made Coram dive headlong into the water as the boiler on the motor launch exploded.

Mountfellon was hit by a section of funnel and knocked into the water beyond his boat, which yawed away on the tide. By the time he resurfaced and shook the effects of the stunning blow out of his head, it had drifted too far away to be swum to, and a moment later was lost in the fog.

Mountfellon swam towards the wreck of the paddle-launch.

Everything was gone down to the water-line, the force of the explosion having been so great, and by the time he was within a couple of strokes of pulling himself aboard, it gurgled once, shuddered twice and then – disobligingly, in Mountfellon's frank opinion – sank in three short seconds, revealing Coram splashing and grasping for air on the other side as he endeavoured to keep afloat, a skill he was clearly not in possession of.

Mountfellon trod water and looked at him with eyes as chilly as the ruffled water between them.

Coram dropped beneath the surface and then bobbed up again.

"I am drowning!" he gasped.

"To elect not to learn to swim is not a rational choice in a world full of water and uncertainty," said Mountfellon, keeping his distance.

"SAVE ME!" shrieked Coram, going under for the second time.

Mountfellon waited until he struggled to the surface again.

"What good would it do me?" he said, kicking away from Coram's frantically outstretched hand.

"I WILL BE YOUR MAN!" shouted Coram. "I KNOW MY FATHERS' SECRETS, CAN TELL YOU THEM. I KNOW WHY—"

And he went under for the third, and traditionally last time. Mountfellon, though of a conservative bent by birth and in many ways a natural traditionalist, in this case flouted convention by reaching beneath the water and pulling Coram up into the air. He held him at arms' length to avoid the commotion as the younger man fish-mouthed for breath and coughed up substantial chunks of Thames water, and then yanked him nose to nose.

"Swear you are mine and will be my spy in your fathers' house," he said, "or the blasted eels may have you."

"Not my real fathers!" coughed Coram. "Am a foundling. Am a poor orphan child."

"Don't give a tinker's damn what bitch whelped you; you will swear to be mine or your next breath will be nothing but river!" hissed Mountfellon.

"I swear!" sobbed Coram, broken. "I swear I will be your man."

"Then stop snivelling like a girl," said Mountfellon, grabbing his collar and rolling him on his back. "This, I now apprehend, is a long game, and The Oversight has not bested me in anything other than a temporary fashion. Your damned fathers have much to answer to me for this day . . ."

He kicked for the riverbank.

"Yes," Coram blubbered. "Oh yes. They are the very devils . . ."

"Just plain devils," corrected Mountfellon. "You will find

we come in all shapes and sizes, and I assure you there is no greater devil for loyalty than I, boy. Cross me and I will have you skinned and displayed, you hear me? Skinned, pinned and displayed."

Only he and the Thames heard Coram sobbing as they made slow progress toward the unseen edges of the great Greenwich marsh on the wrong side of the river.

CHAPTER 73

THE PARTING GLASS

Things happened quickly once Cook, The Smith and Hodge returned from the river. Sara met them as they came in and told them everything that had occurred in their absence. Cook did a great deal of blowing her nose and wiping her eyes when she saw Sara had been reunited with her hand, and they all were vocal about how restored she looked. They had taken advantage of their stop at The Folley to put a soothing poultice on Hodge's eyes and bandage each other's wounds, and so looked a very piratical and chopped-about crew indeed. Of the fighting they said nothing, other than that it had been bloody and brief.

They were much more interested in her recovery.

"When we set out you looked like you were in a shroud and six days dead," said Cook. "And now look at you!"

Sara was again dressed in slender black riding clothes, a tight coat and an oiled silk overskirt, her rings winking on top of her gloves, and her hair, which had looked an hour earlier more like a half-blown dandelion, was now tamed and pulled tight to her head in a thick white plait.

"Quite yourself," said The Smith approvingly. "Just as you should be. And where are the two of them?"

"In the kitchen," said Sara. "And since there are two of them, I have some proposals. The first of which is that I think we might impose on Emmet and ask if he would go back into the river and at least retrieve the Wildfire."

She looked round at them.

"Of everything we have put out of harm's way beneath the water, it is the one that would be better kept close."

"*If* there is a Hand to guard it," said The Smith wearily.

"And take its power," said Sara.

"You are suggesting we make up our number with one of these young people?" said Hodge.

"They are not children," said Sara. "They are both close enough to twenty. And they have true hearts."

"Why is it, Sara Falk, that whenever you say you are making a proposal it ends up sounding as though it is an order because you and you alone have made your mind up?" said Cook, her chin jutting dangerously forward.

"Because I am attempting good manners," said Sara.

"So you want one of these . . . these unproven whipper-snappers to join and make the Last Hand five again?"

"No," said Sara, taking the wind out of Cook's sails. "Not at all."

"Oh," said Cook, relaxing. "That's all right then."

"I want them both to join," said Sara.

Lucy and Charlie heard the raised voices upstairs for a long time, then the noise subsided into more normal conversation, and by the time the feet came down the stairs, there was even the odd short laugh. They were introduced to The Smith and Hodge and Cook, who all admitted to knowing and liking Charlie's parents, and then Cook made a large supper while the proposal was put to them and things were explained.

And then Lucy and Charlie were left alone to decide what they would do. They looked at each other.

"I'll do what you do," said Charlie.

Lucy shook her head.

"You do what feels right for you. Don't make it all my responsibility."

He nodded.

"Fair enough. Didn't mean it like that, but I see what you mean. What are you going to do?"

She looked round the warm room.

"I nearly went with that man just because he knew my name."

"They know that," he said. "And you didn't go. You fought him off."

"Thing is, I don't know everything about my past. I know some things but they're not connected. At least they are connected, but only by the fact that I know I've been alone and running from something for a long, long time."

She took a deep breath. This was harder than she had expected it to be.

"So maybe if I stay in one place I'll find out what that is. Maybe I'll find out who I am."

Charlie grinned and stuck his hand over the tabletop.

"So we're both in, then."

The Smith appeared in the door and caught them shaking hands very seriously.

"I hope that means what I think," he said. They nodded. "Good. And I guarantee you one thing more, Lucy Harker. You won't be alone any more."

Cook found Sara in the passage leading to the hidden cellar where the Murano Cabinet stood open, an ordinary candle in a pewter stick on the floor at its centre.

Sara was standing in the doorway holding another candle in one hand, the other placed within the boundaries of the newest addition to the prints on the wall. *JS* was written below it.

Sara was shaking, and Cook realised with a shock that she was glinting.

She watched Sara's face, the face she had watched grow from a baby through girlhood to the woman now in front of her, and she saw the tear streak out of the eye and splash to the flagstone below, and seeing it she wanted more than anything to take the woman in her arms and tell the child that she still saw within her that everything would be all right.

But she loved Sara too much to lie to her.

So she stepped back, and as she heard The Smith enter the passage behind her she motioned him to stop until whatever memory of himself that Mr Sharp had left as he stood with his hand where Sara's now was had finished coursing through her.

They watched her try and smile through the tears, and when the glinting stopped she jerked her hand free of the wall and turned her eyes to them. She looked dazzled with surprise and something close to wonder.

"He sang," said Sara. "Mr Sharp *sang* . . ."

"He sang to *you*," said Cook. "Only you could provoke that in him."

"He sang farewell," Sara choked. "He sang 'The Parting Glass'."

"Then he will have wished you joy at the end of the song," said Cook, her voice thick. "And you must honour that wish."

Sara wiped her tears away and then turned away again, suddenly bent double. Cook hurried to her and put her hand on her back.

"My dearest child—"

Sara looked up, an agony of incomprehension in her eyes.

"What is this?" she whispered. "What is this pain?"

And still Cook could not lie.

"It is your heart breaking," she said. "It is the worst pain in the world."

"I cannot go on," choked Sara.

"You will," said Cook. "And that is why it is the worst pain in the world, because it *doesn't* kill you. And surviving it makes every day of the rest of your life feel like a betrayal of what you loved and lost. But it isn't."

Sara pulled Cook closer and whispered raggedly in her ear. She sounded ashamed beyond despair.

"I never told him that I loved him . . ."

And then after a long deep breath she shook herself, stood up straight and walked into the cellar.

There was a table on which were Mr Sharp's honing stone, four knives of various lengths and two pistols. Sara slid three knives in her belt and one in her boot, and put the larger pistol into a holster looped under her arm and the other in some arrangement she had clearly previously strapped to her upper leg. Then she smoothed her dress and turned to face them all, Lucy and Charlie too.

Jed led Hodge in and then trotted forward to lick her hand. The Raven sat on Hodge's shoulder and clacked its beak.

"You look just like your mother," said Hodge, his face smiling beneath the bandage blindfolding him.

"You can't see," said Sara.

"Raven and I been sharing eyes since I was a lad, and Jed since he was a pup," he said. "No reason to stop now. You look the spit of her. She broke your heart to look at too."

"What are you doing, child?" said Cook.

"You have The Smith. You have Hodge. You have Lucy Harker and Charlie Pyefinch: you still have a Last Hand," said Sara.

"They are unproven," said Cook, eyes flicking at them. "No offence."

Sara gripped Cook by the shoulders. The tears had been banished by an act of will. Her face was fierce again.

"I was a child when my mother and father went into the

mirrors with eighty-three of their friends," she said, pointing through the door at the tell-tale handprints. "Our friends. Your friends. They all did it to save something they loved, something they believed in. And though they were wrong and misguided, I cannot fault them. The Disaster happened, and I had to make up numbers for the Last Hand. *I* did. *I* was *younger* than those two! You have five. You have a Hand! Keep Lore and Law until I return. I have kept myself safe hiding in this house for too long."

As she turned toward the cabinet and the waiting mirrors, The Smith cleared his throat.

"There is no Ivory to guide you. There is no get-you-home. You will be lost in the mirrors."

She whirled on him, cold fury in her eyes.

"Mr Sharp too is lost! And maybe I will never find him. But then we will be lost together. I will not have my dearest friend go into darkness alone."

The silence in the room crackled with things left unsaid.

"And I will not have you go alone," said Hodge gruffly.

He reached up and let the Raven hop onto his hand. He then put the bird onto her shoulder. The Raven clacked its beak and shook itself.

Sara was unable to speak for a moment.

"Look after her," said Hodge.

Sara swallowed.

"I will," she said.

"I was talking to the Raven," said Hodge. "It's a he."

The Smith and Cook exchanged a look.

The Raven nudged Sara's ear and clacked its beak.

A ghost of a smile lifted one side of Sara's mouth.

Lucy saw it and thought it made her look suddenly invincible.

"She says, 'Whatever gave you that idea?'" said Sara.

And then without another word, perhaps because she hated

goodbyes, perhaps because she could not trust herself to speak, she raised a hand in curt farewell, and stepped into the mirror.

And then she was gone.

As they walked silently back out of the room Cook stopped and pointed at the newest handprint on the wall, next to Mr Sharp's.

"She lied," she said, her voice catching.

"What?" said The Smith.

She pointed at the handprints and suddenly had to rummage in her bloomers for a clean handkerchief.

"If Mr Sharp should ever come back, she did tell him she loved him," she said.

Under the *JS* and the *SF*, midway between the two handprints, were three more letters scratched into the plaster, linking them.

"Who's Avo?" said Charlie.

The letters were A, V and O.

"*Amor vincit omnia*," said The Smith.

"Love conquers all," translated Cook, thundering into her handkerchief. "It's Latin."

"Powerful stuff, Latin," said Lucy.

Cook stopped wiping her eye and fixed it on the younger woman. Lucy didn't blink.

"Don't forget much, do you?" said Cook, a hint of approval in her voice.

"I have forgotten too much," said Lucy, looking at Charlie. "But I intend to learn a great deal more."

EPILOGUE

She stood among the eels in the dark, singing quietly to herself. She could see that it was dusk from the way the light on the river beyond the grilles had dimmed, and she could feel that the eels themselves had become sluggish around her feet.

She sat on the walkway and pulled her legs from the water, still singing. She sang on as she heard someone trying the door. It was early for them to be letting her out but she had no fear of them. They never beat her after she had been alone with the eels. They thought it was punishment, and punishment enough.

· But the door didn't open. It wasn't them. It was someone whose noises she did not recognise. Someone trying to get in. Trying to break the lock.

Someone cold, looking for somewhere to stay the night. Or maybe steal a bushel of eels.

She tried to think who it was, reaching out for them with her thoughts—
And then someone touched her mind back, and she stopped singing.
She felt them listening to her, inside and outside.
Just as she was doing to them.
Hello, she thought, who are you?
She felt them recoil from her mind, a slight feeling like a cobweb being yanked across her brain.

Don't be scared, she thought. I mean you no harm. There is a key hidden on the lintel above the sluice. Don't drop it in the river.

There was silence. She cast about for him. He was keeping his thoughts away.

The eels began threshing in a boiling mass at her feet.

Then the door clicked open. And there he was.

A dark stranger with a tinker's pack on his back.

"Thank you," she said.

He nodded. His eyes were frightened, but not enough to run; they were interested too.

"Do you talk?" she said.

No.

He looked embarrassed.

I am Mute but Intelligent.

And a tinker, I see.

How can you talk in my head?

How can you listen to my thoughts? she replied.

And out loud she said,

"Do you have mirrors for sale in that pack?"

He held up one finger. Only one.

She hid her disappointment.

"No matter. One will do. If you come with me, back to the poor-house garden, I have another one, and then I shall show you a trick which will really impress you."

As he followed her across the water meadow, through the rising mist, she had another thought.

And do you have a knife? A very, very sharp one?

Yes, thought Amos. *Why?*

We shall see. Are you squeamish?

ACKNOWLEDGEMENTS

Thanks to my editor Jenni Hill at Orbit/Little, Brown for her enthusiasm and help in bringing *The Oversight* out of the shadows and into the world, and to Joanna Kramer for her painstaking copy-edit. Any infelicities are mine, not theirs. Thanks to Fergus Fleming, Barnaby Rogerson and Rose Baring for secret reading and encouragement along the way. I'm grateful to Willi Paterson for lending me "Lord" George Sanger's memoir of life in a mid-nineteenth-century travelling show *Seventy Years a Showman*, which was as invaluable a resource for creating the world Sara fell into as Dickens's essays from *Household Words* are for the London that she fell out of. The Sangers aren't in my book, but the Pyefinches are close kin. Na-Barno Eagle and Hector Anderson his great rival did really exist, and Georgiana . . . well she existed too, but what happened to her you'll have to wait and see. In real life she touched royalty.

The Westphalian-born Rabbi Samuel Falk was a Kabbalist and an alchemist and is reputed to know the true name of God, hence his title of "Ba'al Shem" (Master of the Name), and he did indeed live and keep a laboratory in Wellclose Square. He counted Casanova as one of his wide acquaintance. He is reputed to have used his knowledge of the Name to create and animate the only golem ever to walk London's streets. There is no official record showing he had a granddaughter named Sara. But then The Oversight doesn't officially exist either, so who knows?

John Dee is of course an historical character, and his magic paraphernalia is still on display in the British Museum. You've probably unmasked The Citizen's real identity, but if not you'll have to wait, but he too existed and we'll see more of him. The "estimable Mr Henderson" whose "receipt" Cook uses for her Eccles cakes is with us now: I've never met him but I have always deeply enjoyed his restaurants and especially the said Eccles cakes (with cheese), so I hope he doesn't mind being anachronistically thrust back into 1840s London as a bizarre thank you from a stranger.

Anyone who knew my dad and has read this far may have recognised bits of him earlier, if not in The Smith himself, then certainly in his workshop, which is my dad's, minus the blacksmithery. Dad introduced me to Wayland Smith when he shared his love of Kipling with me as a young boy. I think he'd have enjoyed the way I repaid that gift by making him a part of this story, but he died before I finished it. Deaths are tough times for all families, but we and he were greatly helped and served by truly great district nurses in his final illness. Thank you, Siobhan Dickson, Tina Dodd and Janice Colley, and also thank you, Kathy, Karen, Theresa and Cheryl from St Michael's Hospice. I am enormously grateful for the professionalism and enormous patience and good humour of Paul Allsopp, whose visits brightened up some very dark days for both my parents. Special thanks to my wonderful cousin Tracey Little, brick of bricks. You all helped us keep our promise to him, and we couldn't have done it without your graceful help.

And speaking of grace . . . Domenica. Always and forever, thank you. Nothing is ever quite as much fun without you. A.V.O.

Look out for

THE PARADOX

by

Charlie Fletcher

The Last Hand of The Oversight still patrols the border between the natural and supranatural, holding a candle to the darkness. But this new Hand is unproven, its fresh members untrained, its veterans weary and battle-scarred. Their vulnerability brings new enemies to the city, and surprising new allies from across the sea.

But most surprising of all are new revelations about The Oversight's past, revelations that will expose the true peril of the world in which Sharp and Sara are trapped – the secret of the Black Mirrors, and what lies beyond. And the catastrophic danger that will follow them home, if they ever manage to return.

The dark waters rise. The candle is guttering. But the light still remains.

For now . . .

www.orbitbooks.net

extras

orbit

www.orbitbooks.net

about the author

Charlie Fletcher lives in Edinburgh and divides his time between writing for page and screen. His Stoneheart trilogy for children has been translated into a dozen languages. The first volume, *Stoneheart*, was shortlisted for the Branford Boase award and longlisted for the Guardian Children's Fiction Prize. His standalone YA novel, *Far Rockaway*, was published last year to great critical acclaim and has been longlisted for the Carnegie prize and the Catalyst Book Award. *The Oversight* is his first adult novel and the beginning of a new series.

Find out more about Charlie Fletcher and other Orbit authors by registering for the free monthly newsletter at www.orbitbooks.net.

interview

When did you first know you were going to write about The Oversight?

I've always had an idea about those who patrol the unseen line between the natural and the supernatural. I also wanted to tell a story about a brave band fighting against the odds. I put that down to going to see *The Magnificent Seven* with my dad as a kid, and then later discovering *The Seven Samurai* from which it derived (Kurosawa is one of my greatest story-telling heroes in film terms). So I knew it was going to be a multi-stranded tale in which you cared about all the protagonists, which I hope is so. The ultimate catalyst for The Oversight in its present form was (see below) discovering John Dee's magic gear, especially his black obsidian mirror in the British Museum.

You've drawn from magical figures in real life to create *The Oversight*, with characters such as The Smith coming from myth and Na Barno from history. What was your favourite aspect of the novel to research, and was there anything or anyone who surprised you?

I enjoy all the research really, and have to stop it and start writing by a major act of will. I particularly loved redis-covering Dickens's short articles on early Victorian London from *Household Words*. You couldn't get a better flavour of the time in all its minutiae than by seeing it through his sharp and amused eyes. And I really enjoyed reading up about the world of the travelling shows, particularly "Lord" George Sanger's *Seventy Years a Showman* – but again there was a Dickens connection as the impulse to write about them came from wanting to escape the city and have a pastoral section of the story, and I had always loved the showmen in *Hard Times*, particularly Sleary. Georgiana Eagle surprised me because she sort of slid unbidden from real life into the book, which I had not quite expected, but then she is an ambitious, beguiling and opportunistic young thing. I was also surprised and delighted that the Rabbi Falk had, in the real world, been a friend of Casanova, which allowed, among other things, the delivery of the Murano Cabinet to the Safe House and all the consequent peril of the Mirror'd World.

Neil Gaiman, who like you has written books for all ages, recently said that when writing for children he has to be more "precise". You also write for TV and film. How do you feel you have to change your writing for different audiences?

I think I agree with the "more precise" thing. I also don't think you get very far, or at least anywhere interesting, by writing "down" to children. I love writing for kids because I began doing so for my own when they were small, and writing for a younger audience is like talking to your own children: you've just got to look them in the eye and be straight with them, otherwise how are they going to do the same back to the world when they engage with it? Writing for adults is just great because you can play fast and loose with all the tools in the box. Screenwriting is a whole other ball of wax and the rules are simple: if a camera can't capture it, or a microphone can't record it, I don't write it. It's a very boned-out discipline where you're endlessly trying to tell a visual story and looking for fresh objective correlatives for what you can't write. I know some people break this rule, but I never write what a character is thinking or feeling, because a camera or a microphone can't get inside the brain pan and capture that. So you have to find other ways of making the audience understand, hopefully fresh ways (think how many sad scenes happen on screen when it's raining . . .).

Sharp and Sara are something of an epic love story in this novel, and they've clearly got more trials to come. Which are your favourite love stories in fiction?
This is either a great question or I'm wildly unromantic because I realise I don't have a strong contender here. The kind of love story where he/she will just *die* if not loved back by the other always leaves me cold and a bit irritated. My inner cynic is growling, "Oh for heaven's sake, don't be so self-indulgent; show a little grit/backbone/character, etc . . ." So classic pairings like Heathcliff and Cathy, or Anna Karenina and Vronsky end up putting my teeth on edge. On the other hand, I like the strand of strong woman/strong man verbally combative romance that has its start in Beatrice and Benedick in *Much Ado About Nothing* and plays on through characters like Darcy and Elizabeth in *Pride and Prejudice*, and comes to its filmic flowering in the great Hollywood screwball comedies of the forties, all of which I love, but especially Walter Burns and Hildy Johnson in *The Front Page*. And of course anything with Kate Hepburn or Carole Lombard. As a teenage SF junkie I always was rooting for a seemingly impossible happy ending for William Mandella and Marygay Potter all the way through Joe Haldeman's *The Forever War*.

And being a huge fan of the films of Michael Powell and Emeric Pressburger and a great lover of the Hebrides, I am a sad sucker for the love story at the heart of *I Know Where I'm Going!* but am aware it's a mannered and acquired taste! In their film *The Life and Death of Colonel Blimp* (my favourite film), I greatly like the restrained romanticism of the strange triple love story. Emeric Pressburger said somewhere that the British were more romantic than the supposedly hot-blooded Latin lovers because banked-up fires burn hotter than ones that blaze out in a great and dramatic show of flames. I think that's what I like. Banked-up fires . . .

As a native of Edinburgh, Scotland and a graduate of an LA film school, what drew you to write so marvellously about London, and will you be taking The Oversight novels to other locations in future?

London is so layered and ancient and drenched in history that it positively oozes story from every stone. I used to live there when I was working at the BBC, and loved walking around and getting lost a lot. It was cheap entertainment and never boring. More than that, one thing usually leads to another by association, and story builds itself if you pay attention. The germ of *The Oversight* was planted when I went to the King's Gallery in the British Museum and found John Dee's magical paraphernalia on display in what is basically the most wonderful and numinous cabinet of curiosities. That led me to other London mages, which took me to the Rabbi Falk and his golem, and his house on Wellclose Square, and one thing led to another... And yes, the future Oversight novels travel, because the divide between natural and supernatural is global, not local. In the second book we find ourselves across the Channel, somewhere very far from low-lying London . . .

What else have you got in store for us in the next Oversight novel? Give us a hint . . .

Lucy discovers more about both her past and the prehistoric origins of The Oversight. Unlikely alliances are made and new friends appear from unexpected places. Unfortunately old enemies begin to multiply and move in. We find out more about the Sluagh and their grievance, and in so doing perhaps begin to understand why The Oversight has begun to fail, and what the deeper peril is. We haven't seen the last of the resourceful and now vengeful Georgiana Eagle, and we see the first of the foreign allies of The Oversight as one of their number comes to London to warn them of a new impending danger. Sara and Sharp are lost in the mirrors searching for each other, which is bad enough, but the mirrors also not only contain the renegade John Dee, they contain others who live there by choice, cheating the normal effects of time but becoming less human the longer they stay. They're called Mirror Wights, and you *really* don't want to meet them, or pay the Blood Toll they demand for passage through the Mirror'd World . . .

if you enjoyed
THE OVERSIGHT
look out for
THE FIRST FIFTEEN LIVES OF HARRY AUGUST

by

Claire North

Chapter 1

The second cataclysm began in my eleventh life, in 1996. I was dying my usual death, slipping away in a warm morphine haze, which she interrupted like an ice cube down my spine.

She was seven, I was seventy-eight. She had straight blonde hair worn in a long pigtail down her back, I had bright white hair, or at least the remnants of the same. I wore a hospital gown designed for sterile humility; she, bright-blue school uniform and a felt cap. She perched on the side of my bed, her feet dangling off it, and peered into my eyes. She examined the heart monitor plugged into my chest, observed where I'd disconnected the alarm, felt for my pulse, and said, "I nearly missed you, Dr August."

Her German was Berlin high, but she could have addressed me in any language of the world and still passed for respectable. She scratched at the back of her left leg, where her white knee-length socks had begun to itch from the rain outside. While scratching she said, "I need to send a message back through time. If time can be said to be important here. As you're conveniently dying, I ask you to relay it to the Clubs of your origin, as it has been passed down to me."

I tried to speak, but the words tumbled together on my tongue, and I said nothing.

"The world is ending," she said. "The message has come down from child to adult, child to adult, passed back down the generations from a thousand years forward in time. The world is ending and we cannot prevent it. So now it's up to you."

I found that Thai was the only language which wanted to pass my lips in any coherent form, and the only word which I seemed capable of forming was, why?

Not, I hasten to add, why was the world ending?

Why did it matter?

She smiled, and understood my meaning without needing it to be said. She leaned in close and murmured in my ear, "The world is ending, as it always must. But the end of the world is getting faster."

That was the beginning of the end.

Chapter 2

Let us begin at the beginning.

The Club, the cataclysm, my eleventh life and the deaths which followed – none peaceful – all are meaningless, a flash of violence that bursts and withers away, retribution without cause, until you understand where it all began.

My name is Harry August.

My father is Rory Edmond Hulne, my mother Elizabeth Leadmill, though I was not to know any of this until well into my third life.

I do not know whether to say that my father raped my mother or not. The law would have some difficulty in assessing the case; the jury could perhaps be swayed by a clever individual one way or the other. I am told that she did not scream, did not fight, didn't even say no when he came to her in the kitchen on the night of my conception, and in twenty-five inglorious minutes of passion – in that anger and jealousy and rage are passions of their kind – took revenge on his faithless wife by means of the kitchen girl. In this regard my mother was not forced, but then, as a girl of some twenty years old, living and working in my father's house, dependent for her future on his money and his family's goodwill, I would argue that she was given no chance to resist, coerced by her situation as much as by any blade held to the throat.

By the time my mother's pregnancy began to show, my father had returned to active duty in France, where he was to serve out the rest of the First World War as a largely undistinguished major in the Scots Guards. In a conflict where whole regiments could be wiped out in a single day, undistinguished was a rather enviable obtainment. It was therefore left to my paternal grandmother, Constance Hulne, to expel my mother from her home without a reference in the autumn of 1918. The man who was to become my adopted father – and yet a truer parent to me than any bio-logical relation – took my mother to the local market on the back of his pony cart and left her there with some few shillings in her purse and a recommendation to seek the help of other distressed ladies of the county. A cousin, Alistair, who shared a mere one eighth of my mother's genetic material but whose surplus of wealth more than made up for a deficit of familial connections, gave my mother work on the floor of his Edinburgh paper mill; however, as she grew larger and increasingly unable to carry out her duties, she was quietly moved on by a junior official some three rungs away from the responsible party. In desperation, she wrote to my biological father, but the note was intercepted by my shrewd grandmother, who destroyed it before he could read my mother's plea, and so, on New Year's Eve 1918, my mother spent her last few pennies on the slow train from Edinburgh Waverley to Newcastle and, some ten miles north of Berwick-upon-Tweed, went into labour.

A trade unionist by the name of Douglas Crannich and his wife, Prudence, were the only two people present at my birth, in the ladies' washroom of the station. I am told that the stationmaster stood outside the door to prevent any innocent women coming inside, his hands clasped behind his back and his cap, crowned with snow, pulled down over his eyes in a manner I have always im-agined as being rather hooded and malign. There were no doctors at the infirmary at this late hour and on this festive day, and the medic took over three hours to arrive. He came too late. The blood was already crystallising on the floor and Prudence Crannich was holding me in her arms at his arrival. My mother was dead. I have only the report of Douglas for the circumstances of her demise, but I believe she haemorrhaged out, and is buried in a grave marked "Lisa, d. 1 January 1919 – Angels Guide Her Into Light". Mrs Crannich, when the undertaker asked her what should be on the stone, realised that she had never known my mother's full name.

Some debate ensued about what to do with me, this suddenly orphaned child. I believe Mrs Crannich was sorely tempted to keep me for her own, but finances and practicality informed against this decision, as did Douglas Crannich's firm and literal interpretation of the law and rather more personal understanding of propriety. The child had a father, he exclaimed, and the father had a right to the child. This matter would have been rather moot, were it not that my mother was carrying about her person the address of my soon-to-be adopted father, Patrick August, presumably with the intention of enlisting his help in seeing my biological father, Rory Hulne. Enquiries were made as to whether this man, Patrick, could be my father, which caused quite a stir in the village as Patrick had been long married, childlessly, to my adopted mother, Harriet August, and a barren marriage in a border village, where the notion of the condom was regarded as taboo well into the 1970s, was always a topic of furious debate. The matter was so shocking that it very quickly made its way to the manor house itself, Hulne Hall, wherein resided my grandmother Constance, my two aunts Victoria and Alexandra, my cousin Clement, and Lydia, the unhappy wife of my father. I believe my grandmother immediately suspected whose child I was and the circumstances of my situation, but refused to take responsibility for me. It was Alexandra, my younger aunt, who showed a presence of mind and a compassion that the rest of her kin lacked, and seeing that suspicion would fairly quickly turn to her family once the truth of my dead mother's identity was revealed, approached Patrick and Harriet August with this offer – that if they were to adopt the child, and raise it as their own, the papers formally signed and witnessed by the Hulne family itself to quiet all rumours of an illegitimate affair, for no one carried authority like the inhabitants of Hulne Hall – then she would personally see to it that they received a monthly amount of money for their pains and to support the child, and that on his growing up she would ensure that his prospects were suitable – not excessive, mind, but neither the sorry situation of a bastard.

Patrick and Harriet debated a while, then accepted. I was raised as their child, as Harry August, and it wasn't until my second life that I began to understand where I was from, and what I was.

Chapter 3

It is said that there are three stages of life for those of us who live our lives in circles. These are rejection, exploration and acceptance.

As categories go, they are rather glib, and contain within them many different layers disguised behind these wider words. Rejection, for example, can be subdivided into various clichéd reactions, like so: suicide, despondency, madness, hysteria, isolation and self-destruction. I, like nearly all kalachakra, experienced most of these at some stage in my early lives, and their recollection lingers within me like a virus still twisted into my stomach wall.

For my part, the transition to acceptance was unremarkably difficult.

The first life I lived was undistinguished. Like all young men, I was called to fight in the Second World War, where I was a thoroughly undistinguished infantryman. Yet if my wartime contribution was meagre, my life after the conflict hardly added to a sense of significance. I returned to Hulne House after the war, to take over the position which had been held by Patrick, tending to the grounds around the estate. Like my adopted father, I had been raised to love the land, the smell of it after rain and the sudden fizzing in the air when all the seeds of the gorse spilt at once into the sky, and if I felt in any way isolated from the rest of society, it was merely as the absence of a brother might be to an only child, an idea of loneliness without the relevant experience to make it real.

When Patrick died, my position was formalised, though by then, the Hulnes' wealth was almost entirely extinguished through squander and inertia. In 1964 the property was bought by the National Trust, and I with it, and I spent the latter part of my years directing ramblers through the overgrown moors that surrounded the house, watching as the walls of the manor itself slowly sank deeper into the wet black mud.

I died in 1989 as the Berlin Wall fell, alone in a hospital in Newcastle, a divorcee with no children and a state pension who, even on his deathbed, believed himself to be the son of the long-departed Patrick and Harriet August, and who died eventually from the disease that has been the bane of my lives – multiple myelomas which spread throughout the body until the body itself simply ceases to function.

Naturally my reaction to being born again precisely where I had begun – in the women's restroom of Berwick-upon-Tweed station, on New Year's Day 1919, with all the memories of my life that had gone before, induced its own rather clichéd madness in me. As the full powers of my adult consciousness returned to my child's body, I fell first into a confusion, then an agony, then a doubt, then a despair, then a screaming, then a shrieking, and finally, aged seven years old, I was committed to St Margot's Asylum for Unfortunates, where I frankly believed myself to belong, and within six months of my confinement succeeded in throwing myself out of a window on the third floor.

Retrospectively, I realise that three floors are frequently not high enough to guarantee the quick, relatively painless death that such circumstances warrant, and I might easily have snapped every bone in my lower body and yet retained my consciousness intact. Thankfully, I landed on my head, and that was that.

Chapter 4

There is a moment when the moor comes to life. I wish you could see it, but somehow whenever I have been with you on our walks through the countryside, we have missed those few precious hours of revelation. Instead, the skies have been the slate-grey of the stones beneath them, or drought turns the land to dust-brown thorns, or once it snowed so hard that the kitchen door was barred shut from the outside, and I had to climb out of the window to shovel us a path to freedom, and on one trip in 1949 it rained continually, I believe, for five days without end. You never saw it for those few hours after rain, when all is purple and yellow and smells of black, rich soil.

Your deduction, made early on in our friendship, that I was born in the north of England, for all of my pretensions and mannerisms acquired over many lives, was entirely correct, and my adopted father, Patrick August, never let me forget it. He was the sole groundsman on the Hulne estate, and had been so for as long as he had lived. So had his father before him, and his father before him, as far back as 1834, when the newly rich Hulne family bought the land to sculpt their ideal, upper-class dream. They planted trees, drove roads through the moor, built ridiculous towers and arches – folly by name and folly by nature – which by the time of my birth had sunk into moss-crawled decline. Not for them the grubby scrubland that framed the estate, with its rock teeth and sticky gums of earthen flesh. Previous, energetic generations of the family had kept sheep, or perhaps it would be fairer to say that the sheep had kept themselves, on the wide places beneath the stone walls, but the twentieth century had not been kind to the fortunes of the Hulnes, and now the land, though still theirs, was left untended, wild – the perfect place for a boy to run free while his parents were about their chores. Curiously enough, living my childhood again I found myself far less adventurous. Holes and crags that I had climbed along and leaped in my first life, to my more conservative elder brain suddenly seemed places of danger, and I wore my child's body as an old woman might wear a skinny bikini bought for her by a fragile friend.

Having failed so spectacularly to end the cycle of my days by suicide, I resolved on my third life to instead pursue the answers that seemed so far away. It is some small mercy, I believe, that our memories return to us slowly as we progress through childhood, so that the recollection of having thrown myself to my death came, as it were, like a gently gathering cold, arriving with no sense of surprise, merely an acceptance that this thing was, and had achieved nothing.

My first life, for all it lacked any real direction, had about it a kind of happiness, if ignorance is innocence, and loneliness is a separation of care. But my new life, with its knowledge of all that had come before, could not be lived the same. It wasn't merely awareness of events yet to come, but rather a new perception of the truths around me, which, being a child raised to them in my first life, I had not even considered to be lies. Now a boy again and temporarily at least in command of my full adult faculties, I perceived the truths which are so often acted out in front of a child's sight in the belief that a child cannot comprehend them. I believe that my adopted father and mother came to love me – she far sooner than he – but for Patrick August I was never flesh of his flesh until my adopted mother died.

There is a medical study in this phenomenon, but my adopted mother never quite dies upon the same day in each life she lives. The cause – unless external factors intervene violently first – is always the same. Around my sixth birthday she begins to cough, and by my seventh her coughing is bloody. My parents cannot afford the doctor's fees, but my aunt Alexandra finally furnishes the coin for my mother to go to the hospital in Newcastle and receive a diagnosis of lung cancer. (I believe it to be non-small-cell carcinomas confined primarily to the left lung; frustratingly treatable some forty years after my mother's diagnosis but utterly beyond the realms of science at the time.) Tobacco and laudanum are prescribed, and death swiftly follows in 1927. At her death my father falls into a silence and walks upon the hills, sometimes not to be seen for many days. I tend to myself perfectly competently and now, in expectation of my mother's death, stockpile some food to see me through his long absences. On his return, he remains silent and unapproachable, and though he does not rise to any approaches from my infant self with anger, that is largely because he does not rise at all. In my first life I did not understand his grief nor how it manifested, for I myself was grieving with the blind wordlessness of a child who needed help, which he did not provide. In my second life my mother's death happened while I was still under the asylum roof and I was too concerned with my own madness to process it, but in my third it came as a slow-moving train towards a man tied to the tracks; inevitable, unstoppable, seen far off in the night and the imagination of the thing, for me, almost worse than the event. I knew what was to come, and somehow when it came, it was a relief, an ending of expectation, and so a lesser event.

In my third life my mother's impending death also gave me something of an occupation. The prevention of it, or at least the management of it, concerned me profoundly. As I had no explanation for my situation save that, perhaps, some Old Testament god was acting out a curse upon me, I genuinely felt that by performing acts of charity, or attempting to affect the major events of my life, I might break this cycle of death-birth-death that had apparently come upon me. Having committed no crimes that I knew of which needed redeeming, and with no major events in my life to undo, I latched on to the welfare of Harriet as my first and most obvious crusade, and embarked on it with all the wit my five-year-old mind (pushing ninety-seven) could muster.

I used my ministrations as an excuse to avoid the tedium of school, and my father was too preoccupied to see what I did; instead I tended to her and learned as I had never learned before how my mother lived when my father was away. I suppose you could call it a chance to get to know, as an adult, a woman I had only briefly known as a child. It was in this capacity that I first began to suspect that I was not my father's son.

The Hulne family as a whole attended my adopted mother's funeral, when she finally died in that third life. My father said few words, and I stood by him, a seven-year-old boy dressed in borrowed black trousers and jacket from Clement Hulne, the cousin three years my senior who had tried in my previous life to bully me, when he remembered that I was there to bully. Constance Hulne, leaning heavily on a walking stick with an ivory handle carved in the shape of an elephant's head, spoke a few words about Harriet's loyalty, strength and the family she left behind. Alexandra Hulne told me that I must be brave; Victoria Hulne bent down and pinched my cheeks, inducing in me a strange childish urge to bite the black-gloved fingers that had violated my face. Rory Hulne said nothing and stared at me. He had stared once before, the first time I had stood here in borrowed clothes burying my mother, but I, consumed with grief that had no means of expression, hadn't comprehended the intensity of his gaze. Now I met his eyes and for the first time saw the mirror of my own, of what I would become.

You have not known me in all the stages of my life, so let me describe them here.

As a child I am born with almost red hair, which fades over time to what the charitable would describe as auburn, and which is more fairly carrot. The colour of my hair comes from my real mother's family, as does a genetic predisposition towards good teeth and long-sightedness. I am a small child, a little shorter than average and skinny, though that is as much from a poor diet as any genetic inclination. My growth spurt begins when I turn eleven, and continues until the age of fifteen, when I can, thankfully, get away with pretending to be a boyish eighteen and thus skip three tedious years until manhood.

As a young man, I used to sport a rather ragged beard in the manner of my adopted father, Patrick; it doesn't suit and in its untended state I can often come to look like a set of sensory organs lost in a raspberry bush. Once this revelation was made I began to shave regularly, and in doing so revealed the face of my true father. We share the same pale grey eyes, the same small ears, lightly curling hair and a nose which, along with a tendency to bone disease in old age, is probably the least welcome genetic heritage of all. It is not that my nose is especially large – it is not; but it is undeniably upturned in a manner that would not be ill-suited to the pixie king, and where it should be angularly delineated from my face, rather it seems to blend into my skin like a thing moulded from clay, not bone. People are too polite to comment, but the merest sight of it has on several occasions reduced honest infants from neater genetic lines to tears. In old age my hair turns white, in what feels like an instantaneous flash; this event can be brought on by stress earlier than its norm, and cannot be prevented by any cure, medicinal or psychological. I require glasses for reading by the age of fifty-one; distressingly my fifties fall in the 1970s, a poor decade for fashion, but like nearly all I return to the fashions I was comfortable with as a youth and choose rather demure spectacles in an antique style. With these balanced across my too-close eyes I look every bit the ageing academic as I examine myself in the bathroom mirror; it is a face which, by the time we buried Harriet for the third time, I had had nearly a hundred years to become acquainted with. It was the face of Rory Edmond Hulne, staring at me from across the casket of the woman who could not have been my mother.

Chapter 5

I am of a good age to be enlisted at the outbreak of the Second World War, and yet for my first few lives managed somehow to avoid all the dramatic moments of conflict which I would later read about from the comfort of the 1980s. In my first life I enlisted of my own volition, genuinely believing the three great fallacies of the time – that the war would be brief, that the war would be patriotic and that the war would advance me in my skills. I missed being embarked for France by four days, and felt deeply disappointed in myself that I had not been evacuated from Dunkirk, which at the time seemed like a very triumphant defeat. Indeed, the first year of my war seemed to be spent on perpetual training exercises, first on the beaches as the nation – myself included – waited for an invasion that didn't come, then in the mountains of Scotland as the government began to toy with retribution. Indeed, I spent so much time training for an invasion of Norway that by the time it was finally decided that the exercise would be futile, I and my unit were accounted of such little use in desert warfare that we were held back from the initial embarkation to the Mediterranean theatre until we could be retrained or something else worked out useful for us to do. In this sense, I suppose I achieved one of my ambitions, as with no one seeming to want us to fight, I found myself with nothing better to do than study and learn. A medic in our unit was an objector who had found his conscience in the works of Engels and the poetry of Wilfred Owen, and who all the men in the unit, myself included, considered a weak-chinned toff until the day he stood up to the sergeant, who had enjoyed his power too long and too much, and in front of all the men lambasted him as the slobbering perversion of a childhood bully that he was. The medic's name was Valkeith, and he received three days' confinement for his outburst and the respect of all. His learning, previously a source of much derision, now became something of an object of pride, and though he was still cursed as a weak-chinned toff, now he was *our* weak-chinned toff, and from his mind I began to learn some of the mysteries of science, philosophy and romantic poetry, none of which I would admit to at the time. He died three minutes and fifty seconds after we set foot on the beaches of Normandy, from a shrapnel wound which tore open his gut. He was the only one of our unit who died that day, for we were far from the action and the gun which fired the fatal shot was taken two minutes later.

In my first life I killed three men. They were all together, all of them at once, in a tank retreating in a village in northern France. We'd been told that the village was already liberated, that there would be no resistance, but there it was, sat between the bakery and the church like a horsefly on a slice of melon. We'd been so relaxed we didn't even notice it until the barrel swung round towards us like the eye of a muddy crocodile and its jaws released the shell that killed two of us outright and young Tommy Kenah three days later in his hospital bed. I remember my actions with the same clarity with which I recall all else, and they were these: to drop my rifle, to unsling my bag and to run, never ceasing in my shout, down the middle of the street, still screaming at the tank that had killed my friends. I hadn't done the strap up on my helmet and it fell off my head some ten yards from the front of the tank. I could hear men moving around inside that beast as I approached, see faces darting through the slits in the armour as they tried to swing the gun round towards me or get on to the machine guns, but I was already there. The main gun was hot – even from a foot away I could feel its warmth on my face. I dropped a grenade through the open front hatch. I could hear them shouting, scrambling around inside, trying to get it, but in that confined space they only made it worse. I remember my actions, but not my thoughts. Later the captain said that the tank must have got lost: their friends had turned left, and they'd turned right, and that was why they'd killed three of us and been killed in return. I was given a medal, which I sold in 1961 when I needed to pay for a new boiler, and I felt a great relief once it was gone.

That was my first war. I did not volunteer for my second. I knew it likely that I would soon be conscripted so chose to rely on skills learned in my first life to keep myself alive. In my third life I joined the RAF as a ground mechanic and ran for the shelter faster than any other man in my squad when the sirens went, until finally Hitler began to bomb London and I knew I could begin to relax. It was a good place to be for the first few years. The men who died nearly all died in the air, out of sight and out of mind. The pilots did not really interact with us grease men, and I found it all too easy to consider the plane my only care, and the man who flew it merely another mechanical part to be ignored and overcome. Then the Americans came, and we began bombing Germany, and many more men died in the air, where I only needed to lament the loss of their machines, but more began coming back, shot through with shrapnel, their blood on the floor just thick enough to retain the shape of the footprints that had scrambled through it. I wondered what I could do differently, with my knowledge of what was to come, and concluded that it was nothing. I knew that the Allies would win, but had never studied the Second World War in any academic detail; my knowledge was entirely personal, a thing lived rather than information to be shared. The most I could do was warn a man in Scotland by the name of Valkeith to stay in the boat two minutes longer on the beach of Normandy, or whisper to Private Kenah that there would be a tank in the village of Gennimont which had turned right instead of left and was waiting between the bakery and the church to end his days. But I had no strategic information to impart, no learning or knowledge other than a declaration that Citroën would make elegant unreliable cars and one day people would look back at the division of Europe and wonder why.

Having reasoned myself so eloquently into this position, I continued once again to have a thoroughly unremarkable war. I oiled the landing gear of the planes which would destroy Dresden; I heard rumours of boffins attempting to design a jet engine and how the engineers derided the notion; I listened for the moment that the engines of the V1s stopped, and for a brief period for the silence of a V2 that had already fallen, and when VE day came I got horrendously drunk on brandy, which I don't particularly like, with a Canadian and two Welshmen who I'd met only two days before and who I never saw again.

And I learned. This time I learned. I learned of engines and machines, of men and strategies, of the RAF and the Luftwaffe. I studied bomb patterns, observed where the missiles had fallen so that next time – for I felt 60 per cent confident that there would be a next time, all this again – I would have something more useful to serve myself with, and potentially others, than a few personal recollections about the quality of tinned ham in France.

As it was, the same knowledge which protected me from the world was in later times also to put me in great danger and, by this route, indirectly introduce me to the Cronus Club, and the Cronus Club to me.